AN ECHO OF DARKNESS

THE REDEMPTION SAGA

KRISTEN BANET

When echoes of the past threaten to drag you back,
Keep moving forward.
You are not alone.

GLOSSARY

GENERAL TERMS

- **Ability Rankings** - Common, Uncommon, Rare, Mythic. A simple system created to judge how rare abilities are among the Magi.
- **Burnout** - When a Magi uses all their magical energy and must consume life force to continue.
- **Doppelganger** - Magi with the sole ability to shape-shift into other human beings. (Legend)
- **Doppler** – Slang for Doppelganger
- **Druids** - Female Magi with a plethora of natural abilities. They take over large areas of uninhabited land as caretakers. (Legend)
- **Imp** - Derogatory term for agents with the IMPO.
- **International Magi Armed Services (*IMAS*)** – The Magi's military in case of war against non-Magi or an uprising against the WMC.
- **International Magi Police Organization (*IMPO*)** – The Magi's organization for tracking down Magi criminals across the globe.
- **Legend** – A unique groupings of Magi. They are of equal power and have the same abilities per

group. Incredibly rare. Many non-Magi legends have their roots in these Magi.

- **Magi** - Humans with magic. They have anywhere from 1 to 5 abilities and a magical Source.
- **Reading** - A ceremony after a Magi comes into their magic, where a Magi who can 'read' (see Ability Glossary), discovers all the Magi's abilities. This information is then recorded for the Registrar.
- **Registrar** - A documentation system for recording all Magi and their powers during their teenage years. Viewing a Registrar entry requires approval by the WMC. Magi are required to submit to having a Registrar entry made via a Reading. There are lists Magi can join for public use, such as lists of healers in case of a global crisis, also kept with the Registrar.
- **Source** - The well of magical power inside a Magi. It's two-fold in how it can be measured—strength and depth. How powerful a Magi is versus how much magic they can do before running out of energy.
- **Vampyr** - Magi with the sole ability "borrow" abilities from others. They can also become immortal by "feeding" off a non-Magi's life force. (Legend)
- **The World Magi Council (WMC)** – The governing body over Magi. A group of 15 individuals voted into power every ten years.

1

SAWYER

Sawyer thought she was going to get a good night's sleep, she really did. She wanted to remain curled up in black sheets with the warm body next to her, one she was growing more accustomed to sleeping with. Vincent was an easy man to cuddle with, she had learned. She just wanted to press her face to his chest and hope that obnoxious black paw on her head would go away.

The paw just lifted up and fell back on her head. She had one, only one, thing to be thankful for. The claws were put away.

"Sombra, go to sleep," she mumbled. "I'm too fucking hungover for you." She was probably still drunk, but that didn't matter. What mattered was that she was not moving from the bed.

The jaguar wanted to show her something new. And she needed to go outside. Both of these were apparently pressing matters.

"How did you get in here?" Sawyer groaned, pushing her head up to glare at the big cat.

Sombra, who was standing over her, tilted her big head.

She had pushed down the door handle then pushed the door. Like the humans. She seemed to be asking how else she would get in the room.

"I hate you sometimes." She'd somehow forgotten her jaguar knew how to open doors.

Sombra snorted and jumped down with a loud thump that made Vincent groan. Sawyer looked around the room and saw that sure enough, the door was open. Other than that, the room was just how it had been when they went to sleep.

Except Kaar. He was no longer sleeping in his cage, but sitting on top of it, staring at her.

Weird-ass bird.

"Correction," she muttered. "Weird-ass animals. All of them."

"What?" Vincent asked, grumbling.

"My cat. It's not a big deal," she whispered, leaning back down to kiss his shoulder. "Sombra wants to go out, it seems."

"What time is it?" he asked, opening his eyes. She had a special love for those dark olive green eyes. His hair was messy and in her mind, perfect.

He brought up a good point, though, so she reached for the table closest to her. It meant she had to roll away from him, away from the warmth, but she didn't want to force him to move because her cat was an asshole. It was too damn early, she realized, looking at her phone. "Four," she answered.

"I'll go out with you," he said, pushing himself up. He groaned and fell back down. "I'm still drunk."

"Me too," she agreed. She pushed the blankets off and shivered at the cold. It was freezing. "God. Is the heat off?"

"Yeah. It normally isn't this cold this far south." He

2

pushed himself back up and moved off the bed. She followed, collecting her clothes off his floor. They had stayed up drinking and playing chess all night, a quiet evening with just each other's company. That became a night in bed together. "I'll turn it on, and it should be warm when we come back in."

"Thanks." She pulled on her sweatpants and then grabbed her tank. She didn't have a jacket around, but she figured Sombra would just want to go out, do her business, and come back in. The big cat wasn't used to the cold, and Sawyer hoped that worked in her favor.

She heard the heat kick on as she finished getting dressed. Vincent was half-dressed, his pants on but unbuttoned, looking absolutely delicious. He was feeding some treats to Kaar, who ruffled his feathers.

"You know, I go weeks without seeing him and now I see him all the time in the house," she noted, pointing at the bird.

"He comes in for the winter like the rest of our animals," he explained, rubbing the raven's chest. "You know, Quinn and the wolves."

"Quinn is not an animal," she said, chuckling with a shake of her head.

The look Vincent gave her in response had her laughing. All it said was 'Are you sure?' Sawyer's shoulders were shaking as she tried to contain the laughter.

"He's not!" she proclaimed, snorting. "Ok. We'll agree to disagree here."

Vincent's face didn't change. He just finished buttoning his pants and reached down for his shirt. His face had yet to change as he put it on and turned away.

Sawyer was still chuckling as she followed him out of the room. Kaar didn't follow them, but Sombra ran out of the room and nearly knocked them both down on the stairs. As they got to the back door to let the jaguar out, she realized what was going on.

"It snowed," she said to Vincent, keeping her voice down so they didn't wake up everyone in the house. "Something new. She doesn't want to miss it."

"She's probably never seen it."

"She hasn't," she confirmed, opening the back door. Her jaguar ran out and the world, serene and quiet, exploded in a cloud of white, flakes flying everywhere. Sudden confusion ran through the bond. "It's called snow, silly. It's frozen water."

Sombra looked back at her, a tilt to her head. She was trying to figure out how this stuff was water. It boggled her South American cat brain, to the point that Sawyer felt it bleeding into her own mind and making them both confused.

She had to mentally push the connection back to stop it, something Quinn had been working on with her since they got home. Sawyer hadn't had Midnight long enough to explore the bond and what it could be like or do. She'd also been unable to pull away from the bond to preserve the two minds or avoid feeling all the fear and pain Midnight had. With Sombra, she was learning things she should have already known. How to peer into her eyes and see her world, use her senses without Sombra needing to send the information back to her.

"It snows down here like every ten years," he told her quietly. "She's lucky it did. Or unlucky. Let's see if she likes it."

Sawyer shrugged and stepped out, looking down at her bare feet. She should have grabbed some shoes. Part of the porch was covered, so there wasn't any snow, but the wood was still cold. She crossed her arms over her chest and put one of her feet on top of the other to keep at least one slightly warm.

The backyard was a field of white to the woods, which were topped in white as well. It was a tiny little winter scene just for them.

"I should have guessed this would happen, after how freakishly cold November was," Vincent mumbled, also crossing his arms. "Do you mind..."

"You can smoke," she said, shrugging again. "You don't really need to quit with me, you know." She'd been a bit ridiculous that day, taking his pack and crushing it. She knew he hadn't stopped, but they never really talked about it. He just didn't smoke in front of her. This was the first time since they got back from the hot hell of South America.

"You're doing very well with that," he replied, pulling out his pack and putting the smoke in his mouth. He lit it before continuing. "You never smoked as much as me, though."

"Before I met you, I only smoked in stressful situations. I smoked more after coming here. Quitting isn't as hard for me." She eyed the cigarette between his lips. She wasn't interested. She'd meant what she'd said. She was tired of plants that could kill her.

"I can see that," he said, exhaling smoke. "Also, it looks like she won't want to come inside for a long time." He pointed out to her jaguar and Sawyer groaned. She knew. She could feel the pure joy radiating from the feline. She was experiencing something new and exciting. All six inches of snow that had fallen in southern Georgia, the only snow she'd ever seen.

"It's too damn cold," she complained, frowning out at her jaguar.

"It's December," Vincent reminded her, chuckling. "Of course it's cold."

Sawyer sighed. *December*. She *hated* December. She wished for a moment that she could continue pretending it was November - or just skip straight into January. She didn't respond to him as she watched Sombra jump around in the snow. She couldn't share the good mood. Something else had crept into its place: a bone-deep chill.

"What day is it?" she asked softly.

"The second. We're off until January thirty-first. They're calling it a well-earned holiday vacation." Vincent flicked his cigarette. He didn't seem bothered, but why would he? He didn't even realize she was bothered.

Sawyer stopped listening after she heard the day. They had been off for the rest of October, all of November, and Sawyer had missed them entering December. She hadn't paid attention at all.

"This is a really early snow," he continued. "Even when it does get this far south, it's in mid-winter, like January or February."

She shivered, but it wasn't the cold this time.

"Do you need a jacket? I can run in and get us hoodies," he commented.

She blinked and looked over at him, wondering how much she'd missed of him. "No, I'm fine," she whispered, unable to summon even a fake smile. A jacket wasn't going to chase the chill away now.

"Sawyer?" He frowned at her, stepping completely into her sight, blocking her view of her jaguar. "Where did you go? Are you okay?"

"I'm fine."

"You don't lie well to me."

"I don't want to talk about it right now," she corrected.

She should have known not to go with the 'fine' sentiment. He would never believe it from her. "I'm sorry. Later. It's too early, I'm kind of hungover."

"Okay," he murmured. "I'm going to get us some jackets, all right?"

"Thank you." She didn't look in those dark olive green eyes anymore. Now they seemed like too much, too close to the chill settling around her. Too much of a reminder. He probably realized she was avoiding eye contact. He always noticed those types of things from her. He could probably guess what it meant. Something was reminding her of either Axel or Henry.

This time, it was both.

He left without another word, and Sawyer went back to watching Sombra. The jaguar had stopped jumping around and stared back at her with those bright golden eyes. They seemed to glow in the night, too aware. There was intelligence in those eyes that frightened her.

"I don't want to talk about it," she repeated, softer, looking away from the jaguar.

It was a quiet morning and the sun wouldn't come up for a long time. Sombra went back to disturbing the peace, jumping around, so excited about this new white and wet thing on the ground.

Eventually, the jaguar's good mood began to bleed through the bond stronger, as if it was being pushed. Sawyer even cracked a small smile at the ridiculous cat. Her human didn't want to talk about it, so Sombra saw no reason why she should be sad. She couldn't erase the sadness, but she could cover it for a moment. So that her human wasn't so sad when she should be happy about this new stuff called snow.

"Fine!" She rolled her eyes, the small smile turning into

a grin. Something about Sombra made her chest less hollow, and it was easier to break out of the chill thanks to the cat's insight about her mood, even for just a moment. Sawyer reached out and grabbed some snow off the porch, patting it carefully into a good ball. Vincent walked back out at that moment, holding a hoodie and wearing a thick coat.

"Don't you dare," he warned. She wiggled her eyebrows at him.

"I would never. Not at you, anyway." She looked back out at her jaguar and threw, laughing as the snowball exploded against the black fur and the jaguar jumped nearly eight feet in the air. "Got her!"

Sombra was not as amused.

"That's what you get for waking me up too early," she called out.

"You shouldn't throw things at her," Vincent condemned her, but she heard the humor in his voice.

"She knows what she did and it didn't hurt. Just spooked her. That's hard to do, you know." Sawyer was smiling as her jaguar went back to searching around the snow and trying to play in it. "I got to take my chances when I get them. I mean, you can't say she didn't deserve it. Kaar doesn't wake us up at four in the morning."

"No, he doesn't. He just sits awake and stares at us while we sleep." He pushed the hoodie towards her. "Here. I never wear it."

"You own a hoodie?" She took it and pulled it on, inhaling his cologne. She had no idea what it smelled like, only able to pin it as masculine and expensive.

"Apparently. I pulled it out of the closet. No idea when it got there."

"It's mine now," she decided, enjoying how soft it was. She had never been the type of woman who took a man's clothing, but she was fine becoming one. It was another piece of normal in her not normal world. Something ordinary while they were surrounded by unordinary. She wouldn't become her jaguar, though. That cat stole everything from everyone. Sawyer's room was becoming a treasure trove that held El Dorado, which she was pretty sure her jaguar had brought from the Amazon.

"That's fine. I'm missing several shirts, though, and would like them back."

Speaking of the jaguar's sticky paws. "You'll have to convince her to give those back." She pointed out to the black big cat rolling in the snow.

"She doesn't speak English, or at all, actually." Vincent crossed his arms and looked expectantly at her, as if Sawyer was supposed to do something about the situation.

"I'm not going near her pile of shit, sorry." She had tried once, and it was one of the few times her own bonded animal had *snarled* at her. That pile of fabric, which included Elijah's blanket and several of Vincent's shirts, was *not* something Sawyer was allowed to touch under any circumstance. Those were now Sombra's and no one was going to tell her otherwise.

"She's your bonded animal. You do have to take charge and tell her what's right and wrong."

"I mean...is her stealing easily replaceable things *that* bad?" Sawyer shrugged. She didn't think so. That was probably the problem. She didn't think it was such a terrible thing. They all had the money to replace the shit instead of argue with her about it. "I'm more interested in her deciding to finish up what she's doing and come back inside. It's damn cold out here. She can play in the snow when the sun comes up. If it's still here."

Vincent just nodded his response and they watched the

jaguar just continue being ridiculous. She rolled, pounced, and played like a kitten, sending snow flying everywhere. The only thing in Sawyer's favor was that the cat was beginning to also recognize the bone-deep chill of the night.

"Sombra! You're supposed to be using the bathroom too," she called out. "Sombra, it's just frozen water. Nothing special. Go to the bathroom!"

"Keep your voice-"

"Why are you yelling at four in the morning?" a gruff Southern accent asked her. Something very warm got near her. She eyed Elijah, wondering how he was in sweats and no shirt without having a problem. It was probably his fire manipulation. He seemed to always run warmer. She didn't let her gaze linger on his thick, muscular body, the bulkiness that defied logic. "Waking people up and shit."

"Sombra woke us up and now won't hurry up. Sorry, Eli."

"You're all too nice to her," he grumbled. He let out a sharp whistle that made her wince. Sombra stopped jumping around and looked back at the porch. Sawyer was amazed that she stopped just like that for the cowboy, and always, without fail. Respect and a small amount of fear bled through the bond from the jaguar. "Hurry up. You're keeping people awake. We aren't nocturnal, you monster."

Without complaint, through the bond or in action, Sombra trotted out into the woods to get her business done.

"Thank you," she whispered to him, feeling bad he had to come out and order her animal bond around.

"No problem." He just kept staring out to the woods. "You two have a good night?"

"Yeah. Still maybe feeling it," she answered, smiling guiltily, hoping to have a few jokes with him. He was good at keeping the mood light. He always got over his crankiness in seconds.

"Yup." He thumped Vin's shoulder, turned and went back inside.

Her jaw dropped open a little. He just walked away. Not even an attempt at a conversation. She closed her mouth and narrowed her eyes at the back door. This wasn't the first time, but every time shocked her. She had no idea what was going on when it happened either, so she had no idea what was causing it, or if maybe it was something she had missed about his personality before that was coming to light.

"What is his problem?" she hissed to Vincent, turning on her lover. He knew Elijah well enough. They had worked together for years, long before she entered the picture - or even the rest of the team.

"I really don't know," Vincent confessed softly. "He's never been like this, really."

"It's like he's PMSing, and that says a lot coming from me," she pointed out in frustration. "It's so hot and cold with him now. I never know if I'm going to get normal Elijah or pissy Elijah. It's not right."

"It's not," he agreed, but he didn't offer anything else.

She ran a hand through her wild hair, cursing when she snagged a knot and yanked her hand out of her hair.

"Sombra's coming back."

"Thank the gods," she growled, turning to go inside. Her own moods were feeling very erratic now. Annoyed she was in the cold, laughing at her cat, enjoying a quiet morning with a lover, feeling the dread that December normally brought with it, and being pissed off at Elijah. She wasn't exactly sure what was wrong with her. She decided to blame the lack of sleep and the whiskey she'd dived into the night before. This wasn't how she'd planned on spending her morning.

"I'm not sure I'm going to get back to sleep now," she admitted to her Italian. Definitely not with him, with those dark olive green eyes and that thick, curly dark hair. No, her anger at Elijah was only surface anger. Her annoyance and joy were also just surface. Something deeper was riding her now as the chill set back in on her.

"You're going to leave me for the morning?" he asked. They had promised a full night together, but that seemed thrown out the window. She felt guilty for it, but she couldn't anymore.

"You okay with it? I think I need to just go stew in my room a little. Can I leave her with you?" She pointed down at Sombra, who had the nerve to shake her big head in refusal. "Never mind. I guess I'm keeping her." She turned to her door to the attic and Vin stopped her. Neither of them said anything as he held her and slowly placed a kiss on her lips, a loving one, one that promised he would be there for her if she needed it. One he gave her every night, no matter what room she was going to sleep in.

When he released her, she just backed away, turned, and went to her room, Sombra on her heels. As she closed her bedroom door, something broke.

She growled and smacked her hand on the wood. She was all over the place. It was just another cold morning. Just another normal morning, and something was eating at her.

Sombra jumped up on the bed and laid down, those gold eyes watching her carefully, trying to ask what was wrong.

"Henry died in December," she explained softly, giving the only honest answer she could. "That's part of it. It has to be. It ruins every December for me and always will." She wasn't sure if she was trying to reason out her strange moods to herself or the cat, but it didn't matter. Saying the words eased some of it. "Christmas Eve, actually. He had only been awake that night because he was waiting on Santa. He only heard what was happening because of the holiday cheer. He'd never known until that moment just how wrong everything was."

Sadness bled through the bond between her and Sombra. Sawyer had shown the jaguar all the old pictures in the weeks since coming back from the rainforest. Henry and Midnight. The places they had gone and seen. The experiences they had shared. The good times, the bad times, and the ugly times. The very ugly times, the ones that woke up her owner in the middle of the night, crying. The ones Sombra and Jasper had to help her break out of, to remember she was strong enough. Those were better, but not resolved.

Like everything else in her life, the nightmares were another work in progress. Like her relationships and friendships, her place in the world. All works in progress.

Which reminded her of another weird thing from the morning.

"And Elijah. What's his problem? You know what's going on there?"

Sawyer felt the confusion from the feline. She had only recently met Elijah. She didn't know the Elijah before the Amazon. She didn't understand that he'd changed.

That didn't help Sawyer at all. She'd tried confronting the cowboy already, and that hadn't worked. She'd tried asking the guys, but they said he wasn't really talking to them about his shit either.

Sawyer sat on the edge of her bed and leaned over, pressing her face into the cold, wet fur. It was slightly refreshing until she remembered that it was her bed that the wet jaguar was laying on.

"Please get down," she begged nicely, sitting back up. Sombra hopped off easily enough and moved to her favorite corner of the room, that pile of contraband fabrics she stole from everyone. Sawyer chuckled weakly at the sight of her walking in circles and pushing it all around until it was perfect to lie on.

Once the jaguar was at peace and curled into a tight ball to sleep, Sawyer leaned against her headboard and just stared at the ceiling. She wasn't going to get back to sleep, and if this was any indication to how her December was going to be, she probably wouldn't for the rest of the month.

"Fuck December," she said with all the defiant, pissed-off energy she could muster. She knocked the back of her head to her headboard, groaning in frustration.

Now she was going to have a headache to go with her seasonally weird mood.

SAWYER

S awyer was late to breakfast somehow. She hadn't gotten back to sleep, but she was still late getting down; the entire team was nearly done eating when she sat down. Sombra pushed her bowl around in the kitchen until Quinn kindly got up to feed her. No one said anything about their lateness to the meal, just continued on with the normal morning routine. She dished herself a plate without saying anything and got busy on it, looking around at her friends, lovers, and teammates.

Vincent was reading a local newspaper, something she still didn't understand, looking impeccable and put together. Jasper was studying for the finals of those online classes he was taking. She knew he was stressing out over it. The trips in September and October had thrown him off a little, even if he didn't admit it. It stressed him out so much that she barely saw him, and they hadn't had a date since before the trip down to South America. Zander just ate quietly, throwing her a smile when he caught her looking at him. Quinn sat back down next to Elijah, both fairly quiet as well.

It was just a nice morning where everyone was getting along, a blessing on its own.

Normal. It was a normal morning. December hadn't thrown them off like it had her.

"Do you guys do anything for Christmas?" she asked, hoping to divert her energy on anything except stewing in silence.

"Not really," Zander answered, shrugging. "I mean, we get each other gifts, but that's it. Why?"

His answer didn't help her at all. She'd been hoping for more. A party she could help plan, anything.

"No reason." She went back to her breakfast, thinking about it. She decided to correct herself. If they knew, they could help and they were people who were good at helping her. "Guys, December is a bad month for me. You should know that now. I normally find something to do to keep my mind off it."

"Don't like the holidays?" the cowboy asked softly, giving her a look of genuine concern, his hazel eyes pinned on her. That hot and cold shit. Now he was normal Elijah, of course.

"Henry died on Christmas Eve," she whispered, shoving eggs around on her plate. "It gets to me. If I seem a bit off, that's why."

"Thank you for telling us now." Vincent dropped his paper on the table. She knew he'd already known the date. She'd told him before, and she knew that he probably figured out earlier in the morning. "We'll find something to cheer you up, if we can."

"No...I just like to have something to do. Like I threw holiday parties for the kids and the gyms. Fight Night regulars would get gifts and we would do special events and such. I was wondering if you were all into things like that. If you have nothing, there's no reason to get into stuff just for me. Don't worry about it. I'll find something to do."

She had to, or she would go mad from grief. She'd tried one year, just ignoring the holiday, the entire month of cheer and glee. Charlie had found her in her room in a ball, crying. He'd taken her out to buy Liam a gift, and then things for the rest of the kids. It had brightened her spirits just enough to make it through the day, wrapping those presents. The next time her mood dipped, he'd dragged her to the class she was trying to skip to give those presents to the kids. Those smiles had saved her that December and every year since.

She didn't have them this year, so she needed to find something.

"Are you sure?" Zander frowned at her. "I mean, we could totally do more. I'm down for doing more if it's important to you."

She really appreciated that sentiment from him. Of all the big changes she genuinely loved since the Amazon, she and Zander was one on the top of the list. They were working. They weren't arguing as explosively, and now she knew he felt secure. She loved him, and they would work. They just needed some patience with each other.

"It's okay. I'll find something to do." She stood up, her appetite gone already. "I'll get the dishes. Sorry for being so late down here."

"We won't leave you alone." Her eyes fell on Quinn, who stood up as well. "We'll make plans every day to keep you busy. Like you and I haven't hunted yet. We can go do that. And Elijah can take you to his favorite restaurant in Atlanta." He looked down at the cowboy who stopped eating, his eyes going wide. "You've been wanting to, right?"

"I have," he answered, nodding diplomatically.

"Good. Vincent, there are plays in Atlanta too, right?" Quinn was on a tangent now and she knew better than to try and stop it. Once an idea took root in the Wolf, there was no stopping it.

"There are, and I might know how to get tickets this close to any shows." Vincent smiled at the feral Magi and then to her.

"Good. We'll just come up with ways to keep Sawyer busy every day. And plan a party. I've never had a Christmas party. Sounds interesting."

"Well, everyone, Quinn has decided and therefore we shall," Elijah declared, looking resigned to his fate. She narrowed her eyes at him and he cracked a small smile. "It's fine. We'll make sure you make it through this December like you have all the rest."

"You're going to need to give Jasper another week to get through school, but he and I won't let you down." Zander was now giving her a huge grin, all teeth and near-childish excitement.

"Once I'm through finals, you have all my time," Jasper promised, looking up from his books and papers.

"Thank you," she murmured to him, then again to the rest of the guys louder. "Thank you. Really. This means a lot to me." She had already learned to lean on them when she needed it. If the morning was any indication, she was going to need to lean on them a lot this month. She walked away after that, her mind tumbling over what just happened.

They had all just jumped at the opportunity to help her deal with shit that she would never be over. In the kitchen, rinsing her plate, she could hear them making plans for what they could do.

She looked up and thanked whatever gods were watching her for landing her with them. For all the shit they had gone through already together, she was genuinely thankful for them. It wasn't perfect, but they did amazing things for her. This was just one of them.

"Let me," Jasper whispered, reaching around her. She hadn't noticed him come up on her. It was happening more and more. They could sneak up on her, or maybe she was just so used to them, trusted them that much, that she didn't pay attention naturally like she once did.

He took her plate and finished rinsing it off, then loaded it in the dishwasher. She leaned on the counter and watched as he moved on to other dishes he'd brought.

"I can do it. I promised to," she half-heartedly reminded him.

"I've been neglecting my chores around here. I can do this for you today." He smiled at her. "Plus, I'm avoiding going back to reading those books. I think this might be my last semester."

"Really?" She was genuinely shocked. He loved learning as much as Sombra loved chewing on a bone or harassing the wolves and stealing theirs.

"Yeah. There's just so much going on, and I'm losing time with you and the guys over it. I have enough education. This just makes it more obvious. I used to do school since I had nothing else to do."

"And now you do?" she asked, crossing her arms. "Have something else to do?"

"I mean, you're here. I want to spend more time with you. Since we've gotten back from South America, I haven't had the chance. Catching up, nearly failing a couple of my exams - it's been a bit rough for me. I want to hang out more with all of you, but the best I can do is an hour here or there, and you have a lot of us to juggle. I can't expect you to be free whenever I am."

"Yes you can," she replied, shaking her head. "You are the one with the time-"

"You love them. I'm not going to demand your time."

"I love you too," she reminded him softly. "Plus, I still need you." She did. She wondered if there would ever be a day she didn't need him. His kindness. His intelligence. His goodness, that strong moral compass. Even just his normal. He was so much more normal than the rest of them. Just that was a treasure. "If you want my time, if you have an hour to steal away from the books, just tell me. None of them would have a problem."

"Zander might," he said lightly, a smile coming over his face.

"He would want to join in," she responded suggestively, causing a small red blush to hit her golden boy's cheeks.

"That's so-"

"Completely right."

She turned to see the devil himself, grinning in the doorway between the kitchen and dining room. He was leaning on the frame, arms crossed, and watching them with dancing green eyes, looking for trouble.

"That's out of the question," Jasper said quickly, shaking his head. "Absolutely not."

"I mean, it might help you two finally get down and do the dirty deed. Seriously, the sexual tension can be felt across the state."

"Stop, Zander. Not everyone wants to jump straight into bed like you. I like that not everyone just wants to throw my clothes on the floor and yell. Actually, I think I got the order wrong. Yell then throw my clothes on the floor." She gave him a taunting grin. It's not like that had happened too much recently, but it was still something they did. Something only they did.

"You two are awful," Jasper mumbled, still shaking his head. "Sawyer, my last final is next Thursday. Right after it, we're going to the movies again, okay?"

"Sounds perfect. You'll do well. Don't worry about me." She leaned and kissed his cheek. He turned and returned it, a sweet, soft kiss that only he could give her. She wanted that stormy man she saw underneath, had seen glimpses of before - but it wasn't the time. It was never time, it seemed. Every time she got him nearly there in those moments they did manage to have, something came up.

"All right, now come play with me," Zander demanded, taking her hand. She smiled at Jasper as she let Zander pull her away. Her golden boy was smiling back, looking indulgent and accepting of her being stolen from him. "We made a deal. Morning spars every day to keep our skills sharp."

As they made it down into the gym, Sawyer began to feel her blood pump, adrenaline already coursing its way through her. She was looking forward to the physical activity. If her body was tired, her mind would hopefully go with it, and not dwell on that dark winter five years before.

"This is going to be a great way to forget everything," she told him. "I'm glad we do this."

"I think it helps with our more...argumentative and antagonistic tendencies." He smirked as he threw his shirt away, leaving her the sight of his inked and ripped lean form.

"You mean your argumentative and antagonistic tendencies," she corrected, taunting him. "I'm collected, cool."

"You are hot-tempered as hell and you know it." He snorted, then beckoned her on the mat. She pulled off her tank and met him on the mat in her sports bra and sweats.

"How are you really? Probably took a lot to tell us that this month was going to be hard on you."

She considered that. It hadn't been. It had been surprisingly easy. She trusted them. With her pain, with her secrets, with her body, and her soul. There was very little she probably wouldn't trust them with, and nothing came to mind. "I think, with everything else we've gone through, something like this is just a natural progression," she replied diplomatically. "It had struck me this morning. I didn't want to talk about it, not really, but...y'all knowing what I'm going through only helps all of us."

"It does," he agreed, beginning to stretch. She started as well, pulling her arms over her head and holding it for ten slow breaths. "Want to know a secret?"

"Sure," she answered, looking back at him when she finished stretching her shoulders and arms. She sat down on the mat and began to stretch her quads.

"I hate Christmas."

"I know." She wondered why that was a secret. He'd hated Christmas growing up. He'd never enjoyed the holidays. He didn't want to celebrate it or anything else. "That's not something I've forgotten. I'll never forget how you used to lock yourself away and refuse to do any of the holiday stuff at the orphanage."

"The secret is I'm looking forward to this one." She looked up and frowned. He was still smiling and shrugged a bit sheepishly. "It's our first one together in years, since the one before Jasper and I left. And our first one as a couple. Well, in a relationship. I'm not sure if you and I are a couple and you are in several couples, or if we're all some weird fucking unit."

"I don't know the answer to that either, but I'm glad you're looking forward to this one. I don't hate the holiday, not really. Just...this month always reminds me of him and everything else. It's why I focus on the holidays. Something joyful." She lowered her eyes to the mat, something emotional passing through her chest - a tightness, for a moment. Joyful. That Christmas Eve should have been joyful. The next day should have been presents and pretending everything was okay. She just spent the years after trying to make up for it.

"Come back, Sawyer," he ordered.

She closed her eyes and nodded before pushing herself back off the mat. She met his eyes and sighed. "Sorry. It's going to be like this all month. The mood swings, the issues. Everything reminds me of him and that...that sucks, you know?"

"I don't know," he admitted, "but I'm sure as hell going to help you anyway."

"I appreciate the honesty." It was such a truthful admission from him. He really had no idea what it was like to lose such a precious piece of his life like she had. She was actually grateful that he didn't pretend to understand. She stood up, ready to force the entire topic off her mind for a moment. "Now let's do this."

"Can one more join you?" Elijah's Southern accent caught her off guard.

"Sure, man. Having a third means we can do a rotation." Zander waved him over. "Stretch while Sawyer and I get a round in." He turned to her, an arrogant smirk on his face. He opened his mouth and she knew a taunt was coming.

She didn't give him a chance to say anything, sliding into his space, grabbing his extended arm while shoving her shoulder into his chest. Before he could brace for what she was doing, she pushed her back to him and flung him over her to land on the mat.

"Round one to me!" she declared, grinning.

"Fucking cheater," he growled. "That was uncalled-for."

"You were about to say something stupid so I stopped you before you could shove that foot in your mouth." She thought her reasoning was perfectly logical.

"That's just mean, babe." Zander rolled onto his stomach then pushed himself up. Once he was standing, he brushed himself off. "That's not round one. Elijah, think you can call start?"

"Yeah, I can do that," he called from off the mat as he stretched. She made the mistake of looking over at him. His shirt was off now too, and he was holding an arm over his head to stretch his side and shoulder. All-American beef, that one. He was top shelf in terms of just pure size and physical form. It wasn't a form he got from just the gym either. He used his body for real labor, real hard work, which gave it a realness that she enjoyed. He caught her staring and threw her a wink. "Go!"

This time she didn't have the chance to react. She'd been too busy drooling over the bulky, massive body of the cowboy. Zander grappled her to the mat and put her in an ankle hold that had her tapping out in seconds.

"Fuck, let me go!" she snarled, slapping her palm to the mat desperately as he twisted it to the point of near pain.

"Done being a dirty cheater?" he asked. She could hear the laughter in his voice and wanted to strangle him.

"It's not cheating when you encourage me to fuck the other guy," she retorted. It was completely off-topic, but it was all she could think of.

"Oh shit!" Elijah laughed as Zander let her go. Zander was barely able to contain his own laughter as he stood up. She got up last, dusting herself off. There was nothing there, but she felt the need to. "She has a mouth this morning," the cowboy pointed out, chuckling still.

"And the cowboy is in a good mood, outstanding." She crossed her arms and turned on him. "Unlike this morning."

"You woke up me with all of that yelling. Sorry." He said that with an unapologetic air. "You can beat me up for it, though."

She eyed him carefully then pointed to the mat. Zander wisely left the mat without a word. "If I win, you're going to tell me what's going on."

"No, I don't think I'm going to make that bet," he replied, shaking his head as he walked in front of her. "I don't take bets I know I'm going to lose. Instead, we'll do what Quinn said. I'll take you to my favorite restaurant in Atlanta and I'll hopefully be over my own shitty mood. If I win, you pay. If you win, I'll pay. How's that?"

"Is it a date?" She raised an eyebrow at him. They hadn't touched the subject of *them* since before the Amazon. Before they all nearly died, before she had gone through his sketchbook, before she was with Quinn. She silently wondered if he was mad at her for any of that. She'd violated his privacy, and then also laid claim to his closest friend and fuck-buddy. This was the natural consequence. The problem was, when she had asked before, he'd outright denied that was the reason for his mood.

"Between friends," he said firmly. That was shocking, and yet wasn't at the same time. It gave her mixed feelings. Rejected, but also happy he still considered them friends. She just nodded in response and got ready, spreading her bare feet shoulder-width apart. She squared her shoulders and pulled her hands up in defensive positions.

"Go!" Zander yelled like a whip. He must have gotten the strange serious undertone to the spar.

Elijah was fast, which she had remembered from their times practicing with weapons. She also knew he was reasonably flexible, for all his bulk. He wasn't one she normally sparred with hand to hand, though. He always said he didn't have the skill level to be a partner. He preferred Quinn or Vincent.

He'd been lying to her, something that became obvious very quickly. She should have known better, since she'd once practiced blades with him, a long time ago now.

She narrowly dodged his initial attempt at a grab. She barely got away from his swift kick that would have taken her legs out from underneath her. There was a rule not to use magic when they sparred, so they knew they were doing everything correctly, but she nearly broke that rule as he threw a right hook at her head. She blocked it with her left forearm and landed two quick jabs to his gut. Getting those two hits swung it into her favor and made her the aggressor. She pressed the advantage and finally got him in a hold, his chest on the ground and his arm pinned behind his back. He tapped out, breathing hard.

"You've been lying to me," she accused, not letting him up. She was breathing hard too, trying to catch her breath. "You said you weren't very good at hand to hand."

"Well, compared to you and Zander, I'm not."

She considered that answer and released his arm. She stood up and helped him up, keeping her eyes on his and not his broad chest. "True. You left a major opening for me, something Zander and I don't do - not often, anyway. You also pushed too hard as the aggressive fighter in the beginning. You need to wear people down, not burn yourself out. One punch from you can end things fairly easily, you just need to pick the right time to try to land it."

"Good advice," Zander commented. "Listen to her, Elijah. She knows her shit."

"That's why I came down here. I've been getting seriously bored and y'all are still down here working, so I wanted to join you and learn something." He smiled between them. "Y'all really don't mind, right? I know this is sort of your thing."

"No, we're good. Honestly, things get repetitive with just Zander and I. We know each other's tricks too well. Hard to learn anything when you fight the same person over and over." She shrugged. "Come down whenever you want."

With that, they just went back to work. It was refreshing to have someone joining her and Zander, that much was obvious. It gave her a chance to step back and make comments on their form and positioning, and for them to do the same to her. And it kept her thoughts off the dark corner in her mind, begging her to think about it.

They wrapped up sparring two hours later and her body ached with a pleasant soreness that continued to help her mood.

"Same time tomorrow? You two do this every morning, right?" Elijah wiped off his face as he spoke. She was using her discarded tank top, knowing she was going to get a clean one once she was done showering.

"Yeah. We make it down here every morning, no matter what. That includes hungover, right, Sawyer?"

"Yeah, though I'm not really feeling hungover this morning. Got lucky today, I guess." She had hit the bottle hard with Vincent but it wasn't killing her. If anything, her very early morning rise helped her get over it before coming down to the gym. "Today you get first shower, right?"

"Yup. Enjoy being sweaty." He grinned at her as he began to walk out.

"I'm claiming mine," Elijah said apologetically. "You can ask Quinn. He's got the private bathroom."

"I think I might," she murmured, thinking about that. His bedroom still felt very off-limits to her, but she wanted to see him anyway. Zander didn't understand what she was going through, but her feral wolf did, or could relate his own pain to it.

She followed the guys up to the main floor and left them to go to Quinn's door. She didn't know if he was in there, but she knocked and waited patiently.

After several seconds, there was no answer so she went for the back door.

"I thought I would find you out here," she said, seeing him on the back porch. He was clothed, and that almost disappointed her. After the warmer months she'd been here, she'd grown used to his shirtless physique as a constant. Now that the chill had come in, he was in the house more, but he was also more dressed.

"I was making sure those three got their exercise." He pointed out to what he was staring at. She glanced to the field before the woods and saw their animals roughhousing in the melting snow. She could already see mud on them and knew it was going to be an event to get them all clean enough for the house again. "What do you need?" he asked, turning to her.

"Can I borrow your bathroom? Just got done in the gym and Zander claimed ours. Elijah is in the other."

"Of course. You didn't need to ask." He frowned at her, tilting his head as he did. "You can use anything of mine."

"Of course I need to ask. It's your personal space. I'm not going to invade it," she retorted.

"You never invade my personal space," he murmured, his frown shifting into a smile. He stepped closer to her and

28

leaned so he could nuzzle into her neck. "In fact, I think I invade yours, never the other way around."

Her pulse began to race. With only a few words and a simple affectionate action, the feral Magi had her tied in knots. He planted a soft kiss where her neck and shoulder met and then moved upwards to her jaw.

"I like invading your space," he whispered as he made it to her ear. "Feel free to invade mine."

"I probably stink, so I'm going to shower," she declared.

"You smell like you always do after sex, sweaty, so it's not something that really bothers me. I think I might enjoy it." He didn't back off, and she couldn't bring herself to move as his arms wrapped around her waist. His ice-blue eyes caught hers. "The shower can wait. No reason to get sweaty twice," he said with a rough sexuality that made her hot in the cold weather.

"I've made a monster," she teased, hoping it would lighten the now sexually-charged air around them. He was now an unbridled sex god, it seemed. One from her wildest dreams - and that wasn't what she'd expected when she fell for him.

"No, you just tamed one," he purred. "But it only makes sense. Like calls to like."

"We're good monsters." She wasn't sure how this conversation turned to this, but with Quinn, it was an endless game of guessing. He had tricks, that was for sure. Tricks that worked, but she wasn't going to fall for them this time. She really wanted to get clean, not dirtier. "And this monster wants a long shower."

He sighed and released her slowly. Waving a hand, he went back to watching their animals. She felt guilty at his resignation so she kissed his cheek quickly.

That's when she realized this wasn't a trick; it was just a plain old trap.

Before she could back away, he grabbed her again, growling from his chest, and claimed her mouth in a slow, possessive kiss. It was claiming, and with purpose. It was expertly done as well. She knew he was a fast learner when he enjoyed what he was doing. Somewhere in the back of her mind, she remembered he got his GED in November, breezing through it as if he'd never had a problem to begin with.

He'd applied that same driven and intelligent mind to kissing. It left her knees a little weak.

"Are you sure?" he asked, smiling as he pulled away.

She wasn't sure, but she nodded anyway, knowing if she gave any other answer, the outcome would be bedsheets. She only wanted a shower and to talk to him. Sex and talking were not the same thing.

"When I'm done, do you want to hang out? Sombra and I are still practicing letting me in her head and-"

"You must really want that shower," he noted, going back to nuzzle against her neck.

"I really do, and I want to talk to you after it. To say thank you for what you said this morning at breakfast and other things."

He froze and looked back at her eyes. She was trapped there.

"We'll go for a walk when you're done," he promised softly.

"Thank you." She meant it.

3

JASPER

Jasper was sitting in his shared office alone, staring at text that had become blurry. He wasn't even sure what book he was reading anymore. Maybe it was the quantum mechanics textbook. It could also have been the Magi History in ancient Babylon. He had no idea and it didn't matter.

He knew everything in it. He was just hiding in the book now.

His mind wandered as he turned the page. Hiding. There was no better term for it. They had come back from the Amazon, and he'd dug in and hid from her. Not that she realized that. They all believed that school was kicking his ass, even though it had never done so before, so he ran with that and just pretended everything was too much.

Now she needed them, having openly admitted this was going to be a rough time for her. That was a big step for her. He never thought he'd see the day when she would just come out at breakfast and say something so personal was bothering her. It had made him feel guilty as shit. Here he was, avoiding her, and she needed him.

No. She needed them, not him. Not just him. She really didn't need him at all, no matter what she said. Sombra helped her with her nightmares nearly the exact same way he could. She didn't want his advice about seeking professional help, and she had plenty of guys to go to for a companion. He felt expendable, and it was eating away at him. He didn't have Zander's pure sexual charisma, or Vincent's darkness that seemed to call to her like a moth to flame. He wasn't unique or special in any way like Quinn. He wasn't even Elijah, who gave off an easy smile when he wasn't all messed up in his own head.

"Fuck," he groaned, running a hand through his hair. He knew better than to let these thoughts take him over. He knew they all just cared for her as much as he did and she wasn't a liar, not about them. He was just riddled with insecurities, like he always had been. First it was his limp, his disability, and now it was...everything else. Her.

He didn't know how long he sat there, trying to put the thoughts away, when someone knocked on the door. That removed two possible options for who it could be. Zander would have just walked in, since it was also his office, and Sawyer still enjoyed spooking them by walking *through* the door.

"Come in," he called, closing the book in front of him. He didn't even glance at the title as he dropped it on the floor, not caring anymore about it.

Elijah walked in and fell into the chair across from him.

Jasper frowned at the cowboy leaning back in front of him now. "Do you need something?" he asked warily.

"Nah. Just wanted a change of scenery."

Liar.

"Okay." Jasper just stared at him, confused. Elijah just didn't hang out in the offices all that much. At this time of year, it was more common to find him in the workshop, working on something in sweltering heat that Jasper couldn't tolerate.

Minutes dragged on in an awkward silence that he didn't know what to do with. This was strange, unusual for the cowboy. Things had been weird with him for weeks, and this was just another example of it.

"Elijah, why are you here?" he demanded, finally tired of the silence.

"I don't know what to do."

"What?" Jasper didn't like the slightly lost way he'd said that. It sounded not just bored, but nearly depressed.

"You heard me," the cowboy snapped. Just like that, the hint of depression was gone and the agitated cowboy they had been dealing with came back. "And since you're hiding in here, I decided to come hide with you. We can wallow together."

"I'm not-"

"You're hiding from her and so am I, so we're going to hide together. Sorry, did I just ruin your little secret? School is fucking easy for you and I know it. While they've all been panting over her, I've noticed you."

Jasper didn't respond. He should have known. Elijah had always been the one in the house to really look out for how everyone was feeling. With a job like theirs, it was important that one person was paying attention to their mental states.

"Yeah, I called you out." He said it in a taunting way, and Jasper gritted his teeth. He was looking for a fight? Why?

"Go make something," Jasper told him, hoping the cowboy would just leave now.

"I don't know what to make. That's part of the problem. I don't know what to make, what to draw, what to do."

"So you're going to come in here and give me a hard

time?" He narrowed his eyes on the hazel-eyed cowboy. This was not normal for them. They might not have been the closest two of the team, but this sort of interaction wasn't typical.

"Well, the little lady is getting mad at me now. She doesn't bother you, so if I hide in here, she won't bother me."

"She's been getting mad at you," he corrected, muttering it with annoyance. "Maybe you should just tell everyone what's wrong and we can deal with it."

"Nah, I'm not willing to air my shit like that right now."

There was another piece of unusual for Elijah. He was normally the open one, the one who wanted them to air out the dirty laundry and find solutions. Now he was just stewing and no one really understood why. Well, he didn't. He figured Quinn or Vincent probably knew more than him about it.

"You like her," Jasper said quietly, glancing at the door. He hoped no eavesdroppers were around. "Why don't you just admit it? You were torn up when those two were left in the jungle to save you and the soldiers. And now we're back and you've shut down. Just talk to her."

"She gets really close to dying a lot," the cowboy pointed out, trying to make it sound casual. "Of course I was worried about her in the jungle. That place was a shit-show."

"She gets about as close to dying as any of us do. Even Quinn. He nearly didn't walk out of that jungle either."

"Yeah..." He shut down.

Jasper watched as his friend's mind drifted and knew the conversation was over. "I don't get what's going on with you. I'll make you a deal, Elijah."

"Oh really?" With that, the cowboy was focused on him

again. "They won't be bad ones like she likes to make, right?"

"No, this one will be pretty simple. I'll tell you mine if you tell me yours. Just between the two of us."

"I know yours."

"No, you don't," he fired back.

"You are scared of being a virgin and she likes sex."

"That's a base way of putting it. I'm not elaborating until you agree." He knew better than to tell Elijah too much without the promise of something in return. It was a game they all normally had to play with Vincent, but Elijah was just as good at it. Their two 'leaders' had different uses for the game. Vincent used it for interrogations, when he needed information about something beyond them all. Elijah used it to make people admit secrets about how they felt and what they were dealing with.

"Fine, I'll take the deal. Why is Golden Boy hiding from the love of his life?" Elijah waved a hand around, beckoning him to talk.

"She doesn't need me," he admitted. By the expression on Elijah's face, it wasn't the answer the cowboy thought he would get. "It's not just the sex, either. It's everything. She gets everything from everyone else."

"You help with her nightmares when none of us can."

"Sombra can do that same thing I do, and through the bond, so very little could stop that cat from touching her Magi's mind," he reminded Elijah.

"Uh...Damn. You don't really think that, do you? She'll kill you if she learns you're stewing in here, thinking you aren't worth a damn. Because you are, man. You're on this team and a valuable part of it."

Was he? His magic was average. His abilities were decent, but nothing that combined to do any good work, like

Sawyer's set of impressive and cohesive abilities, or Quinn's. His problem wasn't just with Sawyer. The jungle had made him feel weak in comparison to all of them. What had he done out there? He'd been targeted by people they should have been working together with, over an injury, like always. He was a weak link.

No, he didn't think the team needed him either. There it was, another problem for him. Another thing he needed to deal with, another truth he felt like he couldn't convince himself out of. He felt worthless and nothing he did, nothing anyone was saying, helped ease the anxiety he felt over it.

"Look at her and Zander. They give each other passion they need. Vincent gives her a dark refuge she needs. Quinn is Quinn. What role he plays for her is beyond my understanding, but those two are...great for each other, just look at them in the same room. Where do I fit? I'm just here. I'm smart, sure. I'm a guy. I take her on dates. So does Vincent. She lets me in while she sleeps, but Sombra is also doing that. She doesn't...need me."

He needed to feel needed for some reason. He needed to know he had a place, and more and more, he felt like he didn't have one.

"I'll think on what you've told me," the cowboy said quietly, pushing himself out of the chair. "I'll come back when I have some advice, Jasper."

"Wait." Jasper pointed at the chair Elijah had been sitting in. "Stay there and complete your half. I told you mine."

Elijah groaned and fell back in the chair.

"I've loved and been to a funeral before," he admitted. "I'm not willing to do it again. I've been bouncing back and forth between either admitting my feelings to her and hoping for the best or just pushing her away until I know there's no chance she gives a shit about me. Maybe if she hates me, or doesn't care, I'll get over her."

"Now who's being ridiculous? She'll kill you for that, for trying to make her feel a way she doesn't want. She looks at you like her only real friend here. The safe place from the rest of us. Sure, we're her friends, but we're also her lovers." She'd said as much. Something about how he might tease, but there didn't feel like any expectations either.

"Oh yeah, that's part of it. She looks at me as a friend, maybe a fuck-buddy. A fun romp when she gets bored of all of you. If that ever happens. I've always been okay with the distance Quinn and I kept from a romantic perspective, but not from her. From her, it kills me. I just want her to know how I feel, but damn, I don't want to go to her funeral. I don't want to experience being with her, only to watch her slip through my fingers."

"Would rather to have loved and lost-"

"Don't give me that shit. None of you know what it's like to give a piece of your heart away and watch it die," the cowboy snarled out at him. "You lost family and that fucking blows, but they were biological. They should have been with you this very day and further. Zander was abandoned. Vincent had probably the shittiest family I know and deals with that. But I...I gave a piece of myself away, of my own free will. I gave away other shit to be with someone. There was nothing forcing me to love Taylor. And he's dead. I'm not sure I can do that again. I've done the loved and lost shit. Let me tell you, it fucking sucks."

Jasper had nothing to say to that. It made perfect sense, in a way, and none in another. Elijah was scared. The haunted look in his eyes said that much. The pain was obvious.

He was downright terrified.

"We…" Jasper tried to find something to say but Elijah snorted.

"See? A bit harder to just say 'do it anyway,' right?"

"Give me some time to think on it? I'll give you some advice later?" He offered Elijah the same thing he'd been offered in return. "Maybe together we can figure this all out?"

"Sure," he mumbled, staying seated. "So, can I hide in here?"

"Only if I'm allowed to hide in your workshop."

"Deal."

"Is that really all that's going on with you? Just her? Just you trying to figure out how you feel and how to deal with it?" Jasper couldn't imagine Elijah, the free-loving cowboy, really getting so hung up.

"Yeah. Yeah, it is. And now Quinn has gone and signed me up for a date with her. I told her it was between friends, but I'm not even sure. You like the dating thing and I want this low-key like your dates. What do you think?"

"Really? You're asking *me* for dating advice with *her*?" Jasper could have laughed, but he decided to help. "You're taking her to that place in Atlanta, right? You've wanted to. That's going to be an all day trip. Four hour drive there and again back here. You might as well make it a day thing, I guess. Show her the city again, how much it's changed since she left as a teen and barely saw it later. Get a hotel to crash in after dinner. I don't know if she likes dancing or anything, but we know all the Magi-centric clubs. That might be fun. I know she deprived herself of that culture when she was in hiding."

He was just throwing out random ideas, really, but Elijah was soaking them up. He was nodding wisely as Jasper talked. "I was thinking all of the same things, but it seems like it's turning into a romantic weekend getaway and I'm not sure I want to give her that impression."

"Maybe that's exactly the impression you need to give her. I don't think you'll get over her just by making her dislike you. I think either way, you're hung up. Might as well take the risk?"

"Like you have?"

"I'll remind you that I kissed her first." Jasper crossed his arms. He wasn't going to let Elijah forget that it was him who made the first move. He would never forget it either. He'd been shocked by himself, but he would do it again in a heartbeat.

"Damn, you got me on that. That was months ago." Elijah tapped his chin. "I'll think about that. When did you get so smart?"

"I thought I got over her years ago and I didn't. I don't think someone like you would be able to either." Jasper shrugged. The smart comment was a subtle, but friendly, dig at him that he chose to ignore. "Hey, on a more serious note, while I have you here...have you heard from James? I was wondering if there was any news I've been missing out on while hiding in here."

"You've missed out on a lot, but I can't blame you. We're supposed to be on a vacation, not even thinking about work." Elijah sighed, shaking his head. "Vincent and I have talked to him a lot, actually. Now that things have calmed down, he caught us up on what's going on with Axel. We haven't told anyone else on the team. It's not like it's important to us. He just wants us up to date on what's going on with it."

"What is going on with it? Last word was he was sentenced to execution, which would come when he was done being useful to them." 'Them' being the WMC. He once had a lot of respect for them, but that had changed in recent months. Councilwoman D'Angelo had done her best to get them all killed. That had a way of changing someone's perspective.

"He's being very useful. We might be on vacation, but the rest of the IMPO isn't. Three major arrests in November alone. There were more in September and October. We're talking entire trafficking rings have been broken up."

"That's fantastic news. At least that evil fuck can do something good for once." Jasper, wanting to relax more, began to unstrap his prosthetic. He dropped it on the desk and leaned back in his chair to get comfortable. "How's the remaining power vacuum? That's a big hole to be left over."

"Well, since we're arresting all the big guys, none of the smaller ones want to step up. They know it would be very easy for their old bosses to sell them out later on for reduced sentences. Right now, analysts don't know who is going to try and fill the hole left in the middle of the criminal underbelly of the Magi. Honestly, I'm just waiting for someone to and don't care who. We'll always have a job."

"Of course we will. If not organized crime, there's some killer out there no one has stumbled on. Or another assassin. Or any other thing we've run across." He wondered how anyone maintained a positive view of the world in their job. He found it hard. He reminded himself of the numbers. Tiny portions of the population are truly evil. Many are morally ambiguous, but trend towards good. Crime rates decreased every year, regardless of what the news made it feel like.

"I hope there's no more assassins. One is more than enough," the cowboy complained. Jasper couldn't stop a twitch of a smile and covered his mouth. Elijah was similar, a grin fighting to break out.

They both devolved into laughter at the same time. That belly-rolling, chest-expanding laugh that meant the world was good.

"More than enough," he agreed, trying to catch his breath.

4

SAWYER

The shower was hot and long, refreshing and comforting. It felt like it washed off more than just her sweat. Sawyer stepped out, knowing she probably used most of the hot water in the house, but didn't care. She wrapped herself in a towel and walked into Quinn's room, where she'd laid out clothes to change into. He was lying on his bed, looking quite pleased with himself as she dropped the towel and grabbed her underwear.

"Enjoying the view?" she asked innocently.

"I am. Personally, I think humans should go back to a time when we didn't wear so many layers."

"Why is that?" She figured she knew the answer. She wasn't looking at him as she pulled up her pair of clean sweatpants, but she could hear him moving on the mattress. When she did look up, he was closer and reaching for her.

"Because then I wouldn't need to get rid of all of them when I want to be with you," he murmured, grabbing a handful of her sweats and pulling down on them. She grabbed them before they could drop and held them up. He released them, smiling.

"You don't understand the idea of a strip tease, then. The anticipation of seeing, of experiencing something you can't touch." She stepped back from him, hoping to prove her point. She hooked her thumbs in the waistband and pushed them down enough to tease a view of her thong. "There's a certain want for something not available. Leaving things to imagination and playing with the maybes. Slinky dresses that show off the figure but not the details, certain clothing that enhances the look of different parts of the body. All of it coming off slowly, being relished. A show. A game. Even a present. Unwrapping a gift that made itself just for you."

"No, I wouldn't know much about it. My sex life has always been to strip and fuck. It's worked for me. Sex is a physical need. It doesn't need to be complicated."

"You know some romantic things, though. The things that make sex complicated," she countered. "The waterfall, for an example. You just haven't mastered the complete skill set."

"What kind of man would want the slow show when I could rip it off you and have what I want faster? When you could have what you want faster?" His question was oddly serious. She raised an eyebrow. He was trying to learn something. This was newer territory for him, it seemed.

"Someone like Vincent would appreciate it. Think of the way he eats, or listens to music. He immerses himself in whatever sensation is present to him. He wants the full experience to last as long as possible. Clothing and the strip tease is just extending and prolonging that gratification, making it more potent, more satisfying." She knew a thing or two about sexuality and human beings. She'd once told Vincent she'd played the roles for work and hadn't been lying. Sultry wasn't normal for her but she could act the part.

"Hmmm."

She didn't like the sound of that, releasing her sweats to finish getting dressed. He wore an expression of thoughtfulness that let her know that he was already plotting some way to try out what she'd talked about. That was going to be something, for sure. This was not the end of this discussion.

"Elijah never talked about it?"

"Elijah really enjoys the way I do things," he replied. "He likes that I'm...upfront with what I want, when I want it. There's no reason for me to learn other things since he and I don't want them."

"There's a charm to that, and it's normally how I like things as well. Just do it. Be honest about it. But I can appreciate the slowness of other ways of seduction too. Not my regular, but I appreciate them." She was finally dressed and held out a hand. "Want to go for that walk?"

"Ah, yes. You wanted to talk." Quinn grabbed her hand and she helped him up.

"I did, but I'm not..." Sawyer shook her head, trying to find the words. She was trying hard to open up before December got bad, before she fell into her dark hole, but now she was at a loss as to what to say. *Perfect*. She changed her plans. "I just wanted your company, I think. You understand better than most."

"When I'm feeling overwhelmed, I go out to my place, my lean-to and garden, and light a fire. I'll stay out there for a long time. Let's go."

"Are you sure?" she asked softly as he stood up.

"Like my room, you are free to come into my space any time," he promised. "Come. We'll send the animals out. We still haven't gone hunting as well. If you want to stay out there, we can do that. There's some tired, older white-tail in the area."

"It might be too cold for that," she noted. "I mean, it snowed last night. Could very well happen again." She had been avoiding going hunting with him, not because the idea sounded bad, but because she hadn't wanted more nights out of a real bed. The Amazon had been a nightmare. She wasn't sure she was ready for more time playing in the wilderness.

"Ah...I have something that may help you with the cold."

She followed him out of his room and then out into the backyard. They walked in silence to the woods. Sawyer could feel Sombra clearer now. She was deeper in the woods, climbing around, enjoying the sun as it began to warm the world up again. She was already tired of the cold and snow.

"She misses home," Sawyer whispered, looking in the direction of her jaguar. She couldn't see Sombra, but she knew exactly where she was out in the woods.

"She does," he agreed. She knew he would figure out what she was saying. "But she's settling in here well. Sometimes the boys miss where we're from. They had other wolves, they knew the land, and there was freedom. No one to say they couldn't do something, or where they could or couldn't go. It's an adjustment. There must be times you miss New York."

"I do," she admitted. "I miss the kids and Charlie and my home over the gym. At this point, it's all probably covered in snow and looking wonderful. I didn't grow up with snow, you know. Here in Georgia, it doesn't happen very often. I never could find a part of me to dislike it, even with all its inconveniences." She smiled, thinking of New York at this time of year. "The city will be decked out in lights. The

Christmas music should be playing in every building, and kids are excited for presents."

"Sounds busy," he mumbled. She knew he wouldn't appreciate it, since he didn't enjoy cities, but she loved it. It made her miss it all, like an ache in her chest. It was better than being depressed over Henry, though.

"It's amazing," she corrected. "Maybe one day I'll get to drag you up there just for a few days. I think you might be pretty astounded by it."

"Maybe." He didn't sound excited at all by the idea, which meant she was never going to get him there. But she could already see it, them on the Square, his eyes reflecting back Christmas lights. She would love having all of them up there, just once. "You're already considering how to get it to happen."

"No, just day-dreaming about it." She grinned. "It would be fun. We'd leave the animals with someone for just a couple of days."

"So you say. I would go if you asked, but I'm positive I wouldn't have fun. It's crowded, concrete, and too busy. But I would go for you." He eyed her. "Can I admit something to you?"

"Of course?" She frowned at him, confused.

"I'm thinking about getting a haircut."

That took her by surprise. She really wasn't sure what to say in return. She liked his long hair? He was free to do whatever he wanted with it? She went with something easy.

"Why's that?" she inquired, turning to walk backwards on the trail and look at him. She didn't want to seem like it wasn't a big deal. She had a feeling it was.

"Change," he answered softly. "For a long time, I kept it long because it is what I'm used to. But over the last month or so, I've been thinking about it. My mother liked it long, and so did my mate. And I want change. I want something new, something different." He shrugged. "I've always been very resistant to change, but...I have. I'm a different male than the one you met. I'm a different male than the one who went into the Amazon. The male you met would have never considered going to New York just because you wanted it, for example."

"So you want something visual to represent the change. You want to make it feel real." She nodded, thinking about how much he really had changed. She'd been attracted to the man she met when she arrived. She loved the man she was talking to. They were two very different people. Similar, of course - Quinn would always be Quinn. There would always be odd things about him that made him interesting and unique.

None of that changed the fact that she was a little heartbroken to think of him cutting his hair.

"Do...do you want to help me?" he asked softly. "You and Elijah? I'm not sure what I would do." There was such a vulnerability in the words. This was part of the man she'd fallen in love with. He wasn't just a feral man with so much power. He was deeper than that; he was *human*. In one simple, insecure question, she realized the difference between the Quinn she met and the one she knew now. This one trusted her with his deepest worries and fears, things he showed no one except her and Elijah. She saw why the cowboy loved him so much, even just as the closest of friends.

"I'll help in whatever way I can. Quinn, it's your hair. Change it, don't change, just do what makes you feel good. About yourself. Nothing else." She didn't have any other words for him. "I guess Elijah and I can find some styles you might like?"

"That would be nice. Plus, I'm almost tired of it. It's a lot of hair. I have to maintain it. I'm tired of it. Truly."

"Then you sound pretty ready to cut it all off, but maybe the first cut doesn't need to be too drastic? Have you ever cut it before?"

"I trim the ends on my own."

She would have never known. His hair was as long, if not longer, than her own when she straightened it. Probably longer. She would guess longer.

"We'll figure something out," she said, thinking about what would look good on him. She wouldn't let him go as short as Elijah's hair. That would be too different. There were some longer male hairstyles that could work for him, though. Something shoulder-length. She turned again, walking normally at his side as they made it into his camp with his 'lean-to.'

"Thank you." He leaned to kiss her cheek and she smiled in return. "I'll get a fire going and we can just ignore the rest of the world for a little while."

"That sounds nice. It feels far away out here, far away from civilization, people. All of it."

"That's what I love about being out here. Most of the bad things we deal with are in that world, beyond the woods. Here? It's just the wilderness, just a small piece of it. A place where I've always felt comfortable." He moved quickly, grabbing logs from a stack he had next to the lean-to.

She sat down on one of the chairs near the fire pit and waited, knowing he wouldn't want her help. She was trained in making fires and all the other survival stuff he enjoyed, but he thought she was too slow. As he got the fire going, the sun was hanging over them. The day was chilly, a bit too cold for how far south they were.

"Should have gotten Elijah. He could light this in a second," he complained softly.

She realized it wasn't said to her, but she couldn't help making a comment in return. "Is my feral Magi getting lazy?" she asked, teasing him for the complaint.

"Maybe," he admitted, grinning. That beautiful and rare smile. It was a lovely thing and becoming so much more common. She felt like a teenage girl just staring at it and swooning a little. "Is he still being strange with you?"

She groaned and rolled her eyes. "Yeah."

"He really likes you. You know that, right?" Quinn looked up at her as he finished poking the small fire. He rose up and walked to sit down next to her. "He's a good male."

"Sure," she bit out.

She had four wonderful men that she was in love with all for their own reasons. Like the kids she taught self defense to, she loved each of them for their own uniqueness, and there were times when she felt like she didn't deserve any of it. Which was why she didn't question it. She wasn't going to try and convince them that it was ridiculous they all wanted her, or that the future of this weird relationship was probably doomed. She was just going to take the good as it came and turn a blind eye to anything that might end it sooner. It was the only way she could accept it.

That made her conflicted anger and frustration over Elijah puzzling. She felt put out by it. She was in a woman's dream world. Four stunning men who helped her through her rough times, who she trusted more than anyone who came before them, and she was hung up on the cowboy who stopped flirting with her. She was stung by the silent rejection of his recent behavior.

She was messed up.

"Do you like him?" Quinn's question sounded so innocent. She narrowed her eyes on him until he shrugged. "Just a question."

"You don't meddle well."

"I meddle well enough," he retorted, a twitch of his lips telling her that he was trying to hide a smile. She knew a meddler when she saw one, but at the same time, she was glad it was him and not Vincent. He was the person who knew the frustrating cowboy the best.

"Yeah, I like him. He's a good friend-"

"No, Sawyer. Do you *like* him?"

"What is this? High school?" she sputtered, looking at him like he was being ridiculous. Really, she just didn't want to answer the question. She didn't *have* an answer, and that was hard to admit.

"Jaguar?"

With a single word, the conversation became more serious. They only trotted out those nicknames when they were being serious. Since the Amazon, it was something only he called her.

"He's Elijah. He's hard not to like." It was the safest answer she could give. She tried to elaborate, though, knowing Quinn wasn't going to accept that. "I liked the easiness between us, and it's not there anymore. It's evaporated. Poof. Gone. I don't know what I did."

"I don't think you did anything. In fact, I know you didn't do anything. It's all on him, and he knows it."

"I'm going to assume you've talked to him about it?" She pulled her knees to her chest and held them as she looked over at her lover.

"Of course. He doesn't keep things from me. I hold what he says in confidence, but I can tell you, it's all him."

She could smell the meddling over the campfire. She could hear it over the ambient noises of the woods around them. He was meddling quite a bit, her wolf, but she didn't know why. What did he have to gain from nosing around between her and Elijah?

"Wolf?" She turned the serious question back on him. "Why are you getting involved in this? I thought the general rule was that I dealt with all of you as individuals. That while we're a team, the relationships and those problems were something between me and whoever."

"He's not happy right now, Sawyer, and I know it's because of what's going on between you and him." He shrugged, looking off into the woods. "I know you aren't happy with how he's behaving. You both being happy is important to me, so I'm stepping in how I can. I might not be able to give away all of what he asks me to hold in confidence, but I can help you understand that it's not you. He's not upset with you. I promise."

She wanted to believe that, since she was tired of trying to figure out what she did wrong. It was such a fast and drastic change in her friendship with the cowboy that it had thrown her for a loop and had made her unhappy. Every time he blew her off, she was hurt in a way she hadn't figured would come up. Rejected. She relied on these guys and now one was constantly rejecting her, pushing her away. She felt like she lost a friendship, and now was realizing just how much it meant to her.

"I purposefully suggested him taking you out to dinner so you two can have a moment away from the house and the rest of us. I think that might do good."

"Why do you think that?" she asked quietly, hoping to understand the wisdom that she was beginning to expect from Quinn.

"It worked for us, in the village. We were away from the rest of the team, only having each other out there, and strangers."

"Basing your relationship advice on what has been proven to work. Good idea."

"It's not a hard concept. I noticed everyone here does it except you and Elijah. When Vincent needs you, you lock away in his office or room. You go to the gym every morning with Zander, and it's something you both look forward to, something between you. Zander and Jasper play video games on weekends, something between them. It's something friends do." He looked suddenly worried he got it all wrong. "Right? I'm not...mistaking anything?"

"No, I think you have the right of it," she replied, chuckling. "You're right. We all do have something with each other that's just ours. You and Elijah love the swimming hole more than everyone else. Vincent and I love to play chess against each other and talk nonsense. Jasper and Vincent have been known to pore over books they both like."

They continued to throw examples back and forth, talking the day away about their lives and the people in them. Vincent's changes as a person, her work in progress with Zander, Jasper's intelligent mind. How they tied into each other and made what Quinn considered a strong pack. They all had pieces of each other. It reminded her of another thing she had in common with one of the men she lived with.

"Elijah and I both like working on cars," she mumbled. When was the last time she popped the hood on a vehicle and played around? When was the last time she put that hobby into action? It used to be something she could do to pass the lonely hours of her life. It had been a rewarding hobby on top of that, since she could do it and have something to show for it. She felt accomplished when she could get something broken and turn it into something that was wanted.

She had been tinkering on the beat-up truck they used to drive around the property when they had yard work to do, but she hadn't touched it since before the Amazon. Even then, she'd been overwhelmed by everything else and too busy.

"He loves messing with the inside of his truck, especially during 'race season,'" Quinn mentioned. "But I've never seen you two work together on anything."

"We never have," she said, sighing. "Maybe..."

Christmas was coming up, and this had given her an idea. She hadn't been planning on getting any of them gifts, but with this idea, now she had an idea for at least one.

"You seem like you figured something out, which is good. I would rather your mind be focused on the present, the people around you."

She blinked and looked at him, frowning. "What does that mean?"

"You haven't mentioned Henry the entire time we've been out here and it's nearly dinner." He smiled, standing up. A moment later, the fire was gone, swallowed by the earth.

She didn't let her jaw drop, but she really wanted it to. He was right. They had sat out here nearly all day, talking about the people they lived with, and she didn't once think about Henry. She didn't once feel that darkness and cold sliding in her chest and threatening to overwhelm her.

"When I'm caught thinking about my son too much, I find something to divert my attention. Something that requires all my attention."

"Well, it worked." She couldn't deny that, and even now, she couldn't feel the drag of remembering him. Something in her chest was too full for something like that darkness. "It's not like I've never had the same idea but...it never worked, not really."

"You were always alone," he reminded her. "Now, you aren't."

"No, I'm not." She smiled, letting those words wash over her. She was the furthest thing from alone now.

5

ELIJAH

"You only have space tomorrow?" Elijah tried not to growl. Tomorrow was too soon. Way too soon. It had already been a few days since he was cornered publicly into doing this and he still wasn't ready for it. He had hoped he would have another week before he signed himself over to spending an entire day alone with her, maybe even a night.

Not that he didn't see the need to get her out of the house and keeping busy. Just the day before, he'd caught her in the gym alone. He had slept through breakfast and the morning training he'd stupidly signed up for. He'd figured to catch her and Zander before they were done, but he'd missed it. Instead, he found Sawyer, just sitting there on the mat, a lost look on her face. He knew it when he saw it - that moment when a loss felt like it had been the day before and not years ago. He had just helped her stand and walked her out. He found Vincent in their office, and the Italian took her off his hands. He hadn't seen her again until dinner, where she seemed more like herself.

He should have comforted her himself, but that sort of

pain was raw and he'd needed to get away from it. It had only reminded him of Taylor and all the reasons why he was so hung up on admitting how he felt about her. He felt like an ass after the fact.

"Yes sir. It's a busy season with the holidays. We had someone cancel just this morning, and that's the only thing we have for the next two weeks. Unless, of course, you want to schedule something closer to Christmas-"

"No, it works. I'm just shocked. I'll take it, doesn't matter the time. Party of two."

"Then it'll be eight pm tomorrow. Party of two, you say? Would you like us to make any plans for a date or know anything ahead of time?"

He resisted a groan. "No. Just a table for two. It's not...it's not a big date or anything. I just promised to bring her here at least once, and-"

"We'll have something set up at your table to drink upon arrival. Maybe even some flowers." The professional tone of the other person on the line ended after that. "You know, Elijah, you've never brought a woman here before." It was a teasing comment.

"Fuck you, Rogers." Elijah growled this time. "She's a teammate just like the guys."

Well, she was nothing like the guys, but he wasn't going to tell his contact for this place more. Rogers knew he was an IMPO special agent, and so were the guys, but nothing else. And he wasn't going to tell Rogers any more, either. From the years he'd known Rogers, he knew the other man was nosy. It was one of the reasons Elijah stopped sleeping with him. He was always interested in what was going on. That's what Elijah got from making friends with the Magi from Atlanta who knew everything. He played the role of server and host for one restaurant, but he had contacts to every good place in the city and knew all the right people to get the best service around. A call to Rogers meant you were going to get the best Atlanta had to offer, if you stayed in his good graces.

"That's interesting. A new teammate? I hope that's working well for you boys," Rogers commented lightly.

Elijah nearly cursed. He'd given Rogers something without meaning to. He now knew their team was five guys and one woman. He didn't know why it bothered him that Rogers was looking for information, since he always did, but today, it got on his nerves. "Make the reservation. Don't do anything ridiculous."

"Do you need a hotel room for the evening?"

"No," Elijah bit back and immediately backpedaled. "Yes. We'll need a place. There's no reason to try and drive too much after having dinner. Thank you."

"I'll make sure those are handled for you as well."

"Thank you, Rogers." He meant it.

"I'll email everything to you once it's done. Just give me an hour. Have a good one."

"You too," he replied and then hung up. He needed to find his 'date' and tell her the plans now. He didn't like how he felt about all of this. It was just a dinner with a friend. A friend he'd been neglecting because he was a damn coward. Quinn even said as much now. Vincent and Quinn had both now nailed him to the wall over it. Jasper had too, now that he really thought how that went down.

He wondered where she would be now. It was late enough in the day that she wouldn't be in the gym, but he didn't know her schedule anymore. They didn't have much of one, everyone just going with the flow. Sawyer was the hardest to find out of everyone. She could be anywhere from the offices, to her room, to another of their bedrooms, or even in the woods. He was in for a search, he realized as he left his space.

He tried his shared office with Vincent first. Vincent looked up from the book he was reading and frowned at him. "Can I help you?"

"I'm looking for Sawyer," he answered. "You seen her?"

"No, but I'm going to ask why you need her," Vincent replied, narrowing his eyes. "Haven't you pissed her off enough recently?"

"Fuck you. I'm looking for her to tell her we're going on a trip to Atlanta tomorrow." Where he would hopefully grow back his balls and talk to her about what was wrong with him.

"Ah." Vincent visibly relaxed. "Well, I haven't seen her since breakfast. I know she trained with Zander in the morning, but...I would try the woods with Quinn. Those two have been spending a lot of time together in the last few days."

"Don't I know it," he replied. He wanted to spend time with them again, the three of them. He also didn't want to be the third wheel to the Sawyer and Quinn show. There was only one real way to fix that, and therein lay his problem. His shit was keeping him not just from her, but from all of them. They were all wrapped up in her. Everywhere he went, everyone he talked to, he was confronted with her. "I'm trying, Vin, I really am. This trip will be time to air my shit. I promise. Maybe I'll feel better once she understands."

"I'm not the one you need to worry about. Look, we're in a weird situation. We always have been, but she looks at you like her best friend now and you're hurting her. I can understand what you're thinking and going through, I really can, but...This needs to be the time, or I'm telling her the next time she asks me."

"I'm amazed you haven't yet."

"I'm a better liar than she is. I hate it, but you've got the rest of us backed into corners about it, especially Quinn and I. We all know what's eating away at you, at least from some perspective, and we're keeping her in the dark for you. Because it's your feelings that need to be admitted, not ours."

Elijah let the guilt hit him like a bag of bricks. Damn, he was being shitty. He was convincing a group of guys to lie to the woman they loved because he was scared to admit he cared for her. "I'm trying."

"I know." Vin sighed. "But you've got to get over that mental block. It's causing all sorts of problems between people, and you know it."

Which one? The fact that he was crushing on her or that she could die and break his heart? Or maybe that he very possibly could be rejected by her, that she didn't want him like she wanted the rest of them? He felt like the lovesick fool he claimed all of them were. He wasn't even sure he loved her. He cared for her. He'd convinced himself of that, now that they weren't in danger - that nothing was wrong.

"Elijah?" Vincent called out to him and he realized he was just standing there in the office door like an idiot.

"Nothing," he answered, closing Vin back in their office.

He went out the back of the plantation house and into the woods. He didn't need to work very hard to find her or Quinn now. Sombra ran up to him and pounced.

Elijah was a big man, but the over two hundred pound jaguar had momentum and took him down. He hit his back on the earth, groaning as the jaguar rubbed on him, purring. He let it happen, staring at the sky in a small amount of pain. Damn cat.

"Sombra, get off him! We've had this discussion. You

can't jump on people. You can seriously hurt someone." Sawyer sounded frustrated, but when he rolled his head to look at her, he saw the small smile she was fighting off. "Though this one deserves it. Jump on him again."

Sombra obliged and he grunted as she dropped all her weight on his stomach again.

"Thanks, little lady. Really. I get the message." He didn't try to move, hoping his suffering could end soon. Maybe the cat would suffocate him. That didn't sound so bad.

"Good. Get off him, girl."

Sombra did so immediately and trotted back into the woods. He heard even more movement and watched the wolves run after the jaguar and disappear.

"What are y'all doing out here?" he asked as he pushed himself up. A hand appeared in front of him and he took it. Quinn helped him up without a word, smiling as well.

"We're just putting them through their paces. They need to stay exercised," he explained. "The wolves caught your scent."

"Sombra just thought you would make a good practice dummy," Sawyer commented, grinning now. "What are you doing out here?"

"I wanted to tell you that we're going to Atlanta tomorrow. For dinner. Well, maybe sightseeing, then dinner, depending on if we have time. Maybe some dancing afterwards, since we'll be up there."

"As friends?" she asked, raising an eyebrow.

He sighed and looked back at Quinn, who didn't offer him any advice on the matter. He already knew Quinn's advice, and his closest friend knew that. Tell her what he wanted. Just say it. Stop being a coward and start being the male he knew Elijah was.

"No," he said slowly. "Well, if you want it to be as friends.

That's your choice." He corrected to a non-answer. He would rather have her make that decision. It shocked her. He watched her eyes get big, then the emotion disappeared from her face as she covered it all up. It was something she didn't do as much, the blank face, but she pulled it out on him and that worried him.

"We'll play it by ear," was her answer, with no inflection to her voice that told him what she wanted. That frustrated him, but he resisted acting on it. He had wanted her to admit something about how she felt. Friends or something more: make a decision. Instead, she gave him a non-answer to his own.

"All right then, little lady."

An awkward silence settled on them. Elijah wasn't sure where to go from here.

"I guess we're not going hunting tonight," Quinn said, breaking the silence as he turned to her. "We'll plan it for a different time."

"You were going hunting?" Elijah frowned between them. When had that happened? He'd never heard about them wanting go out to hunt. He would have loved to go on a hunt. He grew up hunting with his dad, but hunting with Quinn was an experience.

"We've been planning to, but things keep coming up. And after South America, I haven't been keen to go out and play in the woods away from the comforts of modern civilization." Sawyer was wearing an expression of mock disappointment. "I'm sorry, Quinn."

"Don't pretend to be disappointed."

"Okay!" She grinned and that made Quinn chuckle at her.

He just watched the interaction, happy for them. He had been right about them, that much was certain. He knew

Quinn wasn't going to be able to resist her strength, both physically and of character. He knew she wasn't going to be able to resist giving a piece of her heart to a Magi very few understood and even fewer ever gave a chance to love. Sawyer loved the 'lost' causes.

A pang of jealousy at his closest friend ran through him. A pang of jealousy for her as well. "I'll leave you two. Have a good day and Sawyer, tomorrow-"

"Wait. Hang out with us. It's been a long time since the three of us just hung out." Sawyer grabbed his arm and held on. He hadn't even started walking yet, so she hadn't needed to grab him, but the gesture moved him. She wanted him there, with them.

"Okay, but I'm not sure I can help with exercising the beasts. I'm not fond of being a pounce target, either."

"No, we'll just go to my camp. We've had a fire going all day to battle the chill. I'm certain I have one of your spare sketchbooks; you can doodle while we just talk. She's right. We haven't had fun together in a long time."

He swallowed at the idea of a sketchbook. He hadn't drawn anything in weeks, probably longer. He *knew* what he wanted to draw but he was tired of seeing obsidian eyes looking back at him. Especially now that she knew she was one of his constant subject matters. To combat the urge to draw her, he just stopped.

They walked to the camp and garden, where Elijah immediately made the fire bigger, seeing it was trying to die out. He grabbed a couple of Quinn's logs from the stack and threw them on and brought it back to life. Then he grabbed a chair and fell into it. Quinn brought him the sketchbook and a pen. He took it slowly, unsure of himself. His lover must have noticed, but then, Quinn noticed everything.

"She thinks you draw her beautifully. It brought her to

tears when we were in the rainforest," he whispered. Elijah's eyes went wide as he stared at the leather-bound sketchbook in his hand. "I hope you haven't stopped."

"I have stopped," he mumbled. "I didn't know that she..."

"I know she complimented your work, but she was very touched by your art of her. I should have told you sooner. You should draw something she can keep today."

"Damn you," Elijah grumbled, realizing he was just backed into another corner by the wolf. "Sneaky."

"She knows I'm meddling too, which is why she's wandered off to get the animals back when she didn't need to."

He looked around and realized he hadn't noticed her disappear on him. Shaking his head, he opened the blank sketchbook and began putting the sketch down, getting lost in a mental image of her and those dark eyes and that smile, like every time he drew her. Not even Quinn had been such a captivating model for him.

When she came back with the pack behind her, it felt like normal. They all talked about the animals, each other, and he couldn't resist making some very obscene jokes as Quinn decided he wanted her to sit on his lap, something Elijah had never seen before. She wasn't the type of woman to sit on a lap, but the sight of it made him want her on his. Made him want it enough to put the sketchbook over his lap and hope the animals weren't close enough to smell how turned on he was. He knew they could and then they would tell their owners, because animals didn't keep secrets, not really.

"Jealous?" Quinn asked in a taunting way that made Elijah grin.

"I get her all night tomorrow," he retorted, feeling easier.

"Oh, the pervert thinks he can get a piece whenever he

wants, huh?" She was also smiling and shifted a little in Quinn's lap, like she was trying to get more comfortable. Elijah let out a bark of laughter at Quinn's face, an agonized expression of want and some attempt at control. She was torturing the poor Magi.

"Stop moving," he demanded softly. "Or I'm going to ask Elijah to leave."

Elijah continued to laugh. "Don't stop on my account." He felt the pang of being the third wheel, but he also wanted to keep enjoying the easiness of this.

"That's an even better idea," Quinn murmured. Elijah could see the devious ideas twinkling in his eyes. He knew what Quinn wanted. Elijah had considered that wet dream more times than he could count.

"Oh, that's dirty," she mumbled, getting off Quinn's lap. "I'll sit over here." She placed herself beside Quinn. The conversation was dropped in favor of lighter, less obscene topics.

As dinner approached, he got up and carefully tore out the sketch he'd been working on. He approached her slowly, following Quinn's suggestion and held it out to her.

"I'm going in. You said you like my work and..." He felt like a tongue-tied fool.

She took it slowly and looked it over with consideration. "You always draw me so beautifully," she said, grazing a finger gently over the sketch. He wanted that gentle finger stroking down his chest, or maybe any other body part of his. He had never seen her touch something with such a tenderness. And what she'd said? There was a vulnerability to it. As if he didn't draw what he saw, but rather made her more than what she was.

But he was a realistic sketcher. He drew the world

around as it was and he drew her exactly as beautifully as she appeared.

"Because you are." He wasn't going to give her anything but the truth on that. "Well, you can have that. Good night, you two."

"It's about that time, isn't it?" Quinn stood up and put the fire out. "We'll come in as well. Sawyer?"

"You can stay with Elijah for the night. I think I'm going to bother Zander."

He didn't move as he listened to them. He swore they were reading each other's minds. They made the decision to split and leave each other with different lovers without even needing to discuss it.

"Elijah?" Quinn looked at him, questioning. "You want to come to my room tonight? Or I'll go to yours."

"Yeah," he answered. He wasn't in the mood for anything, but the company would be nice. He would never turn Quinn down, either.

Once they were inside, she disappeared on them. She was good at it, and he still appreciated that she made no effort to stop him and Quinn. Not like it mattered, since nothing was really going on anymore, but it was more him and Quinn, not her.

He walked into Quinn's room and fell on the bed. "Save me," he groaned.

"Only you can save you. Look, we can be normal. You can stop avoiding hanging out with me and her. I've missed you, and I know she wants you around, so you can get over yourself now. Especially now, when she needs us around her, being there for her. She can't be alone."

He growled into the bed. He knew that. He knew and realized all of that. "Are you in the mood?" he asked, rolling onto his back, hoping to change the conversation.

"I am, but I know you aren't. Not for me, anyway." Quinn sat next to him, relaxing onto his pillows.

"I still find you attractive." He would always want Quinn. Something about the Magi made him pretty fucking hard. But Quinn was right. He wasn't in the mood for him at that moment. "I'm getting a hotel room with her for tomorrow night. I want her, and I am going to make sure she knows it. I need to get fucking laid."

"Good. You should also talk to her about everything else."

"That's all you're going to say?"

"What else do you want me to say? I don't erase Taylor and the impact of that loss. I can't erase your fears of her dying on you too. I can tell that you fearing for her like that means she means more to you than I do, or the rest of the team. I'm just hoping you finally admit it to her."

"I do not care for her more than you," Elijah snapped. He would never put anyone above another, especially not over his closest friend.

"The fact that you agonize over her and you never did with me tells me all I need to know. By the way, the agonizing is getting annoying. Ask her if she'll scratch the itch, though, since you refuse to admit you really like her."

"Damn it, it's not just an *itch*, Quinn." He would never look at her like just another pair of thighs he could get between. She wasn't just some chick he was picking up from a bar. She was Sawyer goddamn Matthews.

"But I'm just an itch."

Fuck.

"Quinn, it's not like that." Elijah sat up, feeling awful.

"Our sex is an itch and separate from our friendship. Admit that, please. Then compare that to what you feel with Sawyer."

Elijah hated the truth of it. "I love you. You know that right? I love you as a friend, as a close companion."

"And I love you. But not like I love her. And I think it's the same for you." Quinn gave him a sad smile.

"It is," he admitted. He still hated it. He didn't want to lose one for the other. "You are still a piece of my heart."

"And you mine."

"Why does it feel like we're breaking up?" Elijah frowned at the ceiling. "We were never a relationship."

"No, we weren't, but we need to admit our priorities are different now. If she leaves here one day, I'm going to follow her, not stay with you."

Somewhere in the back of his mind, he knew that already. It almost didn't hurt because he'd figured it out. And he knew, if that came to pass, what he wanted. "I want to leave with her too."

"Then you need to tell her that you're in love with her and it scares you."

"I am and it does, and I promise to tell her. I almost wish I loved you this much instead of her." He wished they would all stop bothering him about it.

"You love me exactly how I need you to." Quinn sighed. "I want my pack together and the only person holding it all back right now is you."

"I'm sorry," he said, meaning it. "Do you think your alpha female will have me?"

"I think that's between you and her. I've been told I should stop meddling."

"Oh, now you stop offering me advice. Well, fine." Elijah laughed, grabbing a pillow and threw it at Quinn. "Thank you. For talking to me."

"I really should have sooner. Now, let's find something to eat. Stay here tonight?"

"Of course."

"I forgot to say this earlier...I'm thinking of getting a haircut. I want you and Sawyer to help me decide on something."

Elijah sputtered, but kept listening to his lover explain what he wanted and why. At the end, he could only agree, even though he would miss the hair.

"Then we'll get you a haircut. No problem." He would stand next to Quinn when they cut off most of the long, silky black hair, and that was that. He would never leave him to it by himself, and Elijah knew if he didn't go, it would happen anyway. He might as well be there for it and help Quinn make his decision.

"Thank you. I knew I could count on you and her for this."

Elijah repeated those words in his head. Quinn knew he could count on *both* of them. Just another damn reason he was so in love with the little lady. Not Vincent, or Jasper, or Zander. Just them.

Feeling easier, he passed out that night across the bed from Quinn. He wondered if one day he'd find Sawyer there between them.

Wasn't that a dream to fight for. He'd just needed to get told off a few times to remember it.

6

VINCENT

Vincent picked up his phone the moment it rang and answered quickly, knowing it was news he couldn't avoid. "What do you have, James?"

"I have an update on Axel's condition." Their handler sounded tired, weary. "He was pretty fucked up."

Vincent held back a groan. He shouldn't feel sympathetic, but he did. He felt awful.

"Someone tried to kill him. He wasn't going to come out unscathed. He'll have scars for the rest of his...his life. However long that's going to be," James continued. "How do you feel?"

"They shouldn't be dragging this out. He's been sentenced. Why is he even still..." He couldn't say it. Why wasn't his brother dead yet? "There's no way he still has information for them."

"He always has information, and they don't even need to torture him for it."

Vincent's heart sank lower.

Two weeks before, his brother had been jumped in

prison. Without his magic, he'd been hurt enough to get put in the medical wing and watched constantly. Since the WMC still found him useful, they healed him as best they could.

And here he was, asking why his brother was still even *alive*. "Do they need anything from me?" he asked softly. "Medical information, anything like that?"

"No, but they wanted me to pass a message along. He wants to see you. Before the end, he wants a day to see you. He's never made a request before and has been cooperative, so they thought it was only fair to pass this one along."

Vincent didn't say anything. His hand shook hard enough that he nearly dropped his cellphone.

"Vincent?"

"I..." He covered his face with his free hand, hoping it would stop shaking as well. He'd never intended to see him again. Never wanted to. He'd hoped once Axel was in prison that it would be over.

"He probably just wants to say goodbye," James said kindly.

"I don't have an answer for you right now," Vincent forced out.

"They'll need one quickly. It's pretty much his dying wish, Vin."

"I'll call you back," he whispered, quickly hanging up before James could say anything more. He forced himself to drop the phone on his desk and stand. He walked out of the room, slamming the door as he left. He didn't know where he was going, but he knew he had to get out. He wasn't going to sit in the office with a chess board, wondering.

This was a game. He knew it. Paranoid, some would call him, but he knew his brother. There was no way seeing him could go well. None at all. Vincent had hung up because he wanted to. He wanted to see his brother again. As fucked up as it was, he wanted to say goodbye.

He couldn't bring himself to say it.

He was out the backdoor before he stopped and bent over, grabbing his knees as he fought to breathe. Something was weighing down on his chest like a stone.

His brother wanted to see him before he was gone. Why? Was it just to play one more game or did he really want to make amends? They were each other's last real family. Sure, they had cousins out there, but Vincent hadn't associated himself with the rest of their family for nearly a decade.

He'd only had his brother, for good and ill. Through losing their mother, to murdering their father, to the dangerous games that resulted in the scar on his chest, they only had each other.

"Vincent?"

He jerked upright to see Quinn frowning at him.

"What's wrong?"

"He...he wants to see me," he mumbled. "My brother wants to see me visit him in prison."

"Oh."

Vincent could have laughed. Even *Quinn* knew just how bad that was. Even the most socially awkward, misunderstanding man who walked the earth could relate to the trouble that Axel left in his wake.

"I want to," he admitted. "I want to say goodbye to him."

"The last time you saw him, another agent had killed himself, Sawyer was maybe dying, and we were all wondering what to do. You said he wasn't your brother. What changed?"

"Sawyer reminded me that it's okay to love the brother

71

he was before he became a monster." It was the only answer he had. Once, there had been a boy who loved his mother and was a good older brother. He'd protected and cared, and had a sharp mind. He loved that boy. His brother.

"Sawyer also admits that the man she loved and the boy you knew isn't there anymore. She'll even say that maybe he was never real to begin with." Quinn touched his shoulder and leaned closer. "Why does this bother you?"

"Because he asked to see me." If it had been Vincent requesting to see him, or anyone else, it would have been different. But Axel had called him out. Axel asked for him, knowing he was going to die soon.

"Do you think he's changed?"

"I don't know. I haven't seen or spoken to him since before he was shipped to the prison. But he's...cooperating for the WMC. He's helping. He's the model prisoner. He's well behaved. He denied protective custody before he was attacked-"

"He was attacked?" Quinn's voice turned hard, his face becoming stone. "Who attacks a defenseless man?"

"Criminals," he whispered. "The criminals he's helped catch."

"Why haven't we been on those cases?" Quinn removed his hand from Vincent and crossed his arms. "We caught him. Why aren't we the team destroying Axel's entire world?"

Vincent sighed, knowing this question was going to come from someone. He understood the Director's reasoning behind it, and so did James. "I'm his brother, and Sawyer was once employed by him. Using us could be seen as me and her looking to destroy his enemies for him, or take his place as powerful members of the criminal world. Perception is important."

"Like we will pretend in public that we aren't sleeping with her."

"Exactly. So I get news of it instead of being directly involved. It took a couple months to get rolling, right after we caught him. They only started making arrests right after we got back from the Amazon, having confirmed the information he gave over."

"And now he wants to see you," Quinn repeated thoughtfully.

"And now he wants to see me." Vincent's hands were still shaking. The idea of it terrified him and yet appealed to him as well. To have one more moment with his brother. To look back in the eyes of another Castello, and maybe they could find what they had lost. The family. Even in his remaining days.

"He killed his own son," Quinn murmured, looking away, back into the woods. "Five years ago this month."

"He did," Vincent agreed. "Sawyer told me the full story of that day a long time ago."

"He might be redeemable for what he did as a criminal, but he's not redeemable for that."

Vincent listened to those words kill any chance of hope he had about reconciling with his brother.

"He's not redeemable for what he did to *her* either. Vincent, drop it. Don't go see him. You have brothers. We're here with you. Let him stay where he belongs. He's not good for you, and he's not good for her. He's not *good*."

Vincent nodded silently, closing his eyes. That's what he'd needed to hear. Axel was a monster, not just to him, but to everyone. He'd murdered a little boy he'd brought into the world, and even if it was unintentional, it was something he couldn't come back from. He'd done unspeakable things to a woman he'd claimed to love. A woman Vincent now truly loved, for her spit and fire, her dark eyes, and her sharp tongue, that wicked dark sense of humor and unapologetic nature of her being.

"Thank you," he whispered, opening his eyes again.

"For what?" The head tilt Quinn gave him was so much like one of his wolves that Vincent couldn't resist a chuckle. The image of it lightened him just a little.

"For reminding me. Speaking of that particular woman, where is she?"

"She left an hour ago with Elijah to Atlanta. For their date."

That had his attention and further pushed Axel from his mind. "Really? How did I miss that?"

"Maybe because you've been locked in your office for two days?" Quinn smiled at him. "Would you like to watch movies with me? Sawyer keeps recommending one called the Godfather. She said it's good but banned from the house? Why is it banned?"

"Of course she does," he grumbled. "Yeah, fine. We can stream it." He should have known she was secretly whispering about that movie to Quinn. It *was* a classic. He would have to get her back for it later, since he knew this was her way of giving him a hard time. It couldn't have come at a weirder time, but he would go along with it. No reason to deprive Quinn of a new movie to experience. As they walked inside, he went back to the discussion of the date. "How do you think the date will go?"

"Terribly," he answered. "I think they will stumble over it like children. I think nothing will really be resolved, but they will at least be on the same page."

"What page is that?"

"He loves her and she doesn't know how she feels about him."

Vincent frowned as he thought about that. "She doesn't know?"

"She said as much to me." Quinn shrugged. "I think they'll fuck. Hopefully. They are more complicated than I ever thought they would be."

"He held off for you and ended up developing more feelings than he had figured." Vincent chuckled softly. "The idiot."

"He didn't have to do that..." Quinn was frowning now as well. "I could see it, though. He probably didn't want me to think the new female was taking away my pack."

"He didn't want you alone." Vincent smiled gently. "I don't blame him, really. I never thought you and she would find anything in the Amazon."

"She...she respects me, not for my power, but for everything else." Quinn looked down at the floor as they kept walking. Vincent watched the feral Magi's face change to one of sadness. "Even you and Elijah sometimes only think about the power."

Vincent opened his mouth to deny it and Quinn waved a hand to stop him.

"It's your job to always account for how useful and capable your team is. Elijah is a direct extension of that sometimes as your second-in-command, at least officially. I get it. I know you also respect me for me. But she...she respected my power, certainly, but respected *me* more. She refused to be scared of my strength, so that she could get to *me*. That's something none of you had ever done."

"I'm sorry," he whispered back, feeling guilty. He'd never known just how much his fear of Quinn's power had been so noticeable in his behavior. He'd figured everyone was like that.

"You tried. It's why I've always accepted you as the

leader. You all tried to ignore my power and deal with me. But I would also purposefully use my power to scare you into backing off."

"I've noticed that's stopped." Not once in over a month had Quinn's power lashed out to shake the house or strike terror in the hearts of the inhabitants.

"It proved to be ineffective with her. Since I couldn't scare her away, there was no reason to keep trying to scare any of you when I ran out of patience or was trying to protect my pride. And the things I was ashamed of are no more thanks to her. And you. All of you."

Vincent crossed his arms and leaned on the wall. He thought of that. This was Quinn reaching out to him, making something private known. Opening up a little. "Why don't we invite all the guys down? We'll make it a group thing while we make bets on how Sawyer and Elijah go."

"A pack event while two are off finding their places together," Quinn rephrased, nodding. "I like that."

"Go get them while I get the movie ready."

He couldn't even blink and Quinn was gone. He'd changed so much. So much, in fact, that it was easier now to make him a part of the group. Not that he'd ever been a real outcast, but he'd always been a little separate. Now it felt like he was molding into them like he'd always been there. At least to Vincent.

"Interesting," he whispered as he went into the basement. She was changing them all. Zander was more focused, maturing, growing. Quinn was becoming more human every day, and bringing his animalistic wisdom with him, able to put it to more use as he understood how to be more human.

And Vincent himself was happier in general. Before her, he'd spent his time completely focused on Axel, but it had always felt like he'd had one foot in the grave. Depression had been his companion.

Who was left?

"Elijah and Jasper," he reminded himself. Elijah had his own issues, and Jasper's relationship with her had seemed to go...stale. He wondered what was happening with that. He could bother their Golden Boy during the movie.

"You meddle like me," Quinn's gruff voice pulled him out of his thoughts. "I can see it in your eyes."

"I do. We all know I meddle," he replied. "I like to know she's happy with everyone."

"Why?"

"I promised her I would do anything to erase him. This is just...an extension of that. I would be fine with her doing anything as long as she was happy." Vincent grabbed the remote for their TV and began flipping to the store page to get the Godfather. He purchased it and began the download before continuing to speak. "In the end, Axel would have never needed someone like her if I had never betrayed him and run to the IMPO."

"In nature, everything is connected."

"As it is in life," Vincent agreed. "So, I meddle. To make sure she's happy. To make sure none of her relationships are like the one she had with him. To make sure her life is as perfect as I can make it."

"You're a good man, Vincent Castello."

"Thank you," he murmured, keeping his eyes on the television. Coming from any of them, those words meant the world to him. "Where are the guys?"

"They will be right down. I beat them here."

"Good. Get settled in. Want anything to drink?"

"A vanilla martini?"

Vincent couldn't stop a laugh from bursting out of his chest. He was still laughing as Jasper and Zander joined them.

Zander chuckled as he saw the drink Vincent was making. "Who lost their balls?" he asked, eyeing the martini.

Vincent pointed and Quinn growled back, making him laugh harder.

"I'll have a beer," Jasper mumbled, trying to not laugh as well.

"It tastes good," Quinn snapped.

"It smells like her, too," Zander pointed out, grinning. "Her and those vanilla candles she lights all the time."

"That's beside the point." Quinn jumped up and grabbed his drink. Vincent put away the alcohol after pouring himself a scotch. "It's good."

"Never said it wasn't," Zander said, still teasing.

Vincent was smiling as he fell into the soft leather recliner and hit play on the movie. He continued to smile as Zander and Quinn bickered about the drink and why it was the one Quinn chose.

"Remember to silence your phones for the movie," he ordered as the title card ended. This led to some shuffling around and a growl from Quinn.

"Is that a picture of her in the gym? Does she know you have that?"

"She posed for it. Jealous?" Zander taunted. Vincent refused to try and glance at whatever this picture might have been.

"Absolutely not. I get to see her in the woods where none of you will go."

He was glad it was Quinn who found him. He had been right to remind him that this was his family. Quinn would know the best of all of them that family, pack, was whoever he trusted with his life, his secrets, and now, his love.

And what a good family it was.

7

SAWYER

Sawyer was locked in a metal death trap. She was going to die. She was certain of it.

"Slow down, you crazy mother fucker," she snapped, holding onto the 'oh shit' bar above the window.

"We're fine," he groaned back. "Stop trying to drive from the passenger's seat."

"Stop driving like a maniac!" she retorted, her foot trying to find a brake pedal that didn't exist. She hadn't been in a vehicle with him behind the wheel in months. When he said he would be driving, since this was possibly a *date*, she hadn't thought about it.

Now she remembered why she made a point to drive herself places, even if he wanted to go with her somewhere. He was batshit insane.

He slowed down, turning to glare at her.

"Keep your eyes on the road too!" she demanded, pointing out the front windshield. That got an eyeroll out of the cowboy.

So far, this *date* was off to a terrible start.

"We're nearly there. I'm not sure why you're complaining."

"We should be an hour out of Atlanta still!" She couldn't believe this guy.

"We're twenty minutes from our destination, actually. You'll like it, I promise."

"I have to be alive to enjoy anything," she muttered.

"My God, Sawyer!" He was sounding frustrated with her. "You can sublimate. It's not like you won't see an accident coming and just turn to fucking smoke anyway while I die. And I'm not out to get myself killed, so maybe you should trust me just a little bit. Good Lord."

She glared at him for that. "I wouldn't leave you here to die. I can sublimate you too, even for a very short period. Not even Vincent can do a full other person." They had tried. She was just powerful enough to do it herself and it was painfully hard to do. "What the hell is your problem?"

His face went stony and she resisted the urge to reach out and smack his damn cowboy hat off.

"Answer me," she ordered, snapping her fingers to get his attention.

"You sit there and nag me for doing something I'm good at, but if the other guys say they can do something, you trust them implicitly."

"This has nothing to do with the other guys," she fired back. How dare he bring them up.

"Sure it doesn't," he growled, cutting her off. "I'm just a fully trained professional racer in my free time. It's not like I don't know how to handle a vehicle at high speeds or anything. It's not like I haven't gone through all the driving courses available to make sure I know exactly how to react to anything happening on the road with complete awareness. But if Jasper tells you that he plays in the jungle without a leg, that's fine. God forbid I drive too damn fast - we're all going to die."

She crossed her arms and sank back in her seat, continuing to glare at him. This motherfucker. "If you were hoping to finally get me to ride for eight seconds, you've now completely lost that chance," she told him, turning back to look out the front.

"Good to know." He was short with her now.

"I do *not* trust you less than everyone else," she muttered angrily. "I can't believe you would think that."

"It doesn't matter," he mumbled just as upset as she was. "Let's just eat some damn food and try to have a good time."

"What is wrong with you recently? What the fuck have I done to deserve this from you?" She wanted to beat his head into the dashboard. She'd hoped that this day to Atlanta would give her back the friend she'd grown accustomed to. Instead she was getting the asshole she didn't know. This wasn't Zander asshole. His attitude had always come from a place of attempting to care, even if it was a little too much. This shit from Elijah was straight-up, pure, unadulterated dick.

"It's not you," he answered, now sounding more upset than purely angry or frustrated. "Shit. We'll talk about it over dinner, okay?"

"Elijah, I can't do this. You know how I feel about your driving."

"I would *never* let anything happen to you or anyone else while in my truck, so I'm asking you to trust me and back the fuck off on my driving. I've never been in a damn accident before."

They entered Atlanta in silence, Sawyer stewing on what he said. As he pulled them off the freeway, she decided to try and say something, something that might make her feel a little more comfortable.

"Have you ever done a defensive driving class?" She hadn't thought it was a very good thing to say, but his answer would maybe mean something. "I mean, you said you were trained..."

"Defensive driving, stunt driving, and several courses through various non-Magi police organizations and the IMPO concerning car chases and using a vehicle offensively. I'm the only person on the team with as much training. The rest just did the basic, mandatory courses. I love to drive and race. I've also never been in an accident. And speeding tickets...well, we normally get out of them. Unlike you."

She was glad to hear a little bit of humor at the end of that, even if it was at her expense.

"I'm sorry. Your driving scares me."

"It scares the guys too, but they don't yell in my ear. They know I know what I'm doing. They trust me."

She closed her eyes in defeat at that. She had been a bit of a bitch to him. He'd been an asshole back, but she'd been a bitch to him first. "I'm really sorry for yelling at you like that," she repeated.

"Forgiven," he said, taking them down a back alley and then turning them onto a driveway. "We're here." That simply, he dropped the topic. She went with it, since she didn't want to keep going on about something as stupid as his ability to drive.

"Where are we parking?" she asked, frowning.

"Valet. Obviously? This is supposed to be some sad attempt at a date," he muttered, pulling them in front of the restaurant. "Not like that's going to work now..." He definitely said that second part soft enough where she wasn't supposed to hear it, but she had.

She didn't acknowledge it, just getting out of the truck once it was stopped. She wasn't even sure why they were on a date. She and Elijah had really only ever joked about that sort of thing. She'd always wanted to finish what they had started, but she wasn't sure he wanted a relationship with her. And she had four men back home. More than she could handle, really.

But she also couldn't forget the sting of rejection when he'd tried to say it was just a dinner between friends. Some part of her was glad he'd rescinded that later on, letting it be her choice.

Too bad she had no idea if she really wanted to date him. She didn't really know how she felt about his past, being overly sexual with friends and teammates. Was this going to be sex and friendship or did he want something more serious? She had a feeling neither of them really knew.

The valet took the truck away as Elijah led her inside, letting the silence over them hang a little longer.

"Elijah!" a young man called out cheerfully as they made their way to the podium. He wore a nice suit, and was definitely a member of the staff.

"Rogers, how are you?" Elijah lightened up immediately, reaching out to shake the other guy's hand. Sawyer waited patiently, knowing the introduction was going to come.

"I'm fantastic. I have everything set up for your evening. You'll have a couple drinks here, a light dinner, then you can go down to that place we've talked about? They have a live band playing. You never get the chance, and tonight seemed perfect since you'll be staying here in the city." The young man with the overly cheerful smile and attitude turned to her. "You must be the newest teammate! I'm Rogers. I know what to see and who to do in this city." He winked. "In case you need any help with that."

"I'm from the area," she informed him, shaking his hand when it came to her. "I'm Sawyer."

"Sawyer? Not the name I would have put to you. I like it. Also, never heard of you."

"I'm glad," she muttered as he turned his attentions backs to Elijah.

"Come. I'll show you your table."

She raised an eyebrow at Elijah, who was still smiling, and he just shrugged one of his massive shoulders. They followed Rogers through the dimly lit, dark velvet restaurant and he led them to a tiny booth in the very back. Sawyer kept that eyebrow raised as they sat down and he gave them menus. There was already a bottle in ice on the table and wine glasses ready.

"Your server will be here to get drink orders. Would you like me to pour you each a glass of wine?"

"Going to tell me what it is?" she asked, trying to give him a hard time for being so on top of things.

"Do you care?" he fired back, smiling down at her.

"No, not really. Yeah, I'd like a glass," she answered him, holding back a smile of her own. She liked this guy.

He poured for them and left.

The silent awkwardness returned. She sipped on the red and waited for Elijah to make the first move. It felt like there was a dam about to break, like something needed to be said, but she was going to let him say it.

"This is weird. I think it was a bad idea," he said, taking a large swallow. "You hate my driving, and I put you through it for over three hours - and this isn't really our scene, is it? More Vincent's thing."

She let the smile out and saw he was smiling back at her. After a few moments, they were both laughing.

"Oh, man. A date? Really, Elijah? Come on. You know I don't need this sort of thing. Sure, some of the other guys do it, but it's because they enjoy it and I'm along for the ride. I like experiencing new things. But you didn't need to do this."

"Well, I've wanted to bring you here and Quinn cornered me into it. So here we are." He kept chuckling as he took another drink. "What would you have wanted?"

"I was actually talking to Quinn recently, that meddler. I remembered we both like working on cars. I've been thinking to get us a fixer-upper to do together." She felt like an idiot for her idea, but the smile he had at it made her melt a little.

"That's much better than this," he told her, nodding. "We'll do that next time."

"I mean, I tinker since it's something to do, and I know you work on your truck for racing, fine-tuning it...I figured we could hang out while having a project for both of us."

"Have you looked at anything to buy for said project?"

"Not yet. We can pick something out together."

"You're much better at this than me."

"Do you really want to date me?" she asked back suddenly. That was the point of a date, but it wasn't the point of her side project. Her side project was supposed to just be something between them, something they could bond over, as friends or otherwise. And she'd meant to keep it a secret until Christmas, but the situation had already grown desperate.

"I do," he responded, swirling the wine around in his glass. "Because I'm an idiot, like every other guy we know."

"Then I should be honest now. I don't know how I feel

about you." She laid that on the table before things could go any further.

"That's fine. I'm just tired of you not knowing how *I* feel. I've been...well, pretty fucking ridiculous recently." He took a deep breath. "I've been an ass and I know it. And I've been avoiding everything so I could figure out how I wanted to deal with it."

"Care to explain that?" she inquired softly. Already, things were looking better than they had in the truck. He opened his mouth but didn't get the chance to say anything.

"Hi, I'm Susan, and I was wondering what I could do to get you started today," a cheery voice cut in. Sawyer eyed the blonde that walked up. Susan was smiling at her, not Elijah. "We have-"

"A water," she answered. "Elijah, what do you think for food? I'm going to be a good date and let you choose."

"That's the nicest thing you've ever done," he mumbled, opening a menu.

Sawyer ignored him ordering as the waitress kept sliding glances at her. She looked down and considered if it was because of what she was wearing. She'd dressed up a little, with a black long-sleeved sweater that had a low-dipping collar. It showed off her scar, certainly, but with the right bra, it gave her passing tits. Add in her black jeans for the day and she looked pretty hot.

When Elijah was done, Susan looked back at her fully. "If you need anything-"

"We're fine, thank you," Sawyer answered, trying not to smile again. The faint red tint on the waitress' cheeks and the way she held herself, even the way she was talking, gave away that she was hoping to get either a great tip or a date.

Once she was gone, Elijah began to chuckle. "Oh, little lady, I think you have a new member of your fan club."

"I don't have a fan club," she retorted, sipping again on her wine.

"Yes, you do. There's five very dedicated members."

"Five?" she asked softly, eyeing him again.

"I've always been included in the count, remember?"

She nodded, remembering that even she had included him in the count, even if nothing happened. "So, want to explain what's been going on with you?"

"You...remind me of Taylor and that's had me unsure of what to do. So I've done nothing except act like an ass."

She put her glass down slowly at that. Taylor, the boy he loved who was murdered. That didn't bode well for them. She waited for him to continue but he didn't. "Taylor was killed," she whispered.

"He was. And...while I've always known I could lose one of the guys to this job, the thought of losing you has paralyzed me."

"Takes some balls to admit that, I'm guessing." She wasn't sure what he wanted to hear from her. She wasn't sure how she felt about what he said.

"Look, it's hard having feelings for someone who lives like they are going to die the next day. And you? You have a high probability of dying on me. On them. So yeah, I've had a hard time because I don't want to see another funeral, okay?" He was stern about it. "We left you in that damn jungle, thinking you and Quinn could be dead. There was a possibility you were never walking out and we'd possibly find bodies. Or nothing at all. You and Quinn, of all the fucking people, nearly already died on me. So I wouldn't say it takes balls to admit that you living such a dangerous life scares me. I think it takes balls to even give a shit about someone who could very well not make it through the next fucking year." He pointed a finger at her and she felt pinned as he went on that little rant. He snapped those fingers next. "That's how fast it could be. I would know."

"I'm...sorry, Elijah. I am." She didn't know why she was sorry and wasn't sure why it was the first thing out of her mouth. She understood pretty well the idea of getting attached to someone and losing them. She knew so well what kind of pain that brought. She could see it now, his behavior being a way to push people back.

"Don't be. This is *my* issue, all right? I'll admit that. So there you have it. I like you. I want a piece of that Halloween candy heart of yours like the rest of them. I'm just not looking forward to wearing black one day."

She wanted to tell him she wasn't going to die one day, but that was a blatant lie. Everyone died eventually. She couldn't even tell him she would die of old age. Her life had already proven it wanted to take her out much earlier than that.

She had nothing comforting to say and he also realized it. That was the issue.

"You remind me of Taylor," he repeated softer, looking away as his hand fell to the table. "I'm sorry for my attitude. I'm hoping you knowing helps you understand."

"It does," she said softly. "I'm not sure what to say."

"Nothing works. It just is what it is, and I feel better now telling you. You know, finding the right time and place to say it was pretty fucking hard, so I became an ass. *I'm* sorry for being an ass. Really." He leaned back in his seat. "Back to lighter conversation, I think we should pick some nice little muscle car. It's the South; there's tons sitting around waiting for someone to love them."

"I like that idea," she agreed. "Both to lighter conversation and the muscle. Good, strong, and American?"

"Of course. Like me." He winked and she grinned, shaking her head.

"Good comeback from the heavy stuff," she noted as Susan could be seen walking back.

The energetic greeting she'd expected wasn't there this time. Instead, the plates were dropped a bit unceremoniously on the table and Susan walked away again.

"That was different," Elijah said, watching the blonde walk away. Sawyer felt insulted. They were supposed to be one of the best restaurants in the city, catering to nearly all Magi clientele who wanted a place where their magic was free to use without getting them odd looks...and the waitress just *dropped* their plates on the table.

"She's not getting a tip," she mumbled, pulling her plate closer to her. "Let's hope the food is good."

"It will be," he promised.

She took a bite of the medium rare steak and was glad they had come to the place, even with strange-ass Susan. She closed her eyes as the steak nearly melted in her mouth.

Perfection. Always trust a Southern restaurant to know a damn good steak.

"I think I did all right with the food then," Elijah said, chuckling more. "I'm glad."

She only gave a thumb up to him, smiling as she swallowed and took a sip of wine. The flavors paired well on top of the quality of the meat itself.

"Elijah," Rogers called out as they continued eating. "May I speak with you?"

"Sure?" Elijah sounded as confused as Sawyer felt. He got up and walked away to Rogers, who stood in the door that must have led to the kitchen in the back. She watched them carefully but couldn't hear what was said.

She could see Elijah's eyes get big. When he came back, he sat down silently and seemed to be pouting sheepishly. "The waitress thing was my fault, apparently," he mumbled.

"Oh really?" she asked, insane curiosity over his admission flooding her.

"I might have fucked a friend of hers once and never called back." Elijah pushed his food around with a fork. "I'll admit now, I haven't been in any sort of real relationship since Taylor. Flings and Quinn have been my life for years now."

"Well, we all make mistakes. Look at mine. Hell, the one I made with you got me arrested." She pointed her fork at him until he grinned at her, nodding.

"True, though let's keep talk of that part of our history pretty quiet. Rogers knows we're IMPO, but nothing else."

"Ahhh." She sighed, shrugging. "One day, I'll be able to talk about anything I want, anywhere I want, and no one will hate me for it. Maybe."

"Now isn't that time."

"Don't I know it," she replied before taking another bite of her steak.

Dinner continued with aimless conversation, the talks of dating and feelings dropped for lighter topics like the muscle car. They debated between the pros and cons of the Mustang as Elijah paid the check. As they walked out of the restaurant, she was having a better time than she had on the ride to Atlanta.

"So, there's a band playing?"

"There is! One I really like actually. So the valet here doesn't just do the restaurant; it's open for anything on the block. We can pick the truck up later and we'll just walk to the bar. If that's all right. I know it's a bit cold and you didn't wear a jacket."

"I'll be fine." She appreciated the thoughtfulness, but she didn't find it that cold with the sweater on. In fact, as they walked into the bar, she figured it was going to get too hot. It was packed and the band wasn't even on stage yet. She let him guide them through to a staircase, past a bouncer, and up onto the balcony, where they found it quieter and less crowded.

"VIP section," he told her with a grin. "I only stayed down there when the guys and I were hunting."

"Women," she said plainly. "When you were hunting women."

"Well, I also hunt for men, and please, like you've never hunted for one of those," he retorted. "I do think you hunted me the night we met."

"I do think I was actually your *mark*. Actually, I *know* I was, so what I was there for doesn't matter." She resisted smiling, resisted letting herself fall into laughter.

"So that's how we're going to play this? You can prowl around for a lay but I can't?" There was a light teasing to the question and she grinned. She never held such an outrageous double standard, but it was fun to joke about.

"I don't need to prowl. I'm popular enough that men just flock to me." She wiggled her eyebrows. Four boyfriends and whatever Elijah was. She didn't *need* to go on the prowl.

"And now she gets an ego." Elijah laughed, throwing his head back hard enough that she would have guessed his cowboy hat was going to fly away. It stayed as firmly planted on his head as the grin he had on his face. "You know, little lady, I wish we had met under different circumstances. As in, I wasn't there to..."

"I wish that had all gone down differently too. As in, I got my orgasm before you decided to handcuff me." She smirked, looking away from him and down to the stage, where the band was walking on and getting ready.

A large hand touched her lower back before moving around to her side. A soft tug pulled her into the broad barrel chest. "We could fix that. I can make up for that," he whispered, hot down into her ear. "We might be bad at everything else, but I'm pretty sure we could bring the damn house down."

There were moments in a woman's life where the idea of stripping and fucking in that exact spot seemed like a great idea. Elijah had one of those voices that made her want to do that. Then again, he'd always exuded that hot, sexual energy that made her more than a little wet. She didn't know where her heart lay with him, but she knew what her body wanted.

"You don't know when to quit," she retorted, disliking that something had made her go soft and airy. She wasn't some simpering little girl. She wanted to climb him like the tree he was, not wait for him to make a move.

"Quitting is for people who don't have what it takes," he fired back.

She turned up and found herself much too close to a mouth she knew was very good at stopping rational thought. "And you have what it takes?" she asked.

"Do you?"

She leaned just a little more. As their lips touched, that possessiveness she knew was in her roared to life. She had no idea if she loved Elijah, but he damn sure belonged to her. Because no matter how good she got, no matter what good she did, she was still greedy. She wanted everything she could have and that included him.

As they battled for dominance through a kiss, his hands found their ways to her hips, holding her flush against him.

She ran her hands up his massive arms to his shoulders, then to his face, holding his cheeks.

A couple of people were bold enough to whistle at them, making Sawyer pull away, her face warmer than she would have wanted. She wasn't one to get embarrassed, but that was also the most public display she'd ever been a part of.

"I think I was right," he crooned.

He was. They were bad at dating, certainly, but there was still enough sexual chemistry there to set the fucking bar on fire. And now she knew who he belonged to.

"I'm so greedy," she whispered against his lips.

"Are you?"

"I've always liked nice things, and now I have five of them." She chuckled, pulling back a little more, before he could seduce her back into another kiss. "I'm a greedy person who wants it all and to leave nothing for the rest of the lovely girls out there."

"I think a love-starved heart wants whatever it can get, and there's nothing wrong with that." He moved a hand to wrap it around the back of her neck. She couldn't turn away from him now. "And if the ones you claim are okay with it, then there was nothing for the other women to have anyway."

Love-starved. She liked that, in a perverse way. She was like her damn jaguar, a cat. They had put food at their door, offered her a warm place, and she had never left, even when she could have easily found a way to walk away. They offered her affection she had grown used to never getting.

And she hadn't gotten it. Her kids relied on her for affection and love, for comfort and safety, but she knew better than to rely on them. She could rely on the guys, on the team.

So she stayed. She would keep coming back for more, even if it killed her.

"I'm glad you already know," she said softly.

"Know what? That I'm yours? Oh, little lady, you think we can't all see the possessiveness in your eyes? We know. We know that you've finally found something with us that you'll never let go of. If anything, what happened, what you went through to get home with the Druid just proved it." He kissed her jaw. She tried to turn and kiss those experienced, full lips, but he held her in place. "I'll say that it was one of the things that scared me about you. You own people, Sawyer. You find ways to fill missing pieces of who we are and live there, refusing to move. You then push and grow and get too fucking big for the spot you claimed and take over."

"Hearing you say that, I feel bad," she admitted.

"Why?"

"Because I don't know where you fit," she reminded him.

"Let's try between your legs first," he teased, shifting until she could feel his bulge pressed against her lower abdomen. "I'm a big man."

She swatted his chest for that comment, causing him to laugh. She was grinning, knowing he'd meant it to be a joke.

"How about next to me, then?" he asked. "Just next to me. It's about time to see what we are. What we could be. I should have started much earlier, and I'm sorry I didn't."

"Thank you for finally telling me what was wrong. Really, Elijah. I don't know how to appease your fears, or ease your heart, I don't, but I'm glad I know. If anything, I understand better than you think."

"I know, and it makes me feel like a fucking idiot for not saying anything sooner, let me tell you. Now let's enjoy this band, and please tell me you know how to grind that ass-"

She cut him off by turning around doing exactly what he wanted, swinging her hips to the beat starting. She laughed at the groan she got in reply.

"Fuck me," he mumbled.

"We'll get there," she promised him.

"I'm glad we're on the same page." He grabbed her hips again to hold her ass to him. She tried to move it, to continue to tease him, but he just held her. "Let's not get me to bust a fucking nut in the middle of the bar, please."

"You asked for it," she reminded him, grinning over her shoulder.

"I should be more careful what I wish for then, huh?" He chuckled and turned them so she could see the band again. He pushed her up against the rail of the balcony and kissed her neck as she watched the band.

They danced there as well, rocking to the drumbeat, each sway making her wonder just how good he was in bed. She had her guesses, her belief that he would blow her mind if she tried to claim that ride.

And she had every intention of claiming it. Tonight, she decided. Tonight, they were going to get rid of the itch.

8

ZANDER

Godfather was a great movie and Zander was glad to finally see it playing in their house. Seeing Quinn completely engrossed in it was a good sign and even Vincent was enjoying it, making comments about how 'that's not how real crime families do things.'

He'd be the one to know.

What worried him was Jasper, who sat silently for most of the movie. When they moved on to the second movie, Jasper tried to excuse himself. Zander grabbed him, knowing his best friend was running off to hide. He hit pause on the movie before saying anything.

"What's wrong?" he asked, demanding an answer. He didn't care if Quinn and Vincent were around. There wasn't much the team couldn't say in front of each other.

"Just...tired, I guess."

"Don't lie to me, man. Come on. You've been sulking; what's going on?"

"It's nothing. I'm going to go crash. It's not a big deal."

"First it's nothing, then it's not a big deal, which means there is something and it's a big enough deal to bother you."

Vincent looked up to the ceiling, leaning further back in his recliner. Zander resisted a smile. Vin knew how to nail someone to the wall over a mistaken comment.

"Is it time for therapy?" Zander asked, the grin unable to be held back. "Come on. Sit back down and let's talk."

"I'm worried about me and Sawyer. It's not anyone's business except mine and hers. I'm going to take her on my own date later this week, so it's not a big deal," Jasper explained, falling back into his seat. Zander was glad they didn't need to try and drag it out of him further. "Let's just keep watching the damn movie."

"Good." Zander pressed play and went back to Godfather Part Two. With that out in the open, they could all go back to ignoring it. He would talk to Jasper about it later.

They didn't make it very far in the movie though, before Vincent's phone began to blow up. Then his and Jasper's.

"What the fuck?" he mumbled, pulling his cell out to frown at the screen.

"Oh fuck," Jasper gasped.

"Anyone else seeing this?" Vincent sounded like the world was ending...and there was no way to stop it.

On his screen was a Magi news release, one that was probably being seen by every Magi with a cellphone, computer or had access to any sort of news.

"How did this happen?" Jasper asked, looking up. Zander didn't have an answer, and it seemed neither did Vincent, who stayed quiet in response.

Sawyer's face was staring back at him. A picture of her and Elijah at dinner came on next.

Words. Shadow's identity confirmed. On date with IMPO agent. Government corruption. Untrustworthy IMPO, fraternizing with criminal who should be behind bars.

He nearly dropped his phone. He wasn't sure how to take this. It sent a variety of emotions through him, like confusion and fear. But really, Zander felt angry. He was furious for her, knowing this was about to blow up in their faces. Knowing that her night was ruined and she deserved some quality time with the cowboy.

Knowing that the news was going to wreck her, hearing people tear her down.

"What are you all talking about?" Quinn demanded, standing up to see one of their phones.

"Sawyer was outed."

"And they are being spied on. We need to get ahold of them." Vincent jumped up from his seat and began dialing. Zander knew he was calling either Elijah or Sawyer. "One of you call Sawyer and the other call James. How the fuck did this happen?"

"I got Sawyer," Zander said, hitting her face in his contacts without skipping a beat. He listened to it ring.

And ring.

And ring.

"I'm not available. Sorry. Tell me which one of you called and I'll get back to you."

He cursed, resisting the urge to throw his phone. He grabbed the remote instead and changed off the streaming movie to a news channel from Atlanta. He knew someone would be covering it live.

"Breaking news. Contacts in the IMPO have leaked that the infamous assassin is Sawyer Cambrie Matthews, who has been living under the cover of being a new Special Agent with the IMPO," a brunette said to the camera before turning to her male co-host.

"You know, Heather, it's even crazier when you hear which team she's on. She's apparently under Vincent

99

Castello, Axel's younger brother. What were the WMC and IMPO thinking?" The guy looked like he was going to laugh and Zander wanted to strangle him through the fucking screen.

"I'm not sure, but thanks to some timely leaks, we know she's currently out in Atlanta of all places, having dinner and drinks with one of those teammates, Elijah Grant.Now, we generally don't follow the Special Agents of the IMPO, due to trying to maintain their privacy, but this seems to be crossing a line I can't imagine." Heather was much more professional. Zander wouldn't kill her if he ever saw her, just chew her out.

"It is crossing a line. We've been talking for months about how we all thought the WMC's sly, no-questions-allowed press release concerning Shadow was a terrible move on their part. How does anyone trust someone who had been wanted for murder to come to the good side? And now look, she's compromised a team of our best."

"What do we know about the leak? It must point to many inside the organizations having problems of their own-"

"Of course they have problems! The people who pay attention have problems. You know, if the WMC wants to step away from rumors of corruption, maybe they shouldn't have kept an assassin out of prison for their own reasons. She should be behind bars, on her way to a speedy execution, not having a fancy dinner with one of the very people we rely on to keep peace and order." The man took a deep breath.

He tried to call Sawyer again. He knew Elijah took them to a bar, to see a band.

"I've got Elijah!" Vincent called out. "You need to get Sawyer into a secure location, out of the public eye.

Someone outed Sawyer and is spying on you. They have pictures from the restaurant. Her face and name are all over the fucking news. They know."

"This had to be done by multiple people," Jasper whispered. "There's no way one person knew who Sawyer was and that she was going to be in Atlanta tonight."

"You're right," Zander agreed, snapping his fingers. "Who is that guy Elijah uses to get stuff in Atlanta? He'd go to him for everything."

"He would know where Elijah and Sawyer *are*, but how in the hell would he know who Sawyer *is*?" Jasper asked in return.

"They are getting his truck and getting out of the city as fast as they can," Vincent declared. "Anyone reach James yet?"

"No, I got his voicemail. He's probably asleep right now," Jasper replied.

"I'll try him. He never misses my calls," Vincent muttered, dialing another number.

"This is bad," Quinn whispered. Zander was impressed by the guy's control and his understanding of what had happened. "I'm going to kill whoever betrayed us for this."

"I'll be right there with you." Zander patted his shoulder as they continued to watch the two news anchors discuss the ins and outs of Shadow, Sawyer, and the IMPO. They dredged it all up - all the public information they could. Her hits, her crimes, Axel's crimes, his infamous organization, the members of it.

"This is ugly. I really hope it wasn't Rogers, but I don't really see who else it *could* be," Jasper said, sighing as he sank back into his seat. "He's never been a problem before. He knew Jon's team too and never made any issue for us before."

"Rogers...Do you have his number?" Zander asked. They could all hear Vincent yelling into his phone at James, but he didn't focus on what was being said, his mind locked on the task of finding who outed Sawyer's last line of protection. Her privacy.

"No. I can search Elijah's room for it, but I'm pretty sure I won't find it."

"I don't," Quinn said as well, still watching the screen.

Zander glanced back at the news and didn't like seeing Elijah and Sawyer, live, walk out of the bar. Her eyes were hard and cold. Elijah looked furious. What he did like was that they kept their chins raised. There was no point in hiding now.

"At least they don't know one thing," he mumbled. "This isn't nearly as bad as it could be."

"And what could possibly make this worse?" Vincent demanded, glaring up from his phone, where James could be heard yelling through the line.

"They don't know we're all sleeping with her. Small miracles, right?"

"No, they just assume Elijah is," the Italian snapped. "James didn't pick up because he's been called into the main office and was getting his ass chewed out. They want to pull him from the team for this." Vincent put the phone back to his ear and sighed. "Yeah, James. I'm not sure why they're trying to do that. They know we're close to her. They know that. We wouldn't have done any of this if we wouldn't have been." Vincent pulled the phone away from his ear and suddenly, they could all hear James.

"Are any of you sleeping with her? Answer me now and answer me honestly. I can help you hide it but I need to fucking know. I'm in a soundproof room right now. No one else will hear it. Right now, they think it's Elijah, and I would be inclined to believe them, knowing Elijah, but I already heard her threaten to end something going on with Zander. I chose to ignore that at the time, because of her history with Jasper and Zander. I wasn't going to stop any of you from dating her, if it came to it. I need to know which one of you is actually with her. I don't care that someone is dating her, but I can't keep having secrets between us all. I can't tell them that she's not with Elijah unless I know the truth."

Zander swallowed on a lump of dread. He met Vincent's eyes.

This was it.

"All of us," Vincent whispered. Stronger, he said it again. "She's with all of us."

The silence was deafening and too long. Zander couldn't believe it had just been said out loud. To someone who probably didn't understand, who would never understand.

"We're all dating her," he said for Vincent, so their leader didn't have to repeat himself again. "Me, Vincent, Jasper, Quinn, and yes, Elijah. We're all..."

"What the actual fuck is going on with all of you?" James snapped. "What the actual hell made you all think any of this was okay? All fucking five of you are dating her? Is she playing you against each other? I'm just...fucking astounded. God damn it." He hung up.

"Well..." Jasper hadn't moved. "That could have gone better."

"Did he really need to know?" Quinn asked, sitting back down as well. "Also, it will be hours before they get back from the city. There's nothing for us to do until they do."

"He did need to know, since he was right. He can't cover for us unless he knows what he's covering. And he needs to cover, since the press is already under the assumption that the outing she's had with Elijah is romantic," Vincent explained. "I...I never considered how he would react to the truth. I never thought we would tell anyone."

"For you, that surprises me," Zander mumbled, sinking down into his recliner with the rest of them. "Sit down and finish your drink. Someone turn the fucking news off, too. We don't need to watch this shit."

Jasper was the one who grabbed the remote and turned them back to the movie. Zander wasn't interested anymore. He just stared blankly at the screen, his mind on everything else.

"I should have been ready for this," Vincent muttered. "I've been so distracted with everything else. We knew this was going to happen eventually. And...I should have known James wouldn't take the news of our romantic situation well. It's not normal. None of this is normal."

"It's...ours," Quinn cut in. "It doesn't matter if it's normal or not. It's ours. And it's what we want. Who cares? It's just sex and dates and our pack."

"The world will care," Zander whispered, closing his eyes. He could see the condemnation in the news anchors' eyes. The hate. The fear. "The world will care," he repeated weakly.

9

SAWYER

S awyer pulled away when she felt Elijah's phone vibrate on her hip. She needed to put some space between them anyway, since she needed to get another drink, but she hadn't expected it would be because of his phone.

"Someone is calling you," she whispered to him, smiling. She would make sure it was on silent when they left the bar, that was certain. "Didn't turn it on silent so you could have the night just with me?"

"Little lady, our jobs are too important for a phone to just go on silent," he reminded her, as he pulled out his phone. "I mean-oh fuck." His face went pale in the dimly-lit bar, and he shoved his phone back into his pocket without saying anything.

"What?"

"Come with me," he demanded. He grabbed her upper arm and she followed him quickly down the stairs, then through the crowd in front of the stage.

"Elijah, where are we going?"

"We need to get somewhere more private." He sounded harried and frantic. She didn't like that, but she didn't know what he saw on his phone to make him this way.

"Is someone trying to kill us? I don't understand."

He pushed them into the back kitchen, startling the cooks and other employees. "I need a way out back," he told them.

"Oh shit, is that her?"

Sawyer felt cold run through her. She looked at who said it: a wide-eyed bartender, staring directly at her. In his hand was a phone.

"It is! Holy shit!" A cook nearly jumped away from her.

"Sawyer, let's go!" Elijah snapped. "Fuck, who's calling me now?" He yanked his phone out and answered this time, holding Sawyer next to him. "If any of you take pictures, I'll fucking break hands, is that clear?"

"There's no way out the back here," someone said.

"Elijah?" she asked again quietly. "Did it happen?"

"Yes," he answered. "Yeah, Vincent, I know what the fuck is going on. We're trying to find a back way out of the bar, but apparently this place doesn't follow the fucking fire code and have a second exit. God damn it. We're going to have to go out the front."

Sawyer stood in relative shock as the staff all stared at her. No one blinked as Elijah hung up the phone.

"We need to go out the front, then."

"Why aren't you in prison?" someone dared to ask her.

Her heart was beating too hard. She hadn't been ready for this. Minutes ago, she was thinking about how she was excited to get another drink and rub against Elijah's body back at the hotel like she was a fucking cat in heat.

She just wasn't ready.

"Because that's not what was decided," Elijah snapped. "You'll learn more when the IMPO and the WMC release a statement to the press, and not a moment fucking sooner. Let's go, Sawyer."

There was one good thing about leaving the well-lit back area and kitchen of the bar. One good thing about going back into the crowd. The drunks, the partiers, the revelers, hadn't looked at their phones, hadn't seen the news.

She closed her eyes for a moment, feeling it in her chest.

"Sawyer, are you okay?" Elijah asked softly, holding her close in the bodies dancing around them. "We need to get out of here."

"This is the last time I'll ever stand in a group of people and be unknown. Be normal," she whispered. "By morning, every Magi on the planet is going to know who I am. I'll never have a normal day again."

"Little lady," he murmured. "We'll give you as much normal as we can, I promise. I'm sorry."

"How did this happen?" she asked.

"We'll talk about it once we get back to my truck and begin driving home."

She nodded and waved a hand, letting him know to lead the way.

"There's going to be press outside," he warned as they got closer to the door. The bouncer there narrowed his eyes on her.

"Get that out of here," he demanded of Elijah, nodding at her.

"You aren't very scary so don't think you can force me or her to do anything," her cowboy retorted. "Why don't you just keep your fucking mouth shut, you two-bit security guard. Probably an IMAS drop out."

"Fuck you."

"He's right," she snapped. "You aren't very scary." That got the pale-faced fear she wanted. She looked back into Elijah's hazel eyes and nodded again. "I'm ready."

"That's a lie, but I'll ignore it."

"Thank you."

There was no being ready for this. Already, just inside the front door, she could hear them: the paparazzi, waiting for her. They knew she and Elijah were in the bar. Which meant someone in the bar had seen her, saw the news, and called it in, gotten everyone's attention. It was moving so fast, she wasn't even sure she could process it.

She was outed.

Elijah pushed the front door open and walked out first. Somehow, it was louder outside, in the middle of the screaming reporters, than it had been in the bar with the band. She kept her chin up. She couldn't show that she was trying to hide now. It was too late for that. She tried not to wince and blink at the flashes from the cameras. She tried to ignore the larger cameras and reporters who were probably live.

"We're not taking any questions right now. You will all need to wait until the IMPO and the WMC release a statement. It's also their call if there will be any interviews," Elijah declared. She just stayed at his side. "Make a path!" he roared.

None of them moved.

She could feel the heat pouring off of him. She heard a yelp and saw a glimpse of a camera drop from someone's hands. "MAKE A PATH!" he roared again, louder than she'd ever heard him.

This time, with heat lashing out from Elijah, threatening to damage equipment, they moved.

She refused to fall to the urge of running. She wanted to. Now that she saw the way out of the mess, she wanted to take off and run, never looking back. Instead, she kept her chin up and walked with Elijah by her side towards the restaurant and valet parking.

They were followed. They were photographed and recorded. Questions were still thrown at them, but there were so many that she couldn't make out what was being asked. She caught that they were angry. Some accused her, she figured, of fucking Elijah. Some accused Elijah, she thought, of betraying his government. Some just yelled.

And with every step, Sawyer realized there was no going back to the normal she had come to enjoy. Or the anonymity that she'd relied on. Never again would she be able to separate the two. She was never going to be able to hide in a crowd, glad that no one knew that she was the monster, the killer.

Never again.

"Where's Rogers?" Elijah demanded as they walked into the restaurant.

"Here. Elijah, I'm so sorry-"

"What the fuck? How did they know? How did they know where we are?"

Elijah was furious, but Sawyer couldn't muster anger as the overwhelming despair continued to consume her. She'd just lost the last thing she had to hide her, to give her any peace. All of her people, every Magi, were going to hate her now, distrust her.

"I...I had my suspicions and asked a friend if she was really her. I didn't think it was going to leak from me. I'm sorry!" Rogers was stammering. "It's not like I'm mad! I don't care who she is, I was just curious!"

"It's fine," she mumbled.

"It's not," Elijah growled. "It's not fucking fine at all. Where's my goddamn truck?"

"On its way already. I knew you would be coming back for it right away." Everything about Rogers' posture and voice was apologetic, frantic, even desperate. He knew what he'd done. "I'm sorry, Elijah, you need to believe me."

"If we weren't already over, we are fucking now," Elijah snarled out like an animal. That, under other circumstances, would have gotten her attention. Rogers must have been a fuck-buddy, someone Elijah went to when he wanted to get laid.

"I know." There had never been a more defeated sentence. Sawyer could relate. She was feeling more lost in that moment then she had ever felt.

There was no way to be ready for this. How was she ever supposed to look people in the eye anymore?

Elijah pulled her out of the restaurant moments later, and she let him nearly throw her in his truck. When he got in the other side, he laid on his horn, causing the people with cameras and microphones to jump and scramble out of his way. "Sawyer, snap out of it," he demanded. "I need you with me."

"I don't…"

"You handled the team finding out. You handled the IMPO, the WMC, and the IMAS. You can handle this. You hear me? None of these people know you. None of them understand. None of them matter. So snap out of it."

She looked over at him as he floored it and they jumped into movement.

He was right. She had handled it all so far. She handled the leaders of their people knowing who she was. She handled the men she loved knowing, her friends. Charlie knew. Liam had taken it well. So had her kids.

"Thank you for saying that." Already she was overcoming the shock. She could feel something strong in her chest begin to form, a wall that she would use to guard her heart from what was about to come. "I mean, what difference does it make? Every time they decry Shadow, they were decrying me. Now they have my name and face. So what?"

"Exactly, little lady." Elijah grinned at her as he had them practically flying through the back streets of Atlanta. "I'm going to get us on the freeway and gun it. Hold on."

"Think we're going to have tails?" she asked, looking out the back window. "Oh, we already do." There was already a pack of cars and news vans trying to follow them. That wasn't good.

"Yup, and I need to lose them before I can take us home. We can't have our house's location exposed to the press. We'd have to move and it'll be a fucking pain. We worked hard getting the place we have for Quinn to have the space he needs. It's our home, ya know? So, while you might be outed, we still have to protect it."

"I get it," she replied, watching him try to make distance. She could feel the acceleration as they hit an on ramp for I-75.

"Put a damn seat belt on," he told her. She nodded and righted herself in the seat, clipping herself in without an argument. "I'm sorry it went this way on us. I can't fucking believe Rogers would out you, or even figure out who you were."

"He didn't out me. He wanted to say he met Shadow and tried to confirm who I was with someone in the IMPO. That person outed me."

"We'll fucking find who it was, I swear. Call Vincent and tell him that, what Rogers said." He took a hand off the steering wheel and pulled out his phone. "Give him Rogers' number too, since Rogers could give us his contact's name. The sooner we move on this, the sooner we can put that mother fucker in his place."

"On it." She called Vincent and waited, hoping he picked up. He obviously had to know what was going on, since Elijah had been on the phone with him earlier.

It only had to ring a couple of times. She pulled up Rogers' number on Elijah's phone during the wait.

"Elijah, make it-"

"We're in the truck, leaving Atlanta right now. He's trying to lose the tails." She glanced at the cowboy. "Might be hard, since they now know what the truck looks like though."

"Yeah, anyone would be able to see you on the road and stop you. This would also be a bad night to get pulled over, so once he loses the tails, tell him to slow down."

"Did you hear that?" she asked Elijah, who shook his head in return. "He doesn't want us to get pulled over, so we should slow down once we're away from the cameras."

"Makes sense. I'll lose them soon enough. None of them can go as fast as me." Elijah threw a grin her way.

"I'm going to die in this truck," she mumbled to Vincent.

"You'll be fine. He's a great, if incredibly fast, driver."

There was a pang of guilt in her chest over being such a raging bitch earlier in the evening. "Let me give you Rogers' number," she muttered, holding up Elijah's phone. She read it off to him. "So, he said he wanted to confirm I was Shadow - he had a suspicion about it. The person with the IMPO he contacted was the one who went public. So he says."

"How did he behave?" Vincent asked softly. She knew when her Italian was angry, and he was fucking pissed.

"He acted incredibly sorry. I had no reason not to believe him, but I only met him tonight for a few moments. We didn't get the chance to ask him for the name of his IMPO friend."

"He knows every Magi of importance that's ever gone through Atlanta. I'll call him and see what I can learn. I'll need to pass this all onto James as well. Oh, there's something you two need to know. James knows about us. All of us. And the press thinks you and Elijah are a thing. Intimate dinner gave them the impression. You know, perception. This is going to get uglier before it gets better."

Sawyer sighed, glancing again at the cowboy. She wished this hadn't happened. She had really wanted to break some of the tension between them, had every intention of acting on every sly, flirty comment, every touch they had ever shared.

The press had gotten it right, in a way.

"Thanks. We'll call you when we're closer," she promised.

"Wait. How are you handling this? I've been worried; so have the others."

"Elijah had to snap me out of the shock, but I'll be fine. I mean, we knew this was coming. Wasn't expecting it like this, but we knew it was coming." She took a deep breath, trying to remind herself to stay calm. "Being in public when it happened, being in the middle of all of that, really did a number on me for a moment. Elijah reminded me of something important, which I'm thankful for."

"What was that?"

"I could handle everyone else who already knew, already judged me. This doesn't really change anything." Even repeating those words made her feel better. "You know, this might just be the distraction I need right now."

"Don't get ahead of yourself. Public opinion could cause us some problems," Vincent chastised her gently. "But I think if we just weather the storm, everything will be clear on the other side."

"Me too," she agreed. "I'm going to let you go. It's a long drive home."

"Be safe. Both of you."

"I'll try to keep him from getting us killed." She grinned at Elijah, who rolled his eyes. "See you later." She hung up and dropped her phone in the center console.

There were no 'I love you's' exchanged, but it didn't bother her. She knew from his concern that it was there. He knew she felt it right back.

"I think we've lost them, so I'll make sure not to kill you on the drive home," he teased and braked, bringing them down to a reasonable speed. "You've been more comfortable, though."

"Well, I'll admit that sometimes you need to go fast, and the road is empty. You drive fast and weave through traffic like a crazy person." She wasn't going to let him think his driving was completely okay. "I drive fast on open road, where no one is going to get in my way. There's a difference."

"Sure there is," he said, humming at the end. They sat in complete silence for a moment then he sighed. "I would turn on the radio but you can guess why I haven't."

"Yeah. I figured." She didn't care. Silence was a blessing after the madhouse they had just left.

"I'm sorry tonight went this way. I know, it's not really my fault, but I'm sorry."

"It's not your fault. Don't feel guilty. Hell, I would even go so far and say it wasn't Rogers' fault either. He just wanted to put a name to a face. He didn't know his contact was going to take those pictures to the press."

"We'll find who outed you, Sawyer. I swear."

"I know. I trust you guys will do everything in your

power to get back at whoever did this." She smiled at him. "It doesn't change anything, though. It's out now. There's no going back. I wonder what the press statement is going to be from our bosses. The IMPO and the WMC. I wonder what they'll say."

"They will probably say how much of an asset you've been to the safety and security to Magi all over the world, even in the short time you've been with us." Elijah continued to hum, as if he was thinking too hard. "They'll trot out your first couple of assignments. They'll talk about how this isn't the first time you tried to go good. They'll talk about how even though it took years after your supposed death, you weren't active. You had already shown signs of wanting reform." He chuckled. "Not like you need to be reformed. You aren't particularly the boogieman people think of you as. Axel was the real monster, and now he's behind bars. Thanks to you. They'll remind people of that."

"The press will try to find ways to drag me through the mud. I killed people."

"You still do," he reminded her. "But, if it's any consolation, they will also drag our bosses through the mud. They will have to defend you to defend themselves, and they can't exactly drop you in a jail cell just because the PR is bad and they need to make themselves look good. They'll probably put us back to work faster, so that people think we're out doing good."

She didn't have a response. He was right, or probably right. Any other response from the IMPO and the WMC would be surprising and unlikely.

They drove home in silence and Sawyer even closed her eyes. She didn't get any sleep, but she tried. She didn't reopen them until she heard the garage door closing them in. Back into the safety of their private plantation house, where no one would bother them or find them.

"Sawyer?" Elijah was talking quietly. "Before we're surrounded by the fan club, I just wanted to say I had a great time tonight, before everything happened. Thank you for coming out with me."

"It was wonderful," she replied, turning to him. She unbuckled her seat belt and leaned closer to him, kissing his cheek. "I'm sorry it didn't end as planned."

"Me too," he groaned, grabbing her chin. She was beginning to realize there was a dominant streak in the cowboy, as he held her there to kiss her slowly. It was like he was trying to drag the moment out, keep it just between them for just another moment, before her 'fan club' came and took her away.

She grabbed his shirt and nearly crawled into his lap, earning a growl as her tongue dove into his mouth. His free arm wrapped around her waist and held her there. She could feel the bulge in his jeans under her.

"Maybe next time," he whispered when she pulled away.

"Definitely next time," she corrected.

With that, they untangled and got out of his truck. She saw Vincent waiting at the door inside, smiling knowingly. She shrugged without a word as she walked over to him and kissed his cheek.

"I'm going to sleep," she told him before she passed him.

"Good night," he called after her.

She found Jasper, Zander, and Quinn in the kitchen and did the same for them. A small good night kiss, just something for them to know she was okay, and that was all.

With the mood she was in, she should have dragged one of them upstairs.

She only saw hazel eyes and a slightly arrogant smile

when she closed her eyes, though. That seemed like such a farfetched idea for this evening. Sex in general, after all of that, seemed like a bad idea.

She was in her room, stripping, when she remembered why she was happy to be home. The press would never find her here and if they did, it wouldn't be soon.

She was down to her bra, some lacy thing, something that had that unique ability to make the wearer feel desirable, when she felt like an idiot. Why wasn't she saying fuck the world and just taking what she wanted?

She didn't bother putting a shirt back on. Her black jeans were unbuttoned, but she didn't fix them. She left her room, angry that she had let what was going on stop her from taking what she wanted. She opened the door to the staircase leading out of the attic.

And there he was. Standing at the bottom of the stairs, holding that door open.

"Little lady," he said casually, looking her over. "What are you doing?"

"Sugar," she replied, her eyes trailing over him. He was shirtless, his belt undone. He wasn't wearing the cowboy hat either, and his boots were gone. He had also been getting ready for bed, she figured. "What are you doing?"

"I think," he began, taking a step up the stairs, "that we both know what I'm doing. The question really does lie with you if I can or not."

"I won't let them stop me from what I want." She didn't move as he made a slow climb up the stairs to her. "I won't let people tell me I can't have something. I'm greedy like that."

"You really are a thief, then, the way you steal hearts and happiness for yourself," he murmured, getting closer. "Are we going to try to find where I fit?"

"You had a great suggestion to that earlier." Their chests touched. She had to look up at him. She had always loved how tall he was, like Zander. They both made her feel a little smaller, and not the five foot eleven she actually was.

"We're on the same page then." He wrapped a hand around her waist and the other up in her hair.

That first kiss was slow and testing, as he backed them out of the stairs. It didn't stay that way. She pulled his belt from his jeans and threw it away in the attic before they made it in her room. He undid her bra and didn't bother to stop kissing her as he yanked it off her. She moaned into him as one of his rough hands massaged one of her breasts.

"Elijah," she whispered as they moved into her room. "I hope this ride is longer than eight seconds." She absolutely couldn't resist making that comment.

"Little lady, I'm going to make sure you ride all night," he crooned, kissing her jaw and down her neck as he pushed down her jeans. He wasted no time in pushing his hand down the front and sliding a finger over her clit. It sent a wave of sensation over her, like a shock.

She hurried to undo his pants, pushing them down with his boxer briefs as well, while also trying to kick off her own, even as he sank a finger deep into her. He was kicking his pants away as her hand wrapped around the tree trunk that was his cock.

"Holy shit," she mumbled. She'd seen it before, but without having her hand on it to really judge the size. She'd seen it hard, but not for long, not enough to really consider it. Not up close.

"Mmmm."

The *arrogance* of that sound.

"Let's hope you know how to use it," she teased. Somewhere in the back of her mind, she remembered he was from Texas - and that stupid fucking saying. *Everything's* bigger in Texas, all right.

Grinning, he pulled the finger out of her and unceremoniously dumped her on one of her couches. She didn't get a chance to sit up as he pushed a knee between her thighs and had her moaning in ecstasy.

"Let's hope you can keep up," he taunted, kissing her roughly afterwards.

There was something dominant in him, for sure. She remembered the last time he'd taken charge in the bedroom, though, and wasn't having it. She pushed him off and they went rolling onto the floor, with her straddling him instead. She ground against him, making him groan this time.

There was no more preamble. No more foreplay. Even with her thong on, she was done waiting. She positioned herself over him, pushing the scrap of fabric out of the way, and slid down slowly. She gritted her teeth at the width of him. It wasn't that she wasn't wet enough. He was just that thick.

"Fuck," he groaned, grabbing her hips to help her. She had to stop and breathe after a moment, refusing to move down further. "You're not done yet."

"Oh gods," she moaned out as he pushed upwards. It wasn't rough, for which she was thankful. She felt full. She wondered if there was a single nerve ending he wasn't rubbing against.

"There you go," he growled, grinning up at her. "Hold on. I like it rough."

She leaned over, nearly putting her head on his chest as he lifted her with her hips and pulled out of her. Then he thrust again, causing her to bite down on his shoulder to ineffectively hide her scream.

For every upward thrust, he also pulled her down on him. And it was rough, he hadn't been lying. He was trying to break her into two, she was certain of it.

She loved it.

She could feel every thick inch slide in then back out of her at a hard pace she wasn't sure she could match, which meant she had to let him control everything, including her. He pushed her into an orgasm as if she didn't have any say in the matter. It just slammed into her without any real warning or true build up.

He stopped thrusting, panting softly as she convulsed, her legs and arms shaking while it ran through her. "You all right?" he asked softly.

"Yeah," she answered. She was more than all right.

"Good. Because I'm not stopping us until you can't walk."

She wasn't surprised to be rolled over on her back. She was shocked when he grinned down at her and lifted her legs onto his shoulders.

She knew what this meant.

He shoved back into her and went deeper than he had before. It was nearly painful, but she didn't want it to stop either. His first thrust was strong enough to move her on the carpet, and she had a feeling rug burn was in her future. She placed her hands on his chest to keep him from leaning down further. She wasn't sure her legs were that flexible, for one, and second, that would only give him the ability to try and get deeper, somehow.

He kept the pace hard, and she went from holding him back to just holding on again, her nails biting into his skin as he fucked her. They were sweaty now, and her hands found it hard to get a grip. He did let her legs fall, as they began to shake too hard to keep up. She wrapped them around his waist instead, crossing at the ankles to keep them there. His body moved like a wave, each thrust was executed like he was just dancing with her, with devastating effect. She closed her eyes, unable to function anymore, as it continued relentlessly.

She didn't come one more time. She came twice before he lifted her, sitting on his ankles with her wrapped around him. He came as deep inside her as he could get, panting as their foreheads met.

"Holy shit," she repeated, unable to reopen her eyes. Now she knew why men and women were always trying to crawl back into his bed, to experience the rough ride he promised.

"Mmmm."

That still sounded so impressively arrogant.

She didn't say anything as he stood up, still in her, still with her wrapped around him like a cat that refused to let go. She didn't say anything when her tender, rug-burned back touched the soft comforter on her bed. She unwrapped her boneless legs and they fell unceremoniously onto the bed as well. Elijah fell next to her, close enough that her shoulder brushed his chest.

"You in there?" he asked softly. "I didn't break you, did I?"

"I'm hard to break," she tried to say. She had no idea if he understood the words. She barely understood what came out of her mouth.

"I broke you, but that's all right." He chuckled arrogantly. "Well, before you think it's over..." He kissed her neck and jaw up to her ear. "I recover quickly and I have no intention of just sleeping the night away."

She nearly whimpered. She wasn't sure if it was in

sympathy for herself or want for more of what had just been done to her.

Either way, she was just glad she refused to let those outsiders take this away from her. Fuck them. She had what she needed in life and it wasn't their approval. It was men like the one next to her.

10

SAWYER

Soreness was the first thing Sawyer noticed as she woke up. Everything was sore. A delicious soreness that she enjoyed, but more than what she was normally greeted with.

Elijah had worked her into not just a second round but three rough rounds that left her unable to stay awake at the end of the last. He'd made her body sing while she screamed in pleasure, and even for a bit of mercy.

She tried to roll, to move out of the bed, but found it impossible. He must have noticed, must have already been awake, since a massive arm wrapped over her stomach to her far hip and pulled her into the broad chest she now knew *very* well.

"Where are you going?" he asked deviously.

"To find someone who isn't threatening to turn me into a puddle of nerve endings," she mumbled. "And hopefully, the bathroom."

"The bathroom is a possibility, but since you only live with men who want to turn you into a, and I quote, 'puddle of nerve endings', I think your overall mission will fail."

She groaned. Wasn't that the truth? Hopefully her guys would have some sympathy for her in this trying time of being unable to move like a regular human being. She had a feeling that walking funny was in her future.

"I'm getting up," she told him, trying her hardest to sit up. She made it, but it felt like she'd been in the gym the entire previous day, working at her maximum without stretching. "What the fuck did you do to me?"

"I think I fucked you like I've wanted to since the night we met," he answered. "And want to every time I get the chance for a very long time."

"Oh gods," she muttered, turning so her feet hung off the edge of the bed. "Do you do Quinn or anyone else like that? Are there countless people out there who will never walk the same again?"

"I normally don't keep anyone else going three rounds with me, no. That was just for you. Well, for me. That was definitely for me."

"Awful," she mumbled. Not like she really should have been complaining. For round three, she had climbed back on top of him, hoping for a slow ride. She didn't get exactly what she'd intended when she'd done that. He'd been just as rough as he'd been since the moment he'd started. "What time is it?" she asked, looking around. One of her couches was not where it had started. That must have been the one he'd tossed her on. Their clothes were everywhere, scattered on the floor with no care. She wasn't wearing her thong anymore and eyed a broken one at the foot of the bed. Well, another pair ruined. Fantastic.

"Nearly ten. We've missed breakfast. I went down earlier to check on things. Jasper and Vincent were up all night on the phone with James. The WMC and the IMPO put out their statements at seven. Exactly what I thought they would be. Talked all sorts of praise about you, about how you've helped them re-establish some connection to some of our wilder people, the Druids, and exposed anti-Magi feelings in Texas. That you've been a model agent for the organization. Those types of things." He took a deep breath before continuing. "Also, that we were just having a quiet dinner, as friends, to enjoy the holiday season. They...they might have said something about how you lost someone important this month and that I was just being a good friend to get you out of the house."

"They didn't elaborate on that, did they?" She didn't want the world to know about Henry. He was gone, but he didn't deserve his name out there. He deserved to rest in peace.

"No, they didn't. They might not like you, but they won't blast a story like Henry's and yours out to the world." She heard him sit up behind her, and a hand rubbed her back. "They had to think of something to say, and wasn't that the truth? We wouldn't have gone on last night's date if it weren't for Quinn coming up with the idea of keeping you too busy to think about Henry."

She stood up before that innocent hand on her back turned less so. She ignored the wobble of her legs and went to find clothes. A pair of clean sweatpants and one of Zander's shirts were what she found first, and she threw them on without stopping to consider the sprawling, nude cowboy in her bed.

"Sawyer?" He sounded worried enough for her to turn and face him. "You don't need to run from me. I don't expect anything from this."

She could only respond with a laugh, shaking her head as she found some socks to warm her feet. The entire room was too cold for her.

"I didn't realize I was so funny," he mumbled.

"I'm not running from you," she said, trying not to laugh through the words. It led to her giving a snort instead. "When have I ever really run from any of you? I'm not the type to run from feelings, unlike someone else in the room."

"Fair point. I'm just saying-"

"I know what you're saying." She didn't need the speech. The 'just because I feel this way' sort of speech. "I care for you. You are a friend, a teammate, and someone I'd kill for. I'm not a teenage girl who needs love to have sex with someone. I'm fine just having sex with a friend. And we'll see if it goes further. Thankfully, the other guys just let me do me when it comes to this stuff, and it's not a problem."

Now it was getting awkward. They had been doing really well and he had to go and say something.

"Plus, we're going to get the muscle car and actually spend more time together. Let's just see where it goes. Sex, no sex, doesn't matter. I'm not running from you, though. I really do need to fucking pee." She turned to leave the room, then waved a hand back at him. "And no, you can't lie in my bed like that all day. That's a no go."

He was laughing as she left. She could hear her bed frame creaking and she hoped that meant she wouldn't come back to him lying there waiting for another round. Not that it was a bad idea; her body just couldn't handle another round. She had a feeling, from the creaking, that her bed couldn't either.

She took her time in the bathroom, washing her face and taming her hair before she walked out.

"Well, good morning." She was greeted by the sight of a grinning Zander in the hallway, leaning on the opposite wall. "How was your night, Sawyer?"

"I think you know how my night was," she answered. "I'll be out of commission for a couple of days."

"Good to know. How are you? In terms of the other stuff."

She hadn't even really thought about it. She considered her feelings and shrugged. "It's just what it is. We'll deal. We'll enjoy the holidays in private, then we'll get back to work. People will...eventually forget about me."

"I was really worried about you last night."

"Thanks, but nothing was life-threatening." She kissed his cheek and smiled. "We're fine."

"And now you're with our cowboy, too," he teased.

"I'm...sleeping with our cowboy. As for anything else, we'll see." She was already tired of that question. He might have been the first to ask about it, but considering Elijah's behavior, it felt like she'd already done this dance number.

"All right, I'll drop it." He was still grinning. "You walking funny?"

"Yeah," she mumbled.

"I've heard men and women praise the heavens leaving his hotel rooms the next day. I've always been slightly curious."

"You couldn't catch," she pointed out. She couldn't see him being interested in men at all, actually.

"You're not wrong. I'll just forever wonder if he's really a god in bed. It's not like I'm jealous or insecure. I know in a few days, you'll be back in my arms."

"This isn't a competition," she snapped, not liking that comment. She didn't want them comparing themselves to each other. Even though she didn't know what the hell was going on with all of this half the time, she knew that if they did that, it would go bad quickly.

"You're right. I'm just trying to give you a hard time.

Want to hit the gym?" He seemed really easy about all of it, smiling as if she hadn't snapped at him.

"I think I'm too sore for the gym. I could use a good stretch, though." She tested that, trying to stretch her arms over her head. It didn't work. "Yeah, a good stretch."

"You just want to pretend like last night didn't happen?"

"Which part? Elijah, or that some IMPO asshole outed me to the press?"

"The press part. Elijah was just something we knew was going to happen. That's not a surprise."

She began to walk away, proving that yes, she did just want to pretend last night didn't happen. She couldn't do anything about it, so she was going to try not getting wrapped up in it. And what he said about Elijah just made her think of something else.

"Why are all of you okay with this?" she demanded as she started down the stairs, Zander on her heels. "This idea that I'm sleeping with all of you, that I'm dating all of you. It's been a while now, and yet..." Sometimes she couldn't accept that someone like Zander would be okay sharing. Or Vincent. Or Quinn.

"Would you rather we all fought and you ended up stuck in the middle of some childish male drama?"

"That's an incredibly mature statement," she muttered. Something about it annoyed her, Zander acting mature. It shouldn't have. He was growing up and that was a good thing. Was he still hot tempered? Sure, but it wasn't the same anymore.

"It nearly happened. I wasn't happy you slept with Vincent - then I realized I was an idiot. I had always known it could never be just me or Jasper. What's Vincent, Quinn, or Elijah? Plus, who cares? It's our life. I told you that you could be with anyone, as long as I got a piece, and I meant it.

I'm not going to get pissy that you've finally ended up with all of us."

"I feel greedy," she admitted. "I feel like I'm hoarding a bunch of good men from the world."

He grabbed her before they made it to the bottom of the stairs. They were chest-to-chest on the stairs, and she looked into his green eyes, wondering what he was going to say.

"Be greedy. You are a reformed criminal. If that's the vice you're going to go with, then be greedy." He grinned at her, that wide, immature, over-confident one she loved. "You know what really helps me deal with it? I can't imagine myself with anyone else. I can't imagine Jasper with anyone else, or Vincent, or Quinn, or Elijah. And they're my teammates and friends, the people I've overcome death with, seen some hard shit with. So, I put my asshole side away, because damn, none of us in this house have ever had much happiness, but we do right now. And it's with you. So I share. So I let you do whatever you want."

"Just as long as you always have a place in it," she repeated for him.

"Exactly."

They all made it sound so easy, and all had different reasons for it. Vincent would tell her it's because he thought he couldn't be with her alone. They would slowly destroy each other with alcohol and depression. They needed others to keep them balanced. Quinn would just say she deserved strong males around her, and that the pack worked best if she cared for them all. She trusted their answers, because she had no reason to distrust them. None of them had given her any reason to think this would end any time soon, and she had a greedy heart.

They were nearly at the stairs to the basement when

they were stopped by Vincent. "Come to the dining room," he ordered.

Sawyer groaned, giving Zander a pleading look that he would let her sneak into the gym. He shrugged and turned to the dining room, not saying a word. She followed and saw Elijah walking down from the upper floor.

"Dining room?" he asked softly.

"Yeah. Any idea?"

"No, he just sent me a message to come down." He tapped his head.

She walked in behind Zander, and in front of Elijah. The first person she saw at the table was Jasper, looking tired. He had dark circles under his eyes, papers in front of him that were disorganized. Unusual for him and Vincent. He wasn't wearing his leg. She could see it propped up against the wall in the back.

She moved to sit next to him, since he was up all night dealing with her mess. She had been fucking a cowboy while he was figuring this out. She felt the pang of guilt she knew was coming as she leaned so her shoulder touched his. "Hey. Sorry about the mess," she whispered.

"Me too," he said dryly, nodding to all the papers. Then he cracked a small smile for her. "It's fine. This isn't your fault, or Elijah's."

"I know, but it wouldn't have happened if I wasn't here." There was no avoiding that.

"James and a few people in New York already have the guy who released the information and the pictures Rogers sent him." Vincent eyed her, but she kept her attention on Jasper. She knew Vincent was fine. He lived for this sort of thing, the mess to be figured out. "There's nothing to be done now. The press isn't reacting well to the statements from the IMPO or the WMC, but there's been nothing serious brought to our attention yet. James has promised they won't pull us off our holiday early. It's actually better that they won't, since any assignment we get right now would be harassed and ruined by the media."

"That's good. What are they thinking for Rogers?" Elijah asked as he found a seat. He was next to Quinn, who looked bored. Zander sat on her other side, rubbing her thigh in a comforting way.

"We're going to let him keep to himself. He might have accidentally caused this, but he didn't do it maliciously. Curiosity isn't a sin." Vincent sighed, moving papers around.

"What's all this?" she asked, reaching for one of the papers.

Jasper stopped her. "Our statements. Well, possible drafts. We aren't sure if we want to give one yet, but it would be good to have something ready if we need to talk to the press." He gave a sympathetic smile. "Including a few mockups and ideas for anything you might be safe saying to them."

"Well damn," she mumbled, pulling her hand back. She wasn't fond of the idea of talking to a camera or doing some press conference.

"We're also to remain on lockdown." Vincent continued on, ignoring what she and Jasper talked about. "No trips to the bar, no visits into town. We need to let Estella go, which is something I'm putting off. She's on holiday herself, so there's no reason to rush to fire her when this might blow over by the time she's due to come back." He sighed heavily, sinking down in his chair further. "But other than some unneeded stress, we're to continue on like normal. We should be fine. Sawyer..." He had such a sad look on his face, and she felt dread fill her chest. "Don't look at the news."

"Can do," she mumbled. "I wonder..."

"What?" he asked, keeping an intense stare on her.

"I wonder what's being said on the Dark Web. I had enemies, and now...well, it's all out there. Who I am, who I'm working with now. It would be good for someone to keep an eye on that, just in case."

"Shit," Jasper snapped. "You're right. I hadn't even thought. Zander?"

"I'll get on it now," Zander said quickly, jumping up from his seat.

"Good idea," Vincent said to her, nodding. "You know your old world better than we do."

"It's all I can think of," she explained softly, hunching over. She wished for a moment it wasn't her 'old world' that was the root of all her problems. It was still her world; she was just on the other side of it now. "Best to keep an eye out. It's probably not just the press dragging me through the mud right now."

"It isn't just the press. We've already had not one, but two Councilmen come out and say they disagree with the 'consensus' of the Council. We've had agents from the IMPO speak against the organization's decision to let you work among us. And it doesn't end with you." Vincent looked around at all of them after that. "Team, many are calling for us all to be fired. It's worse for me than all of you. Once again, having a specific last name seems to bring me more trouble than anything else."

"These aren't problems we haven't encountered already," Elijah reminded them. "This is just on a larger scale. That's all. We can manage."

"We haven't even made it a year into my term," she said, groaning. "A year out of *five*."

"Well, at least it can't get much worse from here," he

replied sympathetically. "You can only be outed once, right?"

He had a point. They could only do this to her once. When the dust settled, it couldn't be kicked back up nearly as fiercely. The team just had to weather the storm.

With all of that covered, she closed her eyes and mentally plucked the bond between her and Sombra like a string of a guitar. It led out to the woods.

"Did she stay out all night?" she asked without opening her eyes. That would worry her. It was too cold for her jaguar to be overnight without someone keeping an eye on her.

"No, she stayed with me and my boys," Quinn answered. "I let them out to hunt for breakfast, to keep them out of the way."

"Thanks. I'm glad to know someone was looking out for her. I should have checked on her last night."

"You had other things on your mind." It was said casually, but she knew Quinn was probably smiling. She peeped at him with one eye and sure enough, he had a knowing smile on his face. He would know exactly what she had on her mind last night, every little detail.

"I'm going to the gym," she announced, deciding not to say any more about her night or stay in the knowing gazes of the men around her. As she stood up, she remembered something else. Looking down at Jasper, she sighed. "I guess this means no date later this week."

"Yeah."

"Maybe we can do something here?" she asked. She really wanted to spend time with him, just to hang out, just to enjoy his normalcy.

"Maybe," he mumbled. "We'll see."

"All right." She walked away, not liking his answer. Why

did it feel like he was slipping away? The date when his school was over was supposed to be a chance for her to be with him, but now she didn't have that. She was pulled in too many directions. Vincent, Zander, Jasper, Quinn, and now Elijah. The job, her past, their future, the press, their bosses.

Things were bound to slip. She just didn't want it to be one of the guys.

Before going down to the gym, she went up to her room and got into the right clothing. She enjoyed being alone for a moment, away from the people and things that pulled her around. She needed to stretch before the soreness became stiffness, and she needed to beat on something.

She could no longer avoid the anger at her situation. It was curling in her chest, festering, and she needed to beat it out. She needed to give it an outlet before she snapped and lost her temper with someone.

In the gym, she grazed her fingers over the punching bag. First she stretched, ignoring the punching bag for a moment longer. Her legs, arms, and back all needed some attention, and she was glad Zander hadn't come down with her this morning.

She was too angry. She could only hide it for so long, and Elijah's distraction the night before had definitely taken her mind off everything, but now? Now she needed to let it out.

She thought about the people with the cameras. The condemnation in their voices, the pushiness of their attempts to invade her privacy. The shocked stares.

She thought about what they were probably saying about her on the news.

She thought about the Councilmen and IMPO agents who were speaking out.

"I hate them," she mumbled to herself. "I hate all of them."

Her fist slammed into the punching bag hard enough to make it swing.

"They have no idea," she hissed, hitting it again. They had no idea how hard it was to wake up some days. They had no idea that she had never wanted it, never wanted any of it. The pain, the blood, the death. They had no idea about the black hole in her chest that couldn't ever be filled, no matter how hard others tried. They looked at her and saw a killer, and that was all she would ever be. Because the world had no space for a woman like her.

She hit the punching bag again.

She knew she was wrong about that last part. The world did have space for her. There were those who understood her and stood beside her.

She hit the punching bag again, ignoring that she had bad form, splitting one of her knuckles open and making it crack painfully.

It didn't stop that the judgment hurt. It always hurt. It would never not hurt. She could shove her chin into the heavens, try to ignore them all, but damn, it always hurt.

It hurt that none of them would ever care that she did it all for a little cat and a little boy. None of them would ever understand the lost ones, the ones she had just wanted to protect.

She was crying as she kept hitting the bag, sinking down as she tried to hold on to it.

All this judgment from them wasn't worth it, because she had failed. She hadn't been good enough to keep them alive. She hadn't killed well enough, pleased him enough to stop him from losing his temper.

None of them would ever know or care. Not about Midnight or Henry. Not about her.

None of them ever cared enough about any of them.

She couldn't stop her knees from hitting the floor, her arms wrapped around the punching bag.

None of them would ever know or care that she was as much a victim as the ones she killed. The only thing she had on everyone else was that she survived - and would continue to survive.

She didn't know how long she knelt there, crying into the bag. Someone must have found her, since a hand touched her shoulder. She nearly jumped, realizing she hadn't been paying any attention. She should have known, heard him, something.

But large arms just wrapped around her and pulled her up. "I knew I would find you like this. What is it, little lady?" he asked softly.

She buried her face to his chest, grabbing on to his shirt. "I failed," she answered. "They condemn me for everything I ever did, and they don't even know I failed. They don't know Henry is dead because of me. Because I wasn't good enough. He's fucking gone and all they care about is the surface. They have no idea. They have no idea how much it fucking hurts."

He held her tightly to him, rocking slightly. "I have you. I understand. Just let it out."

"Not going to give me away this time?" she asked softly, her hands shaking. She remembered how he'd passed her off to Vincent the last time she found herself in the dark.

"No, not this time," he whispered. "I've got you."

She leaned into him and cried. December was going to find every reason to remind her of Henry. It was always going to go back to him. It was going to eat away at her until she was nearly insane - then the month would be over. This was her life.

Even as she cried, she was glad these men did understand. They did know. It was like they were torches in her darkness. They were pointing the way out, offering her warmth on the trip.

"I've got you. We've all got you, little lady," he whispered again.

He sat them down and she practically crawled into his lap. She hated to be vulnerable, but not even Charlie had offered her this. This physical comfort that made her feel like it wasn't so lonely. She couldn't resist accepting it and using it to its fullest extent.

As the tears faded, she just stared at his chest. "Is it ever like this for you?" she asked quietly.

"On the day," he answered. "I drink pretty hard on the day. Grief is funny, though, isn't it? It drives us to act out of character and expose our deepest fears."

"Yeah," she mumbled. "I get it, Elijah. Why you were so uncomfortable with talking to me about...us. It took me a long time to warm up to the kids, truthfully warm up to them, since I always worried they might..."

Die like he did.

He didn't say anything, just pulled her tighter to him, kissing her forehead. She tried to push away, feeling better. She even tried for a weak smile, but it ended with a wince as pain shot from her hand.

"Fuck," she snapped, looking at her right hand. Sure enough, the knuckles were bruised and she poked one. "I think I fractured it."

"Let's go find Zander," he ordered, standing up and taking her with him. He didn't carry her, like he had the other day, only supported her as she steadied on her feet. "You need to be more careful."

"I'll try," she promised.

"Liar. You're going to do this again more than once before the end of the month, I can already feel it."

"You don't have to comfort me, Elijah." She didn't want to burden them. This was her shit, her issues. They just got worse for a little while, and when January came along, she would feel nearly like a new person. It happened that way every year.

"No, I don't," he agreed. "But I'm going to. So are the guys. Ain't no reason for you to be doing this on your own. Depression is a dangerous thing. I'm not going to leave you alone with it. Neither are they."

"I hate being like this. Every year, I hope it'll get easier, and it doesn't. It makes me feel...weak. Out of control."

"There's nothing weak about a heart that loved enough to grieve so deeply." He turned and began walking away. She just let those words sink in before walking after him. He stopped at the stairs and grinned at her. "And they'll never know just how strong you are, and that's their loss. Remember what I said in the truck: the IMPO and the WMC don't matter. The world doesn't matter. They don't know you. They don't know how big your heart is, or how much you love to give it away. They don't know that, yeah, you are capable of awful things, but damn, you always have the best intentions."

"The way to hell is paved in good intentions," she reminded him.

"Then we'll go to hell," he retorted, grinning. "Remember, little lady, you aren't the only one who's resorted to extreme violence over harm done to someone you care about. I don't regret it. Stop forgetting that."

"Fuck. This speech again."

"It's one thing to grieve the loss of someone you loved, but don't fall back into that spiral of self loathing, please."

"Okay, I promise." She held up her hands in defeat.

"Good. I was getting worried for a moment."

She swatted his shoulder and then cursed several times as the pain flared back up. He was chuckling as they climbed the stairs to find the healer.

As he left her with Zander, she watched him go. He didn't know that every time he opened his mouth, he took a little piece of her heart. Damn cowboy.

11

JAMES

"I don't know what to say, sir. They've become friends with her. It's apparent, and I think we all knew it was going to happen."

James finished his speech to the Director and waited. This was the third time they'd had this conversation in the same number of days. Surely this wasn't surprising. The team had always had each other's backs and refused to let any of them get shafted for the good of the others. The Amazon was the clearest example, and it included Sawyer. She was part of the team now, and she was trusted enough by the guys that she was a decision-maker.

"James, if any of them are romantically involved with her, I'm putting them all in handcuffs," the Director whispered. It was a threat that held weight. He could and would have them all taken down if there was anything being hidden. He was so angry he'd have a young team in chains for this.

He was lucky that their Director couldn't read minds. That would have made this meeting much more difficult.

"I don't think that's it. Thompson, you know how teams

are. They choose each other and then stick by that choice. They are trained to completely trust each other, to rely on each other's strengths and weakness, to make a cohesive unit that can do anything. They're our version of special forces." James groaned, leaning back in the seat. "You know that."

"Are you positive nothing is going on?" he demanded, glaring over the paperwork on his desk. "If you lie to me to protect those kids, I'll have you in handcuffs too."

"Even if she was sleeping with them, there's nothing you can arrest them for and you know it. It would be a show to appease the masses, completely unjust and a bastardization of what we stand for." James narrowed his eyes at the Director. "Don't walk down the route of using the power you have to make others bend to your will unnecessarily."

"Why shouldn't I? No one is going to stop me."

"Because we worked so hard to get you behind that desk because the last guy abused his power," he reminded Thompson. They were older men now, having been through too much for this organization and the idea of justice. He would hate to see Thompson throw away everything they believed in now.

"You've got me there. I'm sorry. The WMC is...furious, though, James. They want me to pull the entire group of them up to New York for questioning, or send someone down to have them watched. Is it my sin to abuse my power if I'm dictated to by a superior?" The question held a raw honesty and some despair, even some defeat. James could *feel* it. Empathy was handy in situations like this one, as he tried to judge the mood of his old friend.

"You can just point to the code and hold to it. Thompson, we've been friends since Academy. We were teammates for over a decade. You've never wanted to be in power to abuse it. We wanted to fix this organization. Don't let some hot-button topics ruin that for you. And it will." He took a deep breath, glad that he and the Director were more relaxed now. "They will tell you to do something corrupt, something without justification, then later hang you with it. You know that."

"Thanks for the reminder. And you're right. I'm pissed off that they got outed, but it isn't their fault." Thompson tapped a finger on his desk slowly, looking down at the papers he was tapping. James could feel the anger, certainly, but he could also feel the worry. "How did we find ourselves here? It was always supposed to be you behind this desk and me dealing with teams and doing grunt work."

He grinned and shrugged. "I didn't want it. You know that. I know this is when shit gets hard, but we've got this."

"I hope we do, for them," Thompson mumbled.

James stood up slowly, unwilling to respond to that. It wasn't the kids that Thompson was mentioning.

Once they had been on a team of seven men, men who had met in the Academy and were all screwed, one way or another. James and Thompson were all that was left.

He began to walk quietly out of the room, unwilling to sit in the depression that was beginning to cloud the room.

"Tell me which one of them is in love with her," Thompson demanded before he was able to get out. "I know one of them is. There's got to be one."

"Thompson, we've been friends for a long time, but unless something is pertinent to an investigation or Magi security, I won't violate what any of those kids tell me in confidence. You know that." James smiled wearily back at the Director. "And it doesn't matter if any of them are in love with her. Have you met her?"

Thompson began to chuckle, nodding. James knew

they'd met, and knew what was said. Even though the kids never told him exactly what happened, the Director had told him over a brandy, laughing.

"She's feisty, that's for sure. Arrogant as sin. She's fallen right in with them. You consider her a member of that team now, don't you?"

"Don't you? Look at what happened in October, Thompson. They would die for each other, and considering who we're talking about, that's something to take seriously. It doesn't matter if any of them are romantically involved with her - she's one of them, no matter what. She isn't their charge, someone for them to watch, she's their family, their friend."

"Good point," the Director mumbled, nodding. "You can go. Call them and see how they are. This surely hasn't been easy on them. Also, send her my condolences. I think in the madhouse around here, no one has made sure she's okay."

"You're talking about Henry," James whispered, feeling a sense of sadness fill him, both his own and Thompson's.

"He died in December. You said that the incident with Elijah was about them trying to keep her mind off a personal loss. We, as an organization, need to also be mindful of the emotional needs of our more vulnerable members. We put them through hell, so it's good to let them know that we understand what toll that takes." Thompson sighed, pouring himself a drink at his desk. "Please pass that on? It would also show them that I am on her side."

"But are you, Thompson?" He had to ask. There were few things he and the Director had ever argued about. They all had to do with Axel, Vincent, and Sawyer. James wasn't going to lie to the team that trusted him about the Director's feelings about them.

"They're basically your children; I should have known.

Yes, I'm on their side. Other than PR problems, they've given me no reason to disband them yet. I didn't appreciate the Councilwoman's involvement last time, and I made sure she knew it then too."

James didn't respond, leaving as quickly as possible when Thompson was done. He'd hoped to get out of there earlier. The longer he had to sit in that office, the longer he had to keep lying to an old friend and evading giving more than he should.

Three days since Sawyer's face had been blasted on the news all over the world, and nothing was looking up for the IMPO or the WMC. James was fielding requests for the team to make a public appearance, and if he didn't know what he did, he would have signed them up for it. It would look good. Young successful agents talking about reform, bringing in the worst of their culture to help better themselves and their world. Sawyer, looking nice, and repentant, telling her story for the world to see. It would start a movement to support her, since he knew many would be sympathetic to her story. Hell, he was.

But he couldn't put them there anymore. Not when he knew that they were all fucking her.

All of them. He could only imagine Thompson's face if he'd said that. While the idea was humorous, it would also lead to one of the biggest controversies in the IMPO. It would be a disaster.

He couldn't wrap his head around it himself. The idea of her being with all five of them. What were they doing? Having orgies? It didn't make a damn lick of sense to him, and didn't fit the people on the team. Jasper? No, he would never. Elijah, certainly, but Vincent? He'd be a tough sell, certainly.

James was missing something about it, that was certain,

but he also wasn't really in the mood to call Vincent up and ask for an explanation.

What really bothered him was that he could see it. The way they defended her to the bitter end, the way they looked at her, and the way she relied on them. The way she was so willing to throw herself and the rest of them into a jungle hell, just for them to stay a team, a unit.

He just didn't understand it.

"Damn it," he snapped, slamming his finger on a button when he got into the elevator. He was going home. He'd barely slept for days now. The damned team had no idea the hell they put him through when they were just doing whatever they wanted. He could relate, in some ways. He'd been there once, on a team that could get away with nearly everything. Special Agents, and the teams they were on, could commit murder and claim it had something to do with a case, and the IMPO would turn a blind eye. The handler would be the one who got the ass-chewing. It was funny when he was an agent. It wasn't funny now that he was a handler.

He realized, as he got off the elevator, that he couldn't go home. He had damage control to do, and while he couldn't put Sawyer on display, he knew someone who would jump at the chance to talk about how good she was, how she felt morally obligated to redeem herself.

He focused on that, considering how the press conference would go down. Or maybe just a single interview. She would be furious, but he could protect Charlie if there was blowback. That was the easy part.

He was in front of the gym, staring at the front door for a long time, considering this. He wouldn't ask any of the kids, or even the older boy, Liam. They were non-Magi and wouldn't be very helpful. Magi would say that they didn't understand just how scary Shadow had been at the height of her reign of dark terror as Axel's blade. But Charlie was a Magi, a respected one a long time ago, before his wife passed away. A healer of impressive skill who also turned around and became a doctor, using both skills to help those in the most need.

He walked into the gym, hoping this would help save the reputation of the IMPO and his team.

"Mister James!"

He held back a groan and turned to see Liam coming out of one of the side rooms. Talk about hero worship. Liam was one that James definitely couldn't put on the news. It would be a nightmare. The kid was probably losing his mind over what was going on.

"Hey, son. Where's Charlie?"

"Are you here to tell him about Sawyer being all over the news? We kind of saw that already. What happened? Who did that to her? They're eating her alive, too. Are you going to do anything about that? Can I help?"

"Hold on, young man." James held up a hand, sighing. "First, we're working on it. We did catch the agent in the IMPO who took the photos and information to the press. Second, you can't help. This needs to be handled carefully, and we're still exploring options about how to make this go in her favor. In the end, the press can talk all they want, and her situation won't change with the IMPO or the WMC; she'll just be watched more, as people will want her to screw up. Now, where's Charlie?"

"He's up in his office," Liam answered, pointing to the back. "You know how to get there."

"Thank you for not pressing for more information." James respected that. Normally, the college student was all over him for the entire visit.

"This is the first time you haven't cracked a joke as soon as you walked in the door." Liam shrugged, turning away. "I need to finish this class."

He would have to remember that Liam was so perceptive. He could only wonder who the boy had picked *that* up from. James watched him close himself back into the room before moving to find Charlie. Good kid, even if too exuberant for what was needed.

He knocked once on Charlie's door and then walked in, phasing through the door.

"Well, I should be surprised, but I've been waiting on you," Charlie declared, looking up from his book. "You want me to say something to the press."

"I want you to tell the story of having Sawyer here in your gym and what it's done for kids all over this city. Describe the woman you knew. I think it might help her."

"She'll hate you for asking me, and she'll hate me for saying anything to the press." Charlie didn't move, his nose going back into the book in front of him. "And if you're thinking to have Doctor Charles Malcolm back out there, acting like a hero, you're sorely mistaken."

"No, I'm asking Charlie, the owner of this little gym in the Bronx, to go out there. A broken soul that could understand another broken soul. She healed you just as much, I think, as you healed her. Last I heard, until we found Sawyer with you, you'd stopped using magic completely. You pretended to be a non-Magi. Yet you were fixing her up after every job, weren't you? Every bruise and scrape those kids get - the strays, you call them. Don't think I haven't noticed." James smiled down at Charlie, then sat down on the other side of the desk from him.

"Well, damn. Got me all figured out, don't you. What about you, James Carlisle? Once a golden boy just as much as Jasper. I like that kid, by the way." Charlie waved a hand around, like he was waving away a thought. "You rejected the chance to become the youngest Director of the IMPO and led your friend into the position after the team you guys were on was effectively disbanded due to politics and corruption. You placed yourself in the dead-end role of team handler, the place where older Special Agents die of boredom and never move any further. Then you lost your first team, mind you, to *her*. Well, not her. Her drama. Axel Castello. And now your second team...well. We both have problems, don't we?"

"You are a strange man, Charlie," James mumbled, wondering how the other older man knew all of that.

"People talk a lot at Fight Night. You think I don't get some IMPO agents looking for a good swing? Or IMAS soldiers. It was funny, they never realized who Sawyer was and she never dug in too deep about other Magi that showed up. There are rules to Fight Night and they are followed. Drinks after the event, people get loose lips. Oh, and we had one last night, where Sawyer, and in turn the team and you, were the topic. I already fielded a lot of questions, and now you want to throw me in front of the press."

"I want you to give an interview. I would put her out there, and the team, but they...they have secrets I can't allow to be exposed."

"So you finally know. Her heart was always too damn big, which is funny, since most would think she doesn't have one."

"You already knew." James let that soak in. He was the odd man out. Charlie already knew. Damn, they had kept it from him because of his position. Understandable, but annoying nonetheless.

"Of course I already knew. She gossips to me about those boys like a teenage girl. Once a week, I get my phone call, and she tells me everything is fine but oh, Zander left the toilet seat up. Jasper is too busy with school for her. Vincent is nosy. Elijah is a prick, and Quinn remains weird."

"Huh." He let that continue to process. "Elijah is a prick, huh?"

"Apparently, after their blasted mission in the Amazon, he's been a bit of an ass." Charlie grinned. "Imagine the toughest six people you know. Then throw in that they're actually pretty young, and their jobs have left them bereft of normal relationships. They act immature in private with each other, I'm guessing. There's a psychology to it, I'm certain. Sawyer certainly doesn't know what she's doing. She's never had normal to base it on."

"So, the doctor still lives in there."

"Of course." Charlie shrugged as he put his book down. "I'll do it."

"Really?" James had hoped, but he hadn't been completely certain.

"Of course. You know, you were right. I might have healed her and saved her life, but she also saved mine. And not just mine. Look into the classroom when you get down there. Most of them are still alive because she found them. She doesn't deserve to be left out in the cold and destroyed by the press."

"I agree. I'll get something worked out, then contact you with the details. It'll be fast, Charlie, probably tomorrow or the day after."

"I'll be ready. Need to get a new suit."

"I'll pay for it. We can work something out." James stood back up and held his hand out. They exchanged a firm handshake.

"You need to head home and get some sleep. If I didn't know any better, I would say you're about to drop." Charlie continued to hold his hand, and it warmed up. James felt concern from the Magi and he knew the old man was healing him, feeling the physical toll he'd done to himself.

"We're the same age, so please don't treat me like one of the children you babysit," James retorted, yanking his hand away. "And I'm getting no sleep because I'm babysitting the other children."

"Amen to that. All these kids need more damn father figures in their lives."

He snorted, walking out. He again didn't open the door, instead opting to walk through it. Before he left the gym, though, he went to that classroom and peeked inside.

Rows of little young kids, all non-Magi, were practicing punches and doing jumping jacks. They were smiling and laughing. Teenagers helped them correct their fists and offered hands for them to swing at.

He wanted to make this her legacy. It would never happen, but he could at least make sure it was on the record. People would get the full story before passing judgment on one of his agents.

He headed home alone, almost a little lost. His small condo in New York was all he'd had for years. He had another home outside the city, but it held too many memories for him.

She weighed heavy on his mind, always there, always nagging him. She'd been that way since the day he met her - not just in Atlanta, no. The day his last team started contact with her. She'd always struck him as strange in her communications. She was never what he expected.

That was part of why he wanted to help her so much. And he loved his young team. He remembered the day

Vincent came up to him, young and fresh-faced, but with dark shadows in his eyes. Elijah, there next to him. They wanted a piece of Axel. They wanted to be the team that caught him. They thought James was the only handler that would understand.

And then they found her again.

He wandered through his two-bedroom, modern marble condo, wondering if there was anything else he needed to do for them. Any way he could help, no matter how much work they ended up giving him with their shenanigans.

He needed to make them heroes, not outcasts. Not just Sawyer, but the entire team. They had always been the black sheep of the IMPO, thanks to their collective backgrounds, bad attitudes, and strange behavior. He needed to repair not just her reputation, but the guys' as well, or they would never hear the end of it from the rest of the world.

His kids, that's what Thompson had called them.

Yeah, and he loved the fucking shits, no matter what weird shit they were into.

12

SAWYER

"Would you say she's in any way repentant for the pain she's caused? Do you think she feels guilty, or is this maybe all an act? A show she's put on so she can remain free."

Sawyer gritted her teeth at the screen, glaring at the interviewer. Some fucking rich guy who was well-known for walking his interviewees into corners.

"I know she's repentant, and I know she feels guilty," Charlie answered patiently. "I'm a doctor, Gentry. I wasn't just a surgeon or a healer, either. I worked a lot in psychology as well. I'm not sure what you're trying to ask me that I haven't already answered. I lived with her for four years, from shortly after she was declared dead to the moment the IMPO found her during an unrelated case and took her into custody."

"Now, you say she felt guilty, but she was still a thief, wasn't she? I mean, that doesn't seem very-"

"Has anyone told you what she did with the money she made from that work? She has a very specific skill, Gentry, and made do with it. She did what she could with what she had."

"Why does it matter how she used the money? It's not like she was Robin Hood."

Sawyer closed her eyes as she heard Charlie laugh at the interviewer. Such a good laugh for such a dark conversation.

"But she was! She put it all away. She made college funds for kids. She paid for lawyers to help people escape abusive marriages and pay for their children's needs. Or to get new homes, since they lived in dangerous areas. She might have been a thief, and stealing isn't a victimless crime, but she definitely applied skills you look down on to doing more for the kids of New York than anyone else ever had. Kids in this city, living right under the nose of the WMC and ignored because they have no magic. She didn't ignore them."

"Sawyer?" Vincent touched her shoulder and she nearly jumped. She'd been so focused on the utter betrayal on the screen in front of her that she hadn't noticed him. She was getting so damned sloppy. Comfortable. She turned and saw they were all filing into the room, looking at her.

"Who asked him to do this?" she asked softly, glaring at them. "Who put him in danger?"

"James asked him and we didn't know," Vincent answered. "We had no idea. And from what James said-"

"I don't fucking care what James said," she snapped. "I spent years keeping a low profile so that Charlie and those kids would be safe. So that I could be in their lives and they would be fucking safe." She pointed wildly at the screen, as something unraveled in her. She felt insane, mad as the world she worked so hard to build came apart at the seams. "And now he's on the fucking news, streaming to anyone with a fucking internet connection. This isn't safe!" She was screaming at the end of it. She was breathing hard as her fury ramped up, but the room grew cold.

In front of her, they all stood unrepentant themselves, as Charlie continued to talk behind her about her and her life with him.

"He knows the risks," Vincent told her. "He knows what's at stake."

"HIS LIFE!" she roared.

"No, yours."

She snarled at him. How dare he. There was nothing at risk for her. Her reputation would never be repaired or perfect. She would always carry around the pain and the condemnation. Charlie was safe. He was a respected member of the Magi community, even after he withdrew from it, long before he met her. He could have stayed that way. Now they were always going to look at him as a sympathizer to a murderer.

"I can't believe you. Any of you. You're all okay with this?"

"We are," Jasper said, speaking up. "Sorry, Sawyer, but it's been five days of nothing but hate coming from every speaker in this house. The news channels, the radio, the fucking internet. Sorry, but Charlie was in a position to tell them something they might not believe otherwise. He had a chance to get some of the real truth out there, and we're completely fine with him doing that."

"God damn all of you. He was safe," she hissed it out like her jaguar would have. Her jaguar, who had run off into the damn woods for three days and refused to come back. "I can't watch anymore of this."

She pushed Vincent out of her way and stormed through the group in the way of the door. They didn't try to stop her. She was furious and needed to scream and yell.

She couldn't tolerate this betrayal from them. She couldn't believe James thought this was a fucking good idea. She couldn't believe Charlie went along with it.

She knew what was happening over the last week. It was a ramped-up version of what had happened quietly when it was publicized that Shadow worked for the IMPO. Now they had her face and name; they had a target. They called for those in the WMC to step down for employing a monster, a killer. They called for the IMPO to go rogue and arrest her anyway, for someone to put down the rabid beast that didn't belong in their perfect world.

None of it justified the use of Charlie, exposing him to every Magi in the world who might have a bone to pick with her. Now they knew she was alive because of him. He could have let her die that night. He could have called the IMPO and had her hauled away. Instead he'd healed her and kept her in secret.

He was as much a criminal to the world now as she was. It was one of the things the interview addressed first. Luckily, no one was going to arrest Charlie for just doing what he was gifted with: healing. Plus, it was so far beyond the point that it didn't matter.

She ran out into the woods, deciding to refocus on finding her damn cat. Sombra had torn off one day when Sawyer broke something in their room. The feline wasn't sure what was wrong, but the cat refused to come back until Sawyer did something for her. She just wouldn't tell Sawyer what that was. It annoyed Sawyer, since it was too damn cold for the jaguar to be out at night.

"This will give me something to do at least," she mumbled angrily. "Sombra!" she roared, hoping the cat would answer.

Nothing came back, not even through the bond. The cat was blocking her out.

"Damn it." She hiked further into the woods. She wrapped her arms around her core, realizing she was an idiot for not wearing a jacket. She was lucky she even had shoes on, since she was normally barefoot in the house.

As she moved further away, just following the small tug of the bond, she realized she was going deeper into the woods than she ever had. This was Quinn's territory, all right. She could feel how he was probably the only Magi to go this deep. His magic clung like the Druids' did in their homes. This was where he went to be truly wild.

She found Sombra standing on a log, waiting for her.

"What do you need me out here for?"

There was no annoyance that it took her three days to admit defeat and come find the jaguar. Only expectation. Sombra jumped off the log and began to walk away.

"Don't be weird and just let me know what you want, Sombra. I'm not Quinn. I don't understand a lot of the stuff you send my way." She didn't have his animal instincts to help her understand. He could at least shift into a wolf, which gave him a strong understanding of Shade and Scout. She was just a Magi with one form. Two, if smoke was included, but it wasn't helpful in the manner she needed it to be at that moment.

Sombra stopped and shifted down. She watched the jaguar's muscles tense and relax as the cat shifted silently, her claws digging into the dirt. Then she jumped, flying up into the air. A crunch was the only thing Sawyer could hear.

When Sombra fell back down to the earth, there was a ball of feathers and blood in her mouth.

"I don't need presents," she mumbled as the bird was dropped at her feet. "But thanks."

Sombra then nosed it closer.

"It's a dead bird. You can eat it. There's no reason to waste it. Quinn wouldn't like it."

"She's trying to understand why this killing is good, but not the killing you did," Quinn called out. "She doesn't know why you hurt so badly and why the other humans say such awful things."

"How do you know?" she growled back at him. Of course he'd fucking followed her.

"The animals talk to each other. The boys told me."

"Why didn't you answer?"

"She's not mine to educate."

Sawyer groaned and sat down in the dirt, far away from the dead bird. "I kill other humans, Sombra."

But that didn't answer her question. Sombra saw her kill another human and be praised for it. Why wasn't that bad too?

"Because it matters why I killed the person, and for who. Right now, I am supposed to kill for those in power. They are considered the good guys. They are 'right.' But I used to kill for the bad guys, and they are 'wrong.' Human issues of morality. It's pretty confusing."

Sombra lay down at her feet. She didn't like her human being talked about so badly, which was one of the reasons she came into the woods. She didn't want to feel Sawyer hurt so much again. This was a bad hurt, too. It felt like something was rotting from the inside.

"Oh, baby, I'm sorry," she whispered, running her hand over the slick black coat. Her own pain was being echoed back to her from Sombra's memories. It did feel like a rot, something deep and insidious that could never be healed.

Sombra didn't understand. She didn't know pain could feel like that. She only knew physical hurts. And the feeling was getting worse every day. It had started so small, but now it was big. She hated it.

"I hate it too. I'm trying, baby, I promise." Sawyer kept giving the cat long strokes, hoping to ease her. She looked up to Quinn. "My pain chased her away."

"Yes, it was one of the reasons."

"I need to get help," she whispered, "so my pain doesn't hurt her, don't I?"

"Yes. When Sombra ran off, I went to Jasper. He's already talked to someone about getting you...uh, video sessions with a real doctor."

"Thank you."

"Are you still mad about Charlie?" he asked, sitting next to her.

"Yes," she snapped, her mood turning back to angry. "Damn it," she mumbled, covering her face with her hands. She couldn't believe this, but now with Charlie out there talking about her...there might just be another doctor who could give her a chance to explain her side and get this out. And maybe medicate her ass. That would maybe be nice. "I'm sorry. I'll call Charlie and talk to him. And I'll go back and talk to Jasper about...finally seeing a therapist. It's time. I can't do this every day for the rest of my life. Living with this pain and rot. You guys have been amazing, trying to put me back together, and you've gotten me so far, but it's time I seek professional help."

"I'm glad you understand that."

"I take it you all knew already? That there was nothing else that could be done here at home?"

"Truthfully? I was the last to realize it, and the guys had to explain. To me, pack delivers everything I need, but...they all had solid points. So, I'm just delivering the message." He smiled at her and she couldn't stop a small one from forming too. He was so honest. "It doesn't make you weak, though."

"Actually, it was never that I felt weak," she admitted. "It was that I never wanted to expose myself and my secrets. Now...well, they're all out, so I guess it doesn't matter." She snorted. "Guess there is a bright spot to all of this."

She looked down at her jaguar, who laid her head in her lap, and continued to stroke the silk fur. "I'm sorry, Sombra. I'll get better for you," she whispered. "And now you understand why sometimes killing is okay and sometimes killing is bad."

The jaguar huffed. She thought humans were stupid.

"Can we go in now?"

Another huff, but the big cat didn't budge.

"I guess not," she mumbled. Quinn chuckled, standing back up. "Don't leave me out here with her."

"I'm not," he replied, reaching to grab Sombra's collar and haul her up. "Let's go. You've been freezing out here and no one likes it."

A flash of teeth and a grumpy growl was what they were given, but in the end, they did go back to the house.

Sawyer stopped and checked her phone when they were inside, as Sombra ran off to find a warm place to curl up in. The interview was still going. He was talking about her nightmares and PTSD now. How she was always closing it off, trying to hide the trauma she went through, so no one really knew how bad it was. How she was as much a victim of Axel Castello as anyone else.

"She is a passionate woman who found herself in a situation where she had no hope. Where she was bent and blackmailed into doing terrible things. So when she whispered to me her story while fever ravaged her body and her injuries battled infection, I knew there was no way I could turn her in. She was just a hurt young woman who didn't know how to fix it. That's all she's ever wanted, to fix it."

What Charlie said to Gentry left the interviewer stunned long enough for Sawyer to turn her phone off and not hear a response. He was blasting her secrets to the world, but damn, he had her back and she loved the old man for it. She hoped nothing happened to him for it, and she was angry that it could put him in danger, but a little piece of her loved him so much for risking himself for her.

It eased some of the pain in her chest. Past the anger, she was genuinely happy that someone was able to stand up and say she was good and mean it. With no ulterior motives, no romantic feelings, and nothing to get out of it, Charlie stuck his neck out for her.

She still wanted to kill him for it.

SHE WALKED through the door to Jasper and Zander's office later in the day, right before dinner. She'd spent the day reading the rest of the interview's transcript and cuddling with Sombra, reassuring the big cat that everything would be okay.

That she would be okay.

And she felt like she would be, finally conceding to the very thing she never wanted to deal with.

"Quinn said you were...scheduling a therapist for me," she said immediately, sitting down in front of him.

"I'm glad you're finally going to do this." He smiled kindly at her. "Really, Sawyer."

"Well, my excuse for wanting to keep my identity hidden no longer works," she reminded him.

"I know, and I've had three doctors turn me down for knowing who you are, but there's one I think will work. He's good - and I've actually used him myself. I'm not sure why I hadn't thought of him sooner. He sees the team after some of the harder missions."

"Awesome, so he knows all of you." Something about that was comforting. That she was going to be with someone they trusted and not some stranger.

"And he firmly believes in privacy. No one heals when their business isn't kept in confidence," Jasper whispered.

She watched him close his laptop. "You were reading the news, weren't you?"

"The interview from Charlie. He really put it all out there on you." He looked pained. She wanted to reach out and comfort him. There was no reason this should hurt him, but something held her back. Maybe it was their recent distance. She felt detached from him and didn't like it. "I knew all of it already, and he didn't say all that much, no names or gritty details, but it's pretty much all there if someone knows how to read between the lines."

"I know. I wonder if James coached him on how to walk the fine line of explaining without giving the world everything about me." She had been impressed with how Charlie rode the fine line of mentioning Henry without ever saying Axel's son - or anything else that could have been used to identify the lost boy.

"James did coach him. Vincent called and asked how this came about when it started. He blindsided all of us with this. He's sneaky like that sometimes."

She sat quietly, not thinking about the interview. It was done. There was no going back and telling Charlie and James not to go through with it.

Instead, she thought about how distant she and Jasper

were. "I know we can't leave the house, but I still want us to do something. Your finals are over, so there's no reason we can't...I don't know, have a picnic or something. Just me and you."

His eyebrows went up in shock. Probably from her sudden change in topic. She promised herself not to let this ruin her, and she was going to make sure that included the guys. There were a thousand directions she was getting pulled in, but she wanted to focus on the one that wasn't pulling as hard as the others.

Him.

"Are you sure? I mean, there's you and Elijah now too. You've got to spend some time with him. And Vincent hasn't been able to do anything with-"

"They can wait a moment longer," she said. "I haven't spent real quality time with you in weeks, Jasper, and I want to."

"Tomorrow, then. I'll make us something and we can go to the swimming hole or a field I know nearby and just have a small date." He gave her a bright smile. "Thank you."

"Why?" she asked, confusion taking over everything else she was feeling.

"I know this isn't easy. You being with all of us is already *busy* and then this happened." He motioned to his laptop. "Thank you for thinking to ask *me* to spend time with you."

"Jasper?" She frowned at him. "Why wouldn't I want to spend time with you?"

"Because you don't need me," he mumbled, looking away from her.

The anger was suddenly back, but she pushed it down. "We're going to talk about that incorrect assumption tomorrow over some sandwiches and cake. You understand me?" She pointed a finger at him, pinning him with it. To hell with it. She wasn't going to sleep until she addressed this nonsense. "You think I don't need you? Are you fucking crazy?"

"Elijah said you would be angry," he muttered, looking up to the ceiling.

"*Look at me*," she demanded. She waited until he laid those stormy blue eyes on her before continuing. "I've always needed you. And I'll always need you. We live in a madhouse - I mean, look around us. You're normal. And I love that. Don't be an idiot and think that isn't special in its own right."

"Sorry. I've just been...feeling worthless. Not ignored by you, just not useful for anything. You don't need me much anymore. Neither do the guys, not really. It's been weighing on me. I wasn't very helpful on the last mission, and that's been sticking with me."

"You've been wallowing in your insecurities. You're the smartest person in the fucking house. You need to apply it - that's the problem. You need a confidence check, holy shit. You were really helpful with me in Texas, remember?"

And she promised herself to spend more time with him. He obviously wasn't Vincent, where they could go a week without a private moment and be completely fine. He needed her around, present, in his space, it seemed. He wasn't Quinn, who knew how to claim a moment without stopping them from doing anything else for the day. With her wolf, a simple touch was more important than a long conversation.

He wasn't anyone except Golden Boy Jasper, who held more insecurities than anyone else in the house. And she'd forgotten about those. No more.

"So, a picnic tomorrow?" he asked, seeming wary. He was looking at her and quickly glancing away.

"A picnic. Me and you. Normal." She looked him over. "Thank you for just outright telling me what was wrong. You and Elijah, so good at it." If he didn't hear the sarcasm dripping from her tongue, he was deaf.

"That's not fair!" he protested, standing up at the same time she did.

"It's totally fair. You've both been wallowing in private and didn't tell me what was going on."

"You're being real rich with that accusation." His face was turning a red that was similar to Zander's. She realized he wasn't appreciating what she had to say anymore.

"I tell you guys everything now, so don't go there with me." She crossed her arms stubbornly. "Come on. Tell me one thing I've kept secret since I officially joined the team."

He opened his mouth and she watched him try and find anything. There wasn't shit. She told them everything that was bothering her when it was bothering her.

"Fine. You're right. I'm sorry." He sighed heavily. "Tomorrow, we'll go have this normal date you so desperately want."

"Jasper? You know I've always loved you, right?" She didn't want him to think it wasn't real for her. He was so needed.

"I can always do with a reminder," he replied, giving her a weak smile. "You know I've always loved you too?"

"I love being reminded," she agreed, leaning over his desk to kiss him. He met her halfway and she could feel the storm brewing as their lips met. It was there, just waiting. How she wanted the storm. Her Golden Boy was so calm and normal, but the storm brewing in him wasn't. His eyes were darker when she pulled back from him. He was breathing harder like she was.

"Tomorrow," he whispered.

"See you then. I'm going to get some dinner."

"I'll be out in a...few moments," he said, chuckling. She dared to look down but the desk blocked her view. Raising an arrogant eyebrow and smirking, she turned to leave the room. One day she was going to get that calm to break and she was going to get to that tempting storm underneath.

Even though she didn't really do anything productive, she felt like she'd accomplished something for the day, and it washed away the negativity that she had started with.

13

SAWYER

Sawyer was ready to go the next day at noon, standing in the kitchen as she waited on Jasper to come down. She looked over the food she'd prepared, then the stuff he'd done. Then she began putting it away, in a duffel bag since they obviously didn't own a fucking picnic basket.

She was going on a fucking picnic. And it was her idea. The world was ending, that was for sure.

"Excited?" Vincent asked her as he walked in. She smiled, looking him over as he drew closer. He hadn't shaved, hadn't combed his hair, and his shirt was unbuttoned and untucked. She loved when he looked so completely like a mess.

"Yeah. I've never been on a picnic," she answered. "After my day with Jasper, you and I need to work something out."

"We play chess on nearly every Wednesday and Sunday. We don't always play chess either," he murmured, leaning down to kiss her neck. Shivers raced down her spine as his coarse stubble tickled her neck.

"We should be more spontaneous," she said, tapping his chest.

"I think I like consistency. I know when I'm going to see you and it's just us. It's our time. The guys don't bother us most of the time." His hands found her hips, sneaking under her tank top. "Living out here doesn't give us many options on more spontaneous things to do, and my plans to have you in Atlanta for a couple of days have been ruined... by Elijah's plans to have you in Atlanta for a couple of days."

"Touché. Now go on. I'm waiting on Jasper, and you are a major distraction from my planned distraction."

"Yeah, I can't stay." He sighed, looking away. "Back to the phones. The public is already changing. Small groups of people are beginning to ask more about you, your story. More people want you to give an interview. James and I are still keeping that option off the table, but it's a good sign."

"I don't want to hear about it today," she reminded him.

"Okay." He gave her a small smile. "Have a good time."

"We will," Jasper said as he walked in. "Keeping her occupied?"

"You're late." She crossed her arms as Jasper threw his up in exasperation. She grinned at the look on his face. It was obvious she was teasing. Even Vincent was snickering as he walked out.

"I live here. I can't be late for anything. I said sometime in the afternoon. You've just been sitting down here waiting on me." He walked into her space and kissed her cheek. "Thank you for yelling at me yesterday."

"Any time. Now let's go before we end up with a party."

"Good idea," he agreed, grabbing the duffel bag. "What did you put in here?"

"Salads. Caesar and fruit." She liked refreshing foods, and she thought they would go well with the sandwiches he'd made. "There's also a bottle of wine in there."

"Of course there is," he said, chuckling.

As they walked out the back, Sawyer pulled her jacket out of the bag. It was chilly - of course it was. "This is what we get for having a picnic in December," she mumbled.

"It was your idea," he reminded her casually. She eyed him, in his comfortable hoodie and jeans. He'd been more prepared than her. "At least it's sunny, and it's warmer than last week. No more snow in the forecast."

"Yeah, I didn't appreciate the cold snap. I'm glad it's not freezing, just a little chilly."

They walked out to the field quietly and she let Jasper find the perfect spot. Before they did anything else, she opened the wine and poured them each a glass.

"This will warm us up."

"You like to drink too much," he teased, taking a sip. "This is cheap-ass wine, Sawyer."

"Of course it is. It's the stuff we used to steal."

She watched the memories pass over his face, smiling to herself. Once upon a time, there had been three orphans. They had no money, but they had connections. They could get moonshine every now and then, and they were also good at stealing cheap-ass strawberry wine from the grocery store.

"I haven't had it in years," he whispered, looking down at the drink.

"Me neither, but if I remember right, it was all you really would drink. You didn't like the moonshine we got ahold of."

"I'm amazed you remember that."

"I never forgot." She met his stormy blue eyes, hoping he knew she meant every word. "Now let's eat, before we drink too much. I'm sure no one would appreciate if we got drunk out here in the woods by ourselves."

"Quinn would find us and drag us back, but you're right.

Do you mind if I take this thing off?" He gestured to his prosthetic and she one-upped him. She didn't answer, just moved closer. She pushed his pants leg up and reached underneath it to get to the straps. It meant her hands were on his thigh. "Sawyer..."

"Let me," she murmured, undoing the leg's straps. She slid her hands back down his thigh slowly and pulled the leg off. "I can't imagine it's comfortable wearing it all the time."

"I got used to it. I need to make sure I keep it dry, and that I don't make it too tight. You know, general stuff so I don't give myself a damn rash or anything." He was rambling on her now. She could tell by how fast he said it, a tumbling of words that reminded her of a waterfall. "It's better than the stuff most people wear. It's responsive, acts like a real damn leg. I love it. I wish I didn't have it, but it's the best that can be done. Though there's a reason most aren't like mine. Too expensive and-"

She rolled her eyes and moved to straddle his thighs, silencing the rambling with a kiss. When she was done, she smiled at him, wondering what he was going to say now.

"You really don't mind the leg, do you?" he asked softly. "I fucking hate it more every day."

"I'll never mind the leg. You know why I was so pissed out in the jungle when they fucked with you? First, it was just mean, cruel-hearted. You are a damn good Magi, and we were on a serious mission. Second, you lost that leg for me. I'll never judge you for a sacrifice made for me. I think you only mind it because it's strengthening this idea that you're worthless."

"Maybe we should eat," he said against her lips.

"Trying to avoid the difficult topics?"

"Always," he confirmed. She laughed at that, knowing

just how true it was. Years of him just bottling things up, badly at that. Where Zander was explosive, Jasper put it all away, and not even well, unlike Vincent.

They nibbled on sandwiches, picking a lighter topic: her, and everything else.

So light.

She quickly evaded it. "So, how was school?" she asked, curious. "That seems safe."

"That might be safe. I've passed all my classes, straight A's. I'm done. I didn't register for anything in the spring. It's time for me to look at other options for my intelligence than just collecting degrees."

"You mean like...work for the IMPO!" She grinned at him, but he surprisingly shook his head.

"No, I mean leaving the IMPO."

"What?" She didn't know what to say to that. If he wasn't on the team, she didn't know what to do.

"It's a small idea, and not a serious one," he promised. "I'm just hitting a point where I'm feeling a little lost, if that makes any sense."

"We'll think of something, but I don't think you would be happy out of the IMPO." She knew she wouldn't be happy with him leaving. And that's what it sounded like. If he left the IMPO, it felt like he was leaving her. Not like she was always going to be an agent, or whatever she was, but it was what she had now.

"You think?" he asked, leaning to her. Their lips were too close for her to resist licking her own lips, causing her tongue to brush against his. "Maybe this was too heavy for us too."

"How long have you been thinking about this?" she asked back softly.

"Since the Amazon. You know that mission really

fucked me up, Sawyer." He sighed. "Can we talk about this later? I can promise you that anything I decide will be after you're done with your contract. I can promise that. When you're looking for what's next, so will I. And hopefully, it's not so different as you might be thinking it will be."

"We can talk about the future later," she agreed, kissing him to end the conversation. He didn't resist, but he didn't push back either. She took control of it and climbed on his lap, wrapping her arms around his neck. So normal, a make-out session during a picnic.

She loved him too much to think about a future without him. She'd been there before, not having him in her life. Not having his goodness and acceptance of who she was. She wasn't going back to it.

She was pleased when he grabbed her hips and pulled her flush against him. She could feel his cock between her thighs, and she knew the storm was right there underneath the surface. She moved one of her hands between them and undid his pants before he could stop her. He groaned as she touched the head of his cock. She moaned as he grabbed her ass roughly, forcing her to grind against him, her hand trapped between their bodies.

"Sawyer, I need to tell you something," he murmured against her lips between her attempts to keep kissing him.

"What's wrong?"

"Nothing, but I'm a virgin." He chuckled, his head falling where she couldn't see his eyes anymore, his blond hair falling over his forehead.

She stopped and pulled away so slightly. This was a shock, in a way. She had heard that he never finished the deed with random hook ups, but she hadn't considered that he'd *never* finished the deed. "This is why you stop us," she said, realizing it. "Why it's heavy make out sessions, then you find a reason to end the date."

"Yeah. I didn't just want to rush into bed with any woman out there, and I didn't just want us to be about sex. So it's just never happened." He sounded so...insecure.

"You know what, Golden Boy? I'm going to blow your mind, then," she decided. She pushed him onto his back, hard enough for him to thud. "But not right now. Outside in the cold isn't a good place for it."

"So you're just going to torture me?" he asked.

"Well, I'm damn sure not letting this end with blue balls," she retorted, grinning. She leaned down and claimed his lips again, grinding against him like she was in heat. He smartly moved a hand to unbutton her jeans and slide in.

"I'm not a total idiot," he whispered, sliding a finger into her as his thumb gently rolled over her clit. She moaned into his shoulder. She had to grab his wrist and make him stop so she could readjust her position over him. When she was done, he went back to what he was doing. She wrapped a hand around his cock and stroked him.

It had been a very long time since she'd just fooled around, but something about it was nearly more erotic than just stripping and getting down to business. They had too many clothes on, and that was part of the fun for some reason.

He finished first, but she didn't say anything, too wrapped up in what he was doing between her legs. There was now a second finger thrusting into her, finding her g-spot and pushing her quickly over the edge.

She was panting over him as he pulled his hand away, and she watched with heated eyes as he licked them. He looked like he was imagining some dirty shit behind those stormy blue eyes. "I might never have had sex, but I've done a lot of other things," he murmured, smiling.

"We'll take things at your speed," she promised, putting her forehead on his chest. "Feeling any better?"

"Well, knowing I can give you an orgasm as good as the other guys is definitely a positive." He sounded like he was joking, but she wondered if it really was a joke.

"The orgasms don't matter. Just being here, with me, on my side, and in my corner...that matters."

"I'll always be on your side and in your corner, even if you never want to see me again."

"Don't let those insecurities drive you away from us. We're a team, a family." She closed her eyes as she kept her forehead on his chest. "You're the first family I've ever had, you and Zander. I just got you back. I can't lose you again, not now."

"I'm sorry." He wrapped his arms around her. They stayed there for what felt like hours. She couldn't help but see the faces of those she'd lost already.

Fucking December. Always a bad month.

She buried her face into his chest, hoping the smell of him, alive and well, would drive away the rest.

"Ready to go in?" he asked her gently. She hadn't been crying or anything, but her silence must have told him where her mind had decided to go post-orgasm.

"Yeah," she sighed. They packed up quickly, making sure they grabbed any trash, since Quinn would kill them if they missed anything. Jasper reattached his leg as fast as he could, deftly, no longer fumbling over the straps like he once did.

As they walked back, she left the sadder part of her mood in the woods. A smile took over her face as she snuck in a kiss to his cheek, making him grin at her. When they were out of the woods, they were laughing, talking about how bothersome Zander was, and how Sawyer decided that Jasper actually had one thing on him. Jasper knew what the word foreplay fucking meant.

"That's just mean!" Zander yelled out from the back porch.

"Oh, I think someone is waiting on us," she whispered to Jasper. "I think we should just throw our shit to the ground and run back into the woods."

"You know how he is. Can't be alone for too long. I guess Vincent got tired of him."

"I think Elijah is with Quinn, too. Poor bastard has probably been waiting on us since we left."

"More than likely," Jasper agreed, still grinning. "Netflix and chill?"

"Sounds like a plan. Maybe you can teach him something about how to get a girl worked up properly."

"And without violence," he muttered.

She laughed harder at that. "Well, I kind of like the violence. Just a little. Sometimes." She loved a good fight, in and out of the bedroom. It really brought her alive sometimes.

"Oh god," he groaned. She would have worried he thought she was insane, but since he was still smiling, she knew he didn't.

They went straight up to her room and she decided to curl into Jasper's side as they turned on some show she hadn't seen yet. The day ended just as she had wanted, relaxing and pretending the rest of the world didn't exist. It was exactly what she needed. For a single day, all her problems seemed so far away. The guys were pretty damn good at making everything seem pretty good.

"I'm going to bed," Zander said late into the evening.

"You two have a good night, and thanks for letting me crash your time together."

"Any time," Jasper said, yawning afterwards. It ruined whatever else he was trying to say.

"Yeah, it's a good time to crash," she agreed, uncurling herself from his side, and stretching her arms over her head. "God, I'm tired."

Zander swooped down and kissed her, then darted from the room. She looked at Jasper beside her, wondering if she needed to ask the question on the tip of her tongue.

"I think I'm going to my room for the night," he answered, standing up. "Next time?"

"Any time," she said this time. "Whenever you're ready." She didn't want him to feel pressured into getting into her bed. She wanted it. She knew if she had him there, she would be all over him, exhausted or not.

And she appreciated his idea of waiting. It was sweet, in a really innocent way. Take a girl on dates, getting to know her, treating her right, then approach adding sex to the relationship. She didn't have enough real innocence in her life and god, Jasper gave her that normalcy she never got the chance to experience.

She figured she would always need it.

"Such a gentleman," she murmured to herself as he cleaned up her coffee table.

"I heard that, and I try to be." He smiled over to her, and when he was done throwing away the trash from their snacking, he gave her a kiss goodnight.

She grabbed his shirt to keep him from pulling away too quickly, forcing open and claiming his mouth like she owned it. He braced himself over her, his arms reaching to the back of the couch as she kissed him. When she was satisfied, and newly horny, she let him pull away.

"You should go before I don't let you," she whispered.

"You make it hard," he retorted, glancing down quickly.

"I know." She gave him an arrogant smirk as a blush moved over his cheeks.

"Damn. I'm going. Good night, love."

"Good night," she called as he practically ran out of her bedroom. As he left, Sombra ran in, already knowing the plan. Sawyer got up and began to strip as the cat went to her pile of things and started getting ready for bed herself. "How was your day, girl?"

Sombra had tons of fun running with the wolves, Quinn, and Elijah. She even got to see Quinn and Elijah wrestle. For humans, they were strong males.

"Oh, I bet you saw them *wrestle*," Sawyer muttered, rolling her eyes. She couldn't deny she was a little jealous for missing the sight herself, but she wouldn't say anything out loud either. "Good night, Sombra."

Sombra just sent back a wave of love, but nothing else. The cat's eyes were already closed.

Sawyer turned off her lights and crawled into bed, feeling better on a chilly December night than she had in years.

SHE WAS DREAMING, and it was a pleasant one. That was the first thing she realized, finding herself in her own room - but not quite. Sombra wasn't there, and none of it was real. Something hazy was all over, making the details of the room slightly obscured, not quite as crisp as the real world.

And even though Sombra wasn't there, that didn't mean she was alone.

"I shouldn't have left," he whispered to her from across the room.

She looked over at him, not sure what to say. So she just beckoned him closer.

Jasper wasted no time, storming across her dream room in just a few short steps. His mouth crashed onto hers as his hands found her hips. She pulled him towards her bed. It might have been a dream, but they were both as real as they could be. This wasn't a dream Jasper, but the real deal, there with her.

And she would take him any way she could have him, dream or no dream.

She twisted them around before she ran into her bed. It caused him to fall back instead and she straddled him, finding she liked to top her Golden Boy. She held his chest down so she kept the control, kissing his neck up to his jaw, then his ear. She kept him down, teasing him with those kisses, just to see when he would break. She wanted the storm.

His hands grabbed her ass and held on tight. He even was bold enough to thrust upwards, causing him to grind against her and pull a moan from her.

Then something else touched her mind.

"Wait," she said, sitting up.

"Sawyer? What's wrong?"

Another brush. It was Sombra.

"I don't know. Sombra is trying to pull me out. Surely she would know nothing is wrong in here..." She frowned, looking around her dream room. Sombra couldn't enter her dreams, but she could tug on the bond and ask Sawyer to come out, recognize the dreams aren't real. It was something she liked. She liked that only Jasper joined her fully, but

Sombra was still useful in the effort to help with the nightmares.

The tug came hard, making Sawyer gasp.

There was danger. And it was very real.

"Wake up. Push me out too. There's something very wrong in the house."

Jasper only nodded, then it was over. The dream faded in only a few seconds, all except him. "I'm going to run up."

"No. Get Zander. Get the guys. Make sure they're okay. Plus, you can't hobble on one leg. I'll run a check of the rest of the house."

"Quinn should already know something is wrong, thanks to the wolves and his power. It'll be okay."

As she watched him fade out, she fucking hoped it was all okay.

14

SAWYER

The first thing Sawyer realized when she woke up was that Sombra slammed her with the order to *not move*. Not a single muscle. Don't change the breathing. Pretend to be asleep.

Sawyer sent back only confusion, but did as her cat advised.

She got back something from Sombra she didn't like, not at all. Someone was in the room. She could smell the other human, but she couldn't see the other human.

Sawyer's heart began to race. She concentrated on bringing it down as she tried to feel any sort of magic that wasn't her own, or the guys'.

It felt like there was nothing there. Nothing at all.

Too much nothing.

On the left side of her bed, there was a spot where not even her magic existed. Because someone was in the spot, giving off no bleed of magic. But they still took up space.

Sawyer waited for a moment longer, until she heard her bed creak as someone gently put their weight on it.

She sublimated right in time. Through her black smoke form, an invisible arm drove a knife down into the bed.

She didn't need to say anything. Sombra was already in action, since the attacker had given themselves away. With a vicious snarl, the black jaguar jumped and Sawyer flew across the room, reforming to see the black massive body of Sombra hit something still invisible. She even got her teeth on something.

A scream of pain and a flicker. Suddenly, the cloak was dropping and Sawyer called her own before the man could turn around to see her. Sombra roared, but the man phased, falling down through the floor.

"Stay," Sawyer snapped, falling down as well. She knew everything about this house now, and knew exactly how to get around it with magic. She had long planned different escape routes and knew the easiest places to walk through, drop, or sublimate to get through the vents.

Some things never wore off. Sawyer's need to have plans was one of them, even if she never intended to act on them.

Zander's room was right below hers, and he was wide-eyed as she dropped in. "He went out the fucking wall before I could stop him. Outside, not the hallway."

"Get the rest of the team," she ordered. Then she left him, running for his window. She phased through and sublimated on the other side as she fell to land. She could still see him, which was promising, as he ran for the woods. She wasn't nearly fast enough in her sublimated form to catch him, since the wind was going in the wrong direction, so she reformed and took off running seamlessly. He was out of her blink range, but she was able to halve the distance with a quick one, not breaking her stride as she covered nearly fifty feet with just a bit of magic.

He trained just as hard as her, fast enough to keep the distance between them. When he hit the woods, she grinned viciously. The fool was running into a domain he had no business being in.

She followed, her feet pounding against the earth in a flurry of kicked-up dirt and leaves. She knew the trails, she knew the fallen logs and the terrain well now. If he stumbled over something, she had him. She couldn't blink in the thick brush, but she knew it well enough to keep running, and that was all she needed.

She kept him in her line of sight, just in case he decided to cloak. When he stopped in a clearing, she slowed down, keeping him nearly twenty-five feet in front of her. Her mind ran the numbers quickly, judged the distances, and knew that if he tried anything, she could make the blink easily and have him.

He faced her and in the moonlight, she knew who she was looking at.

Naseem of the Triad. The wind of death himself.

"So, was this a personal hit or a professional one?" she asked softly, her temper growing cold in the December night. She took a vicious satisfaction in the blood that poured from his arm, dripping into the soil. Sombra had gotten him and left a mark. Good. It meant he would never forget the encounter.

"Professional, of course. The Triad has never killed professional rivals for sport. Why would you think it was anything else?" He didn't sound angry. He was rather calm, actually. It pissed her off more.

"I'm no longer in the business," she reminded him. "I work for the good guys, remember?" She moved onto a better question. "How did you find me?"

"I'm not going to tell you that," he scoffed. "Now, why don't we finish this with honor? We can do that, right? No animals, no friends. Just me and you."

"You aren't finishing anything tonight, especially not with honor," she retorted. She wasn't sure she could win now. Not against Naseem. His mastery over the wind was stronger than Jasper's. She was lucky he hadn't gotten her when she sublimated. He must have been too distracted by Sombra. He had a few other tricks as well, like his phasing, and she knew he was exceptionally well-trained in hand to hand combat.

And now she knew why she couldn't feel him. She hadn't been able to process it earlier. The Triad was famous for it, that ability to totally mask their magic, making them invisible to other Magi on that front.

Naseem was a dangerous opponent.

"Are you sure? You forgot a weapon. Getting rusty in your retirement?" He gave her a cold smile and she curled her lip at him. He was right. She'd forgotten a weapon. Now she just needed to trust that Quinn would come to help and stay alive. "I never thought his whore was his assassin. Such a surprise. Axel has always had so many surprises, always kept everyone guessing. To think, people are scared of you, the whore who hated her master but still got on her knees." He scoffed. "I'm the most dangerous thing in these woods. You shouldn't have come after me."

"There's more dangerous things in these woods than you," she whispered onto the wind, knowing he would hear it.

At that exact moment, wolves howled. She grinned.

"Your little friends." He sighed, nearly sounding bored.

The earth began to shake and she knew that Quinn had

found her. Naseem glared down to the earth. She couldn't feel the other assassin and that meant Quinn probably couldn't either. Even with Quinn's strength, there was no reading something that seemed to not be there.

But he could feel her. She had a feeling her feral lover always knew where she was in his woods.

"We're at a bit of a stand-off. I can't catch you without a weapon." She showed him her bare hands. "And you can't kill me because you've run out of time. They're in the woods now."

"My employer will be upset. Until next time, Shadow."

"Until next time," she agreed softly, watching him disappear. At the same time, earth came up around her, walling her away from the world. She knew it was Quinn trying to protect her. She also knew Naseem would be long gone and impossible to catch now.

As she stood secure in the earth, she considered what had just happened. If she had been nearly hit by the Triad, that meant two others, somewhere on the planet, were also targeted. That's how they worked. They rarely did missions together, as a team. They were like a club. They did synchronized hits together, any time, any where. If one member was seen taking someone out, you just needed to wait for news to break about two other deaths.

She'd never run into them before, not professionally. She'd met them at a few parties Axel had thrown. Funny enough, she'd known who they were, but since Shadow had no face, they hadn't known who she was, standing at Axel's arm. His arm candy, the woman who took care of his son. His whore. Certainly not his assassin.

And she knew that for a fact. They had once asked him to introduce them to Shadow, so they could meet another assassin who had made waves in their industry. Purely professional, maybe even as allies.

She'd been standing there as they inquired and Axel just laughed them off, shaking his head.

"Shadow likes her privacy," he'd answered. "If she wants to reveal herself, she will."

She never had. She'd never wanted to be one of those who found pleasure in the work.

"Sawyer!" Quinn called out, pulling the earth down. She turned to him, but didn't move. He threw his arms around her. "Where is he?"

"Long gone. He wasn't going to test trying to take me out with you coming." She looked back out into the darkness. "Don't let the wolves go after him. They could get hurt. He won't think twice about killing a nuisance."

"Okay." He whistled, and in a split second, both wolves were right next to them.

"Was anyone injured in the house?" she asked.

"No. You appear to be his only target." He growled in frustration. "How did I not know? I know when anyone is here."

"I'll explain when we're safely in the house." Not like the house was really safe anymore. Not with assassins showing up in her fucking bedroom. The house only had space for one assassin, and that was her. "Let's go."

She should have been freaking out, but a calm had settled over her. This was it. Her identity outed, people wanted her dead. She'd known it would come to this. She faced it with a stone cold attitude. If they wanted her dead, they were going to have to try harder.

They walked back in silence. For once, she had a feeling that Quinn was deferring to her. She was the expert on the matter. Assassins were her bread and fucking butter.

And it kept ringing in her head.

Someone wanted her dead and they hired the Triad to do it. Which meant they wanted more than just her dead. Already, she could smell the conspiracy. There were going to be bodies in the morning. Those would tell her a lot. The who's, the when's, and the where's.

Her mind was racing as they left the woods and she saw the rest of the team on the porch.

"You shouldn't have chased after him!" Zander yelled and she sighed, weary of it.

"I nearly had him," she retorted patiently.

"He was here to fucking kill you!" he roared, pointing a finger at her chest as she walked up onto the back porch. "And you ran off alone into the woods after him!"

"Everything is fine," she snapped, losing her patience already. "I knew what I was doing." Softer, she reached out to him. He worried. He wanted her safe and she couldn't begrudge him that. "Remember the trust thing, Zander." She kissed his cheek. "Thank you for worrying. It all happened quickly and I was following my instincts."

"I know," he sighed, kissing her back on her forehead. "God. A fucking assassin."

"Yeah," she whispered, glancing back out to the dark woods. Still the adrenaline from the encounter didn't abate.

"We'll talk about it inside," Vincent interceded, glaring at her. She scoffed at his face, pushing through the group to get inside. "Basement. It's the most secure thing we have."

She turned and went down the stairs. Her blood was pumping too hard through her veins now. She'd met with an opponent, a professional rival, and they had both walked away. That *never* happened in her world. It was why she always considered herself lucky to never have to deal with another assassin. They were fights she could have very easily lost.

She went into the entertainment room and just stared blankly at the far wall, her mind still racing.

What really bothered her? The rush of adrenaline, the taste of her old life back in its purest form. She kind of liked it. This was nothing like the vast unknowns of the Amazon. She hadn't know the place well, or the people, including her opponent.

But this felt like something else. And whatever that was, she kind of liked it.

"Why did you run out after him?" Vincent demanded as the guys flooded the room. "Why not just let him run?"

"Because I could catch him," she answered softly, still staring at the wall, her mind going back to that moment. She'd felt rage at being the target. How dare he come into her home and try to take her out. She'd felt like it was her duty to chase down whoever it was and catch him. It would have solved a lot of problems. "And I nearly did, until I realized who it was. Without a weapon, it became a much more dangerous game at that point."

"Who was it?" he asked. She noticed none of the other guys were even trying to say anything. Vincent was being the leader, the chess player, looking for how the pieces moved and wondering where he needed to put his own.

"Naseem."

Something clattered at the small bar. Elijah cursed and she dared to glance at him, watching him wipe up whatever he spilled.

"The wind of death," Vincent murmured, looking away from her. "Damn. That means-"

"There will be two other deaths tonight and somehow, they're connected to me," she finished for him. "Quinn, that's why you had no idea he was there. Sombra could smell him, which is something he can't mask, but the three Magi of the Triad can mask their magic so it feels like there's nothing there. You have to look for the spot that's too empty. It isn't natural. Look for that, and you'll know where one of them is."

"Sombra could smell an intruder and pulled you out," Jasper mumbled, sitting down in one of the recliners.

"Explain everything," Vincent demanded, crossing his arms. She had seen this before. It had been a long time since he'd been like this, now that she thought about it. When they met, he was like this. All business, all focused.

But then, when they met, she had been similar to how she was tonight. Silently waiting for her chance. Plotting. Considering. Her mind racing over all options and ideas, just like his was.

"I felt his weight on the bed, just slightly. He was careful. It wouldn't have woken me up. I sublimated to avoiding the dagger that would have buried itself in my chest." She felt clinical repeating the encounter to Vincent. Detached from it. "Sombra attacked him then, and I got across the room and reformed. She got a bite off on him, shoulder or arm. I could see blood from it. He must have been too distracted by her to grab me with his control over air. He phased down into Zander's room. I followed him all the way into the woods. He stopped in a clearing and I stayed out of any of his possible range. That's when I saw who it was." She looked down at her hands. She'd forgotten to grab a weapon.

Rusty. She really was. She wouldn't have done that before. "Naseem is a dangerous man, but he's not a fool. Once he realized I had backup coming, it was over."

"Why didn't he just suffocate you?" Vincent asked. He

leaned against the back wall of the entertainment room, those dark olive green eyes pinned on her.

"It's a slower way to kill. I would have woken up, and a fight would have started anyway." It seemed simple to her.

"It also takes a lot of power to manage something on that small a scale with air control. It's very exact and that's not normal for us. Axel could do it easily, but I'm not sure most of us with that elemental control can." Jasper leaned forward, putting his elbows on his knees. She watched him cover his face, rubbing it. "We're lucky he didn't, either way."

"He might have also wanted to send a message, giving me a bloody death in my own bed...like I gave bloody deaths to other people. It would have been something he was hired to do, though. The Triad doesn't pick personal fights. They are too professional for that." She chuckled darkly. "I even asked. He was hired, which meant they all were. So it's not like those three want me dead, but they are paid to make it happen. And this is going to happen again. They aren't going to let me slip away; it would ruin their reputation. They will work to complete the hunt."

"We need to get to a safe house. I'd say we're safe until dawn, maybe even the day, but we won't be spending another night in this house." Vincent pulled out his phone and began to dial. "I'm calling James to get the ball rolling. Someone turn on the news. Keep an eye out for any high-profile deaths or murders."

"Vincent. He didn't tell me how he knew where we were." She felt he needed to know that. It was a big, gaping problem.

"I figured. It means there's a bigger leak in the IMPO or the WMC than originally suspected. The person who ratted you out to the press didn't know our official location. Someone higher would, though. Consider that."

She didn't like the implications of it. There was someone in New York that they couldn't trust. They had already figured it was pretty much them against the world, but this meant someone in power in the IMPO or the WMC. She had no idea how long the list was about who knew what.

"How many people know where we are?" She hoped it was a short list. Something easy to deal with.

"Thanks to you being here? Way more than normal." He sighed as they all listened to the phone ring on the other end. James wasn't picking up yet. "Dozens more than normal. In case you killed us and ran or something like that."

"Fuck," Elijah groaned.

"I can't fucking believe this," Zander muttered.

She could agree with both of those sentiments, but still, something in her kind of liked the adrenaline that refused to leave her.

Vincent must have noticed, his eyes seeing all too much. "Go to the gym with Zander," he ordered.

She didn't say anything as she walked out of the entertainment room and entered the gym across the hall. Zander barely kept up with her. "Need to hit something, Sawyer?" he asked, grabbing her before she made it to the mat.

"Yeah, I really fucking do," she snapped. "Someone tried to kill me tonight and I couldn't even get my fucking hands on him. Sure, how it ended was actually the safest way it could have, but damn! I could have had him and I forgot to grab a fucking weapon."

"Then hit me," he told her, spreading his arms.

"Get on the mat," she growled, then she added something softer. "And thank you."

"Always. Sorry for yelling at you, by the way."

"Don't be. I was stupid enough to forget a weapon. You were well-justified." It galled her to say it, but she had fucked up. Next time she wouldn't.

And there would be a next time.

Something in her liked the idea of that, too.

15

QUINN

Someone had encroached into his territory and he'd missed them.

Quinn held onto that fact as he settled down in a recliner next to Jasper. Elijah fell into the one on his other side. They were all staring at the news going in front of them, hoping anything came up that they could understand.

But he was distracted by his mistake. An assassin coming for his female had walked into his territory and nearly killed her. Sombra had saved his mate's life.

It caused anger to curl in the pit of his stomach. He'd never messed up so terribly, not even in the Amazon. Not ever. He didn't get fooled or tricked like this. He was the most powerful Magi in North America that wasn't a legend. This wasn't supposed to be possible, him getting fooled by a cheap trick.

"Quinn, are you okay?" Elijah asked softly.

"No. I'm going to kill this Naseem if I ever see him again." He meant every word of it.

"Me too," his friend agreed. Quinn could hear the passionate truth in the quiet words.

"I can't believe I was tricked, Elijah. I can't believe it. No one has ever come onto this property without me knowing. *No one*, not even her. If anything, the more powerful the Magi, the better I know they're there. He's supposedly powerful and I had *no idea*." Quinn bared his teeth as he looked down at his hands.

"No one knew, Quinn. No one could have known. Don't let this get to you." Elijah threw an arm over his shoulder. "No one is blaming you. We're all fucking shaken. We all missed that someone was in the house."

Quinn closed his eyes, growling. Elijah was right, but he needed to do something. He couldn't just sit here in the quiet while Vincent tried to get ahold of James. He couldn't just watch the news. "I think I should go out there and track him."

"Absolutely not," Vincent snapped from across the room. "We're staying in this house, with each other, until dawn. No one is going out there to see if he's still around."

Quinn turned and looked at Vincent through the space between his recliner and Jasper's, snarling. Vincent stared him down, the phone still to his ear. He resisted the urge to rumble the earth beneath, remind Vincent who was the more powerful Magi. He knew if he did it, Sawyer would feel it and come in, wondering what was wrong. She would agree with Vincent.

"Do you understand me, Quinn?" Vincent asked in a hard voice that Quinn hadn't heard in a long time. Something else was on their leader's mind. That meant this went beyond just an attacker and other possible victims. He wondered what Vincent was hiding. There was something, even if it was just a suspicion of his, that he hadn't shared with the rest of them.

"I do," he answered, looking away out of respect. He

reached for his wolves, who were upstairs with Sombra. None of them wanted to come down. They were patrolling the house, finding the intruder's scent and his path through the house. They were making sure no one else came in without them knowing.

Shade touched him back through the bond, a comforting brotherly poke. The wolves were okay. They would protect their cat if someone came back.

He cracked a small smile at that. Their cat, as Sawyer was his. They had competition. Kaar was also quite taken with the jaguar, even though she continuously tried to eat him. Not seriously, or the raven would have already been a snack, but more to torment the poor bird.

He liked the distraction of the animals. They knew something happened, and they had a reaction. Protect the pack. They knew he couldn't tell if the man was there, so they would pick up the duty. It eased him a little.

"Fucking James. Finally!"

"You woke me up at three in the morning, why?" James groaned back. Quinn turned back to Vincent. The phone was on speaker for them to all hear.

"Naseem of the Triad broke in less than an hour ago and tried to kill Sawyer. She's fine, he got away. No one was injured in the event except him. Sombra apparently got a bite in."

There was silence from James.

"You're kidding," he whispered, sounding very awake now. Quinn could only imagine the shock their handler was feeling. The poor man was going to have a heart attack one day.

"No. And we don't know who the other two victims might be. It wasn't any of us. Only Naseem was here."

"We need to get all of you in a safe house," James said. "You know that already. What have you already planned?"

"I'm going to give us until tonight to get out of here. I'm keeping everyone locked down in the house until dawn, then we need to move quickly to get everything we need for an extended stay away. And a move. We can't live here anymore, obviously." Vincent ran a hand through his hair. "James, you need to find who the other two victims are."

"I will. I'll also pick the safe house personally and only tell-"

"Tell no one. The Triad was hired, which means someone with wealth and power called for this."

"How do you know they were hired?"

"He told Sawyer it was professional, not personal. That told her what she needed to know. To them, she was just another hit."

Quinn was glad that Sawyer understood the terminology. He was catching up, but she was the expert on these sorts of things. For a moment, he realized he was on the back foot in the situation. She was the expert this time, not him. He was rarely the expert at anything concerning criminals and murders, but this was purely her domain like the Amazon had been his.

"Well, damn," James muttered, barely loud enough for the other Magi to hear him. Quinn even had to strain his ears. "I'll go into the office and find the Director immediately. He'll need to know what happened, and it gives us a warning that two more either just happened or will happen before dawn. Fuck. Godspeed, you all. I'll text you when I'm safely at the office and call after I've talked to Thompson."

"Godspeed," Vincent replied, hanging up. Quinn knew he didn't believe in God, but he didn't ask why he said it.

"I'm going to check on Sawyer and Zander. Then I'm going to go upstairs and pack my bags. I recommend you all start doing the same."

"Roger that, boss." Elijah stood up, elbowing Quinn in the process. "You can help me, then we'll get yours done."

Quinn didn't respond, standing up to follow Elijah out of the room. They glanced into the gym as Vincent went inside, to see Zander and Sawyer sparring. Jasper hobbled behind them.

"Did you get your leg on right?" Elijah asked, looking back.

"No, I was moving too quickly."

"What you did was quick thinking," Quinn said, holding out an arm for Jasper to lean on. "Coming straight into our dreams and throwing us awake. Very smart. Without you, it would have taken even longer for us to rise." Jasper tentatively took his arm. "It's okay to lean on a packmate."

Something flashed over Jasper's face as he nodded in return. Quinn eyed Elijah, who was watching them carefully.

"You can help me too," the cowboy declared. "We'll do me, you, then Quinn. We've got plenty of time."

"What all are you thinking of taking?" Jasper asked, holding Quinn's arm tightly. Quinn glanced down at the leg, noticing that it was so quickly put on that it seemed to be barely hanging on, wobbling hard when Jasper put weight on it.

"Clothing, weapons. Not much for personal items. We need to keep this light in case we need to keep moving."

That started up a quiet conversation about what would be best as they made their way up to Elijah's room. Once inside, Quinn closed the door as Jasper fell on the bed. It only took a couple of moments for him to fix his leg, something he could have done earlier.

"I think I broke it," he mumbled, looking down at a buckle.

"Let me see." Elijah reached out and called the leg to him. It flew across the room into his hands. "Yeah, you snapped a buckle, probably from rushing. No worries. Five minute fix."

"Thanks."

"You feeling any better about that stuff we talked about?" Elijah put the leg down on his desk. Quinn perked up, looking between them. They had talked about something? Now he was curious.

"Yeah, a bit. She was pretty pissed off with me when I said something to her. She said some things that really set me straight."

"Told you." Elijah grinned. "Dumbass."

"What happened?" Quinn couldn't resist getting nosy now.

"Jasper here thinks that he's not needed by her. Or us. The idiot."

Quinn growled at the Magi in question. Jasper raised his hands in defeat immediately. "Not needed? You are my pack. You'll always be needed."

"So everyone keeps reminding me," he replied, lying back on the bed. "And tonight, you were able to get moving to keep her safe in the woods because I was able to wake you up quickly. I get it."

"Exactly. You might not be a great warrior like her or me, or Elijah, but you are a member of this team for your intelligence, like Vincent. You are better at people than most of us as well. You don't intimidate them like Vincent, who meets someone new and considers how he can use them. You are just good."

"You're not telling me anything she didn't." Jasper rubbed his face in exasperation.

"I knew she was a good female." Quinn huffed, looking back at Elijah. "And you? You've slept with her now. Did you tell her what was wrong? Was she mad at you for keeping it from her?"

"Yes and yes. And she and I are going to try just going out and doing stuff together, to hopefully build something. Thank you, Doctor Quinn." Elijah chuckled, shaking his head. "I wish everything came so easily for us as it did for you."

"Nothing came easily for me. I just didn't deny it once it happened." Quinn went to the closet and began pulling out clothing he knew Elijah would want. "Jasper, if anything I'm upset you felt that way, since I think everyone here has their place, and I also understand it now. Tonight, I was confronted with being useless. She was out there with *him* and I could only feel her. I should be powerful enough to feel anyone coming onto my land, and I couldn't. We're not perfect. We all have our strengths and weaknesses. This is why we're pack hunters, not lone wolves."

"She's a lone wolf," Elijah muttered.

Quinn turned back to him. "No. She's a jaguar. There's a difference." He thought that was obvious. "She accepts the pack and she belongs with us, but her skills are formed and tempered by the idea that she's working alone. It's where her strength lies, being able to take care of herself."

"Then what's her weakness?" Jasper asked softly.

"Her weakness is that a group can take her down. She's best in one-on-one fights. She can't fight back against multiple attackers. Which is where we come in, if needed."

Quinn threw the clothing from the closet on the bed, then went to Elijah's dresser. He knew the cowboy was doing a quick fix on the prosthetic. "Is this enough?"

Elijah glanced over and nodded. "Yeah, that works. Here, J. New buckle on it." Elijah sent the leg hovering back to Jasper, who grabbed it from the air.

The conversation died off. They finished collecting everything for Elijah to pack then went to Jasper's room to do the same. They would inventory, then bag it all up.

When they were done in Quinn's room, dawn was breaking. Sunlight was dripping in through his windows and he looked out to the woods. To think, he couldn't go out to them since it was no longer safe. His own woods.

"We should get the others moving," Elijah said, sighing as he looked out the same window. "Want to check on everyone with me?"

"No, I'm going to make sure I have everything I need. Just in case," Jasper answered, leaving the room quickly. Quinn knew it was because he was uncomfortable in his space. Not many came into his room, not very often.

"I'll come down with you," he said to the cowboy. Elijah nodded, and together, they walked down back into the basement. He checked on Sawyer first, sticking his head into the gym. He raised an eyebrow at the sight of Sawyer picking up her shirt off the floor, her bare breasts revealed to him at the door. He could smell sex and sweat, the heady vanilla that she gave off when she was worked up. "That's one way to destress."

"Yeah," she answered. Zander was next to her, pulling his pants up. She smiled guiltily, but Quinn only shrugged. He wasn't going to give them a hard time, nor was he jealous. He would have her later. She would come to him, or the other way around. He was confident in the feelings between them.

"We're just checking on everyone," he explained. "Begin collecting clothing and other items for relocation to a safe house."

"I'll help her," Zander said, looking over his shoulder. "Let us clean up in here."

"Okay." He closed them in again, smiling at Elijah.

"Should have known that was going to happen," Elijah commented, chuckling. "Now for our fearless leader." He opened the entertainment room door and the first thing Quinn heard was Vincent's phone ringing.

And ringing.

And ringing.

He walked in behind Elijah and his eyes fell on Vincent, who was sitting in front of the TV, looking terrified. He wasn't moving. He rushed to the Italian's side, trying to find out what was wrong. There were no injuries. What had happened?

"Vin-"

"Oh sweet Jesus," Elijah mumbled.

Quinn frowned and looked up at the screen.

BREAKING NEWS
TWO WORLD MAGI COUNCILMEN DEAD
ASSASSINATED IN THEIR HOMES

SOMETHING COLD RAN THROUGH HIM, something scared.

"It...hit the news before anyone could tell me," Vincent whispered. "That's probably James."

Quinn ran for the phone, answering it as Elijah turned up the volume on the TV. "Yes?"

"Oh, Quinn. Where the fuck is Vincent?" James sounded pissed off and harried. "Have you seen the news?"

"Just now. Vincent is a bit shell-shocked. What happened?"

"Someone leaked it as it was getting to us. We were just as blind-sided. There was no way to keep the news quiet anyway. Already, there's a press statement going out saying that the Triad is responsible and that Sawyer was the third victim, also the only one to survive. I know we discussed a safe house, but right now, the Director is calling a Code Black. All Special Agents are hereby commanded to report to the main headquarters and join in the investigation and protection of the WMC. IMAS is flooding the city with guards already, ready to take orders from us. I'm sending Trevor down to pick you all up in about an hour. Get packing."

"Yes sir." Quinn knew this was the end of the call. They had their orders and it was time to move.

"Godspeed to you all. I'll see you when you arrive."

James hung up and Quinn pulled the phone down from his ear, slowly turning to Elijah and Vincent.

"What did he say?" Vincent asked softly, still staring at the television.

"We're all going to New York. It's a Code Black."

"May the gods have mercy on us," Elijah whispered.

For the first time in nearly two thousand years, members of the WMC had been murdered. Quinn was glad he'd finished up his schooling. Even he could understand the sheer weight and severity of the situation. The attempt on Sawyer's life seemed to be a part of something much bigger now.

He didn't have the heart to tell her.

"Someone has to tell the others," he said, swallowing. It couldn't be him. He wasn't even sure what he would say. He didn't know how to convey such severity to others.

"I'll tell them," Vincent whispered. "When the news first broke, they were theorizing it was Sawyer."

"James said that the IMPO is about to put out a press statement saying she was the third victim, though she survived. That should clear her of guilt." He should have said that first. Sawyer was more important than the orders to New York.

"That's good. She'll be happy to hear that. I'll deal with her if one of you gets the other two."

"I'll tell Jasper and Zander. We need to get moving. Quinn, did he say anything about transportation?"

"In one hour, Trevor will be here to make us a portal to New York."

"Fuck, we need to move," Vincent snapped, jumping into action. Quinn looked at Elijah as their leader ran out of the room.

"I think he knows something," Quinn said, hoping Vincent wasn't in range to hear him.

"If he doesn't know something, he suspects something. It would explain why he hasn't said anything. He doesn't want us running with half-baked theories. Now, let's get moving. Our holiday is officially over."

"That it is," Quinn agreed, glancing back at the television. He turned it off before following Elijah from the room.

16

SAWYER

Sawyer took a quick shower then got to work getting ready for going to this safe house they had planned. She hated that she was being sent out of her home, sent to go hide, but there wasn't much they could do. She understood the practicality of it. It's easier to protect someone in a secure and private location.

But what was really bothering her was that she needed the protection. Again. This was how she met the guys, got caught. They had thought she needed protection from Axel. How right they had been.

She went to her closet and opened the safe. She couldn't leave any of this behind. She pulled out daggers, her kukri, and every other black weapon. She dumped it all on her bed without care, then went back for the mask.

When her fingers grazed the front, she nearly pulled away. She didn't want to take it, but leaving it meant it could get stolen, and the last thing anyone needed was someone pretending to be her. She was walking out of her closet with it when Vincent walked in, looking a shade paler than was healthy. She dropped the mask on her bed with the rest of her things and rushed to him, touching his cheeks.

"Are you okay?" she asked. "Vin?"

"We're going to New York," he whispered, sounding tired. "Oh, gods, Sawyer, we're going to New York, not a safe house."

"Why?" she asked softly, wondering why he was acting the way he was. He seemed like everything had gone to hell.

"The Triad's other two targets were WMC Councilmen. Sawyer, someone hired the Triad to kill you and two members of the WMC. We're in Code Black. All Special Agents are to report to New York to investigate and give manpower to the IMPO to protect the WMC."

Her hands began to shake as she released him. She took two steps back and sank down onto the edge of her bed. She didn't move back far enough, her ass sliding off and sending her to the floor.

She sat dazed for a moment, her mind reeling.

There were hits that not even Axel would send her for, people he hated but would never kill. There were unbreakable guidelines to the Magi world, even for the criminals. There were unspoken rules in the lawless wild west of Magi crime. There were lines their people had never crossed, not for a very long time.

This was one of them.

"Oh my god," she whispered, looking down at her hands. She pressed her face into them, rubbing, hoping to scrub off the news that Vincent just told her.

"I'll help you pack. Trevor will be here in less than an hour to get us."

"Who's packing for you?" she asked, not moving.

"I did, while you were in the shower. Elijah and Quinn

told the others, so don't worry about them." Vincent reached down for her and got her elbow. She looked up at him as he tugged. "We have to move."

"Fuck," she groaned, grabbing him to haul herself up. She was thankful for his support at her elbow, since it helped stop her sway. "Here I was thinking I was going to get a nap eventually."

"I'll find you a place when we arrive. They aren't going to make you run on fumes, and I'm hoping they keep you minimally involved because of your status as a target."

She nodded silently as they turned to her bed. Now she was packing with a purpose, a goal. She knew where she was going and why. That made this much easier.

"We don't have a full Council anymore," Vincent said, as if he was trying to convince himself that it happened.

"No, we don't." She wasn't sure how to feel about it. "This is only going to get worse before it gets better." She began putting her weapons into a bag while Vincent got her clothes packed.

"I know."

"With the Council on the menu, this is going to be a nightmare. If they can suddenly be killed, then it's going to be free-"

"*I know*," he snapped. She stopped moving and looked over to him. He had closed his eyes. "I know," he repeated softer. "This will put them in emergency state. They will be voting without a full Council. The magic will be weaker. Their lives are at risk. New York will be a madhouse with you right in the middle of it, since you were a target of the Triad, which means whoever is killing them wants you dead for some reason. That's not taking into account the criminals who are watching this happen as well. A Code

Black means we're dropping whatever cases we're working on all over the world. They will have no one keeping them in check."

"The wild west just got a whole lot more wild," she whispered, looking back down to her hands. Once, she would have been on the other side, playing an event like this to the hilt at Axel's orders. The amount of power he could have gained in a situation like this would have been indescribable, and he was already one of the most powerful crime lords on the planet. "You have any ideas?"

"I do."

"Tell me. Between me and you." She could keep a secret, depending on why it needed to be kept.

"I think another WMC member is behind this."

She froze for a moment then continued like he hadn't said anything. The very idea was treasonous. "Someone could arrest you for even saying that," she reminded him.

"I know, which means I'm on my own working it out. The IMPO is going to be completely focused on just catching the assassins, playing like they haven't been paid. No one is going to ask the big questions until the threat has ended. I want to be able to hand them anything I've learned from now until then, hopefully leading to a speedy resolution. But I have to be careful. The guys can't know. They aren't careful and they can be distracted."

"Do you need anything from me?" she asked, holding one of her daggers. She tested its edge, considering what she could do to help him.

"Keep your eyes and ears open all the time. You'll be under protection too, and you'll know more about this sort of situation than most of the agents in New York. They'll come to you for things, I already know it. But...be careful with what you say. I don't want you dragged into the middle, Sawyer."

"Always," she purred, smiling. She would never say the wrong thing in a situation like this. Keeping her mouth shut was a skill she'd developed over the years. Secrets were easy. Lies were child's play. "I'll help. I'll bring you whatever I learn."

"Thank you."

They didn't continue talking as she finished loading her small armory and he packed the rest of her clothes. She stopped at the mask again, her hand hovering over it. With a deep breath, she picked it up and laid it on top, zipping up the bag with its black visage staring back at her.

"Are we ever going to come back here?" she asked softly, looking around her room, hoping she got to. This had become home for her, a place where she felt like she could be herself with a fucked-up family of men who were lovers.

"Probably. It'll take time for us to line up a new secure location to move into," he answered. "And once we discover the person who exposed the location to the Triad, we'll be able to remove them from the equation, hopefully keeping us safer longer."

"Yeah..." She picked up her bag and motioned for him to leave first.

"I need to finish some things, then I'll meet you out back." He took her bag of clothes with him.

Assassins and chaos. That's what waited for them in New York. She wished her room goodbye in silence, just running a hand along the back of the couch as she walked to her door. She would miss it. She would miss the time they had on holiday, and the fun things they got to do. She wished she had confronted Elijah and Jasper about their issues sooner, had more time with them, exploring her feelings and whatever was going on between them all. Now they would all need to put their personal lives aside to deal with whatever was going on.

She didn't stop to check on any of the guys as she walked through the house to the back door. When she walked out, she was hit with Sombra through the bond. The feline had been kind enough to give her space since Naseem ran off and Sawyer disappeared with Zander. Now she wanted to make sure her human was really okay.

She scratched the jaguar behind her ears, but said nothing.

Quinn watched her from a chair on the porch, his wolves lying at his feet. "How are you?" he asked, those ice blue eyes pinning her where she was on the porch.

"I'm fine," she admitted. "I should be freaking out more over someone trying to kill me, but I'm fine. I'm more surprised by the WMC than I am about myself."

"You knew this was coming. Someone attacking you."

Had she? She knew things could go sour easily on her at any point during this attempt to gain a pardon and walk away from crime and her past.

"I did," she whispered, looking out to the woods. "I figured it was going to come. Maybe not how or when, but I knew someone would want me dead. Someone who wasn't Axel. I made a lot of personal enemies while I worked for him. A lot of people blaming me for the deaths of their loved ones who crossed him, and other things."

"We'll keep you safe," he promised.

"I don't need you to keep me safe, Quinn. I need you to back me up."

"We'll do that too. We can do both."

Everything was so easy to him. She chuckled, shaking her head at it. He just confronted a problem with a confidence that was unmatched. He knew what to do and when to do it. It was black and white to him in a lot of ways.

They waited on the porch as the rest of the team came out, dropping their bags. No one spoke much as they waited for that portal to show up in their backyard. The air was thick with tension as they all considered what would be in New York waiting for them.

"At least we aren't going commercial," Zander joked quietly, leaning against the porch's railing.

"Amen to that," Elijah replied, a smile breaking over his face.

Sawyer couldn't stop a small smirk.

"Yeah, it could be worse. WMC Councilmen assassinated, our location exposed, Sawyer attacked...but we're at least getting a portal to New York. The WMC and IMPO doesn't have time to make our lives harder than they need to." Jasper was trying not to laugh as he said it.

"Maybe they realized there are bigger fish to fry," Quinn muttered. Sawyer snorted, smothering laughter. Nothing about this was supposed to be funny.

"I mean, someone did try to kill Sawyer. Maybe they feel sorry for us. We're now targets of someone else. They failed to kill us, so now no one else can. They're petulant children like that." Vincent said that and she lost it, doubling over in a fit. That brought Elijah and Zander down with her, both of them laughing harder than they should have.

They were all laughing when Trevor showed up, the portal forming in their backyard. He looked at them like they were crazy as they grabbed their bags, still chuckling and snorting at the situation they found themselves in.

"You know, at least it won't be hot and humid," she told

them. "And Quinn, you'll get to see the holiday lights of New York!"

"Oh joy," he groaned.

Vincent went through first with Kaar, and the mood sobered quickly. Then Elijah went through and Sawyer realized they were all leaving any semblance of happiness here at home. She could feel it, as they locked it all away. Quinn, then Zander and Jasper.

She had waited to be last on purpose.

"Are you going through?" Trevor asked, frowning at her.

She turned to him slowly. "Did you give up our home?" She met his eyes. This was her best chance to ask him.

"No. No, I didn't say anything, Sawyer. Promise."

She believed him and stepped into the cold dark of the portal.

ONCE THROUGH, she left the small room for portals and walked into the hallway. Immediately, she noticed the madhouse. From peaceful, backwoods Georgia into a flurry of activity that seemed like it would never end.

"We need to get to the central meeting room. They've picked a big conference hall where the Director does big announcements to be the main area of the investigation." Vincent grabbed her elbow. "We need to stay close together and not get separated. We don't need any drama from having you here. You've already been announced as the third victim of the Triad, and who knows what sort of response that will get from people."

She only nodded, following him as the team fell in around her. She stood in the center, not something she was particularly used to. People glanced at the group as they walked.

"Remember, someone was just arrested for exposing sensitive material. The person who outed you to the press. Tensions concerning you are already high," Vincent whispered back to her. "Keep your head down."

"Of course. Like I ever do anything else."

Elijah snorted, shaking his head next to her. He had a silent point. She had a tendency to make something of a scene.

They got to the elevators without any incidents, but that changed quickly. Overcrowded with people and animals, they were all packed together like sardines. Once closed into the elevator, some IMPO desk jockey ran his mouth.

"Look, it's the person who got Collin arrested." The words dripped with anger and condemnation.

"Is Collin the guy who took my photo to the press? Then fuck him. He got himself fired." She eyed the other guy.

Vincent spun to glare at her, then at the guy in the suit. "Lawrence, I'm going to recommend you don't say another word while on this ride," he said with an animosity that even she couldn't muster. "We're in the middle of an emergency, so there's no time for the petty shit - or I'll report you to my superiors."

Lawrence slammed his mouth shut. He must have decided it was better to remain quiet, making Sawyer pleased. When the doors next opened, Vincent led them off and she took a deep breath, glad to be off the overstuffed elevator.

"Over here!" James called, waving them down from the center of the new floor they were on. He was in the middle of a massive crowd, all yelling things at each other. She beelined for him, even leaving the guys behind, since she could cut through the crowd around them easier.

"Who the hell is in charge here?" she demanded, waving around at the other agents. She dropped her bag on the table he stood at. It was her table now. She noticed all the others were completely full.

"The Director," he answered. "He's in charge of the entire operation and will be assigning tasks per team. We're to deliver him anything we learn during our assignments. Vincent, he wants you and Sawyer to him pronto. Everyone else, get your stuff put down and find something to eat. Everything is going to be moving fast."

She glanced over her shoulder to see the Italian there, his eyes dark. Behind him was the rest of the team, though they began to spread out, dropping their bags at the circular table as well.

"Can do. What's our current assignment other than that?"

"Actually, he's going to give you our team's assignment. I have a feeling none of us will like it. We're either going to be tossed to the side for Sawyer's protection-"

"Or thrown into the thick of it? Bring it on," Elijah said, cutting off their handler. "Go on, you two. We can hold down this table in here for us to sit at, get something to eat and hear the word spreading through the other Special Agents. We got this."

"Come on," Vincent ordered her. She went without saying anything, glad to be going. Already, eyes were falling on her, watching her carefully. Whispers broke out underneath the yelling. One or two dared to point.

She walked through them, wearing their uniform, and even had one of their badges in her wallet, the wallet she kept on her at all times, in her back pocket. If it weren't for her past, she'd be just another agent. Her past did exist, though, so her very appearance brought the whispers and glares.

"Naseem went after you?" one of them asked as she and Vincent passed him to find the Director. There was a slight Russian accent that reminded her of Varya. It made her interested in the agent.

She also, for a moment, wondered where the Russian woman and her bear were. She hoped they were well. She hadn't seen them since they left South America.

"Yeah." She wasn't sure what he wanted to hear.

"They say you let him go."

"I didn't have a weapon on me and backup wasn't going to get there in time to help me take him down." She shrugged. There wasn't much to say about it. "Walking away with my life is victory enough at that point."

"Good point," the other agent agreed. Then he lightly hit her arm with a closed fist. "Good work on surviving. It gives us a lead of sorts, a heads up to who the players in this are."

She frowned at him, stopping completely to stare at him.

Vincent began to chuckle softly. "Not everyone hates you," he whispered to her.

"Oh? Is that..." The other agent looked between them. "No, I wasn't going to give you a hard time. I know a lot of people will, but I get it from them too, or used to. I was a thug for the Russians before IMAS pulled me out. Joined the IMPO right after. I get trying to survive by doing wrong. It's the only way to make it in Russia. It's that or get hauled to the labs."

"Yeah..." she nodded slowly. "Another reformed criminal, then."

"Yup. I did it to save my younger brother. He was able to

have a good life, and I got him out of the country. Then IMAS caught me through an IMPO investigation."

"We need to get to the Director," Vincent finally cut in again, ending the conversation. The other Special Agent nodded, waving them away. Sawyer looked back at him as they continued walking.

Interesting.

"He's going to be in here," Vincent murmured as he pushed open a door.

Inside the small meeting room was more chaos as agents screamed at each other. Her eyes fell on the Director, though, looking annoyed as he stared at the other, older men in the room. He looked like he wanted to say something, but wasn't going to find the chance or had given up on silencing the others to speak himself.

"Director!" she called out over the others. "You needed to see Special Agent Castello and me?"

The room went quiet as the other agents looked to see who dared speak over them. Added to the fact that she had used Castello, she had given away their identities in a simple statement. A pin could drop and it would be the loudest thing in the room now.

The Director raised an eyebrow at her. "I did. Come in and have a seat. Tell me about last night. I've heard the secondhand from James, but I want your retelling of it."

"Yes sir," she replied, finding an empty seat at the boardroom table. Quickly, she recounted the entire incident and her thought process behind every action she took. From the moment Sombra pulled her out of her sleep to getting back in the house, she didn't miss a detail.

"See, I told you she's the one we need to talk to," the Director said to another older man near him.

"I'm not sure we can trust her."

"I don't trust her," another fired out.

"Looking for expert advice?" she asked, leaning back in her chair.

"We don't need experts. We catch killers all the time," one snapped at her. "We are the experts."

She glanced at Vincent next to her.

He sighed, shaking his head at the scene. "We're not experts at catching assassins," he said, calling out the obvious reason they had her in the room. "In fact, we've only caught one in the last century." He gave her a pointed look.

She snorted, rolling her eyes at that. Yeah. Just one. Her.

"We've caught hitmen before and that's all assassins-"

"Don't even finish that," she snapped out, pointing at the man about to make the offensive statement. It nearly had her out of her chair, sitting up and on the edge as she practically shoved her finger into the guy's eye. "Hitmen are not assassins and assassins aren't hitmen. We aren't just there to kill an unruly ex-wife or husband. We don't do small time. We take it big. We're the best. Hitmen are child's play. You treat the Triad like they're hitmen and they will run you over and take their targets without a sweat."

"Explain," Director Thompson ordered calmly.

"Hitmen don't have the skill or resources to get through lots of security. The Triad will have both. They also have the magic to back them up. Most hitmen are weaker Magi or non-Magi. They aren't as threatening. The Triad are powerful. They are all incredibly gifted in terms of magic. Naseem, for example, got into our house, all the way to my bedroom in the *attic*, not only under my nose but through four animal bonds and *Quinn*. He was about to stab me in the chest when my jaguar even noticed he was there. She could smell him. That was the only thing to give him away. He got close enough for her to *smell him*." She curled her fist, remembering just how close it had been. Adrenaline was already working its way through her system just at the memory of it. "Hitmen? An accident is their best work. A bloody murder is their worst. An assassin? We'll kill you in your bed and no one will ever know we're there. No one will ever know who it was unless we want them to. Don't think this will be easy, like taking down some small time, fucking cheap-ass hitman."

No one said anything in return when she was done until the Director again spoke up with another order for an explanation. "How would you do it?"

"I haven't thought about it," she answered, sinking back into her chair as the question felt like it bounced in her head.

How would she do it? She would spend months researching the target, learning the patterns of the guards and their personal habits. She would know what types of cars they all drove, how they moved around the city. She would work up to the target, finding ins and outs. Then she would find blueprints of the location she chose for the hit. It was always their home. The idea of getting them where they felt safest? Axel enjoyed that. He would always provide a lot of this information as well, though he let her out to do any groundwork she needed.

"If this tied to my information going out to the public, it went too fast." She tapped a finger on the table. "I'm slow. I like research. I like perfection. I like knowing. It made me a great thief when I...uh, *died*. It made me a better assassin, when..." She stopped for a moment. She was going to talk about her old work in a room full of people she didn't know. "It made me an even better assassin when I worked for Axel. He would supply much of the information I wanted faster than I could get my hands on it. Which brings me to one of the biggest differences between assassins and hitmen. I was trained to do what I did. Grueling hours of having it beaten into me how to get it done without being caught." She took a deep breath. "As for how I would do it...not like this. It's too fast, too sudden, and too *big*. But I can consider why I was a target. I know how these things work. I know how to look at security and find its weaknesses, or at least the ones assassins would exploit."

"And that's why you're in this room," Thompson explained for her. "I'm going to put you in all of the strategy meetings. I want your input on everything. Vincent, you know why you're here."

"So much for keeping you out of the middle of things. He wants you deep in this." Was what Vincent sent to just her. She wanted to laugh. She'd known, somewhere deep in her, that she was going to get center stage for this mess.

"I had a guess, sir," was what he said to the Director.

She didn't. She had no idea why Vincent was also in the room with her. To keep an eye on her? He would have told her.

"Good. You think of anything and you tell me. James keeps telling me how damn smart you are, and now that you aren't focused on your brother, I want you to put all of that into this."

"Yes sir."

That made a lot of sense. She looked at the Director with more appreciation now. He knew the people in his organization and knew how to use them. It also made her respect the hell out of Vincent. She knew he was good at people, finding the threads and how they fit together, but they hadn't gone on a case where that mattered yet. Texas? That was easier to put together, and they had stumbled on it following the sheriff's situation around. The Amazon? Not much to put together there. It was a kill squad, not an investigation.

This? She had a feeling Vincent was going to thrive during this.

"First, we're already bringing in every member of the WMC from their holiday homes. They will be roomed here in New York together, where we can keep an eye on them. They understand they need to follow a strict schedule with security, and none are complaining about it."

"Good plan," Sawyer muttered. "Unless they all get blown the hell up."

"Excuse me?" One of the older men glared at her.

"Keeping them together, in a single spot where we can keep them contained and watched is a great idea...unless one of the Triad gets frisky and tries to blow them all to high heavens." She thought it was an obvious problem.

"They won't. We don't know who they're working for or why. They might be just taking out a few key targets and leaving some. They aren't the type for collateral damage, you know that," Vincent replied, tapping a pen on the desk. "It's not their MO."

"Or they could have been hired to take out the WMC. Completely. Leave the Magi communities around the world in complete disarray. Hell, the last time the Council was shy of a full table was when one died of a sudden heart attack over a hundred years ago." She crossed her arms. "We've never held special elections, not in living memory. Not since before we've been public to the rest of the world. You think we have problems now with two missing? Imagine the hell we'll have if we lose our entire governing body. There's already going to be anarchy out there with the IMPO dumping their resources here. Imagine if there was no one paying the IMPO, therefore the IMPO didn't exist."

"You both bring up points we've talked about extensively," Thompson cut in before Vincent could respond. "They won't all be kept together unless they are in council, discussing the future of the Magi and how to fill the two empty seats. We're thinking a few groups scattered all over the city, in hidden locations-"

"There won't be anything hidden about those locations." She shook her head in pity for the man. Did he really think they could secret WMC Councilmembers across New York? "Don't pretend to think those locations are secret. They won't be. I bet the Triad is already scoping them out, if you have people in them already. Man them like a prison. Don't get caught undermanning them because you're trying to keep some secrecy."

"You seem positive."

She glanced at the person who said that and shrugged. "I am. First thing I would do? Find out where the WMC Councilmembers are going to be sleeping. Now, I don't think there will be any danger for at least twenty-four hours. You have a chance to regroup and prepare. Use it. What's IMAS doing in all this?"

"Pure guard work. Guns at doors and windows. We're going to be in charge of the more nuanced protections, while they have kindly taken grunt work."

"Are their generals okay with that?" Vincent asked thoughtfully.

"It's Code Black protocol. They don't have a choice. And plus, if we fail, they don't look bad." He nodded to Vincent. "You can go ahead and go. I've provided a work space with several things we've been working on that might be tied in. You and the rest of the research team I've made have access to all our files to uncover whatever you can."

"I'll be working with others?"

Sawyer stayed leaned back, reclining as Vincent stood up.

"Yes. Other bright minds. Can you handle that?"

"I'm going to bring one of my own in. He's insanely intelligent."

"Approved. Sawyer, the rest of Castello's team is yours." Thompson looked down at her and she just gave a thumbs-up.

"You're giving her *authority* over the agents who are supposed to be keeping her out of trouble?" one of them snapped, glaring at their collective boss.

"I'm giving her the only resources I can to make sure she can help us to her fullest ability. I can't give her authority over anyone else or I would," the Director fired back, his gaze just as heated. "Don't test me. Dealing with Shadow is the least of the things I'm worried about when it comes to stopping the Triad from killing more of the WMC before we catch them."

"If," she corrected softly.

"We'll catch them," he growled at her.

"You'll try, but don't lose sleep at night if I end up killing any who cross my path. I'll try to capture first though, have no doubt on that. I'm just not willing to let them get away if it's between that and killing them. This might have started professional for them, but it's personal for me." It became personal the moment Naseem called her Axel's whore. Or maybe before that, when he dared to walk into her *home*. He had exposed a security issue of her home and could have killed one of her guys. It was very personal to her. She stood up, intending to follow Vincent out. "I'm going to go now. Need to get my half of the team ready to go over blueprints." And a plan started to form in her head. A dangerous one. One that required Shadow's level of perfection and attention to detail. The same attention to detail that had led her to successful hits and a solid career as a thief.

"Yes. You may both go. Sawyer, across the hall, a team is already looking over locations around New York. I would like you to as well, and approve any they think might work. Disapprove any and give me reasons why they don't."

"Yes sir." She gave him a fake salute, making him shake his head. Vincent was trying not to smile, she could see it in his eyes.

When they were nearly out, she could already hear the argument fire up about whether she should even be on the case, Code Black or not. "This is a nightmare," she whispered immediately to Vincent.

"Yes and we're both down teammates." They began walking back to the main area where they left the rest of their team.

"Zander, Elijah, and Quinn are better with protection like me. Good call getting Jasper."

"I wasn't going to leave him to the wolves," Vincent retorted. "Not just for his leg, but this isn't his type of mission. He's more useful with me."

"I know, and I appreciate that you were looking out for him." She smiled gently until Vincent nodded, looking away. She wanted to kiss him, so bad. "We're going to need to be careful."

"Just like the last time we were here. Just keep your head down."

"Going to be hard to do when I'm in the middle of the plans." She pointed to her three. "Elijah, Quinn, and Zander, you're all with me. We're going to be approving the protection detail plans and the locations."

"Jasper, you and I are investigating the who behind the

Triad and anything else we can use to catch them. We're split, but we can make this work."

"And me?" James spread his hands, looking between them. The fact that their handler was asking them for something to do made Sawyer feel somewhat uncomfortable.

"Go take a nap," Vincent answered, leaving with Jasper.

"I mean, don't you have a thing you can do?" she asked him, as he stood up.

James shrugged in return, rubbing his eyes. "Most of us handlers are just twiddling our thumbs. We don't have much going on in this. We're retired Special Agents. I'll go mess with Thompson." He threw a grin at her. "He and I used to be the Vincent and Elijah of our own team. There's a fun fact you can overthink today."

She was left gaping at him as he walked away.

Elijah chuckled softly, then tapped her shoulder. "We never told you? A shame. Yeah, it's why we think he's the best handler. Sure, he's a right pain, but he looks out for us and helped us build this team. He also has the ear of the Director, who claims that James doesn't sway his choices - but we all know better."

"That's wild." Sawyer looked over who she had left. Just over half the team. "You all ready?"

"Ready to stop assassins from killing our government?" Zander sighed, looking up to the ceiling as if he were silently praying to a god.

"No, are you ready to catch them?" She thumped his arm and started walking away. She might approve the security plans, but she wasn't going to let herself get stuck on guard duty. She was going after these motherfuckers. Naseem walked into her house to kill her. She had a bone to pick with that SOB.

And she refused to acknowledge how much she liked the idea of going toe to toe with someone who held just as much of a professional reputation as she did. Something about just the idea of it sent a thrill through her that got her nearly as high as sex.

Serial killers, fighters, Druids. None of them had the same thrill as going after one of her own kind.

17

JAMES

James walked away from his team, knowing something was wrong. They had been split up, which was never good, but not only that, they had been given positions that would put them in the thick of it.

He went directly to Thompson, hoping the meeting was finally over. When he reached the door, he could already hear the arguing. Shadow, of all people, couldn't be so involved in security. It was unacceptable. Thompson was crazy for thinking she was trustworthy.

With a deep breath beforehand, James walked in and grinned at all of them.

"She's not so bad!" he chastised lightly. "If anything, she's dedicated to whatever she's doing, and now you've focused her on this. Good idea, Thompson."

"Director. He might be your old teammate, but he's still the Director of the IMPO," one of the old farts snapped.

"I'll remind you that I was offered and given this job because he refused," Thompson muttered, glaring at the old man. Then he looked up to James. "What do you need, you fool?"

"See, I don't want *Sawyer* in the thick of this either." James crossed his arms, closing the door behind him. He made a point of saying her real name. The more people said Shadow, the more they separated her from being a real person. Sawyer Matthews was a real girl. An orphaned Magi with a heartbreaking story. Shadow was a figment of death. "They tried to kill her, Thompson. Why are you going to put her in their line of fire?"

"If she wants to be an IMPO agent, then she needs to act like one."

"I just got that team back from hell. And the Amazon was hell. I don't want to lose another team, Thompson, and I already nearly have twice this year." He ignored that the others were in the room. They all knew the story, had been working with the IMPO for just as long, if not longer, than he had. "I've lost two too many already."

Thompson narrowed his eyes. "You get attached too easily."

"I do, I'll admit that. And these kids are a pain in my and everyone else's asses. I think it's why I like them so much." James laughed, shrugging. "I'm not looking for them to get killed when they should be in a safe house, Thompson. A safe house I would prefer far away from New York."

He wanted them to be heroes, but not like this. This was too much. This had the stink of death on it, and he wasn't going to see another team of his get caught in a bad place.

Their graves.

"James-"

"I watched them get dragged into the Amazon, Thompson. I got calls about how Sawyer and Quinn couldn't be found. I remember reading the body counts from that mission." James' voice turned hard. "You will not get them killed here. I've invested too much into this team."

They glared at each other now.

"Too bad." Thompson walked out and James walked after him, refusing to drop this.

"I'm not letting you do this to them." He tried to grab his friend's arm, but Thompson yanked it away.

"They're all I have!" Thompson roared in the hallway. People stopped and looked, but neither of them cared. "I need experts. We have one. *Only one*. And I get that she's also a target, but she's also already proven that she can take care of herself. And you were always the one telling me how fucking good this team is. Their record also speaks for itself." He lowered his voice. "I know, James. I do. You were destroyed by the loss of your first team. I know these kids mean the world to you. I know they're very young compared to most Special Agents, but they are all I have. I need Sawyer's expertise, and we both know that I can't just have her. They will all come following her if I tried."

"Then I want to be shifted into an active role. With Vincent and Jasper on the intelligence team, put me on protection with Sawyer, Elijah, Quinn, and Zander."

"You want me to make you an active agent again? Are you insane? We haven't seen active duty since two thousand seven, James. A decade ago."

"Doesn't mean I don't know what I'm doing." James held out his arms. "I'm not too old for it. We have Special Agents and teams older than both of us."

He wasn't letting these kids die in this mess, and he had such a bad gut feeling that they would. He had felt similarly about the Amazon. That entire mission had made him sick to his stomach. He'd worked his hardest to get the IMAS and Councilwoman D'Angelo off their backs, and he'd failed. He'd nearly lost all of them in the process.

He wanted them to be heroes and live through it. He wanted them to ride off with the world at their feet.

He didn't want them to be recognized for the good people they were long after they were gone. He wanted them to have it while they were *alive*.

"You're mad. Crazy. James, I can't-"

"We're talking about young men and a young woman who have survived the worst this world has to offer. Orphans, backwoods prejudice, terrifying family legacies, lost families and loves. They are so young, Thompson. If you're going to make them active in this as much as you seem to want, then I want to be in it with them. To keep them safe."

The Director sighed, looking over him. "At least you stayed in shape." He chuckled weakly. "You always had a big heart."

"It's a handler's job to do whatever is necessary for the team they are assigned. From their mental health to their professional careers. We had a shit handler - a couple. I won't be that for them. You know, since this team formed, my entire goal has been them. I don't give a shit about the politics, or my job past them. You should have known this was coming."

"Yeah...Makes me wish you and I had a handler like you." Thompson ran a hand through his hair. "Go. Approved. Godspeed, James. And tell those kids they're lucky to have a man like you looking out for them."

"Godspeed, Thompson." He'd never had much of a family, much like Sawyer and Zander in that regard. While he could never be truly in their lives, he looked at the team as his family, from a distance. Kids he had to watch grow up, try new things, get in trouble. Messes, and pains in his ass. He was like a detached parent or older brother.

And he'd put them where they were. He'd let Vincent make this team. He'd helped them get the members they wanted in Zander and Jasper. He'd been the one to convince Thompson that Quinn was an asset, not a danger to the organization. And he'd let them keep the stray that was Sawyer.

This was his team, from a distance.

He walked into the room across the hall, just in time to see the assassin herself lose her patience.

"You can't put that few guards in this location. I keep fucking telling you that you need a guard nearly at every fucking corner and you keep fucking ignoring me, you stupid shit. If you want the Councilmembers here to die quickly, you might have missed the reason we're in Code Black."

The room was silent as an older agent stood up and looked to the door. He glared at James as if this was somehow his fault. He just walked in.

"I won't take orders from a criminal," he said, growling the last word like it was a curse.

"Too fucking bad," she snapped, crossing her arms. "I'm the only person who can look at the blueprints and see all the options. This place is fine to hold like seven of them, over half of the WMC, but you need to put the right amount of guards on it. Seriously, not one on every corner, two. One will just get killed or incapacitated. Two at least have a chance to get word out if something happens."

"It's a waste of manpower," the older agent said. "You think too highly of your kind."

"I think highly of them because none of you have

stopped them. Reminder, I'm the only assassin the IMPO has caught in a very long time, and it was a fucking accident, on just about everyone's part, including the team who caught me." She pointed at the blueprints on the table again. "They will walk in and they will destroy you. They will get in, kill who they please and walk out if you don't listen to me."

"Why is this even a problem?" Elijah cut in. "Why can't you just swallow your pride and follow the advice? We have an expert on assassins. She literally survived a run-in with Naseem last night. What is your issue?"

"She shouldn't even be here," another agent yelled out. "She's a murderer."

"So am I, but we all ignore that," a Russian accent said into the argument. "She's come to our side."

"You did all of that for your brother."

"I'm sure she had her reasons as well. If some guy in the Bronx, a doctor and healer, is willing to speak for her, then I see no reason why we shouldn't."

James watched her face while the bickering continued. He'd seen it once or twice, just glimpses of it. He'd been told by all the guys on the team that her dark eyes could get so cold, so endless. Dark depths of horror and pain, endless abysses of the night. They weren't black, her eyes, but when the light wasn't hitting them just right, they were like cold obsidians, giving away just as little emotion as the stone itself.

He saw it now. As she also listened to the bickering, her eyes were hard. There was an emotionless quality to her entire face that honestly frightened him a little. She could lock it all away, and well. The only reason he knew what she was feeling was his empathy. Her pain. Her regret. Her shame. Her heartbreak. And underneath it was pride. For herself or the guys standing up for her, he couldn't tell, but it was there.

"Do the changes," James said. He was the ranking member in the room. None of them stopped bickering. "Do the changes!" he snapped louder, his eyes still on her. He didn't like how cold she was. He didn't like that the temperature of the room had been dropping either. That, he had felt before, in the meeting with D'Angelo and the General. He hadn't liked it then either.

"Yes sir," the old agent growled. "We'll put two to four IMAS soldiers at every point. What about this one?" He pointed to a single hallway.

"There too," she whispered. "Now with that location taken care of, let's move on to the second one. Will there be a third?"

"We think two locations are best. Three might stretch us too far."

"Okay. Two we can make work." Her arms stayed crossed. James narrowed his eyes on a hand that found itself on her back. Quinn was rubbing her back slowly, the sight blocked by Zander and Elijah from most of the room.

Quinn, of all people, was touching someone else.

"James, what are you doing here?" Zander asked him and he blinked, refocusing on why he was actually in the room.

"I've been moved to active service during the Code Black! I'm officially a Special Agent without a team, though I'm hoping mine will have me."

"Oh my fucking god," Elijah muttered. "James, are you serious?"

"I am. I'll remind you that I once did your job. It'll be

fine. I wanted to give a helping hand, and the IMPO needs the manpower and the experience." And he needed to keep them alive.

"Well, we're glad to have you," she whispered, still looking at the blueprints. She sent him a small smile, one that didn't reach her eyes. Eyes that had dark circles underneath them. He reminded himself to find out where his team could get some sleep. They had been up much earlier than everyone else, since they had been attacked.

The meeting continued without much more issue. He figured it was because of his rank. It was obvious he was there to keep his team in charge and alive. If they were too busy planning, maybe they wouldn't try to go out into the field. He gave them more weight. If one person tried to scoff at a change she wanted, he would order it to be done anyway. And there was no arguing with James, the old friend and teammate of Director Thompson. No one was that stupid, not in the IMPO. The WMC and the IMAS, certainly, but not in their home organization.

As people began sending out the orders and plans, others started to wander out, looking for places to sleep.

"You can all come to my condo," James offered as they were left alone. "I know you all need sleep. I have a few couches and a spare bedroom."

"Seriously?" Zander perked up immediately. He felt for the reckless redhead. He wasn't much of a planner, and the day must have been wearing on him.

"Yes. Let's find Vincent and Jasper, then you can all come with me. I'm only two blocks from the headquarters, and I'm actually in a good halfway point between here and one of the safe houses. It should work out."

"And the animals?" Quinn asked, pointing to the zoo

following the team. A jaguar and two wolves. He knew Vincent probably was already letting Kaar figure himself out but the collared big predators needed a place to stay and bunker down.

"My building has a rooftop garden for Magi animal bonds."

"Then it's acceptable." Quinn's ice blue eyes were tired, more tired than James had known the feral Magi was capable of.

"I just sent Vin a message that you offered us your place. He says he and Jasper will be right out." Zander sat back down, kicking his feet up. "Today sucked."

"It's only going to get worse," she whispered, not looking at any of them, her eyes glued to the blueprints in front of her.

James felt a chill run down his spine. Something about her, in this sort of situation, made him wonder how the entire team was into her. She was downright terrifying. In that moment, the only emotion he got from her was a cold pleasure. While her face gave none of it away, nor did her posture, something pleased her.

Something wasn't just pleased, it was excited. He hadn't gotten that from her before the Amazon mission.

What was she so happy about?

"Let's get out there and meet the guys," he said quietly, breaking his gaze off her. That feeling from her was going to stick with him for a long time, that much was certain. It worried and concerned him. Why was she happy? Excited?

It made no sense.

He walked out of the room, the rest of them following in silence. She was last, her mood not shifting, but none of the rest of the team seemed concerned in any way over it. Quinn was annoyed and uncomfortable from being in the city, a general feeling that always happened when he saw the feral Magi in a crowded place. Elijah was worried, probably over the mission. Zander was feeling down, weighted, something James was picking up from many of the agents in the building when he reached out to check the general mood.

"Hey!" Jasper called. "Thanks, James, for the place to stay. I hear the hotel is taking in a lot of us, but I was hoping we wouldn't get shuffled in with the rest."

"No, I wasn't going to let that happen. The hotel might be more comfortable than my condo, but it would also expose you all to the madhouse. I think my condo is better for Sawyer as well. The hotel isn't secure enough, in my opinion."

"Thanks for looking out for me," she said quietly from behind him. "Means a lot."

"Of course." He grinned back at her, but wasn't feeling it. He remembered a time when his grins were genuinely happy and his jokes were more than just a cover. With her, they always had to be. Even the time he met her and didn't know who she was, he'd been uncomfortable with the emotions flowing through her.

He was too old to be so happy, but he knew it was reassuring to such a dark group of people like Vincent's team. Even though ones like Jasper and Zander seemed normal, he knew better. Like calls to like. Vincent had found men for his team who had at least a little darkness that echoed his own, even if he did it unconsciously.

"Let's go. Elijah, Vincent, you both know where I live. You can drive there with a couple of rentals I've secured. I got them while you were getting ready for pick up." He worked too damn much. "You can take the animals in the SUV. Sawyer, I want you to ride with me."

The idea made him uncomfortable, but there were still things he needed to talk to her about. Things he was being asked to keep secret for them. And he wanted to make sure the newest addition to his team wasn't going to be the thing that ruined it.

"Sure?" She frowned at him and her confusion washed over him. He pushed it away, locking out his empathy. He was tired of being bombarded by the emotions of others for the day. It was a neat trick he'd learned as an agent, the ability to separate from his empathy, which always wanted to be on. He'd basically learned to ignore it.

They walked down quietly to the parking garage. Vincent told them that he and Jasper would give them a brief back at the condo. Good. He wanted to know exactly what they were up to. He'd never seen his team truly in action, so his curiosity was also very much invested in this entire situation.

He tried to keep it like that. A situation. He couldn't get caught up in thinking about it. His government had been attacked. His team had been attacked, but as an agent, he had to remain focused. This was just another case.

He hoped they were all remembering that lesson as well. He'd made sure, during their training, to teach it to them. A case is a case. An agent had to be able to step back and look at something objectively, with no emotions clouding their decisions.

He got Sawyer's door for her and closed her in.

"Are you going to interrogate her about...what's going on between us?"

He looked over his car at Vincent, staring at him from the SUV. He nodded once before getting into his car.

"Be kind to her, James. Don't give her a reason not to trust you."

"Vincent is telling me to make sure I don't make you distrust me," James said, turning his car on. He looked back to make sure no one was in his way then pulled out. "Personally, I think it's the other way around right now, Sawyer."

"I was told you know, so let's cut to the chase. Am I sleeping with them? Yes. Am I using them? No." She sounded so sure of it.

He didn't say anything else until they were on the road. "We don't have much time for this, so I'm also going to get this said quickly. Do not lie to me. I don't want...details, but I need to know..."

"I love them," she whispered, looking forward still.

And he stopped ignoring his empathy and was hit with the full force of those words. He saw tears come to her eyes and knew they were honest.

"They are everything to me. My family, my friends, my lovers. There's...problems, sure. Elijah and I have things we need to work out, but I'm beginning to see where I want him, where he fits." She tapped her chest. "He once told me I give away pieces of my heart like Halloween candy. He's not wrong. I do. I just never expect to get a piece back from someone."

"And they gave you pieces back."

"They did." She looked at him and smiled. "I've been so lonely, James, that now I'm greedy. And I won't apologize to you for that. I loved Zander and Jasper my entire life, and I'm finally experiencing that. And gods, don't I know what the reaction would be if the world found out I was sleeping with Vincent Castello? But he and I understand each other so well. And I fought that one. I fought him. He's fucking Axel's brother." She took a deep breath and he just felt the love and pain fill her chest. The hurt of being so in love that it couldn't stay contained. And some sadness he couldn't place.

"What about Quinn and Elijah? How did you really end up with five people? And are you sure it's love? Can you even...do that?" He was curious, but now he didn't think it was a ploy. He just thought it was outside the realm of his experience.

"I don't know when I fell for Quinn," she admitted to him like it was a secret. "One day I was scared of him and the next I was seeing this totally different side of him. He couldn't read and that...I could relate to that. I took care of kids, you know? I...taught Henry how to read." She choked over those words. "And then when they were saying he was going to go on a fucking suicide mission...I couldn't let that happen. And if that meant risking all our lives, then that was how it was going to be."

"I know he has his GED now. Thank you for helping him."

"He's very intelligent - he just needed a different approach than the guys were trying. Plus, they let him push them around, and I don't blame them for that. I didn't let him push me around and that made a difference."

"And you have things to work out with Elijah."

"I love that dumb cowboy, I do, but I don't know if it's... on the same level as my love for the others. He's a great man and a good friend." She smiled, looking out of the car. He tried to ignore the sickening, to him, sexual pleasure from her. He didn't need that. Something about whatever she was thinking of made her feel very happy.

He felt like an old pervert. He couldn't look at this girl like that. Sure, she was in her mid-twenties, but he was way too old for that, no matter what. He shut his empathy back down.

"But he loves me and I know it. He's been an ass because he was avoiding his feelings, thanks to his past. But we're working on it. I can say I don't see a life without him and right now, that's what we're going with."

"Shit, I missed my turn," he muttered. "To my own damn house. I make this drive every day."

"Didn't do it on purpose?" she asked, giving him a look.

"No, actually I didn't. I have empathy. I know you aren't lying to me based on the strength of your emotions. I just needed you alone to make sure I wasn't being clouded."

"Ah..."

"I already knew Zander was in love with you. I knew the others held strong feelings, but only whispers. I didn't know how you felt, and I didn't know you were...*with* all of them. Don't ask me to begin to understand that. As a man, I can't comprehend it, but I'll let it go." He turned down a side street, cranky over the traffic he was having to deal with for even longer. His short drive was already bad enough thanks to New York. "Look, I don't...care. I just had to make sure we weren't all being played by you. I'm not around you guys as much as I would like to be, to watch this all and see how it works, just you being on the team, so I have to be nosy when I get the chance."

"I get it." She shrugged. He could feel some small amount of hurt from her, knowing that he couldn't one hundred percent trust her, and he hoped to make that up as time went on.

"I look at them as sons, as younger brothers. I used to be in their shoes. They are my priority, and in turn you are, as a member of the team. I'm sorry."

"I get it, James."

"How are you, otherwise?" he asked softly, deciding to use this extra time to dig about something else.

"I'm fine. This is a big thing but I'm not-"

"Not this. How are you about December? Henry?" Vincent had let him know, and now he was going to do his job for her. He needed to know she was okay.

Silence greeted him for nearly a block. When he was turning onto his street, she finally opened her mouth. "I'm distracted from it, and that's all I can ask for. It's always there, in the back of my mind, asking me to think about him, asking me to remember how I screwed up, how I failed him. The best I can be is distracted enough to not give in to seeing how he connects to everything. And I mean everything. Everything leads back to a little boy who looked like his father and uncle." Her voice got shaky at the end. "I miss him, but there's no bringing him back, so I just need to be strong and stay distracted. In January, I can let myself think of him, but not this month."

"Okay. You tell me if you need a day, though. You tell me if there's anything I can do." He meant it. Every word.

"Jasper is getting me scheduled with a therapist, to finally get to the root of it and find some peace. Maybe in time, I'll be normal, living a semi-normal life."

"Good. I'm glad these guys are looking out for you too. And...I'm glad you look out for them. I know you do. You all work well together."

He meant actual work, but the more he considered it, the more he realized he meant their relationship as well. Broken souls, hurt people, all coming together to find something that works for them. He honestly couldn't find a way to begrudge them that.

He pulled into his parking garage and parked. He saw

Elijah and Vincent had both beaten him here with the rest of them, waiting at the elevator across the concrete.

"I hate parking garages," she muttered.

"Why?" he asked.

"They tend to go boom."

He couldn't disagree with that, and they were living in dangerous times.

18

SAWYER

T he night at James' house had been blissfully peaceful in a world that felt like it was falling apart. They had made a large meal in his kitchen, talked to their handler about their relationship, explained some of the nuances so he understood better, then watched a movie before everyone passed out.

James had made one thing clear before they all passed out, though. No 'hanky panky' in his condo. Sawyer was given the bedroom alone.

The next morning, she was getting ready when Vincent walked in. "I avoided giving a briefing last night because I thought we all needed a break, but I'm going to tell you now that right now it looks like the IMPO is run by a bunch of idiots."

"Oh, yeah. I could have told you that," she replied, pulling on her shirt. She'd already showered and just needed to get dressed, and he wasn't telling her anything she didn't already know.

"Funny. The team they put together to investigate who hired the Triad is useless. They are looking externally and none will even begin to acknowledge there might be an internal threat. When I brought up the exposing of our home's location, they all glared at me, like it would change anything. They think someone leaked it to a criminal, or maybe just was careless enough to let it get out. They aren't taking it seriously."

"What's on the agenda for today?" she asked. "Other than you dealing with idiots. That just means you and Jasper need to work on your own, and work well. We're counting on you."

"The WMC members that are alive are arriving at their safe houses. You should know that."

"I probably already did, but I want you to tell me, fearless leader." She was trying so hard to keep the mood light, hoping it would make this all easier. But in the back of her mind, she was so excited for this to get painful and rough. She was perversely ready for the Triad to try again, and she was keeping her plans close to her chest.

He stepped closer to her, rubbing his hand over her hip and pushing her shirt back up to expose skin he could touch. "You hate when people tell you what to do."

"Maybe we're both gluttons for punishment," she whispered. She'd once called him one. She kissed him slowly. James hadn't said no to that, and she'd made a point to use that loophole. She kissed all of them the night before, even Elijah, who seemed surprised. She had to use her time wisely, so when she could steal a moment to remind them that she owned them, she did.

She was pulled in so many directions, but only five really mattered to her. Six if she included the current situation looming over New York and their people.

"No hanky panky. We promised," he murmured against her lips.

"Then stop standing in there kissing and get out for breakfast," James snapped as he walked by the guest bedroom.

"Wow, he really is like a dad," she muttered, glaring at the door.

Vincent chuckled. "The less he sees, the easier it is for him to lie."

"I would rather him just go back to not knowing."

"Too late for that."

She huffed in some small frustration and went out into the living room. She leaned down to scratch Sombra.

"I know you won't like it, but you have to stay here, girl. I don't want you getting hurt in all of this."

She adamantly disagreed. It hit Sawyer like a punch to the gut.

"Please. I can't have you getting hurt, and there's going to be so many people. If things happen, bullets will fly and you can get shot on accident. I'm sorry."

"I'm doing the same to the wolves," Quinn called out from the living room. "She'll have company."

Sombra just didn't want Sawyer out there alone. She also hated the metal building she kept being stuck in. She hadn't liked them the first time she had to go through New York either.

"I'm sorry," she whispered again. She just couldn't have Sombra in danger, not during this. "I've already lost you once."

Images of a little black cat went through her mind. An understanding bloomed in the jaguar. She still wasn't happy, but she understood that Sawyer's fear would not be appeased, no matter how strong the new form was.

It amazed Sawyer that her jaguar knew she was once Midnight, but had no memory of it. The abuse, the pain that

Axel tortured her with. Small blessings, in her mind, that her jaguar didn't know what her previous form had been through all because of her.

"Thank you." She straightened up and looked over the team. "I heard James snapping about breakfast?"

"I could go for something to eat," Elijah teased, his eyes heated for a moment. The hazel eyes moved down her body and looked directly at the spot she knew he wanted his 'breakfast' from. She could have gone for that, grinning at him.

"No." James growled it out, pointing a spoon at the cowboy. "None of those types of jokes either."

"Roger that," Elijah said, chuckling. He wiggled his eyebrows at her and she rolled her eyes. Zander and Jasper were chuckling as well as they found seats at James' dining table.

"Today, we're splitting up again. Sawyer, you'll be going to look over the safe houses, right?"

"Yup. With all of you." She pointed to the four coming with her, including James. "You can throw your rank around for me. Thanks for that."

"Of course." James shrugged, dropping a massive plate of eggs down in the middle of the table. Zander sat on one side of her and Elijah on the other. He glared between the two of them. "You two need to find other seats. I trust Quinn, Vincent, and Jasper more than you."

"Damn," Zander mumbled, his hand leaving her thigh as he stood up.

She knew they were all just messing with James, and it was childish good fun in the middle of a mess. Elijah didn't move though, leaning back and putting his arm around the back of her chair.

"Make me," he taunted.

James narrowed his eyes, but just shook his head after a moment and walked away.

"Y'all be nice," she told them. "He's trying."

"He's weirded out and it's hilarious."

"We have more important things to deal with than messing with James," Vincent countered, walking in finally. He looked so put together.

Except he hadn't shaved. He leaned down and gave her a swift kiss, letting his stubble run over her cheek. From his smile, she knew he didn't shave since she liked it, and that he was also looking to mess around.

Jasper took the place next to her, and he reached out to take her hand. "I'm going to miss you today. Be safe?"

"As safe as I ever am," she promised. He pulled her hand up and kissed it, keeping a hold on it until all the food was on the table, Quinn helping James.

They ate breakfast like a family, like they did every morning, just this time under the watchful eye of a man who was trying to be their father in a weird way. He made sure they ate enough, pushing the plates at them. She held back a grin when he narrowed his eyes at Vincent, who was just nibbling on toast with his coffee. Finally, Vincent sighed, loading his plate with eggs, bacon, and hash browns.

The mood went as they loaded up to leave. Vincent released Kaar into the city for the day, his little ankle tag back. Sawyer gave Sombra a blanket to sleep with and she hunkered down with the wolves on either side of her.

They loaded up, this time with her group cramming into the SUV. James took his own car, while Vincent and Jasper took the smaller rental.

"I'll drive," she told Elijah only once. "I know New York better than you."

"Fine," he sighed, handing her the keys.

The drive to the first safe house wasn't a long one. Really, they didn't pick safe houses that far from the WMC building, since the Councilmembers still needed to get to work. That situation was being handled by IMAS, who knew how to securely transport people around better than the IMPO.

"I'm thinking, once I clear that these places will work with the amount of guards chosen, I'm going to start putting myself on night watch here," she told them. "Are you all okay with that?"

"So we would sleep at James' during the day, then get here for the nights. You want to be in the middle of this." Elijah crossed his arms in the passenger seat. "Vincent won't like it."

"I do, because I have a bone to pick with the Triad now," she admitted. "But it's not just that. The night watches always tend to get lax at places. They think it's dark and no one is watching. They can slack off. I want to be there to make sure."

"We'll be there with you," Zander cut in. "I personally like it. It means we can make doubly sure all this shit actually works and if anyone is going to catch the Triad in the act, it's us."

"It's Sawyer," Quinn corrected. "But yes, we should make sure."

"What if they hit during the day?" Elijah asked the obvious question.

"They would do one of the transports to or from the WMC building at the beginning or end of the day. There's nothing I can do to stop that. And they won't just hit the main WMC building. It's always been too heavily guarded." She was certain of that. If the Triad hit a transport, she was effectively useless. She didn't do moving vehicles. That was just too dangerous. She could only account for the safe houses, and she had a trick up her sleeve to make sure it all went according to her plan.

But she couldn't tell the guys that yet, not until later in the day. They would kill her - and somewhat justifiably.

Not that it was a bad plan, either. They wouldn't like it because it was putting her not just in the middle of things, but in the direct path of the Triad. She knew they were going to come back for her eventually. She was just speeding up the process.

When they arrived at the first safe house, she jumped out without saying anything else, knowing she couldn't give too much away.

It was just a hotel, but not like the one where the IMPO were staying. It catered to Magi, but it didn't have the magic-enchanted walls, since those would interfere with the ability of the agents and guards on duty. It was securable, but not in the same way like the big fancy-ass place was.

She walked the halls, looking over the rooms. They were good enough to please the rich shits of the WMC. She would have been fine with a cheap-ass motel as long as she didn't get killed in it, but she was fine playing around the tastes of the WMC Council as long as she got what she wanted in the end.

She ignored murmured comments from others as she walked past without a word. They took over the entire second floor. Some were close and easy to run out of in case of emergency. It had its drawbacks, though, being close to the ground level, but that's why she had so many people in the building. If they were all doing their jobs, nothing would get missed.

"Sawyer?" A soft Russian accent.

"Varya?" Sawyer spun and grinned at the blonde. "How have you been?"

"Good, and you?" she asked back, walking closer. People looked at them like they were crazy - mostly Varya, though. Who was this soldier who smiled at the infamous Shadow?

"Busy, but you can see why."

"Yes, and I saw the news. My new unit was very interested in hearing about my time with you. I told them the truth. You are a dedicated soldier who can throw a good right hook." The grin Varya had matched Sawyer's. "My unit was brought here last night to assist in the protection of the WMC. We were assigned to this building and will be sleeping on the fourth floor. I still have your dagger, by the way. I didn't know how to send it back to you."

Sure enough, Varya pulled the dagger at her belt and it wasn't standard issue. Black and sharp, well cared for. One of Sawyer's blades.

"It's good someone thought to buy out the entire hotel. That keeps civilians out of the way." Sawyer nodded wisely, considering that. Then she considered the last part of what Varya had said and the dagger in front of her. She just ignored it as Varya kept talking.

"Oh, you must have missed it. Every Magi who isn't a part of the Code Black has run from the city. They don't want to be in the middle of this. That includes civilians."

Sawyer had a feeling Varya was right, except in one case. Charlie was probably still sitting in his gym, his arms crossed. He would be glaring at nothing as he listened to the radio over the gym's speakers. He would be paying attention, but he wouldn't leave his home or those that relied on it.

"Of course they did," she replied. "I have to finish my review of security here. I hope to see you around..." With a deep breath, she pushed the dagger towards

Varya. "Keep it. Tell your grandkids about it one day, if you have any. Scare the assholes you work with. If it keeps you alive, it's doing better work than it ever did for me."

"Thank you. You stay safe as well." Varya waved as she backed away and turned towards her unit.

Something about the interaction brought a bit of happiness to Sawyer. She was glad that Varya was also recovered from the Amazon trip and healthy, back on track with the IMAS. And now, separated from the awful place, she liked the blonde a bit more.

"How are the soliders' floors?" she asked Zander when she saw him in the lobby.

"They'll live. They'll be doubling up, but it's all we can do about the space."

"The lobby is too open," Elijah said quietly, looking between them. "You need more guards down here."

"No, I don't. They won't come through the lobby, and the staff of the building is still here. They'll be wandering through. I wish I could get them all out of here, too, since they expose possible ins for the Triad, but the WMC requires amenities I can't convince anyone to take away from them."

"Spoiled children," Quinn growled. "On to the second place?"

"Let's go." She waved them to follow until Elijah asked the obvious again.

"Where's James?"

She narrowed her eyes on their handler, who she could see talking to one of the soldiers, an attractive man around the same age. And there was something about his body language that made Sawyer pause.

Was he flirting?

"My god. Is James gay?" she asked, her eyebrows going up as it hit her.

"Took you long enough," Zander muttered.

"No fucking way." She crossed her arms and watched the soldier write something down and hand it to James, who gave an award-winning, shit-eating grin.

"No," Elijah clarified, rolling his eyes at Zander. "He's not gay. He's good at playing people, though. He knows body language and how to play off other people's emotions thanks to his empathy. That guy probably thought he was attractive and he's using it."

"So our handler is...manipulative."

"I mean, have you met Vincent? We live in a world of manipulative people, little lady."

He had a point. She didn't say anything to argue with it.

"Plus, James isn't out to get anyone. He's a good politician, in a weird way. He just likes having contacts in the different organizations. It helps him help us."

James saw them watching and *winked*. She held back a sigh of disappointment. He was supposed to be the old, mature one, but he always did weird shit where he could have been a stupid-ass teenager. Then he would turn concerned old man on them.

It took nearly twenty minutes for James to get to them.

"He's the officer in charge of the soldiers. You'll want his name, rank, and number," he whispered as he walked past her. "You're welcome."

"Thanks." She hadn't planned on messing too much with the soldiers, thinking they would be best served if they just did their jobs.

"After the Amazon? I'm not letting any of us just ignore them. We'll need to make sure they are doing their jobs, and therefore, you need the names of their superiors in case anything happens." James waved the phone number at her.

"And you had to hit on him to do that?" she asked.

"You thought I was..." James brought his eyebrows together. "I'm happily divorced and I'm not interested in people for that anymore."

"But you-"

"I wasn't flirting. I knew him already. He was IMPO before he went to IMAS, looking for something different." James sighed, shaking his head.

She filed that all away. New things about James. Interesting things. She decided not to press for more though, even though her curiosity was getting the best of her. "We're going to head to the second location. Also, I saw Varya," she said, pointing the second part out to the guys and not James.

"Really? How is she?" Quinn asked her that, smiling. "Good female. Strong bear."

"She's good. Her unit is assigned to this building. I'm glad for it. I hope Anya is ready to fuck some assassins up that...aren't me."

She would never forget the fear that had hit the moment that bear broke the shield around her in the Amazon. Then the fist that slammed into her face a second later.

Quinn chuckled at her the entire way back to the vehicles. She glared at him. She knew why he was chuckling. The time in that hole in the dirt with her in the Amazon. He'd heard all of it. He hadn't witnessed the fight, but she was certain someone told him about it later.

Varya also threw a mean right hook.

"I read reports of the time out there. Varya and you had a fight?" James looked at her with interest as they walked out to their rides. "I mean, I know you did, but other than reports, none of you ever tell me anything *important*."

Sawyer eyed the rest of the team with her. "It was nothing. In the end, I think I made a somewhat friend that I'll never really like." She didn't really have much else to say. Varya Petrov was a Russian-born IMAS soldier who had been rescued from the labs that were infamous in that country. She was a hard-ass, by the book type of woman that had nearly zero personality and a very large stick up her ass.

But damn, she threw a mean right hook.

And down in that hole, Sawyer found somewhat of a connection. They were just two sides of the same coin. Two women who outstripped the men around them. Two women who lived a hard life and had to be tough as nails to get through it.

"Well, let's get to the second location. We've only got a couple more hours until the WMC start being brought in by IMAS." James waved them all to load up, but Sawyer was way ahead of him, already halfway in the SUV, getting behind the wheel.

She waited patiently and the moment seat belts were on, she got them moving, her mind on the second location.

The location of her plan.

It wasn't that she was keeping the guys in the dark to do something stupid. Instead, she wanted the groundwork in place before telling them her idea. If they hated it, she could easily wipe the plan away without a trace before the end of the day. She just needed to see the safe house to make sure it was as viable in person as it had looked on the blueprints.

When they arrived, they made quick work of running through guard positions and logistics. She didn't care much for how the soldiers got it done, only that they got it done the way she wanted. The only way any of this worked was if they listened to her and followed orders. Nothing she'd suggested was impossible by any stretch, and if they were smart, they would see she only had the WMC's best interests at heart.

Seriously. She did.

She had to remind herself of that, but she really did. She didn't like a world where only the criminal existed, and while the WMC wasn't the most forthcoming or nice government, they were needed to maintain the balance of the Magi community. Without them, their world would be mayhem.

And she thought of Dina. That woman pissed her off, but in the end, wasn't she just trying to do what was best for the Magi at large? Sure, Sawyer could be pissed at how Dina did it, trying to get her behind bars, but in the end, that was actually the least corrupt move the WMC could have pulled.

Sawyer was a murderer. Murdering for the right people didn't make it any better, only different. Killing others to protect loved ones was still killing, but Sawyer felt much less guilty over it now than she once had.

She was changing, she realized. Sawyer looked down at her hands as she stopped in one of the bedrooms. When had this happened? There was a time she had been wracked with guilt over killing, no matter what it was. It had been the right way to feel.

But somewhere in the jungle, something shifted, and this was the first time she'd realized it. Truly realized it. Something had changed. Some of the guilt felt unnecessary. Elijah had been right every time they ever talked about it. She had always killed for others, not to serve them, but protect them, to be with them, to love them another day.

The road to hell was paved in good intentions, and she consciously decided she was fine with hell. She would kill to protect those she loved, those she respected, and those who needed her that she didn't see. Maybe someone like Dina was a great mom. She obviously just wanted to make their people better than the criminals that they combatted. Maybe saving Dina would change someone else's life.

And with that strange realization, Sawyer looked back up and turned to see James watching her. "What are you planning?" he asked softly.

"I'll tell you and the guys in a moment," she promised, smiling. "James? Is it possible for an assassin to be good and still be an assassin?"

"I think if there's anyone who can answer that question, it would be you. Why do you ask?" He frowned at her, stepping in and closing the door.

"Because I remembered...I've remembered that I enjoy this work. The details, the perfection. I'm on the other side of it, but it's the same. I stayed a thief because that was a job I had...enjoyed, and it involved less death. It's the thrill of the hunt in this urban world." She chuckled. "It's the idea that I make a plan, and they make a plan, and those two forces clash and one remains victorious. Whether it's me stealing and them trying to stop me, or me trying to stop them from doing something. I missed this. And here I am, thinking about how I fully intend to kill Naseem if I run across him, and I don't feel bad for it. I didn't feel bad about Camila." She shrugged. "I was wondering if something was wrong with me or if maybe...Maybe I can use the more dangerous set of my skills for good. The idea that if I kill Naseem, someone like Dina remains alive and she's better for this world than he is."

"Sounds like you might be playing god, and we both know where that leads people."

Megalomaniacs like Axel Castello.

"No, not like that, but...maybe."

"I'll say that soldiers kill every day, and to them, it's their duty, orders, and they are just extensions of the finger pointing them in a direction. You've been the soldier before, and it didn't work for you. I've had more than one case in my time with the IMPO where ending a criminal's life saved others, in direct harm and maybe in the future. Those are decisions made in a split second. I don't carry them around. I think I ended an evil that walked on this earth. And if you do it right, then yes, maybe an assassin can be...good." He smiled gently at her. "Now tell me right now what you're planning so I can shut it down before you get *yourself* killed."

"I'm not stupid enough to get myself killed," she retorted. "Really. This isn't about doing anything stupid, but rather, making a neat little trap."

"You're invested in this more than I want you to be, and I think more than Vincent wants you to be. And probably more than the Director intended." James crossed his arms and leaned on a dresser. "Let's hear it."

"They made this personal - maybe not for them, but for me. They walked into my home and tried to kill me, but that's not why this is personal. They exposed a danger to the guys brought directly from my past. They should have known better than to take a contract on me." She met his eyes and said it all without hesitation. "I'm not in the business anymore. Any attack on me is considered personal. Any threat to the guys is personal. I'm going to capture or kill them for it. I am."

"What's the plan?" he asked softly.

"I left an opening in security with the intent to make sure it's their only opening. If they want to get paid, they have to take it or deal with soldiers at every turn - and they don't play like that. Like me, they like the easiest, open route." She waved a hand around, trying to dismiss the look on James' face. "I can easily cover the hole if no one agrees with me, but it's a solid plan, if I have backup. I had no intention of sitting here alone to catch one or more of them. Like I said, not in this to get myself killed."

"If you can get the guys with you to agree, then I'm okay with this. If not, you plug that fucking hole and never try something like this again." His voice was hard and left no room for argument.

But something in his eyes was impressed.

"It's not a hard plan, but most of the IMPO wouldn't go for it, so I've kept it...quiet."

"It does put the WMC at risk. You're using them as bait without telling them."

"I know." She nodded at that, unable to deny it. "And the hole I left in the security, the gap, is one they didn't even recognize. In the end, they would have left it and more open. So, it's not like I haven't helped. I just plan on filling the gap unofficially myself."

"Vincent is going to kill you." He sounded like he was going to laugh now.

"Vincent has his own things to worry about." She had no doubt that he would be okay with her plan, especially with what he was working on quietly behind James' back. He couldn't even say it out loud, for fear that someone would take him down for it. No one could incriminate a member of the WMC; that was madness.

She hoped it didn't spell their downfall, but the two groups had different objectives. She had to trust Vincent with his investigation and he needed to trust her with this.

With the conversation over, James let them out of the room as the first WMC member showed up with little fanfare. Hushed conversation passed her as the Councilwoman was taken to her assigned bedroom, surrounded by guards. She didn't even glance Sawyer's way.

But Sawyer would always recognize Dina D'Angelo. She would need to ask Vincent his thoughts about her later. Maybe she would be in the running for who was behind this. She despised Sawyer working for them, even if they had somewhat of a truce at the end of the Amazon mission, something Dina could twist in her favor.

Then her eyes fell to two young boys following her.

"Lucius. Adrian. Please, boys, we must get you safe." Dina turned and waved them closer, smiling. She looked tired, worried, but the smile was there. "I know this isn't what you wanted for the holidays, but it's what we have to do."

"It's okay, Aunty. We were just looking at shadows," one whispered, turning to Dina and giving her a bright smile.

"Oh, were you?" she asked kindly, leaning down. One of them pointed at Sawyer, who tried to turn away before she got into more trouble than she needed.

"Sawyer. Her name is Sawyer." Dina sounded softly chastising. "And she's here to protect us, and herself. Don't move."

Sawyer had a feeling that last part was directed at her. She didn't move, looking back to them. Sure enough, Dina was still looking at the boys, but a finger was pointed at her. Dina straightened, brushing her front off. Lucian and Adrian looked back at her as well, their eyes wide with interest. They had interesting eyes. Their curly hair was much like Henry's, which nearly gave her a gut punch since they were the same age Henry should have been. But their eyes were gorgeous. Central heterochromia was rare, and they had smoke and fire eyes. A ring of orange around the pupil and then dark gray on the outer ring.

Sawyer felt nearly captivated by those eyes.

"You shouldn't wear your mask. It could break, and you'll need it again for something else."

She felt the blood run from her head as she stopped looking into a set of those eyes and up at Dina, who carefully put a finger over her lips then continued like nothing happened. "How are you? I heard you were also attacked. You might not believe it, but I was worried until word came that you came out unharmed."

"I'm fine. Decided that I would rather help in the protection than get put in a corner. I need to get back to work. You all have a nice day, and stay safe."

And Sawyer was going to try and forget the thought that whispered through her head the moment she looked away from the kids, who were still staring at her strangely.

Dina had her own secrets, it seemed. Ones not even Sawyer would risk exposing. One of those children obviously had an ability that wasn't even publicly registered. The ability to see the future was like necromancy. Sure, it was possible, but no Magi wanted to confirm with the rest of the world that it was.

"You as well, Miss Matthews. Come, boys."

Sawyer watched them walk away, her chest too tight. She had to put away the strange occurrence, though, because now she and James, who had watched the entire encounter carefully, had to talk to the rest of the guys about her plan.

19

JASPER

J asper tapped his pen on the table, contemplating what was going on with everything around him. The 'investigation team' was for show, that was certain. The IMPO was more worried about just catching the assassins than they were finding out who was behind it.

He glanced at Vincent. He had secrets, ones Jasper needed to be in on, but they hadn't yet found a safe time to exchange thoughts on what was going on. Even in James' condo, they were uncomfortable talking about it, thanks to James' constant hovering. Plus, they had to address the five man and one woman elephant in that room as well, or it would have never gone away.

"Vincent? When was your last smoke break?" Jasper asked softly.

"I don't really..." Vincent looked up to him, his reply trailing off. "I haven't had a chance since early this morning, before breakfast."

"Come on. We can spare ten minutes while the analysts finish compiling the information we requested." Jasper stood up and Vincent followed him. They were out of the room in milliseconds, and hurrying to get outside and talk. They even took the stairs. "So, you're really quitting?"

"Slower than Sawyer. I cut back a lot. Hoping I can finish it off before the end of the year, but we'll see."

"Big of you to quit for her." Jasper looked over the Italian's face.

He gave nothing away. "Not just her. It's a bad habit. I have to say, once I didn't care if it killed me. Now, I kind of do."

"Understandable."

"As much time as we can get, right?" Vincent tried to smile, but it failed. They both remembered the Amazon, certainly. Leaving her out there, maybe dead, maybe about to die. They remembered the assassin, less than forty-eight hours ago.

"As much time as we can get," he agreed. "But I need you to keep smoking while we're here. It's a good chance for us to talk."

"You're right. I'm surprised it hadn't crossed my mind earlier. I have a pack on me, thank god."

They went out a back door and into an alley. As Vincent lit his cigarette, Jasper looked around, making sure there wasn't so much as a homeless person hanging around. "The IMPO is treating our group like a joke," he started the moment he knew they were alone.

"Because they don't want to look too deep. None of them will enjoy finding a WMC Council member at the center of this." Vincent met his eyes. "Yes. I just said that."

Jasper blinked a couple of times. He didn't say that.

Vincent didn't move.

He did. "I..." Jasper tried to find some words. Vincent just went back to using telepathy. Probably for safety.

"Look at the information that would have had to get in the wrong hands for this to happen. Look at the timeline. It's not plausible. The only person who could have known all of it from the beginning is a Council member. It's the best bet."

"And it's treason to incriminate them. You know that. If you're wrong..."

"I'm Vincent Castello, the younger brother of the maniac crime lord, Antonio 'Axel' Castello. They would have a very easy time pushing me to the side, arresting me, and making themselves seem like the victims of a terrible ploy. Yes, I know."

Vincent seemed so ready for that to happen. It was in his eyes, the posture he held.

"What can I do to help?"

"Help me dig without getting caught. You've got a mind to look at details I don't understand. I analyze people, but you're better with data - and data is all we have."

"Roger. How right do you feel about this?"

"I don't see any other options." He took a drag from his smoke. "Damn, Jasper. What have we gotten ourselves into?"

"Something life-threatening, which is pretty par for the course at this point." Jasper wished the joke landed. It didn't. It was too honest.

"When the assassin first hit and Sawyer was coming back with Quinn, I thought it was a single hit. Someone in the WMC or IMPO was trying to take her out. Fine. We could have handled that. Then the WMC members turned up dead and..." Vincent shook his head. "This reeks of something I can't figure out. This feels deeper than I expect, but I'm not sure what lies beneath."

"We can focus on the WMC first, then move on to whatever else might be hiding in this mess." Jasper felt like he was getting minor whiplash from Vincent's switching between speaking and telepathy.

"You're right. You'll need to help me stay focused. You know how I am. There's something hiding, somewhere, and I need to find it."

"I haven't seen you like this since we met Sawyer." There was no avoiding it. He was going back to the way he had been when they were in the midst of trying to catch Axel. It wasn't a good look for Vincent.

"You'll notice I'm not the only one who seems a little bit like how we were at that time." Vincent sighed. "The only thing grounding me right now is her and you guys, all of us. Knowing I can rely on you."

"You mean..."

"She's focused, like she was when we met her. In her eyes is a focus. On a task, like when she was trying to get away from us. Trying to figure us out and keep moving on with her secrecy. It's there again."

"This hits a little close to home," Jasper reminded him. "For her."

"It really does, so I can't blame her. It also falls a little too close to home for me."

That gave Jasper pause. It did?

The more he thought about it, the more he could see it. This was the type of scheme Vincent had grown up around. Assassinating people to get certain others on top. Eliminating competition and twisting things so it didn't look like it was the perp.

"Damn. I'm sorry."

"Axel was always better at understanding these things than me. He would have figured this out in a couple of days, max. He's very good at the chess board. The way he was in that last year before his capture was...extreme for him. He had an unusual focus on Sawyer and killing her - that wasn't like him."

"Let's not talk about him. You're good at this too." Jasper swallowed. He didn't like talking about Axel. He'd prefer the man was dead already, but that wasn't up to the team. "We got this. Our team. You and I will dig as deep as we can until the Triad are taken care of. Maybe we'll even crack it, but either way, this team can do it. Sawyer and our friends can handle their end."

He didn't know he was going to have to be the voice of reason and confidence.

Vincent's eyes seemed hollow for a moment until he nodded and they came back to life. "Thanks," he mumbled, putting his cigarette out on the concrete wall of the IMPO headquarters. "Let's get in and get this done, then."

Jasper nodded, feeling his own speech rebound on him. As they walked back into the building, he felt good about him and Vincent figuring this out, especially since he knew exactly what Vincent was thinking. He could see why the Italian was sitting on it for so long. He had probably mulled it over for hours, debating on if he should say anything. Reasonable, since even the thought could get them in trouble.

They went back into the room that had been given to the investigation team. They had a large whiteboard on the wall, which Jasper and Vincent didn't mess with, and several boxes of paperwork lying around. It was a general meeting room, with a long table and leather chairs.

It didn't fit the work they were doing. Just another sign that the IMPO had their priorities messed up.

"Are you two going to get anything done in here?" one of the agents asked as they retook their seats.

"Yes, when the analysts get me the information I want,"

Vincent retorted, leaning back in his seat like he owned the room. Jasper liked how much Vincent put off in the gesture. He was better than the others, was his message. He was better than this job. He knew what he was doing. It was really a quiet confidence, something that couldn't be missed but wasn't arrogant or cocky. It wasn't boastful.

Jasper wished he could put on that act.

"The information you want isn't pertinent to the Code Black," one snapped. To a woman sitting next to him, he muttered. "God damn this fucking team."

"Put them in their place, please?"

Jasper sighed, looking back to Vincent, who nodded. Jasper reached down and pulled his pant leg up enough to remove his leg. It was itching him and he didn't want to deal with it. He dropped it on the table in front of him, while the others watched. Some went a little wide-eyed. Jasper never made a public thing about his missing leg, or a public scene in general. It wasn't what they knew him for.

Once his leg was off, he looked back at Vincent. Did he really want Jasper to do this?

Vincent nodded again.

"Do you know who any of them are?" he asked casually.

"No. Please tell me. I'd like to know more of my colleagues." Vincent knew who everyone in the room was, their strengths and weaknesses. He didn't know the numbers Jasper did though.

"Nicholai there is on a team with a startlingly bad rate of capture. At last review, I read they were considering revoking the team's privileges and sending them back into training, or demoting all of them to a more consistent and easier role as a city-based detective, if that." Jasper stopped for a moment for the one who made the comment to turn a little red. "Laura is from Dallas, actually. She's not even a

Special Agent. We'll be kind to her; she's here for an interesting time. Just transferred to this city and she's in the middle of this. She was in Dallas while we were." He pointed to an old guy. "Old guy there is Old Guard. He went to Academy with Jon Aguirre, and they hated each other. He's got a competent level of success in murder cases, but don't let him anywhere near organized crime or white-collar crime. He's abysmal. We're talking it takes him and his team three to four times longer to close one of those cases...if they do. His team has the longest list of open cases in the IMPO."

"We get the point," one of them snarled out.

"No, I don't think you do," Vincent whispered.

"While our team has a long open case average thanks to having Axel's case open from the day we formed, none of our other cases have been open longer than four months. We have a one hundred percent catch rate, though I would make that higher since we're the ones who stumbled on and caught Sawyer. What do you think, Vincent?"

"I would agree."

Jasper grinned. He figured he would. "We've handled cases that cover the spectrum as well. All with a perfect capture and close rate. We're also the two smartest people in the room based on the test scores of this organization. We're also the most educated people in this room, and that's from personnel files."

"So *this fucking team* is going to wait until we get the data that we requested from the analysts, and if any of you have a problem with that, please show me why I should trust your judgement over my own. Or Jasper's." Vincent was sneering now. It wasn't a common look, and Jasper didn't like it on him. "And while we're in here finding out who did this to the best of our ability, not yours, the rest of *this fucking team* is out there making sure the WMC lives through the fucking week."

The silence from the other agents was deafening.

"I'll make the quick reminder that we're the ones who woke up with a member of the Triad in a secure home, trying to kill someone on our team. Regardless of who that was, we can all understand how very bad that is for an IMPO Special Agent." Jasper tapped a finger on the table. "We all make enemies out there. There's no reason to sit in here and make them. Don't fuck with us, though; we will run you over. If there's one thing we have a reputation of being good at it, it's running people over."

Eventually, the other agents got back to their own work, and it was nearly an hour before the analyst brought them the documents and data they requested.

No one asked why they had requested WMC transactions in the last month, and Jasper hoped no one would. He knew Vincent would have a good excuse if someone asked. Until that came to pass, Jasper stuck his nose in the numbers and hoped he would be able to find something, anything.

20

ZANDER

"**A**re you sure about this?" Vincent asked again. It was probably the third time.

"I trust her," Zander answered again. "Look, you can ask all you like, Vin, but we're doing this. I like the plan. I think it's ingenious. Now, I'm not a planner, so that might be something you should take into consideration, but James, Elijah, and Quinn were all okay, so why wouldn't I be?"

"Because it puts her in danger."

He sighed, straightening up from tying up his boots. He spread his hands in defeat. "Then she's in danger. She'll either be in danger with me around or without me around, and...the jungle taught me I would rather be around for the danger and see it than be in the dark. And I can help her. My abilities are perfect for this work." Zander picked up his shirt and pulled it on, then a black long-sleeved shirt. "Vin, are you really that worried about this?"

"You did yell at her for running into the woods the other night to go after Naseem." There was his answer. He was worried. Vincent was very worried, if he was trying to get Zander to be an ass and stop this plan.

"And I apologized literally a couple of moments later. I freak out, I know, but going into this with a plan should help me keep my head with her. I'm slow to learn, but I can be her teammate and know that she's very much capable of taking care of herself." He had to learn that lesson the hard way out in the Amazon. She'd been fine, in a loose sense of the word. Sure, he would love to hide her away and keep her safe, but he knew it would only upset her. It was also unnecessary. She was tough; she always had been. "Vin, you need to trust us."

"I do, but I guess with everything else, I have a feeling this could go bad. It has me worried."

"The likelihood we're going to see any action tonight is very small," Sawyer said as she walked into the bedroom. She must have heard them talking. "Vincent, tonight will be more of a stakeout on the guards, than waiting for the Triad. Even with how fast they move, it took them a few days to come after me when my identity went public."

"I hope you're certain." Vincent reached out to her, and Zander watched her walk into his arms, running her hands up his chest.

"I'm never certain, per se. I can say the probability is in my favor. I'm armed to the teeth just in case."

"I know," he murmured, leaning to kiss her neck.

Zander held back a growl, not of jealousy, but of want. Damn, he thought it was hot to see her getting loved on by the guys. It made him think she was taken care of. Even when he couldn't, someone else was making sure she knew exactly how fucking beautiful she was.

Vincent's eyes met his over her shoulder and an eyebrow went up. Zander must have looked like an idiot.

"I'm not into whatever you're thinking."

He nearly laughed. *"I was thinking how it's good to see her so taken care of by all of us."*

"I bet you were."

Zander snorted, looking away.

Sawyer glanced back at him, frowning. "What are you two saying?" she asked perceptively.

"Nothing of any importance," Vincent murmured, kissing her cheek. "You should go before I try to keep you, something James wouldn't appreciate."

"Of course," she agreed softly, kissing their leader back, holding his face so he couldn't pull away. It was so tender, like her lips were showing how she intended to caress the Italian later. There was always something so private about the way those two interacted.

Damn, he liked watching her kiss them too now. Zander shifted uncomfortably. He liked watching those dark eyes grow warm with a heat when she looked at the others. He never thought it would all work out so well for him. He figured he would have bouts of jealousy every now and then as this went on, but so far, he was perfectly okay. He even enjoyed it.

"Let's go, everyone!" Elijah called out.

"Ah, yes, saved by the cowboy," Vincent crooned. "Go. I'll try and sleep, I promise."

"You might want to tell James what you're up to," she said as they walked out of the bedroom.

"I'm...considering it, but there's too much of a risk he might trust Thompson with it. That I can't risk at all. Thompson would have my head."

"Are you sure?" Zander brought his eyebrows together.

"Positive, because while he's in charge of the IMPO, he's also the WMC's dog and there's nothing anyone can do about that." He waved them away as he entered the kitchen and they crowded at the front door. "All of you stay safe, okay?"

Zander wanted to brush the concern off, looking away. He was uncomfortable with just how close they all seemed to be getting. Something in the group had only grown tighter together since Sawyer stormed into their lives.

It wasn't a bad thing; it just made him a little uncomfortable. Like how comfortable the relationship was with all of them in her bed and her heart. He got uncomfortable with the comfortable. It made no sense to him.

But it was good for them, and that was something he couldn't deny.

They left, shaking hands and giving the other guys well wishes before heading out.

"James isn't coming with us?" Quinn asked softly as they loaded into the SUV.

"He's going to keep an eye on the other building tonight for us, so we're all together." Sawyer turned on the vehicle. "It's no problem."

"Okay."

Zander looked back at Quinn to make sure he was really 'okay' and sure enough, he took what Sawyer said without any sort of complaint, vocal or visual.

They drove to the safehouse in silence after that. Zander mentally prepared himself for anything to go wrong. He knew everyone in the car was. They had been through too much at this point to not be prepared for anything. The Druid had taught them to take nothing for granted, even a night that seemed peaceful.

Sawyer beat them inside when they arrived, parking and jumping out without a word. He caught a glimpse of everything she had on her. From the daggers to the kukri and her throwing knives, she was armed like she was going to war, and in a way, he felt like she was.

Something was different about her. When she told them about her plan with trying to bait the Triad, the only thing he could think was that it was something *he* would do. She was in a zone he wasn't used to seeing: the professional, the best in the business. While it was a plan he would make, it was done better by her, since she knew all the ins and outs. She'd found weaknesses in the security that he didn't understand.

She had a reputation for a reason.

As they walked inside, he sent a grin to Elijah, trying to keep the mood somewhat light. "So, you've been better since the trip to Atlanta. I'm sorry for how that ended."

"I'm not," Elijah replied, grinning as well, his eyes going down as they walked inside.

Zander followed his gaze to her ass and chuckled. "I mean about the press," he said lightly. "But I can agree with the sentiment."

"She likes it rough," the cowboy purred, as if he was imagining that night all over again.

"Don't I know it." God, he loved when she was in the mood to play dirty and get a little painful. Zander fell for that sort of violent passion hard, and she had it. Not always. He could see why she also liked the intimacy of Vincent, but when she needed the harder passion, he liked knowing she came to him.

"As for the press." The cowboy sighed heavily. "Well, look where it's gotten us. She'll be fine, though. I think. She was hit pretty hard with it at the moment, but she's done well getting on with things. I can't even begin to relate, you know, but I tried that night to just remind her that hey, none of those motherfuckers matter."

"They don't. They can take their opinions and shove them up their asses." Zander snorted, shaking his head as he remembered how people were talking. Now, he didn't know what was being said. The situation had them all pulled away from looking at the news and keeping an eye on it. He did know that the world knew she was nearly assassinated in her home, and maybe that was changing things. "I'm glad you were there with her that night. You're big enough to be intimidating as hell."

"Yeah and I might have committed assault against a cameraman. I melted his camera and made him drop it to prove I was capable of violence if they didn't let us go through to get to the truck."

"Why didn't you say anything earlier? Think anyone will press charges?" Zander crossed his arms, considering the cowboy.

"I didn't say anything because they weren't going to press charges. No one is going to press charges on an IMPO Special Agent, no matter the situation. Please."

"Guys, focus," Sawyer ordered. "Come with me."

Zander went to her and they followed her to a room on the top floor of the hotel. It was completely empty, except for several chairs.

"There's a few rooms up here that didn't get filled. Being so high up, the idea of someone climbing up to get in the building is very slim. The other agents didn't even consider thinking up, but I did. Coming in from the top is the easiest way to get anywhere, since most places don't consider it." She pointed down at the floor. "Three of the four floors below us are all soldiers, but one is the Councilmen."

"And this room is above one of them and not over an

officer's room on the same floor," Elijah muttered. "Damn, woman."

Zander wouldn't have considered that.

"I once made a multi-floor phase drop - the job I was working when Axel showed up and led to all of this. It's possible. They will move slower and quieter, but this is their best way of getting in a Council member's room. From this, they can get into all the other rooms and do what they need to do. Since they can mask their magic, something I wish I fucking knew how to do, no one would even know they're there."

"I'm beginning to see why the IMPO has always had such a hard time catching assassins," Zander mumbled, looking down at the floor still. Christ. No one ever considered this sort of shit. It was just too ridiculous. Coming in from the top and going down? Phasing through floors like this? Having the ability to mask their magic so no other Magi could feel them?

"Now, all but three rooms on *this* floor are also full. So, they will choose to go through the empties instead of an occupied room, if they can. They could try the stairs, but I've put guards in there. They'll need to do the drops and hope they don't wake occupants."

"And why don't they just hit the transports to and from the WMC again?" Elijah asked it but Zander was also curious.

"Because not even the best assassins want to deal with a crowd of alert, armed soldiers ready to open fire on something that blinks at them funny. We all know that IMAS is very good at transfers, where the IMPO falters in it. It's why IMAS is in charge of that side of security." Sawyer shrugged. "Just call it a professional rule. We don't fuck with armed IMAS vehicles. The soldiers work in larger, more coordinated groups than the IMPO and they're highly trained. You do know that it's Spec Ops that are doing the transports, right? Yeah, no thanks."

He really couldn't find a fault in her logic, but then, he wasn't Vincent or Jasper. He figured Elijah and Quinn were also at a loss. "So you want...what?" he asked, sitting down in a chair.

"One person in each room. If anything happens, raise the biggest fucking alarm you can. Take down whoever you can without getting hurt. We're all so close together that it'll be simple to get where you are. One of us, probably Quinn or I, will be roaming the hall instead, ready to be the first person jumping in to help."

"Me," Quinn said. "I'm the most powerful here."

"It's easy to get the jump on you, though," she whispered, reaching out to him. "Remember Camila?"

"Remember I'm immensely more powerful than you, and she was immensely more powerful than me. She also caught me in the dark." Quinn sighed. "You know I never really thought I would win that fight, only give you all space and time to run. We've spoken on this."

"And you think you'll be better here? Without bringing the building down?"

"I'll be fine."

Zander never thought he'd see the day when someone would question *Quinn*, of all people. But she did it and he just took it, like he was ready for her to judge him for the best outcome for their...pack, as Quinn would call them.

"Then you can be in the hall. I like the idea; I just needed to make sure you were confident in it." She smiled. "All right, everyone. Places."

Zander took two steps closer to her and kissed her for as long as possible, until he felt her push gently on his chest.

When he pulled back, he saw her hooded eyes staring at his chest, her fingers curling into his shirt. "Be safe," he whispered. "If anything happens, we'll get here as fast as possible." He couldn't just walk away without saying it. He needed her to know, always, that he would fight for her like a fucking madman if the situation called for it.

"And I'll get to you," she promised in return.

He left, the other guys also saying their 'be safes' and such before following him. He picked the room towards the end of the hall, figuring that with his telepathy, it would be easy for him to get help even at the distance. He was still in range of his team for his telepathy to work, so it didn't worry him. He could also shield and heal, so if they took time to get to him, then he could remain safer.

He settled into a chair in the room and just waited, keeping his mind awake and alert only through the training he'd received with the IMPO.

It was a long night - and a boring one at that.

Sawyer, at dawn, was pleased to be right with her assumption that the Triad wouldn't attack yet, but for Zander, it was almost bad. It felt like the stakes grew every second that nothing happened.

21

SAWYER

After two nights of nothing, Sawyer was beginning to lose her patience, but she didn't allow it to affect her focus. Getting ready for the third night, she had an itch, something whispering to her that something was going to happen, but she ignored it. It was an itch she had every night.

And every night, she reached into her bag and her fingers grazed her mask. She itched to wear it for this, but the words of the boy haunted her. It might break, and she would need it later.

Fucking future sight. She had no idea if the boy spoke any truth, but it stuck in her mind like a knife carving a scar. Even when the knife was removed, it would always be there, haunting her.

"I don't like this schedule," Vincent whispered, looking at her from across the room. "I don't like you all there every night without Jasper and I."

"We're fine," she reminded him. "Seriously. We've got this. We have a ton of backup in the building if anything goes fucking tits-up."

"I know, but that backup isn't us."

"How's your investigation going?" she asked, hoping to hear anything other than his worry.

"We haven't found anything, which is getting quite disappointing. It would be nice to have one of them captured and forced to talk."

She had a feeling capturing the Triad would be the easy part, and even that was going to be one of the most challenging things she'd ever done. Getting one of them to talk? That was going to be nigh impossible. She didn't say any of that to Vincent. She knew, with or without a Triad member, he would figure it out. She believed in him.

"You're also working around not giving anything away. Look, maybe tomorrow you should take the leash off and just go wild. You're holding yourself back, trying to play this quietly." Sawyer watched him as she said it. She watched his eyes narrow just a little, enough to make her realize her words landed the way she had hoped.

"I'm not holding myself back."

"You are. The secrecy, the lack of trust. Get wild. Be the leader you know you are. And shit," she really didn't want to say this next part, "channel some of Axel. He got what he wanted because he ran through it with the exact same sort of perceptive mind you have, but he didn't let anything hold him back, like the possibility of getting into trouble."

He was glaring now, and she felt bad, but it needed to be said.

Axel was a maniac, an abusive monster, but none of them had ever denied that he was very good at what he did as a criminal. If his intelligence and abilities had been good, he would have been a force no criminal could have stood against. Sadly, he'd gone down a darker path thanks to insanity.

Vincent had the same keen mind, but he was quieter and rougher than his brother. He was holding back so people didn't compare him to Axel and she could understand that, she really could. But they needed the mind he and his brother were both known for, not the man who wanted to shed the mantle of being one of the two Castellos.

"I'll think about it." He dropped whatever he was holding and walked out of the room, leaving her to finish putting on her weapons.

She had a feeling he was upset with her, and that was fine. They would talk it out when this was over. She just said what she felt needed to be said, because it wasn't time for the word games or the playing around.

She left the room and found Jasper in the kitchen with James, who was going to stay in, feeling comfortable with the security at the other safehouse now. She wrapped an arm around Jasper and leaned on him for a moment.

For three days, they had barely seen each other. Normally, she wasn't a needy person, or clingy at all, but the last time she'd been without them had been thinking they could possibly be dead in the jungle. Now, not having them all the time sort of worried her. She couldn't keep her eyes on them. Something could happen to them, and that would kill her.

"How are you?" she asked softly, her forehead on his shoulder.

"I'm good. Miss you, miss being home, hate all of this, but good otherwise." He gave a weak chuckle and kept cutting the carrots for some stew that was being made. She would be eating those leftovers at dawn.

"Same to all of that," she said, sighing heavily. "Vincent may be mad at me tomorrow, but don't freak out if he's acting differently."

"Oh?"

"I told him to stop holding back because he's scared of being compared to his brother," she whispered, hoping James didn't hear.

Jasper stopped cutting and looked at her on his shoulder. He didn't say anything, but those stormy blue-gray eyes were full of concern.

And James did hear. "Bad move. He hates knowing he and Axel have similarities. Thought you would know that."

"I do. It's why I'm assuming he'll be in a mood." She glanced at their handler, wondering why he was staring at her so oddly.

"I mean, with everything going on, I think reminding him of Axel right now is a really bad idea, especially since he got that invitation."

"What invitation?" she and Jasper asked at the same time.

James looked between them from his spot over the stove, comprehension dawning over his face as he realized they didn't know what he was talking about. "Fuck," he muttered, shaking his head. "Forget I said anything."

"No, finish that," Elijah snapped, walking in. "What invitation?"

"My brother asked for me to go visit him," Vincent said, following Elijah into the kitchen. "I hadn't had the thought to tell them yet, James. Thanks for that."

Sawyer turned her gaze on him. She knew she was glaring, but didn't soften it for him.

"Don't," James ordered, waving a hand at her. "He was undecided about it. I'm-"

"You were invited to go see him and didn't fucking tell me?" she demanded, pointing at her chest. "This month, of all months?"

"He was attacked in prison a few weeks ago and it left him severely injured. Scarred. He'll be fine in the long run." Vincent was trying to remain cool with her, but she could see it cracking. "I was planning on turning it down. Quinn and I spoke about it."

"You didn't tell me-"

"And what would I have said?" he snapped, losing his composure. "'Oh, Axel wants to see me for the fucking holidays?' He made a request that the WMC decided to pass along because he's been a model prisoner. I'm not planning on visiting. I found out the day you went to Atlanta with Elijah. Other things obviously fucking came up. 'Oh, Sawyer, your identity was exposed last night, but let me tell you what happened with the man who gave you the damn reputation that doesn't let you have a normal fucking life?'" He was even yelling at the end of it.

"Yes." She was still glaring at him as she stormed out of the kitchen and grabbed her bag from the dining room table. She went down to the SUV without saying anything else for the night, her anger driving her to just leave. She would talk to Vincent again at dawn. She was going to use the anger to focus on her job instead.

She couldn't fucking believe he would keep something like that from her. She could have helped him. She could have said something, anything to make him feel better. It would have kept her from bringing Axel up again, so that Vincent didn't have to have that shoved in his face again.

She was just angry, and she needed to focus on the case.

When they got to the safehouse, she went to her room without a word, waiting. Another night in the dark, just wondering if they were going to take her bait. If they never did, that worried her. It meant they had other plans, ones she couldn't get a grasp of. Like Vincent, she was moving nowhere in all of this. She had a plan and it needed to work. She couldn't afford to fail, not in this. It would leave her dead, not because of the danger involved, but because she was another target.

If the Triad succeeded for whoever they worked for, her head would be on the proverbial silver platter.

"I hope you're doing okay, babe. I know you're mad at Vincent, and I am too, a little, but he didn't think it was a big deal for everyone."

She cracked a small smile at Zander's words. Damn him for growing up and being the fucking rational one. When the fuck did that happen on her?

"I'm harassing Elijah right now, because I'm very bored."

She snorted. Of course he was. There went that idea that he was suddenly mature and serious.

"I'm not stupid enough to mess with Quinn, or I would. Did you know he doesn't really like telepathy? He loves the wolves and the animal bond, but telepathy kind of freaks him out. He's fine with it when it's necessary, but you'll notice Vincent never uses it to call him anywhere."

She hadn't known that, but it made sense. It would be an invasion, in a sense. It wasn't as bad as mind reading, but there was no way to block someone shoving their thoughts into your head.

"I should stop messing with Elijah." He said it with a mental sigh. *"When we're done with this, I want first dibs to have a day with you."*

She wasn't even going to address that later. There were no dibs, but mentally, she knew she needed to spend time with Vincent and Jasper since they were separated from the team. Maybe Quinn, since he was stuck in New York with her. In December.

In the quiet night, with Zander finally done being

ridiculous, she realized that outside was a Christmas wonderland. She'd been ignoring anything that wasn't related to the case.

They were in New York for the holidays. Wasn't that something.

Her smile broadened as the night continued. When this was over, she needed to make sure they all took a day to go see the lights. She wanted to see those ice blue eyes of Quinn's dancing in the Christmas lights. She wanted to see what sort of trouble Elijah and Zander would get into with all the snow. She wanted to drink hot chocolate with Jasper and have Vincent visit her kids with her. They weren't Henry, but they were hers and maybe he would like it. She had them because of the impact Henry made on her life. He would understand, she hoped. Maybe even appreciate them for that.

There was so much she wanted to do with them.

A small thump in the room, but she didn't react. She continued to stare into the darkness like it didn't happen. She remembered how angry Vincent had made her and refocused it on the Triad. They were the source of her problems at that point. If it weren't for them, Vincent would have eventually told her about Axel. The team wouldn't be here, where she had to play a game to catch whoever hired them.

A second thump. The room grew a little colder as her anger grew.

Then a third.

In her room, which she had let her magic take over and make cold, were now three very empty spots. She felt nothing from them.

Got 'em.

"Well, well." A smooth voice whispered. "I wondered if

the whore was smart enough to make a neat little trap for us. I guess Axel wasn't the entire brain behind the Shadow after all."

Naseem.

Her fury boiled, but she didn't move. The room just grew so much colder.

"If you knew it was a trap, why are you here?" she asked softly.

"Because we have unfinished business."

That had her moving. Her kukri was drawn before she even stood up, spinning to deflect a short sword aimed for her ribs. She didn't have time to stop the dagger from slicing her left arm, though.

She jumped away, able to see in the dark after hours of getting used to it. Before her were all three of them, the members of the Triad.

And they weren't there for the WMC. They were there for her. They had figured her out.

This was about to get very messy.

22

ELIJAH

Elijah heard several large thumps and stood up, moving quickly to his door.

"HERE!" she roared and he knew.

The Triad was in the building. They had taken the bait.

He shoved out into the hallway and ran for the door to Sawyer's room. Quinn was already there, yanking it open. Zander was down the hall, falling out of his room and hauling ass.

Elijah was right behind Quinn, as he shifted into a wolf and jumped into the room, a vicious snarl startling whoever was in front of him enough to make them pause. Fangs met flesh and a scream tore out of a terrified throat.

Elijah manifested a fireball to throw at another of the dark figures in the room, knowing it wasn't Sawyer. There was no magic in the area where he aimed.

Zander came in last, and shields wrapped around them, tight, close to their clothing. It was a tricky way to make shields, something Zander had practiced with for years, but it drained his magic considerably and was even harder to do when they were active.

He was impressed.

"I'm the target," Sawyer called out, grappling with the third member on the far side of the room. "They're here for me."

Elijah didn't need to hear any more. He wasn't letting that fucking happen. This was what they had wanted, but something about them going after Sawyer specifically pissed him off. The flame in his hand grew and he sent it for the one he wanted. It didn't make it to his target, whose white grin could be seen in the dark.

"I'm the fires of hell, boy," a feminine voice taunted. "Don't think you can blow me up."

Fuck. He should have known better.

The fireball rebounded back to him and he took his to his chest, but it didn't hurt. Instead, he let go of his control and let the fire lick over his skin like it was part of him. It proved he was more powerful than her. She didn't take the fire like he could.

"Well, doll, looks like we're at an impasse, then." He knew it was burning off all his body hair. It always did when he let it play on him like this. He never let it touch his hair. He saw her eyes go wide, then narrow in anger. "Did you think you were going to be the strongest Magi with fire in the room? And why the dramatics? The fires of hell? Really?"

"I'll kill you," she snarled.

She jumped for him, but he knew how to handle a little spitfire. She didn't have the muscle mass of Sawyer - or the height. She was a tiny thing. He made sure not to underestimate her speed as she tried to slice open his gut. He grabbed her wrist and twisted, hoping to disarm her, but she did a fucking sideways flip thing and took him to the ground.

Holy shit. Thank god for Zander's shield, because it made her blade bounce away when she tried to drive it into his chest.

He could smell smoke in the room now as his fire took over the carpet. Fuck. He put it out before the chick had the chance to think of ramping it up and taking the building down. As he removed the fire, water soaked the carpet, probably from Zander.

He jumped up before the little brat could try and stab him again. This time, he didn't make the mistake of putting his hands on her, using his telekinesis to pull the blade from her hand and throw it into a wall, loud enough to hear the twang of metal vibrating.

"No more of that," he told her, pointing. She glared at him, glancing over to another section of the room. Then he saw her eyes go wide.

He turned to follow as well, to see Quinn back in his human form grab the third Triad member by the hair and slam his face into the wall.

"Stay down," Quinn snarled.

"Adaih!" the little fire user gasped. "Naseem!"

Elijah didn't have a chance to say anything, as something invisible shoved him into a wall. He was able to see Quinn keep hold of the one she called Adaih, as Naseem tossed Sawyer back into a wall as well. Elijah winced at the sickening crunch of her making a large dent in the plaster.

He didn't have the chance to find his feet before Naseem grabbed the little woman and they sank through the floor together.

"Fuck!" Sawyer snarled. "Quinn, Zander, keep that one and get fucking handcuffs on him. Elijah, you're with me."

He didn't have the chance to say anything or react as she blinked to his side and they also fell through the floor.

He'd never phased before, and the sensation wasn't pleasant. He wasn't sure how anyone really liked using the power. It made him feel sick, as he could tell he was in something and something foreign was in him. He was lucky he didn't fall face-first to the floor below. Sawyer had somehow yanked him into a standing position before they landed.

"Move," she ordered and that got him going. They ran out of the room to catch the backs of Naseem and the woman running into the stairwell. They took off after them, letting their legs fly as guards came out to look at the ruckus. Most were smart enough to come out armed but not shoot the two IMPO agents hauling ass.

In the stairwell, Sawyer jumped into the hole in the center, grabbing Elijah's arm at the same time. One moment, he was standing there and the next, he wasn't anything. She had sublimated them and flown them to the bottom of the stairwell in a matter of seconds. He wanted to puke when he was solid again, but Sawyer was already moving and he had to keep up.

This was what she did. Urban runs, fights in tight corridors, using her abilities to make distance and find ways to get places.

They ran out the fire escape door at the bottom of the stairs, instead of the door to the lobby.

"Fuck, a getaway car!" she growled as they ran down the dark alley after an Explorer that was trying to speed up and get into the parking lot.

"SUV. Give me the keys," he demanded and as they ran, she tossed them to him. As they detoured to the SUV in the main parking lot, he could hear her making a call.

"I need everyone in this city on a black Explorer. It holds two assassins who just made an attempt on the life of the

WMC. They are armed and dangerous. The license plate is YHX 8988." She took a breath as they hit the SUV and jumped in. "We are in active pursuit. Get a visual."

Elijah got them moving. He was in the fifties before they left the parking lot.

"Visual acquired. They took a left here." Sawyer pointed and he made the turn. He slammed the gas, focusing on the road and only the road. "They have a helicopter over the getaway car. Roadblocks being put up by IMAS."

"Won't be fast enough," Elijah countered, keeping the pedal down as far as he could get it. Part of him wondered if the automatic was going to be able to handle what he was doing to it. He hoped the engine didn't blow from his treatment.

Finally, he had the Explorer in his sight. He kept the speed, dodging any unfortunate civilians on the road. He could hear the helicopter above them, but it wasn't a distraction.

"Get us close enough and I can sublimate into their car and get it stopped."

"Roger that, little lady." The getaway Explorer wasn't driving nearly as fast as he was, probably trying to dodge and avoid traffic. Or the driver wasn't as experienced as him.

He was pulling up on them so fast that he caught up to them in a turn, nearly hitting their tail lights with his front end. Sawyer cursed.

"There's three fucking people in there. They had a god damned driver waiting for them."

That meant they had more help than expected. They would talk more about the implications of it later. He did know that if they had a driver, she would jump into that vehicle and go against Naseem and the woman at the same time.

"Sawyer, you can't make the jump," he told her, keeping on the Explorer's ass. "You can't do it. Naseem, if he's not driving, will kill you if you become smoke."

He heard her curse.

"I can't blink into a moving vehicle. It's the only option!" She sounded like this was the only chance they had.

It wasn't even that.

A shield formed, only feet in front of him. It appeared too fast. In a second, a very long second, he hit the brakes.

"ELIJAH!"

A hand tried to grab him. It grazed his shoulder before falling away, unable to find a grip.

The front end of their SUV slammed into the shield, causing the magic to blast out from the impact. He was thrown forward, then slammed back into the seat.

The shield shattered, and still they kept going forward.

He wasn't wearing a seatbelt. He lost consciousness as he left the seat and went through the windshield, glass raining around him.

23

SAWYER

There are moments in life where there's no time. They seem too long, those moments - every second dragging out to feel like an eternity. Yet, no matter how long those moments feel, there's no time. The body can only move so fast, and in those moments, it's like everything is weighed down. Slow motion.

Too slow.

She was always too slow.

She screamed, reaching for him, trying to find a way to grab him.

The impact knocked her into the door and dashboard. She shut her eyes against the pain and was thrown one more time, out the windshield. She sublimated the moment she knew she could, instinctively knowing it was safer to be smoke, through the pain.

Even in her smoke form, she had enough momentum to go nearly thirty feet, the crumpled metal following her. Reforming as soon as she could, she staggered in the debris around her, dazed.

She couldn't focus on anything. She must have hit her

head in the collision. Something warm trickled down her forehead. It had to be blood.

Smoke came off the wreckage. She didn't recognize the SUV she had just been in. Blinking, hoping she could focus enough to see anything, she looked for him. Where did he go?

If she went thirty feet from the SUV, she thought he would have landed between her and wreck, but that wasn't the case.

She turned away from the wreck and saw him, another twenty feet down the road.

Not moving.

She stumbled as she tried to run for him. She tripped on metal pieces and nearly fell when she reached his side. Everything hurt, but none of it hurt so much as her heart, seeing the twisted form of her cowboy on the asphalt.

Not moving.

"Elijah?" she asked, croaking it out. She didn't touch him. She hoped his back wasn't broken. She couldn't risk hurting him anymore. He was face down. She couldn't even see his wonderful face. "Cowboy? Elijah?" She could hear the tears coming to the surface as the realization finally settled in.

She resisted the urge to pull the big body into her lap, only leaning down and touching her forehead to him. She could already hear sirens, but none of it mattered.

"Elijah, baby, you can't die on me. Please."

Nothing else mattered. Her heart felt like it was being torn in two.

"Please. Please don't leave me. I can't be left. I need you. Oh god, please." Every sentence was punctuated by a sob. "No. Not like this. No, baby, I love you. Come back. Don't go. We're not done. Please."

Blackness began to take over her vision as dizziness set in on her. The adrenaline was wearing off.

"Please!" she begged, her hands tangled into his shirt. "I love you. Please come back. Don't go!"

Hands grabbed her, pulling her away. She fought against them, screaming for him. She couldn't leave him. No matter what, she couldn't leave his body there. She had promised. She had promised him she wouldn't let this happen to him. She wouldn't leave him like that, and let him die.

She was still screaming incoherently as a needle jabbed in her. Her fight left her body, but not her soul. She was being pulled away, but she just wanted him.

She needed to hold him.

This was her fault.

She couldn't lose him so fast.

Not like she lost Henry.

She didn't want to wake up the next day and know he was gone.

She needed his smile.

His laughter.

His fun.

His love.

She lost her ability to stand, her knees slamming into the asphalt as whoever had her couldn't hold her up.

She loved him so much.

It broke her heart into a thousand pieces, watching him being treated by the strangers.

Everything went dark after that.

24

VINCENT

V incent couldn't move, his eyes wide on the television screen in James's living room.

They had been woken up with a call saying there was a pursuit of the Triad. That one had been detained, but two of his team went after those running.

Elijah and Sawyer had been in the chase.

All he saw now was wreckage. Twisted, smoking metal scattered all over the road.

"Vincent?" someone whispered.

He didn't move.

Something whimpered at his feet.

Sawyer and Elijah had been in that mass of metal and debris.

His chest felt like it was caving in. The last thing he and Sawyer talked about was an argument, concerning Axel of all people.

And then she nearly died.

"They were taken to a hospital, but we still haven't learned which one," the voice continued. "I do know both their hearts were still beating."

"Two IMPO agents were injured in the accident," the news anchor was saying. "We do have their identities confirmed, but the IMPO and the WMC have requested that we leave off an update on them until there is more concrete information about their health."

"The accident was caught on video by a non-Magi who happened to be walking home on the street as the chase passed. It seems a shield was erected right in front of the SUV. No amount of training could have stopped this." The other anchor sounded sympathetic. "There was no chance they were going to stop themselves or have time to prepare for an accident."

"The IMPO might want the identities unconfirmed by us, but there's no holding back that video now," the first one said, tired. "Everyone in New York, please be careful and keep the agents in your hearts and prayers."

Vincent still couldn't move, and again, there was more whimpering at his feet.

"The video. I have it. It's rough," another voice choked out. "Oh god. They caught her...fuck."

"What is it?" the first voice asked.

"She was screaming over Elijah's body. 'I love you' and 'don't leave me.' Things like that." The voice faltered over the words several times. "Oh, Sawyer..."

Vincent couldn't blame her. It's all he'd wanted to say to both of them since he turned on the television to see live footage of the accident site. He could hear the video playing from somewhere. Her screams echoed in the condo. The gut-wrenching pain. The proclamations of love.

The desperation.

He glanced down at Sombra, who was lying as close to the floor as she could. He didn't know what to do or say for the cat. If anyone knew how Sawyer was, it was the jaguar.

"I have Quinn and Zander. They had IMAS secure the only captured one in the safe house and are trying to find out which hospital it is, too."

"Vincent?" the second voice asked. A hand touched his shoulder. He turned slowly to see stormy, emotional blue eyes looking at him. They were red with unshed tears. "They're alive right now. We need to find out what hospital they're at and go see them."

He couldn't say anything, and another whimper punctuated the silence of his mind. It was like the jaguar was making every sound for both of them.

"I just got a text. Apparently Sawyer had to be drugged to let EMTs handle Elijah. She fought them. They were both transported to New York Presbyterian Hospital." James stepped in front of him, blocking his view of the television. "Vincent, go put on clothes. You too, Jasper."

The television was turned off and Vincent felt like a zombie walking back into the guest bedroom for his bag. He didn't know what he ended up putting on.

Elijah and Sawyer.

His oldest friend.

His only real love.

He hadn't been this scared for a life since the Amazon and then, he'd trusted Sawyer to do what she needed to do. He had been there and known she was going to fight and come back.

This time it felt like his heart had been ripped from his chest.

It happened too fast.

It happened way too fast.

He didn't know how Jasper was holding it together.

A hand ran over his back, comforting. "They're alive."

"For now," he whispered hoarsely.

"No. They're alive. Period." Jasper snapped it at him. Vincent looked up and saw the belief there in those stormy blue eyes. Jasper wasn't going to believe otherwise. Not until he was holding a corpse.

"Okay." Vincent wasn't in the mood to argue.

It felt too fast, Jasper pulling him from the room and all the way out of the building into the parking garage. James was already waiting, his car running. Vincent was nearly tossed into the backseat, Sombra climbing in next to him and the wolves following. It was like they refused to be left behind. Not for this. Not for more of their humans being hurt.

The drive to the hospital seemed like nearly a dream, the large cat nearly climbing into his lap.

Another hospital to visit his team members.

He was tired of this.

He was tired of knowing that if one more thing had gone wrong, he wouldn't have them. He didn't have much of a family. They were all that mattered to him.

He wished he said something more often. He always felt uncomfortable with the guys, rarely telling them how much they meant to him, as the men he chose to go on such a journey to catch Axel with him. He found it hard to open up with them like he could with Sawyer.

He needed to change that.

They had caught Axel, but the journey was still going. They were brothers. He needed to tell them that more often.

When the car parked, he didn't need Jasper to pull him out. The first people he saw were Zander and Quinn, both looking exhausted and worried. The wolves took off for their Magi. Sombra stayed glued to his side as Kaar swooped down, landing on his shoulder as gently as the bird could.

People looked at them as they walked in, a dreadful silence still weighing on them. He could ask the guys about the one they captured later. Everything else could wait.

He had to see them.

"BOYS!" A booming voice broke him out of his fear in a single snap, like a whip cracking. Vincent spun, making Kaar caw in frustration at the speed. Walking down a hallway was fucking Charlie. "I just saw Sawyer. She's just been put under. A bit beaten up, bruised. She obviously didn't sublimate fast enough to avoid getting thrown around a little in the vehicle, but she'll be fine. Maybe a minor concussion, but that's the worst of it."

"And Elijah?" Quinn asked softly.

Vincent wondered how Charlie got there faster than them, but he also knew that Charlie knew everyone in every hospital in the city. None of them would have denied him the information he needed to find Sawyer, patient confidentiality be damned. He was the closest thing she had to a father.

"A bit worse," Charlie said, sighing. He shifted uncomfortably. "He had a punctured lung and bleeding in his brain. Broken ribs, a broken tibia. Dislocated shoulder. He...should make it. The bleeding in the brain is... complicated to deal with. I'm about to go in there and do some healing on him myself, but I knew you were going to be here and wanted to stop in. The doctors and healers with him have him stable for a little while longer before we need to do a trade."

Vincent's stomach dropped. He swayed, and two strong, but different hands grabbed him - Charlie's on one side and Quinn's on the other.

"Why don't we find a place to sit down?" Jasper asked softly.

"Go on. I'm going to see Elijah and offer my hand." Charlie turned, beginning to walk away.

"Let me help!" Zander demanded, walking off after Charlie. "I'm not a doctor but I can heal, and-"

"Let's go."

Vincent watched their reckless redhead walk away with the older African American. God, Zander would kill himself to make sure Elijah came back. Something about it was comforting. Zander would do anything. He wouldn't give up.

"They'll let us go into Sawyer's room," James murmured, leading them away from the main desk of the hospital.

Vincent didn't pay attention to anything. He was loaded onto an elevator and ushered off. He was led into a room and saw her. Kaar flew to sit on machines and watched her as closely as he did.

Bruising, light from healing, was on her face. He could see the new scar on her forehead, cutting into her hairline where she must have gotten the concussion. He stumbled and sat on the bed next to her thighs, leaning down slowly, his head touching her chest.

Alive.

She was alive, and would remain so.

God, he was so in love with her. Every part of him ached to just hold her and know she was okay. The only thing that held him back was not knowing where Elijah was. The damn cowboy deserved to hold her too. After hearing how she screamed for him, Vincent knew that her love for him ran deeper than she probably realized.

"How long until she wakes up?" Jasper asked someone.

"It could be a couple of hours, but her magic burns off the sedative quickly, it seems. Doctor Malcom told us not to dose her again, let her wake up when she wants to."

"Thank you. You can go now."

"We'll have Mr. Grant brought here once he's out of ICU."

"Thank you," Jasper said softer.

Vincent didn't move as the other Magi sat on the other side of the bed. He didn't move as Sombra climbed halfway up, and lay over Sawyer's legs. He didn't move as Quinn and the wolves nestled into the corner of the room, huddled together like they were fighting off a bitter cold winter.

He didn't move for hours. He listened to the updates on Elijah as they were brought, but he refused to move from her, perception be damned.

"Vincent?" a hoarse feminine voice made him open his eyes and lift his head off her stomach.

"Hey, love," he whispered.

Her dark eyes were there, slightly unfocused. "Tell me," she demanded weakly.

"He's stable and will be here soon. He'll live. He'll be fine." He knew she needed to hear it. Those awful screams on that video meant she had thought he was dead, and he couldn't let her keep thinking that.

"Good," she mumbled and he saw them, the tears. He reached out and wiped one that escaped away. "Good."

"Say it," he whispered. "Say it."

"I love him so much," she sobbed. "I can't..."

"I know," he continued to whisper, wrapping his arms around her.

"I love him like you. And Zander and everyone and god, he nearly died. I thought he was dead and it..."

He held her as the rambling continued. Never had he

seen her so vulnerable. Never had something shaken her so hard. And she was shaken. Her shoulders moved with the violent wracking of her sobs.

He knew. He understood.

It had been so sudden. In just an instant, she could have lost him - not to a fight they knew they had, but to a dirty trick, something that couldn't be fought, something that couldn't be conquered.

It took a few moments, but the crying stopped and a sniff happened. She pulled back, wincing.

"You have some bruising that will need to heal on its own, but you're fine otherwise. And there might be a concussion you have to worry about."

"Good." She sighed, looking around him. "Hey, girl."

Sombra took that as a sign to belly-crawl up the small hospital bed, and Vincent watched Magi and jaguar embrace, the jaguar's head over Sawyer's shoulder as her arms wrapped around the slick black body.

"I'm fine, girl. I'm fine." She kept holding the feline as her eyes moved around the room. "Jasper? Quinn? Where's Zander?"

"He's been helping with Elijah and was offered a place to get a quick nap in private," Jasper explained, moving closer. Quinn was right behind him.

"Am I allowed to get up?" she asked. He would have said yes, but she didn't wait for him to say anything, pulling the IVs out. She was out of the bed before he even knew what was happening. She always did this to him: just up and moving the moment her emotions were taken care of and neatly put away again.

"Sawyer, you need to-" Poor Jasper tried.

"What time is it?" She looked around the room and found the clock that hung over her bed. "Fuck, already six am? You guys have to go to headquarters. We caught one of the guys. The-"

"Others are handling it," Vincent cut in, watching her. He didn't want to be so callous as to go and get back to work. He wanted to be there for them. He needed to be there with them.

"No." She stared at him and he realized something unmovable was in the word. "No, Vincent. You and Jasper will find those assholes. You will find who hired them. You will get handcuffs on them."

"Sawyer-"

"You have until nightfall, Vincent."

The room couldn't be this cold if Elijah was going to stay in it.

"Or what, love?" he asked softly.

"I'm going to go after whoever I need to until I find out who it is."

God have mercy on him and whoever else heard that. Jasper's eyes were wide. Quinn sat up a little straighter.

Sombra growled, almost in agreement with her Magi. They wanted blood, and they were good at getting it. Deadly predators were possessive over their territory.

And Sawyer's territory? The team. Him, Elijah, the rest of the guys.

He had until nightfall. He hoped he had enough to at least convince her to slow down.

"Why nightfall?" Quinn asked, standing up.

"Because I want the day to make sure I'm not hurting too bad and...Elijah. I need to see him."

"Let Jasper and I see him before you throw us out," Vincent beseeched her. He wouldn't leave just because she ordered him to, but he felt the need to get her permission to stay anyway. She was angry and he knew that much of what she was saying was driven by that. But she wasn't cruel, so he reminded her of that. "You're not the only person in the room who needs to see him."

Something flashed in her eyes, something warmer. The room's chill left.

No, she wasn't cruel. He knew she would remember that Elijah was important to him and Jasper, too.

"I'm sorry. I'm...so fucking angry," she whispered, looking down. "Stay for a little while, please. I didn't mean you need to leave right now. Well, I did, but you're right. God. I'm sorry."

"Sit down," Jasper ordered gently. "Please. With what happened last night, I'm positive we can take a moment to breathe."

"It's all my fault," she mumbled.

Vincent's heart clenched. "No. The plan was solid. You caught one of them. The other two were forced to run. You couldn't account for the way the accident happened. Based on reports, none of the Triad ever showed the ability to shield."

"There was a third person in that Explorer," she explained. "The driver wasn't one of them. Naseem and Kalama were in the back seat."

"Good to know. That means they've brought someone in to help them, who probably isn't as well trained as them. They needed help, which means this is too big for even them."

"I was the target last night. They knew I had set the trap." She looked down at her hands, and he wondered what she was seeing there. He wondered where she had gone in her own head. He wanted to be there with her. "They played me. If it weren't for the accident - you're right,

I would have come out the winner in a nearly fair fight." She curled her hands into fists.

They sat in silence for a long time. He decided to just sit next to her and wrap an arm around her waist. Later, after all of this, they were going to have to worry about other things, like her proclaiming her love for one of the team to the world. But for now, he was happy to feel her lean on him.

"Boys," James called in. "Ah, Sawyer. Elijah is coming in right now. He's already awake, but a bit out of it."

Vincent jumped up at the exact same time she did and they nearly got tangled up in each other, stumbling for a second.

"He shouldn't be awake," Charlie grumbled as he walked in. "Hey, kiddo."

"Charlie," she sighed out, walking over to him.

"I helped heal your boy. He'll be fine. A bit beat up, but a couple of weeks and he'll be all right. He got to the hospital in time. Took a whole hell of a lot of magic to pull it off, but we did."

"Thank you," she whispered, holding him. "You're burnt out."

Vincent just smiled, glad to see those two together.

"Me and your other boy, Zander. He's asleep, but once we let him in the damn room, he wouldn't stop. He's got skill. He's good. Someone should convince him to get his license to do it professionally. Send him to school."

No one could stop from laughing at that suggestion. Zander was not a school type of guy.

Then Elijah was rolled in.

Vincent made it to him first and grabbed his massive hand. They smiled at each other.

"Hey. I got into my first accident. Sorry about the rental."

"Are you fucking serious?" he asked, trying to not laugh as Elijah tried to joke with him.

"No. Where is she?" Elijah's eyes shifted and found their target. "You get over here. Right now, little lady."

"Is he doped up?" she asked Charlie quietly.

"Yes. He shouldn't be awake, so we doped him with painkillers instead of knocking him back out."

She was nodding at that as she walked to the cowboy's other side. "Can I help you?"

"Yeah. You can repeat what you said. I thought I was dying, so you can say it again. Please."

A bright smile bloomed over her face and Vincent felt like he had never seen such happiness. There were tears in her eyes as she sat on the edge of his bed and leaned close to him.

"I love you. You can't leave me yet. I need you."

"Fucking finally," he groaned. "I love you too, little lady."

"No funerals," she whispered, leaning close, kissing his cheek.

Vincent swallowed, looking away. He was happy for them, but he wanted them to have this moment alone. Even James and Charlie had the decency to look down at the floor and not try to stop it. Out of the corner of his eye, he saw Quinn grinning like a fool.

"No funerals," the cowboy promised.

There was a peaceful, happy silence as everyone let Sawyer and her damned cowboy have their moment.

Vincent was so glad it happened. Those two deserved it.

"Well, I hate to have bad news, but..." James began talking after the long moment.

"Then don't have bad news," she muttered, looking around at him at the foot of Elijah's bed.

Vincent hid a smile with his hand and heard a choking laugh from Jasper behind him.

"You were caught on tape screaming how much you love him. We're going to have to deal with it." Their handler sighed, shoving his hands into his pockets. "It could get you taken off the team."

"No," she said simply, shrugging. "No."

"What?" James looked startled.

"James, look at him." She pointed at Elijah. "Really look at him. This happened to him because of the work he does for our government. To protect them and uphold their law. And the Amazon, where we were cornered into taking a mission where we could have all died, and Quinn nearly did." She shook her head and Vincent realized where she was going with this. "And I've been with this team for all of this. As Jasper lost his leg upholding their law. I've been beaten on. I've been tossed aside. I've been condemned. I've nearly lost my life. And that's only in the last few months... while upholding their law. With this team. This team who is willing go the fucking distance to get something done." She looked down at her hands again, then back up at James. "Tell them the truth and then tell them that if they try to take me from this team, they don't just lose me. They lose a team that has been broken and bled for them, that has fought for them, only to earn their distrust and their vitriol. And then I'll take all of that to the press."

"That doesn't-"

"If they try to do it before this case is over, we'll take Sawyer to our own safe house and we'll leave them to sink or swim," Vincent cut him off.

James looked between them, swallowing, then nodded.

"Then I'll tell you what else you've all missed."

Vincent frowned. They had missed more?

"You know the WMC has been in private sessions, trying to address the open seats on the Council, correct?"

"Yes," Jasper said, sitting down on Sawyer's bed.

"Well, today they plan on announcing their decision. They voted that special elections should be done immediately, to help repair the government as quickly as possible. So good news."

"That is good news," Vincent agreed softly, nodding. "Did anyone vote against it?"

"That's not public knowledge. Sorry."

"Damn," he sighed. "Fine. Well. Jasper and I will get to the IMPO headquarters and get back to work."

"Be safe," she said to him, leaning over Elijah. He met her halfway for the kiss. He was nearly out of the room as Jasper did the same, saying goodbye to her.

He loved that she, for all her toughness, took a moment to do that for them. To tell them to be safe, or goodnight, or to have a nice day. It made him feel like it was a genuine and real relationship.

"Wait!" she called out, following him and Jasper out of the patient room.

"What do you need?"

"You don't need to catch them today. That's unreasonable. Get me something, though, Vincent. Anything. Even just a suspicion. Then...well, we can work on a plan that maybe I can use to dig up the rest."

He smiled, a small one. There she was, the professional.

"Of course. Then we can do what needs to be done. Safely. No collateral damage."

"Exactly." She ran a hand down his upper arm and he loved the casual, calm touch. He figured Elijah being alive had brought her out of the anger for a moment. It would return, but he was glad that she was finding some balance.

There was nothing wrong with being possessive, but he didn't want her to scar her soul more while defending them to the bloody end. She turned to Jasper and gave him a similar touch, placing her palm on his chest. "You two can do this."

"Thank you," the Golden Boy whispered.

Then she went back into the patient room, and Vincent looked at stormy blue eyes. "We're on our own."

"We are, and we need a lucky break."

"We do," he agreed.

25

QUINN

Quinn stepped closer to Elijah's bedside as Sawyer walked back in. He'd heard, thanks to the wolves, what had been said out there. He was glad she was considering the pack, how they worked together. It was easy for something like the jaguar to decide to go out on its own.

But Sawyer was remembering the pack. She was stronger with them backing her up, even if her actions were her own.

"Quinn," Elijah murmured, extending a hand. Quinn took it, a firm grip, knowing what the cowboy wanted. "I got into a car accident." The words were slurred from drugs the wolves could smell. Quinn knew what hospitals were like. He knew there were chemicals in Elijah that weren't natural. They eased the pain, though, so it didn't worry him.

"You did, and you nearly died," Quinn whispered. It had hurt to know Elijah was nearly gone on him. Like losing a limb, or losing one of his wolves. "Don't do that again. Sawyer doesn't like it."

"Haha." The cowboy snorted, looking at her. "Hey, little lady. I'm stuck in bed. Come be stuck with me."

"Oh good gods," she muttered, a small smile taking over her face. "Charlie?"

"He's fine. We stopped the bleeding in his brain, set and healed the breaks. Closed the lung, which actually did require cutting him open to set the rib that had punctured it. Then we healed that closed too. As long as he stays in bed and doesn't hit his head again, everything will heal just fine."

"No sign of long term problems?" James asked that. The wolves could smell their handler's worry and even a tinge of uncomfortable feelings, probably over the displays of affection between all of them.

"No. No signs of dead tissue. Since it was being watched and IMAS was all over the city, the first healers and EMTs got to him quickly enough." Charlie smiled at them. "Before I get out of here, I'll get Zander to come in so everyone is accounted for. He's burned through everything. Tried to get him out of the room when he burnt out, but he refused. Boy doesn't play anything safe, does he? Touched his life force like an idiot and then three of us forced him out."

"He's...known for reckless behavior when he's healing," Quinn explained.

"He's known for just being reckless in general," she corrected, grinning. "But it's a good reckless. We know he'll never let any of us die."

"Well, with that all taken care of, I'm going to let you guys keep an eye on this one." The big black man pointed at Elijah. "I need to get home."

"Be safe, Charlie." Sawyer walked to hug him and it was a good solid embrace. "I hear you might be the only civilian Magi in the city now."

"Like a fucking assassin is going to chase me out of my city. The others are just fucking pussies. They didn't know one had been here for years already." Charlie shook his head. "Plus, I can't leave the gym to fucking Liam - who, by the way, has been up my fucking ass about everything going on. Boy loves you too damn much. Oh, and all the older kids have been rooting you on and telling everyone they can about you. Shadow's kids, they call themselves."

"Save them from themselves," she muttered, letting him go.

"I'm trying," the old man grumbled back. "I'm going to take a fucking nap first."

"I should also be going," James said, looking between them. "It's...been an interesting night. I'm glad everyone here is okay. I think I need to start working on making sure this isn't all broken up. It's the only thing I can do for you right now."

"Thanks, dude!" Elijah grinned. "Wait. Fix what?" Elijah frowned, a dopey frown that looked like something Quinn had seen in a cartoon one of them had made him watch before.

"It's not memory loss. He's super drugged," Charlie said, leaving the room.

"Us being broken up because I'm with all of you in a romantic relationship that is not only inappropriate, but... against conventional standards," she explained, smiling as she sat on the other side of his bed again. Quinn enjoyed how close they were in that moment, around their injured packmate. Everyone had their places. Vincent and Jasper were on the hunt for the pack's safety. Zander was resting from saving a member of the pack. He and Sawyer were supporting the injured pack mate as he recovered in a safe environment. Such a natural way for them all to fit together.

"Oh. That. Fuck them. I got plans. She's staying with me." Elijah said it simply.

"Plans?" he asked softly, sitting down on the bed as well now.

"Yeah. Those plans." The cowboy gave the most exaggerated wink of all time. It wasn't hard to figure out exactly what those plans were, not for him, but the cowboy decided to elaborate. "You know. The plans where we both-"

"Let's not talk about those plans here," he said quietly, eyeing James. "If you don't want to be uncomfortable, you might want to leave."

"Yeah. I'm going. Need to speak to Thompson immediately. I'm sure that video is now viral. I've been avoiding checking the news...or answering my phone." At that, their handler did look down at it and groaned. "Yup. Ten missed calls. All Thompson. Forty-two texts."

Quinn didn't have anything to say to that.

James waved at them, wished them well once more and left.

When he was gone, Quinn finally relaxed more, leaned down further and placed his forehead to Elijah's. "I'm glad you're going to be okay."

"Yeah, bud, I'll be fine." He dragged fine out. "Now why don't both of you relax with me. There's space."

There wasn't, but Quinn backed off so Sawyer could crawl a little further on the bed. Something about the sight of that made him growl in pleasure. Sawyer crawling into a bed with them in it.

"Those plans," he murmured, looking between them.

"Oh." Realization dawned on her face. "By the fucking gods, you two."

"Yeah, the *fucking* gods," Elijah said crudely, grinning.

"You can't...do that," Zander said walking in. "No

fucking. You'll lie in that bed and fucking heal, you god damned perverted cowboy."

Zander looked exhausted, too worn, something that was common since the man couldn't resist doing literally anything in his power and beyond it to help someone.

"Go sleep on my bed," she ordered softly. "And thank you for helping Elijah."

"Of course. You love him. He's my teammate, my family. I was going to keep him alive. No reason to say thank you, babe." Zander smiled wearily. It was an attempt, at least. Then he walked to her empty hospital bed and collapsed, snoring in only a few moments.

"We should turn the news on and keep an eye on it. Watch out for that WMC announcement. Work." Quinn was already reaching for the remote as he said it.

"Of course. We can brainstorm while Jasper and Vincent are safe at the IMPO headquarters."

"And I will keep us safe here," he promised her. He glanced at Elijah, noting that he was silent already, and saw that the cowboy had passed out between sentences. Just out like something flipped a switch. It was good to see him resting. "You all need rest. I am fine."

"Thank you, love," she murmured, her head nestling gently next to Elijah. He saw she was careful to not put any sort of weight on him.

"Of course."

He watched her eyes drift to a close.

Soon enough, he had three people all giving him a melody of the quiet snores of sleep. Not the animals, though, who took that moment to get up and stretch. He eyed Sombra, the dangerous jaguar. He couldn't feel her like his wolves - that was up to Sawyer - but he hoped his boys would tell him if anything was wrong. So far, the only thing they had told him was that she worried about her Magi. Her human had been hurt and one of her males had been hurt.

He watched the news while the animals jumped around. Even Kaar was hopping around, staying inside with them. It was unusual for the raven to stay when Vincent left. He tried to peck at Sombra, who gave him a lazy swat, making the bird puff up, trying to be bigger. The wolves found it humorous.

"Don't you know that cats eat birds?" he asked, his eyes on the news.

Kaar jumped on Sombra's back like it wasn't a big deal. The jaguar bared her teeth, but nothing happened.

He had gone from hunting assassins to babysitting the animals. He wanted to think this was an unusual occurrence, but really, it felt more normal than anything else had in New York.

Hours passed, and he got no word from anyone. Sawyer woke up at one point, pulling up a chair to sit next to him between the two beds. It was an amicable silence, their shoulders touching. Every so often, he would reach out to touch her hand, hold it for a moment, to let her know he was there. She would squeeze it, letting him know that she knew.

That was all he wanted, really. He liked the quietness. There was no great public passion between them, though the possibility was there. In the months since the Amazon, they had become silent. The silence wasn't bad; they had just moved on from needing to say anything. A simple touch told them each what they needed to know.

He loved her.

She loved him.

They were pack and belonged with each other. They could support each other and would always do so.

"I am glad you have...found peace with Elijah." He wasn't sure how to word it. "I had hoped you would love him. He needs love."

"You all need love. Everyone needs love." She smiled. "God, listen to me. 'Love fixes everything.' What have I become?"

"I like it," he murmured.

"I do too," she whispered, keeping her eyes on the screen. "Oh, fucking finally. Thought this was going to be a morning release."

"New from the WMC today. They have decided not to do special elections to refill the seats of the Council, and instead elected a Head of Council, Councilman Suarez. This is due to the state of emergency that the Council is facing. The attack on a safe house where over half of the Council members are staying, and the severe injuries sustained by Sawyer Matthews and Elijah Grant, has led them to this decision." The anchor looked pale and his face was pinched, as if he knew something the viewers didn't. "Have a nice afternoon, everyone."

Quinn frowned. That hadn't been what James told them would happen.

Sawyer was on her phone in a second, talking away with Vincent.

Quinn just kept frowning. Politics of this sort weren't his expertise. He would do as the team told him.

26

SAWYER

Well, what the actual fuck.

"Just saw it. No one was warned," Vincent said as he answered the phone. "I'm going to guess that you have an idea."

"Yeah. Let's talk to Dina." Sawyer couldn't believe those words were coming out of her mouth.

"What?" He sounded just as shocked as she felt. She heard a growl from Quinn, but had to ignore it for a moment so she could explain.

"We know Dina. This is obviously some behind closed doors politics. This could very well be, and possibly is connected to what's going on." She took a deep breath. "And Dina owes us. She owes me." For the secrets she planned on keeping for the Councilwoman. For the things Dina had put her and her team through.

She owed them.

If Dina was as morally righteous as Sawyer believed she could be, then this was just a way for the woman to help do what's right. If it was connected, anyway.

"You're right. I haven't made any progress here. We've been

looking through financial records, but we were downright refused the records for individual Council members." Vincent groaned. "Damn it. I was going to call you the same moment to say I think this had something to do with it all. You just shocked me by saying Dina. It's a solid idea. Jasper and I-"

"I'm going too. We'll leave Quinn to protect Elijah and Zander, while we handle Dina."

"Should we bring James?" he asked. "Don't answer that. I'm going to bring him as well. He's been stalking around the building, yelling at people. We're getting some dirty looks because of what happened last night. And the Triad member? Adaih? He's not talking, so everyone is pretty pissed off at everything."

"Okay. Come pick me up." She hung up. She had known that assassin wouldn't talk, but she had said it on the first day in New York: this was all moving so fast.

Too fast.

Something, in the back of her mind, realized why. It clicked.

The Triad weren't making the rules. No, they would want to slow down. They would want to wait for the heat to cool and drop off before going after another target. They wouldn't roam into a building full of guards. They weren't stupid.

They were being pushed to go quickly. But by who?

That was the important part.

She chewed on that thought.

Too fast. Too bold. Too big.

The Triad were also out of their depth. That's why all three of them had come after her. They had assumed she would set the trap, but did they have time to plan for who on her team would be there with her?

And now a major political shift. The person behind the scenes?

"Quinn?" She looked to her beautiful man, who was frowning still. The frown hadn't left since the announcement.

"Go. I will protect them here. If you get a lead, I'll stay. You, Vincent, and Jasper can handle anything."

"Are you sure? We could leave Jasper here and take you instead." She was fine either way with who was going to dig deeper with her.

He shook his head in return. "I don't like the city and don't think I can serve you well here. Let me..." He glanced at Elijah. "Let me stay here."

She leaned down and kissed his forehead. He tilted up to capture her lips before she could pull away.

Oh, she understood the need to just curl in with those who were hurt and protect them, to viciously guard them. It didn't help that Quinn was so out of his element.

"Keep the animals safe as well?" she murmured against his lips.

"Of course. Take Sombra, though. I'll keep Kaar for Vincent, but I think you need your jaguar."

She resisted. Their training wasn't done. She and the jaguar had a hard time achieving certain things in the bond and...

Sawyer didn't want to risk losing that piece of her soul again.

He seemed unmovable about it, though. He wouldn't let her walk out of the hospital room without her jaguar and it was apparent.

"Okay." She looked over to Sombra, who jumped up immediately.

She would fight with her Magi. She would be perfect. She would keep the males from being hurt again.

"Well, baby, we're not going to fight; we're just going to see an old...friend." Everything they were doing was just precautionary. Keeping someone to protect their guys who were down, having people together. It was all precautionary. "I should get down and meet them at the visitor's parking."

"Okay." Quinn stood up and kissed her slowly.

She couldn't find words, just grazed her hand over his cheek. It was all that was needed.

I love you, and be safe.

She found her weapons and put them on. She got her boots and laced them up. She felt like she was preparing for war. It was just Dina. How bad could she be?

"I HATE THIS," James muttered. "God, you kids are just asking for trouble."

"How bad could it be?" she asked, looking back at him from the passenger seat of his car.

"You three are considering blackmailing or coercing a WMC council member to give up private information. All of these votes have been behind closed doors, and that information is supposed to stay with them. Forever. It's..." James shook his head. "Breaking laws."

"To save their lives."

"Oh, that I know. I know your intentions. I agree with them, but there has to be better ways than going after Dina."

"And those are?" Vincent asked softly.

"I don't know." James sounded defeated. "It's why I'm driving. I hate this idea, but it's what you have."

"I seriously can't believe everyone else is just...on auto-pilot." She shook her head. "It feels like we're alone in this."

"In a sense, we are," James reminded her. "I still can't believe, Vincent, that you didn't tell me your suspicions earlier."

"I was afraid, and we were trying to play things quietly."

"I get that, but I would have been able to help. I could have talked to Thompson, told him that you had a lead that you felt safer delving into on your own, without the rest of the IMPO agents around you. As for the rest of them... others might be thinking on it, but no one is going to act on it like you kids do. They care about their careers, looking good, not making enemies in the WMC. On top of that, there's a problem with...what's that Southern saying? Passing the buck? They want others to take risks like that, jeopardize their careers and lives."

"Cowards," she snorted, shaking her head with disdain.

"Most IMPO are also WMC loyalists. They'll turn a blind eye to anything, since to them, the WMC is the moral center of our community. The WMC versus criminals." Vincent sighed heavily. "Yeah, we are alone."

"It's why you're such a good team, though," James said kindly. "You all offer different perspectives that most agents don't have. Sure, there's some other reformed criminals in the IMPO. Same for IMAS, but not a concentrated group of different like you all are. It's why you guys get the hate you get. It's why you're the outcasts that you are."

Sawyer just let that all sink in. During her time with the team, it had been nearly withdrawn from the rest of the IMPO, except for the short trip before the Amazon, and the two times she had seen Jon Aguirre's team in Atlanta. Most of her time had been spent at their plantation home, away from it all.

"Vincent, how does the chain of events work here?" their handler asked, curiously.

"A member of the WMC has been plotting against his or her political opponents. Maybe they also disagree with Sawyer being let to walk free, much like Dina. Sawyer's identity goes public, causing a shift in public perception for the WMC, making them seem even more corrupt than usual, which leaves them vulnerable. He or she hires the Triad to take out his political enemies, and there are a couple of options as to why they would go after Sawyer."

She knew both these options, so she said it. "One, they want me dead because justice or whatever, but they hired assassins. That option would make them hypocrites. The second idea is that they find me a threat to their plans. I know assassins. I was one. I am still considered one by many, because those aren't skills that just...poof, disappear."

"Second option is more likely. If this was someone who despised the idea of criminals near the government, they would have gone a different route." Vincent leaned back. "But, since I don't know the who, I don't understand the end game. Are they trying to just pick off certain members? Are they trying to take out the entire Council? I need to know what's happening in the Chamber. I need to know the players. Dina can tell me that."

James muttered something about vigilantes that she didn't understand as they pulled into the parking lot of the hotel turned safehouse.

"Is she even going to be here?" she asked.

"Yeah. After the announcement, most of the WMC decided to head out, since the important business of the day was done. With it also being the holidays, they don't have a lot of the general administration they normally have in the busier seasons, like spring." James got out and she followed.

Vincent and Jasper climbed out of the back seat. Together, a unit, they walked into the safehouse. James did all the talking, requesting if Councilwoman D'Angelo would speak to them.

She couldn't resist the mental chuckle of the name, remembering how she teased Dina when they met for it. Sawyer was never going to like this woman, but today was supposed be a day of partnership. Of hoping that they could work together.

"I don't think Dina is behind this. Do you?"

Sawyer shook her head at the telepathic question. No, she felt Dina had too many of her own secrets for a plot quite like this one. She seemed to want to protect her nephews, and this would risk exposing them.

Though, a boy with the ability for prophecy...

No. Dina wasn't behind this. Sawyer was convinced of that.

They were escorted to her room where the IMAS soldier on guard knocked only a couple of times.

"Come in," the feminine voice called out.

The door opened and James led the group in. It looked better that he seemed to be the 'point,' since he was their boss, the one who did these sort of meetings with those in charge of the IMPO and WMC more regularly than someone like her or Vincent.

She looked tired, immediately, to Sawyer. Worn down and trying to relax after an exhausting day. The boys were bouncing on the bed, watching something on the television.

"Oh, what can I do for you all?" she asked, perking up, putting on a professional mask as she stood up from her chair.

"We need to speak to you alone," James said gently,

nonthreatening. She waved the guard away and soon, they were closed in alone with Dina D'Angelo.

"What is it?" She sounded expectant.

"We need to know...any strange occurrences recently in the Council Chamber," Vincent said carefully. "I have a... strong suspicion that what is going on is rooted very close to the center of our government."

"I thought so. I'll tell you what I can." Sawyer raised an eyebrow, and Dina must have seen it. "A family member gave me a word of advice recently." Sawyer swallowed. Her eyes drifted to the boys, who ignored her. Dina didn't say the advice. "So, you think one of the Council is killing off the others."

"We do," James confirmed.

"I'm inclined to agree after today. Councilman Suarez is someone you should look at. First, he was vocally for special elections. He's friends with everyone, and so when someone offered the idea of electing a temporary Head of Council, we went with him. There was no reason not to. He's a moderate, can play both sides, get all the votes, and keep things reasonable between everyone." Dina groaned, shoving some papers around on her small desk. "Then, he took the position and immediately flipped. Now, there won't be any special elections. Actually, he wants us all to stay where we are, in a holding pattern. He wants the IMPO to continue as they have been. Even after last night's incident, special elections are important. We *need* to plan for after this. Everyone on the Council agreed on that."

"Anything else unusual?" Jasper asked.

"Have a seat, young man. I bet that leg isn't comfortable." She waved to her chair, but Jasper politely declined. "I tried. And no, but I have..."

"A feeling," Sawyer murmured. Then she watched Dina glance at the boys. One even looked from the television.

"Sometimes, you just have to go with your gut," he said brightly. "In the end, we're all animals with instincts, and those very rarely fail us."

Shivers ran down her spine.

"Yes, Lucian, sometimes we just need to do what feels the best, what feels right." Dina smiled gently. "They told me earlier that my suspicions would help you...and that, uh...if this didn't end very soon, it wouldn't."

"We'll investigate him," Vincent promised. He was also looking at the young boys, a little confused. "Councilwoman...is there anything else except a gut feeling?"

"Look, I can't tell you anything more than that. There's nothing to tell, honestly, that would help you from a legal standpoint. I'll say that if this goes wrong, I will tell everyone that I sent you against Suarez. We can all go down together, or you'll be seen as victims of a WMC trying to get back at another one. Something."

There was something harried about that. Something that made Sawyer think Dina was right, not just because of cryptic hints from the boys, but rather, because they told her, plain and simple.

"We'll investigate."

"You three will investigate," James corrected. "Councilwoman, do you mind if I stay and put myself on your personal protection? I worry that you publicly having us as visitors, and Sawyer's place in this investigation, may make you more of a target. I would feel...a tremendous guilt if it happened and we left no one here with you."

"You may, and thank you for the concern, James, especially after everything I've done to your team."

"It's in the past. Right now, we will only focus on this situation and the future. We can always be better people tomorrow, even if we can't change the past."

Sawyer looked down to the carpet at that, as Dina looked at her.

"Yes, yes we can be better people tomorrow," the Councilwoman murmured. "Please have a seat. We can play cards while the boys watch their favorite show until their bedtime."

"Of course." James smiled kindly, then looked at the team. "I can't know what you plan, but I hope those plans see you to victory."

The boys, Lucian and Adrian, said nothing, something Sawyer was thankful for.

"We'll keep you updated on everything, James," Jasper said, patting their handler on the shoulder.

"Good. Go on. Godspeed."

Sawyer shook his hand before walking out, the guys all doing the same, and Vincent gave Dina a small thank you. They didn't slow down, just walked straight for their car. They didn't want to get stopped by any of the IMAS soldiers for updates.

When they got into the car, she looked at Jasper in the back, since Vincent was driving. "What were the other IMPO agents saying at Headquarters today?"

"They gave us a lot of well-wishes for you and Elijah, actually. They thought you two did everything possible to catch the Triad, were impressed that you apprehended one, and hoped you didn't die. It was...surprising, at least their sympathy to you." Jasper gave her a gentle smile. "Seriously. They were all impressed with it. Many begrudgingly, mind you, but they still offered their condolences to the injuries and the public scene."

"Thompson pulled us aside, though, about the video of you and Elijah," Vincent said, not even glancing over. He was driving, and after the accident, she was glad he didn't look over, even for a millisecond. "He's...well, he was worried for you both, even though you'll both recover, and also upset about the other stuff. He was told by James there was nothing romantic going on, and that's now...definitely a lie. It doesn't help it was Elijah, who you were on a date with."

"No, I bet it doesn't help..."

She remembered that moment, the smoke and twisted metal. The fear, the pain, physical and emotional. The suddenness. Even in that moment, it gave her a pause. She had to force herself to think of him in the hospital, drugged up and dopey.

"He said any major discussions will come after this is all over, but he's unsure with how he'll fall on it." Vincent sighed. "Now, what do we want to do tonight?"

"I say an office break-in, like we did with the sheriff in Texas. Or set up surveillance on him." Sawyer leaned back in her seat again.

"What was with Dina's nephews?" he asked, that confused look back on his face.

"One...has future sight, prophecy," she whispered, almost like if she said it too loud, it would get out, go public. "I don't know which, but they are...strange kids. I ran into them the day she arrived in New York."

"Are you certain? They are way too young for their powers to manifest."

"One had telepathy and told me...something. It wasn't anything important. Something about my mask breaking."

"Well, fuck," Jasper muttered. "Let's get back to the hospital and plan a break-in on the WMC building tonight."

"Sawyer?" Vincent looked at her expectantly.

"Yeah, I can get us into the WMC building tonight." She had no doubt of that. When this had all started, she had been feeling somewhat perversely excited about stretching her skills out, dusting the rust off them. Now she felt honed and ready.

A break-in? That was child's play.

27

SAWYER

In the end, the plan wasn't difficult. Sawyer's solution to their problem was honesty. They would tell the guards they were investigating a lead and walk through the front door.

"You guys always think I'm going to come up with some outrageous plan, but it's not that big of a deal. Vincent, you have Thompson on the line?"

"Yeah. Sir, are you-" Vincent stopped as Thompson spoke on the other end, but she couldn't hear anything. "We need this to stay between us. I want to go in without fanfare. I want no one to know until we're in the building. It'll stop them from hiding anything, if they're there to try and hide anything...Yes sir, I understand. I know this puts you in a very difficult position. You brought me on the investigation side of things because I look in different places. If James thinks this is plausible-"

It went on like that and she just leaned back in the chair. They were back in the hospital. She took a few pills to battle a headache, but it was the only thing that the concussion had given her yet, and it might not have even been that. The bruising from the accident was sore, but she had been in rough places before. She didn't think it would hold her back, if push came to shove.

A large hand reached out and rubbed the top of her head. She side-eyed the owner of the hand. Drugged-up Elijah was grinning at her.

"You be good," he ordered.

"Never," she promised, a grin taking over her face at the dismay on his.

"She's teasing you," Quinn mumbled, a small smile playing on his full lips.

"Thank you, sir. I really appreciate this." Vincent hung up. "He's good. He's willing to validate our investigation if anyone decides to call him about us. We're not going to be breaking any laws. He's...wary, but he's got a lot riding on this."

"If we're wrong, we all go down. We're not wrong." She was confident. It was one of the WMC, maybe even the one Dina had a feeling about. First they needed the evidence.

And Sawyer wanted to know, so bad, what idiot pushed the Triad past their limit, forced them to get sloppy. Those three were unstoppable, given time and their resources. They had a failure rate of zero, until her, and she had a feeling that she was only still alive because they were being pushed to do things that didn't show them as the professionals they were.

"Let's head out." He waved her and Jasper to follow him out of the room, but she didn't immediately jump up. Instead, she looked towards the window. Night had fallen. Her fingers itched. Her mask would be great for this.

No.

She was here as a Probationary Agent of the IMPO. Not a professional criminal. The mask was unnecessary.

She jumped up and followed him after reminding herself of that. It was time to do her job.

They rode in silence. They already knew how this would play out. They would investigate the new Head of Council first. He was top of the list thanks to Dina and her boys. Thank the gods for them, that entire family. She never thought she would think that. Thank the gods for the D'Angelos.

She shook her head at the thought. Ridiculous and appropriate.

"I have a feeling," she said finally, as they pulled into the parking garage across the street, "that something is going to happen tonight."

"Why?" Jasper asked. "After what happened last night-"

"Exactly. Whoever is behind this is pushing the Triad, and pushing them hard. They're sloppy, in a sense. Mind you, if me and the guys hadn't been there, there would be dead WMC Council members. They aren't bad, but they had to get a getaway driver."

"I think you surviving the first attempt fucked up their plans," Vincent added. "And now they're off the plan. They're trying to catch up. You were the target yesterday. It means they really want you dead before continuing. They sent all three after you. You get in their way, unlike anyone else."

"I know - just look at how good I made the security for the WMC. And look at you guys. We're riding their asses, and whoever it is, well, they're about to know. If they had killed me back at the house, you all would have been ineffectual in this. An entire strong team of IMPO Special Agents, out of the problem. Instead, we all came to New York."

"So you think they will continue to try and push and pressure. To get their plans back on track."

"Yeah, because the Triad isn't stupid, but whoever hired them sure is." Sawyer got out of the car and began walking for the WMC building. The guys jumped out and followed her.

She walked up to the first guard, flanked by Vincent and Jasper, but didn't say anything.

"We're here to continue our investigation of who is behind the assassinations. Please, let us in." Vincent sounded so much better than the IMAS guards, like he lived in a different world, one that was leagues from the foot soldiers.

"Sir, no one is allowed in the building after hours."

"You can take that up with Director Thompson."

"No, sir, you don't understand. Councilman Suarez has expressly stated that under no circumstance can anyone enter this building. He believes it's a security risk." The guard sighed. "If anything, he's very paranoid of someone, like...bombing the building. That's the reason he gave, anyway. He thinks it could be anyone on the security teams too, or even the IMPO. He's been in there all night, thinking it's safer than going to the safe house made 'safe' by the assassin." The guard's eyes fell on her and Sawyer raised an eyebrow. The gaze quickly fell. "I don't think that. But seriously, I can't lose my job. You'll have to come back tomorrow."

"Interesting..." Vincent murmured, turning away. As a group, they walked back to the parking garage, but once out of sight of anyone, she grabbed each of them and cloaked.

"I can't hold this long, but we're all trained. If we hurry, I can get us into the building."

"There's no color," the Italian noted, looking around.

"I should have warned you."

"I noticed the same thing my first time too," Jasper said to him, as they turned again and began walking back towards the building.

Sawyer had gotten a good enough read on the guard to know he was a weak enough Magi that she could get nearly twenty feet from him before he even could begin to feel her magic in the night. That gave her more than enough space to get the guys to the side of the building.

They watched a roaming patrol walk away at that moment. Since she'd been a part of the security team, she had spent some time looking over the guards for the actual WMC building. She didn't have a say in it, but she knew the system they had.

In less than a minute, another patrol would walk around the building.

"Move," she hissed, nodding to a window. Neither of the guys questioned it. Once there, she was pleased to see Vincent and Jasper each get in by their own ways. Vincent sublimated and slid through a tiny crack, the window not sealed properly. Jasper walked straight through the wall. She went Jasper's route, going through.

"Where are we?" their leader asked inside.

"A restroom, obviously," she answered, going to check the stalls first. No one was there and the guards were outside. "Fun fact, the building should be fairly clear now. Most of the security is outside. There's no cameras in here."

"Suarez is here, so his security team should be as well," Vincent reminded her. "Also, quite paranoid of him to decide to hide in this building and keep everyone out of it, no matter the reason. I don't like his implication that it's someone on security trying to do this."

"Think the paranoia might make him innocent?"

Sawyer frowned at Jasper's question. It was a solid point. Getting power in a situation like this made Suarez a bigger target. He could have easily freaked out and gone off the deep end.

"We'll keep that in consideration." Vincent was diplomatic about it. "How do you want to do this?" That was directed at her again.

"I can keep us cloaked, but it's a drain. I think we might just be able to sneak. We're not the Triad, so another Magi could feel us anyway and it's all over." She didn't really see them getting out of this without being caught. It was why her plan had involved the 'proper channels' originally. Sometimes, to get something done, you had to go with the right way. "You know what weirds me out? This Suarez didn't tell anyone outside the building that they weren't allowed in. Like, that's something the IMPO needed to know."

"I won't argue with that; it is uncomfortable." Vincent leaned on the wall, crossing his arms. "I'm going to text James, let him know, before we get moving."

They all waited for that and, as a unit, left the restroom together. She was right; there were no guards patrolling the hallways that she could see. There would be cameras and a security team watching them, but she had a feeling that in a building the size of the WMC, not all the cameras could be watched at once.

She had never studied the blueprints of the WMC, because they weren't public record and would never be available to the public. She knew the few copies of them that existed were kept under lock and key, only pulled out if renovations or repairs were needed. Even then, the person viewing them only saw a small portion of the full picture, the part they needed.

She did know where the cameras were, though, and kept her head down, knowing the guys would follow her lead.

They took the stairs to the third floor, where the Council members' offices were, but they didn't leave the stairwell immediately.

"Should we each do a room? We would move faster." It had been their plan to do each room as a team, but that had been when they were planning on legally being in the building. Now, she figured they needed the speed.

"Yes. Let's move."

She opened the door to leave the stairwell and narrowed her eyes at a completely empty hallway. There should have been some sort of security if Suarez's office was on the floor, but there was nothing. No one. She couldn't even hear a guard walking around. The silence was almost too much.

"We got lucky," Jasper muttered, sliding past her. She watched him phase into the first office. She didn't find it lucky.

She found it out of place.

She watched Vincent go to the next closest office and sublimate to slide underneath the crack of the door. This was why they were the ones doing this. The three of them had more elusive abilities, and it was hard for anyone to keep them out of anything.

She didn't go in the third office, her gut telling her to find out why there was no sound. She rounded a corner, then another. Still no guards. She eventually lost the tension in her shoulders, the one where she knew she was slinking around and could get caught.

There was no one to catch her.

Her eyes narrowed on a door with a name plaque. She'd passed a few of the Council members' offices at this point and was near the one that should have had guards posted at the door.

There was still no one.

She stepped closer to the door and began to listen, something going cold in her. They would know she was out there, and for a moment, under her fury, she was okay with that.

"How is she here?" a rich, masculine asked. "No one should be in the building. I'm the Head of Council. They should all be following my orders. And *she* should be dead. He said she would only get in my way, every step of it, and he was right."

"She's a rogue," Naseem whispered. "She was, from all the rumors, never very good at following the orders of her superiors. She's also an expert. Axel made her very good at what she does. I knew killing her would be a challenge."

"Yes, that was mentioned once by Axel in his interrogations. It made me wary of her working for the WMC and IMPO."

She pulled open the door at that, staring down the man behind the desk. That was a name she hadn't wanted to hear tonight. Suarez was an attractive man, Latino with brilliant brown eyes. He was put together and looked every bit a Councilman.

Naseem stood to his left, like he had turned to look at the door when he'd been facing Suarez previously.

Before she could step inside, a shield slammed down in front of her.

That just pissed her off. She turned to the third body in the room, her eyes narrowing. He was wearing an IMPO uniform, the standard black, but without the heavy firearms the IMAS soldiers carried around.

Fucking dirty-ass cops. Dirty politicians.

The WMC didn't need her to ruin their reputation. They were very good at doing it themselves.

"I take it you're the getaway driver," she crooned. "I have a bone to pick with you too." She turned for a moment, knowing that shield kept them all safe from each other. "Vincent! Here!"

"Coming. Jasper as well."

She waited patiently, that something cold in her taking over. She went back to giving the Councilman, the assassin, and the IMPO agent the blank stare she knew she had on her face.

It took Vincent and Jasper only seconds to find her, and in turn, the group shielded in the office. Vincent narrowed his eyes at them as Jasper pulled out his phone, took a quick picture and sent it to someone.

"That was to Thompson," he explained. "Should be enough evidence."

"Naseem, make sure you take care of that for me," Suarez said casually. "Tonight."

"Of course," the assassin whispered. Then he phased down through the floor.

"Go," Vincent ordered her. "Stop him. We'll handle these two."

She didn't bother giving a response, dropping down as well, before anything else could be said to her. She landed in a large meeting room, Naseem in front of her.

"Are you ready to finish this, Shadow?"

"Are you?" she asked, unsheathing a dagger. She hadn't been unarmed since that night. Even in James' condo, her weapons had been close enough to have them within a second of waking up.

The rust had worn off. Now it was time to see who was better.

28

JASPER

"Who is this agent?" Vincent asked softly, pointing to the IMPO agent in the room with the Councilman.

"Special Agent Deacon," the man answered. "You're Vincent Castello and your buddy is Jasper Williams. Now that introductions are out of the way, I think you two should turn around and walk away from this."

"Why?" Jasper asked, glaring at the other agent. "Why are you working to undermine everything our people have built?"

"Because the world is a fucked up place, tied up in red tape. Suarez believes that with a single ruler, the Magi world can be better. One vision, and everyone working to that goal. Not fifteen ideas of what's right and wrong and everyone arguing about it."

"Power." Vincent's answer was much simpler. "You're power-hungry. Tell me, had any long chats with my brother? He's power-hungry too. Believes he can rule the world, make it in his image. The only reason he was ever caught was due to a moment of insanity, an obsession that wouldn't release him from its hold."

Such a casual reference of Axel, but Jasper knew the reason. The WMC had Axel, and Axel was charismatic and intelligent. He also was helpful now. The model prisoner. It would make sense that someone looking to overthrow their government would go to him.

"Naseem should be done with Shadow now," Suarez said casually to Deacon. "Handle these two for me while he handles the Director. Can't have Thompson in power anyway. He's too good. I need someone a bit more...flexible."

"Where's Kalama?" Vincent asked softly. "Tell me. If I'm going to die, let me hear the plan that I couldn't figure out."

Jasper didn't like the way he was talking. He didn't like that Vincent felt like he didn't know.

"Kalama is taking care of the rest of the WMC. Heard you had a chat with D'Angelo today. Interesting, since you and she hate each other. She'll be going first."

"I'm so fucking tired of power-hungry maniacs." Jasper crossed his arms, but it didn't make him any less ready for a fight.

"Me too," his friend whispered. "Well, Deacon. Come try to kill us."

The shield dropped and reformed over just the Councilman, who stayed seated in his chair.

"He has shielding, petrification, and-"

A boom cut Vincent off. Jasper figured out what the last power was. Sound manipulation. Deacon had only snapped his fingers. The boom shook the building and was strong enough to send both of them back into the wall on the other side of the hallway.

Jasper scrambled to get moving, pulling his sidearm. He felt a shield clamp down over him, preventing his first shot from hitting its target. He'd been bubbled in, and the bullet ricocheted around him.

"Shit!" He tried one more shot, hoping to crack the shield. That bullet bounced and sliced over his arm. "Fuck me!"

Deacon went for Vincent, who sublimated and got around behind him before reforming. When he was human again, Vin already had a small blade out, going for a strike at Deacon's back.

Deacon spun, just as well-trained, his fingers finding a grasp on Vincent's wrist, skin to skin.

Jasper knew the moment Vin lost the internal battle of who would petrify who. Vincent was still breathing but nothing else. His eyes were narrowed, still locked in the focus of attack.

The traitor grinned. "Kids. You think you can win every fight." He took the dagger out of Vincent's hand.

Jasper roared, firing the rest of his magazine into the shield, and Deacon slid the dagger into Vincent as the last two shots made cracks.

Out of ammo, he kicked the shield as hard as he could with his fake leg. It would tolerate the force he was putting into it.

The shield shattered, sending a small shockwave of power out.

Deacon stumbled, glaring at him, the dagger out of Vincent's gut already.

Jasper rushed to his feet and tackled the man before he could react. He disarmed the enemy, taking the dagger. He had it in Deacon's chest before anything else could be done.

"No. Not another one of my teammates." Jasper growled down at him as the life left the agent's eyes. He felt feral like

Quinn. Angry like Sawyer. He thought of what this man had done to Vincent. Thought of what he did to Elijah.

A thump behind him had him turning from the dead body underneath him.

Vincent was on the floor, holding the wound on his stomach. Jasper jumped up and pulled up his friend's shirt to look at it. Blood was everywhere.

He glared at the Councilman trying to walk out, taking Vincent's gun and aiming at the man. "If you move from that spot, I'll just shoot you."

Suarez raised his hands and went down to his knees in defeat.

"You don't have any offensive magic. Telepathy and aura reading. Good abilities. Worthless in this case." Jasper was furious. "You have dishonored our people. You have destroyed the trust I have in the WMC. I'm going to watch you fall for it."

"Jasper...call nine one one." Vincent groaned.

Jasper cursed, keeping his gun trained on the Councilman with one hand as he pulled out his phone. He dialed, put it on speaker, then dropped it on the floor. He pressed his free hand to the gut wound, hoping to slow the bleeding.

He yelled at the operator. He needed someone to get to him, and he needed them now.

29

JAMES

When night fell, James watched Dina send her boys to bed. Her nephews. Her very odd nephews.

"Do you really think its Suarez?" he asked calmly. They hadn't spoken of anything important the entire time the children were in the room.

"I know it is," she admitted softly. "But...I can't risk my nephews."

"Of course. I would never ask you to." He would never expose children like that, no matter the situation. The adults could handle it. Those boys deserved happy lives, good lives. "We can talk about something else, then."

"The team. The news. Elijah Grant and Sawyer Matthews." Dina gave him a shrewd smile. "You think I never thought something was going on there? I have empathy like you. I just paid attention and read between the lines. I'm also a woman. I think I know how another woman feels about the men around her."

"Why are all Magi politicians and schemers?" he asked himself softly, leaning back in his seat.

"We're not. You just live in the part of our community that is full of the best of them." Dina's smile softened. "Give me your reasons why the WMC and Thompson shouldn't split your team, James."

"They need each other. Together, they are nigh unstoppable. They have complimentary skills and a bond tighter than most teams I've ever seen." He didn't say that bond was because they all loved her, or she loved all of them. It was something he was still wrapping his head around. To be in a real relationship with five men? It screamed...*inappropriate*, but this was a more modern time. If anyone could pull it off, it was them. "And look at what they've already done together. Look at what their accomplishments have led to. And they never take any of the credit. They go home. They live private lives. Jasper continues his education. So does *Quinn*, who, mind you, is now finally caught up in some form of mandatory education."

"We've established contact with more Druids in the last month than we've ever had. We're building the bridges with a new understanding, and reconnecting families through it," Dina said as she took her seat again.

"And the IMPO has been its strongest in terms of organized crime in recent months. Because they caught Axel." He wasn't going to let her forget that. "They have taken every hit. So, I don't see why my team should be broken up because they got into an accident and Sawyer got emotional. Isn't that what you want to see? That the infamous Shadow has a heart that led her from a life of crime? That she can *feel*? So you can know that she regrets and understands guilt?"

Dina grabbed the deck of cards they had been playing with and began to shuffle them without a word. He was strangely impressed with her ability as she dealt them hands.

"Are you going to say anything?" He took his cards, not really looking at them.

"I'm not going to break them up. As long as they don't say anything about my nephews, I made a promise and I intend to keep it. I tried something dirty and underhanded. I look back on it all the time. She was smart to remind me that people...died for my scheme, and I..." Dina sighed. "I messed that all up, then I had to salvage it. Those soldiers would have gone there without Special Agent Judge, certainly. They would have been more severely injured, I believe. But still, I put more at risk." She gave him a vulnerable look. "I've had to live to regret that, even if my colleagues find it a normal day's work."

He wasn't sure if he believed the speech about regretting it, but he could see that she wouldn't risk pissing off Sawyer or the rest of the team. No, her nephews obviously meant the world to her. While all of the other Council members left their families at home, Dina brought those boys to keep them right at her side. She obviously cared for them like she was their mother.

"Let's play cards," he said, dropping the conversation.

It was a few hours later, too late in the evening, when his phone went off. He held up a finger to Dina, who looked tired herself, as he checked it.

It was a text from Thompson, who had forwarded him something from Jasper.

"Well, Dina. Your gut was right." He held up the image on his screen for her. Naseem with Councilman Suarez, who looked at ease, not in any danger. "This should all be over tonight. I bet they are arresting him right now."

"That's good-"

The blast blew open the door, sending it into the window, and flying out into the night.

James reached for Dina, grabbing her and pushing her head down with one hand as he pulled his sidearm with his left. He fired blindly at the door.

"STAY DOWN!" he roared as he pushed her towards the boys' room next door. "MOVE!"

She did, staying bent over as they got to the door. He didn't bother opening it as he fired another shot blindly at a now-building fire at the door of Dina's room. He pushed Dina through, keeping his hand on her so they could both phase using her magic.

Once inside, she ran for the boys as he positioned himself to stop anyone from coming through the door.

"Move!" one of the boys yelled and he did, jumping to the side as that door was blasted into the far wall. These fucking boys.

"Dina, get them out of here!" he demanded.

"No, I don't think so," a cruel, feminine voice said politely. James turned for the door. He hadn't felt any other Magi. He hadn't been looking, truthfully. The fire, the explosions. Those had mattered more. He saw her as she tried to plunge a sword in his chest.

It's very hard to phase when an object is coming towards someone at an unknown speed and force but he managed, jumping away before he lost it and the sword ended up in his chest.

"Go," he snapped to Dina, who nodded, grabbing the hands of the children and running for the door. Kalama practically hissed in anger as James took a potshot at her for her attention. "You'll have to kill me first."

"Fine."

She pulled fire in from the blaze in the other room and

tossed it at him. He rolled, taking a shot as he went. He didn't have anything except his sidearm. She dove at him with a short sword that was blazing.

He had less than a second to make a decision. None of the options were good ones.

He took the sword to his chest as he pulled the trigger, hoping for the best. She yanked it out, her eyes wide.

He looked down at the bleeding on her chest, falling to his knees as she stumbled back.

He heard a thump.

Fire consumed the room, wildly out of control.

He couldn't feel the heat.

30

SAWYER

Naseem made the first move, and it wasn't for her. He phased down again, a dangerous grin on his face. She followed, running after him the moment her feet touched the floor.

Her mind reeled. Was he really going to race her to Thompson? Was that the game they were going to play?

Yes. As he phased through a wall and she kept after him, she decided that it was exactly the game he wanted to play. She wasn't sure why, though. Thompson would already have the text. It would be on his phone. If he was smart, he would send it to others, as backup to the evidence.

She knew he was working in his office late, waiting on them to report to him. Well, he'd gotten his report in a single text, a single picture.

Naseem ran through the last wall to leave the WMC building and she followed close behind. They both made short work of the small alley and phased into the IMPO building. She knew this building better and went straight for the stairwell. It was a tall building, but she could make short work of it.

She lost Naseem, not knowing how he was going to scale the massive building. She looked up the center of the stairwell for a moment and blinked upwards, finding herself five stories up and about to fall down. She sublimated and got back on the stairs before doing it again to go higher. It took a lot of concentration to blink like this, knowing there was nothing to catch her at the spot she wanted to be at.

But she still made it up the stairwell much faster than an elevator could get her.

She burst out on the top floor and ran for Thompson's office, phasing through his door. He was just standing there, frowning at his phone, looking tired.

"Sir." She was breathing hard as she walked closer to him.

"Sawyer? What are you doing here?" He turned his frown on her.

"Sir, Naseem is coming for you. We need to get you to safety."

"Really?" Thompson dropped his phone on his desk. "I sent a copy of that image to James and several others, to make sure that everyone was on the same page at dawn." He pulled open the top drawer of his desk and pulled out a small pistol. "Do we want to bunker down here?"

"Yes..." She glanced at the door as she walked closer to him. "Stay away from the windows. Find a place..." She pointed to a corner near his fireplace. "There. You'll be able to see the entire room."

"I know." He seemed so relaxed. "I used to be an agent, Sawyer."

That explained it. He was trained. Like James. They had once been agents like the guys. They knew what they were doing.

"Don't shoot him. I want him alive," she said.

"I'll shoot him if I think you're going to die. Or I am. How's that?"

"I would prefer you just sit in the corner and pretend like you don't exist." She glanced at him. "Just...let me handle this."

"Because it's personal?"

She didn't want to say yes but it was the truth. She was taking this assassin down personally. For a thousand reasons, it seemed like, but now, the only one that mattered was her guys. He was a threat to her guys and she couldn't allow that.

She felt sweaty. Her palms were clammy. Her shirt stuck to her uncomfortably as her heartbeat refused to slow down.

Something had her anxious.

She had beaten Naseem to the top, which gave her the advantage. What was bothering her?

She closed her eyes for a moment, rubbing her temples.

A split second to catch her breath.

The sword sliced across her ribs and a laugh echoed in the room as she staggered away, shocked by the attack.

He had gotten in at some point and she hadn't even realized it. She hadn't been careful enough to look for the empty spot. The energy, the race, the adrenaline had distracted her.

"Axel's whore. You're fast, but please, you aren't better than me." Naseem attacked her again. She had to pull her daggers and deflect faster than she ever had before, forcing his sword off to her side. She responded, trying to get in his guard and deliver a quick hit to his gut.

She felt the push, the pressure.

A strong air manipulator could gently push people off their trajectories. A bullet, even a fraction over, would become ineffectual. A punch would land wide when it should have landed.

She had fought against them before, but air manipulators were a serious weakness for her, especially those with such minute control. Her secondary form was crippled by them, on top of her inability to land a hit.

He took the chance to slice open the other side of her ribs. Neither wound was fatal, by any means. He planned on wearing her down, making her hurt, proving he was the best there ever was in their business.

She blinked to get behind him and delivered her own hit on his back, scoring it open. He spun, going low and sending his blade upwards to strike her. She had to stagger back, her ribs aching.

"I've killed a Druid in open combat. What makes you think I'm going to die to you?" she demanded, watching him dance away after his slash didn't land. "While I'm asking questions...why are you so sloppy?"

"Why am I sloppy?" he repeated softly, then chuckled. "The Triad took this job on a dare, not because Suarez offered as much money as he did. What we didn't account for was how you really do refuse to die, or how pushy Suarez would be once the plans slipped up a little. At the end of the day, we had a professional reputation to uphold. We couldn't back out on an unfinished hit."

"Reputation." She was tired of hearing about reputations. "Who would harm your reputation so much if you walk away that you would rather die?"

"There's one or two people out there with that sort of power."

She used to work with one, but he was out of the game, so then who could it really be?

The conspiracy was much deeper than she had

anticipated. There was someone else, someone not in this part of the game. There was a bigger picture she was missing. She would need to tell Vincent that later.

She didn't need to hear any more, blinking closer to Naseem and delivering a swift hit to his temple with a right hook. She didn't go for anything fatal because she wanted information. She wanted a name at the end of the night.

He took the punch and stabbed upward again with his sword, slicing her hip as she moved to the side. He got a grab on her shirt, which was bad news for her. As long as he held on, he was going for a ride if she blinked.

She decided to use it, blinking closer to the giant windows and swinging him into them as his sword missed, jarred by the impact. She slammed him into it again, making him lose his grip and stagger.

She bent him over and brought her knee up into him. She didn't know if she hit his face, chest, or gut, but it didn't really matter. She was a brawler and she knew how to fight close. He might have stopped her ability to sublimate, but blinking worked just as well.

And she was better than him.

She pulled his face eye level to her and delivered one more hit to his temple, letting him drop to the ground.

"Handcuffs?" she called out to Thompson. They flew across the room and hit the window with an unnatural accuracy. She didn't know any of his abilities – well, now she knew one. He must have telekinesis. She rolled Naseem over and handcuffed him, leaving him there as Thompson met her in the center of the room.

"You have...an impressive set of skills," Thompson said, a little uncomfortable.

"I was born lucky, I guess." She knew her abilities had made her a target for Axel to exploit. Not many people in the world, if any, had the combination she did. And if they did, they didn't use them like she did. She knew that because she never heard of them.

They stood in an awkward silence for a long time.

"Come sit down. We'll put him...somewhere. Other agents should be coming soon as well. I hit an alert on my phone, so everyone should be coming."

"All right."

She'd won, but none of it felt finished. She needed an update from Vincent or Jasper. She wanted to get in touch with Quinn, Zander, and Jasper.

She wanted to finish the mystery too. Who would dare the Triad to take this on and they were afraid to back out of it?

They moved Naseem and propped him up against a wall. Then, she took a seat opposite of the Director at his desk, as if they were going to have a normal meeting. The silence was uncomfortable and she didn't know what to do with it.

"So...you and Elijah?" he asked softly, pouring a drink. The weirdness of this wasn't missed by her and it must not have been missed by him either. "We can't leave until backup arrives. Might as well talk."

"Me and Elijah. Elijah and Quinn. Me and Quinn." She cocked an eyebrow at him. She wasn't in the mood for this. "Me and Jasper, and Zander, and Vincent. What are you going to do about it?"

He had been moving to take a drink and stopped. He set the glass down slowly, threading his fingers together as he leaned on his desk.

"Nothing. You and that team have-" His phone began to go off. He picked it up immediately. "Director Thompson."

He was quiet as someone on the other spoke frantically.

At that moment, she could hear sirens down on the street. She needed to investigate. Unable to resist the urge, she stood up and went to the window, looking down on the street. She could see the ambulance, the non-Magi police forces.

"Sawyer? There's been a fire at one of the safehouses." Thompson sounded...sad. He shouldn't. They had won. Naseem was handcuffed on the wall. Jasper and Vincent should have Councilman Suarez in cuffs, waiting for backup as well.

But there was an ambulance on the street. In front of the WMC building, just next door to them.

There was a fire at one of the safe houses.

"What happened?" she demanded softly.

"From that report, Kalama attacked them. Dina and her nephews were the first targets she went for."

"James is protecting them," she said, something dark settling in her.

"He was. Firefighters pulled out his body, along with Kalama's." Thompson must have been working hard to sound steady. She could hear the tremor. The pain. But he put so much effort into keeping it steady.

She was shaking as she kept her eyes on the ambulance.

"I need to check on my team," she said, her chest growing tight.

"Sawyer. James is dead," Thompson said, clarifying.

"I heard you!" she snapped, turning to storm out of the room.

Once her feet began moving, they didn't stop. She ran through walls to the stairwell and jumped over the rail and began to fall. She was smoke before she hit the floor. She was human again to keep running, through doors and walls, past agents who were scrambling to get up to the

Director's office. The IMPO headquarters were coming alive.

And she felt like everything was falling apart.

She kept running as she broke outside onto the steps. She found the ambulance and didn't stop. She needed to find her team.

Who was in that ambulance?

She ran into him. Strong hands took her upper arms. "Sawyer. He'll be okay. He'll be okay."

"Who?" she begged. "Who?"

"Vincent."

She blinked and looked at the stormy eyes, whirling with emotion, staring directly at her. The blond hair, the classic good looks.

"Jasper, what happened?" she asked softly. "What happened?"

"The IMPO agent, Deacon, stabbed him. He'll be okay. Lost a lot of blood but he'll be okay." He looked around, seeing the chaos now. She was ignoring it.

Still, something felt like they hadn't won tonight.

"Sawyer?" Jasper looked back at her eyes. "What don't I know? What's going on?"

"I stopped Naseem," she whispered. "And there's a fire at one of the safehouses."

"Shit. Kalama? Suarez said something, but..."

She nodded. God. They hadn't won tonight. They hadn't won. There would be no winning. She looked at his hands on her. Covered in Vincent's blood. He had been too busy to worry about Kalama because Vincent had been hurt.

"Okay. Tell me-"

"James is dead."

31

ZANDER

Zander was waiting for them to get back when he got the text from Jasper. Vincent was coming in with an injury. Case closed, but bad news.

Bad news.

"Well if Vincent is injured, I expect there's going to be some bad news," he mumbled to himself. He left Quinn and Elijah in the room, knowing they would be okay. He wanted to be at the main entrance to hear this bad news. And see Vincent. He couldn't help, not burned out from helping Elijah, but he needed to see. Another brother hurt. God, this entire thing had been a fucking mess.

Case closed meant it was at least over.

The entire day, he'd been out of the loop. It didn't help that he slept most of the day. It also didn't help that once Vincent, Jasper, and Sawyer left for the WMC building, no updates came. From anyone.

He saw their rental pull up and waited.

He tried not to think about how Sombra's attitude had been so low when he walked out of the room. He tried not to think about it because the first thing he noticed about his friends was the hollow looks in their eyes.

Sawyer's was the worst. Not cold or emotionless. Hollow.

Jasper looked at him and he saw the Golden boy's shoulders jerk from something.

"Bad news?" he asked softly. "Where's Vincent?"

"He'll be coming in on an ambulance. Gut stab wound," Jasper said quietly. "I can't..."

It was Sawyer, in a tone that matched the hollowness of her eyes, that said something. "James is dead."

Then she stepped around him and kept walking inside.

Zander felt everything fall apart as Jasper reached for him. He leaned into his oldest friend as the tears came. As the shock broke him.

Men didn't cry?

Fuck that. He bawled.

James.

The man who had given them a chance.

The man who had put up with their shit.

The man that genuinely cared for them, even as they made his life hard.

He had done everything in his power to take Zander and Jasper out of the IMAS. He'd let them go with Vincent, a new enigmatic friend, someone they weren't sure of. But James was there for them, every step of the way, even from a distance.

He'd been *constant*. They knew they would end a case and he would be there. He would ask how they were, the youngest team in the IMPO. The team no one liked.

He couldn't be gone.

"No..." he groaned. "No."

"Kalama..." Jasper took a deep breath, albeit a shaky

one, one choked by emotion and tears. They just stood there, holding each other. "Kalama got him, but he got her back. Only a few soldiers went down, but casualties are surprisingly low thanks to him."

Zander kept his eyes closed, his face pressed into his oldest friend's shoulder as the tears came back. His shoulders shook hard. His knees were weak.

He felt like they had failed.

Case closed. At a cost.

A cost that was *too fucking high*.

"Let's get inside," Jasper said, raspy and tired. "Please."

He nodded, pulling away. They weren't done yet. Vincent was coming in on an ambulance. God, Sawyer was probably already up there telling Quinn and Elijah.

They were nearly at the hospital's elevator when the ground underneath them rolled like a small earthquake.

Oh yeah, she had just told them.

They made it into the room to see her sitting on the edge of Elijah's bed, Quinn on his knees in front of her, his arms wrapped around her waist. His shoulders were shaking roughly as well. Elijah looked lost as Zander walked to him, trying to hold it together as he sat on the other side. Jasper huddled in as well.

"I..." Elijah's eyes were unfocused. God, he was still drugged up and getting the news.

Zander reached for him, grabbing his hand. "I'm sorry," he mumbled, pushing a little more magic than he should to make Elijah go to sleep. The last time he'd pulled that trick had been Jasper during their fight with Axel, to stop shock. He tried to convince himself it was for the same reason here. Elijah couldn't process any of this while doped up on painkillers. He needed to be sober.

They sat in silence, all past the tears after a moment. He had a feeling they would come back soon, but for a moment, they were all just hollow.

"When are we getting word on Vincent?" Quinn asked softly.

That brought the flood of tears back to Zander's eyes. James normally would do that sort of moving around and questioning when he was around.

Jasper just stood up and walked out, the door closing behind him too quietly.

Zander stared at the wall, leaning back to have physical contact with anyone. It was the unconscious cowboy, but that didn't matter. Sawyer was leaning forward, hunched on Quinn, still wrapped around her waist on his knees like he was a boy who needed someone.

It's about how Zander felt. Like a boy who just lost an older brother.

He'd always been there for them. They had never faced a day without him. They never saw a mission or a case without talking to him.

He dropped everything, no matter what, for them. Through frustration and anger, he trusted them. He gave them a chance. He brought them together, helping Vincent build this team, and then he backed them up.

Zander felt like a boy who lost everything. He felt small. And the tears wouldn't leave his eyes. They wouldn't spill over again. They just stayed there, overwhelming him.

"He's with healers," Jasper said quietly, sitting back down next to him. "Shouldn't be more than an hour."

They waited. No one came to see them. No one called their phones. They didn't turn on the television to check the news. He had a feeling, a far-away feeling, that they had done it. That his team had pulled it out. Not that he was the most helpful.

God.

He could have healed James. He should have gone with them to Dina. He should have offered to protect her with James. Instead, he sat in the fucking hospital, recovering from healing Elijah like a bitch.

He leaned over, sick to his stomach.

When they brought Vincent in, he jumped at the sudden commotion outside their door.

"I'm fucking walking in there!" Vincent yelled. "Let me out of this bed."

Really? This was when Vincent got stubborn?

He stood up and went to the door, opening it. He knew the rest of the team, those awake, were watching him.

"I'll help him to a seat," he told the nurses who were trying to hold him to the bed.

"We shouldn't have let him wake up. The healers say he'll be fine, but bruised but..." The non-Magi nursed looked like she didn't quite believe it.

"After a century of us working in these hospitals, you non-Magi still have a hard time believing in magic healing. Yeah, I get it. He'll be fine if they say he will be."

"Thank you," Vincent said, swinging his legs off the bed.

Zander didn't miss the wince. "Bruising," he reminded the Italian. "You still need to be somewhat easy on yourself."

Healer mode. It was easy to hide the grief in healer mode.

He helped Vin walk in and got him to sit on Sawyer's neglected bed. It took Vin all of ten seconds to realize something was wrong, very wrong.

"Guys? We closed the case right? Sawyer, you got Naseem?"

"I did," she whispered.

"Amazing. Um..." He frowned at her and the hollow response. Zander saw his eyes fall to Quinn on his knees, unmoving, arms locked around her waist like it was the only thing he had. He went to the animals as his raven hopped up to him and bumped his little head on his Magi's shoulder. "Kaar?" His eyes flew up to Zander's face. "What. Happened?"

"James is dead."

God, there was no easy way to say it.

Zander watched him crumple over in shock. He touched his back, the tears in his eyes refusing to break over and fall again, but also refusing to stay gone. They just taunted him. Constantly.

Vincent's tears were quiet. He just rubbed his friend's back.

James had brought them together.

And now they were in a world without him.

Quinn removed himself from Sawyer slowly and it looked like a statue was coming to life. Zander watched him stand and walk over. He pulled Vincent up and into a bone crushing hug.

Sawyer was next, not touching anyone, she just lay down on the extra bed and curled into a tight ball, her hands over her head.

Zander knew she had faced loss before. He could tell she wasn't coping.

He went back to Elijah's bed and found a way to lie down next to the cowboy. He needed to be there when he woke up. He was the healer. He had to be there for the injured. He would focus on that.

"What are you doing?" Quinn's soft voice broke the silence.

"Getting...calling..." Vincent wasn't able to speak, to finish a sentence.

"No. No, you must rest."

"I need-"

"Vincent, please," Quinn whispered.

"I need to talk to Thompson!" Vincent roared, startling everyone except Sawyer. No one said anything as Vincent pulled out his phone and dialed. No one tried to stop him. "Thompson. Do you need...anything? Is there anything I can do right now?" A pause. "Yes, I've been fucking told. I need...I need something to do. Please. Please give me something to do. I can't..." Vincent was obviously holding back tears as he spoke. "What..." Vincent put the phone on speaker. Zander could suddenly hear the tired Director.

"Go to his condo and relax. You're all off the case. The case is over. Plan to stay in New York for a few days, at the least. Now, without a lawyer, I can't promise this, but I'm nearly positive James named you, Vincent, in his will to take over his condo anyway. Stay there. I know Elijah is injured, but I'm sure he'll be fine in a wheelchair there. Get out of the hospital and go somewhere private and grieve. All of you, since I'm now on speaker phone."

Director Thompson was tired but clear. Forceful even. Zander was angry at it. His condo? The last small gift James had given them? A place to stay that was more like a home than a blank room?

He didn't know if he could handle that.

"Come dawn, I want you all out of that hospital. Is that clear?"

"Is that an order?" Vincent asked, looking over the team, full of despair. Zander had to look away.

"Yes. Godspeed...and I'm sorry."

"He's grieving too," Jasper mumbled. "James used to be

his teammate. He doesn't have the time or energy to deal with us."

"Let's..." Vincent ran a hand through his hair and turned away from them. "Fuck. At dawn, we leave for the condo."

And that was that. All they could do. Sit in silence and grieve, then go to the fucking condo.

32

SAWYER

Sawyer didn't want to be there. She didn't want to be in New York. She didn't want to be in the same room as anyone. She didn't want to be in his fucking condo, staring at a picture on the kitchen counter.

She jumped when someone touched her. She spun, nearly thinking it was someone to kill her and saw Jasper and those broken stormy eyes.

"Why don't we try to eat?" he asked carefully, rubbing his hand over her back. She swallowed, her stomach doing flips. She could only shake her head in response. "How about you sit with everyone on the couch then. I'm going to make something and we can all get to it as we want it."

How could he be like this? How could he find a way to keep walking forward at this exact moment?

She put her mind to that instead of her location. It was a good distraction, because all she could think now was fuck December. Fuck this month and its holidays. Fuck the cheer and goodness. Fuck all of it.

First Henry, whom she'd loved with everything she had

in her. A boy who had never seen the darkness and just loved her back.

Now James, who had touched her with the way he cared for her men. A man who saw the darkness, had been affected by it, and gave her a chance anyway. And let her love five wonderful men who were all going to be hurt by his loss.

Fucking December.

"Stop being so..." She tried to find the word. Nice?

No, Jasper wasn't being nice; he was just continuing to move forward. Good for him. He was just trying to be there for them.

She was angry at it, though.

"Go sit down, Sawyer," he whispered, running a hand over her cheek. "And let someone look at those cuts."

"They're just cuts," she snapped. They stung, but they weren't deep. She would clean them eventually, but at that moment, the pain made her feel more alive than anything else. It was the only thing that wasn't somewhat numb, the only thing that kept her sane, in a sense.

Jasper's patience with her was still not done. "Come on. Let's get you on the couch."

So perfect. So normal. Such a good man.

She would rather he blame her, get upset, something. He'd broken down on the way to the hospital, as she made the drive somehow. She looked at his hands. They still had Vincent's blood on them.

It dawned on her then.

He was taking care of them because it was all he could do. Her Golden Boy. Her normal, loving man. Her sweetheart.

"I'll sit if you wash up," she mumbled, looking away.

"Oh. Of course." He turned on the kitchen sink as she walked out and fell on the couch. Vincent was next to her on one side, and Zander on the other. Quinn had taken Elijah to James' master bedroom for sleep. While it was fucking morbid, they didn't know what else to do. Get a hotel?

She heard the sink turn off, then the fridge open. Cupboards and dishes. Jasper was focusing on an easy task. Making food.

She couldn't handle the quiet anymore, grabbing the remote. Taking a deep breath, hoping to steady herself, she turned on the television.

The news was on, first thing. One of those twenty-four hour channels, where people could get a constant stream of 'the world is fucking shitty,' whenever they wanted it.

The anchors talked about Suarez and the assassins. They talked a lot about the fire at the safe house. She teared up when they talked about James, a hero.

A fucking hero.

Why couldn't people ever be heroes when they were alive? Why wasn't that a thing? Why did he have to be dead to be a hero?

Fucking Dina was doing a live interview, describing how James had bought her and her nephews time to run. How if he had failed, the assassin would have come after her nephews and her, and she didn't want to lose them. She was eternally grateful to the man and even said she would do anything in her power to honor him.

Sawyer's gaze at the screen was only broken by Jasper placing a plate on the coffee table. Zander was now snoring next to her, worn out from his grief. Vincent was staring at the screen with an intensity she didn't understand. She wasn't sure she wanted to. There was something she had to tell him, but it escaped her. When she remembered, she would make sure to get it to him.

Already, in a way that felt too soon, too early, she was coming back to herself. She still felt hollow and cold, but her mind was picking up speed again.

Then Thompson came on, and so did pictures of her team.

"Guys," she whispered. "It's us."

Vincent nodded slowly. Jasper turned his back to her, looking at the screen.

She didn't catch the details. Her mind was working, but it wasn't that fast. She caught the big points. Heroes. Best of the IMPO.

"Turn it off," Vincent demanded, glaring at the screen. She did, without debate or arguing. "Tomorrow, I'm going to go see my brother."

She had no response to that. She wasn't sure what to ask, or even if she wanted more information.

Jasper turned back to them, though. "Why?"

"I couldn't say goodbye," he mumbled.

Her heart cracked and the hollowness was replaced with a pain that she wasn't ready for. Goodbyes. No one ever got to say goodbye.

"And I think he knows something. So it's a double visit." Vincent stood up and left the living room, going onto the patio and staring out over the city. She watched him light a cigarette and couldn't blame him for that. This was a time where even she resisted the urge to steal one and feel it wash away some of the anxiety.

"Fuck," she moaned, rubbing her face. She had to tell him about what Naseem said. She jumped up and grabbed one of the small sandwiches Jasper made. He smiled gently at her as she passed him. She didn't take a bite of the sandwich, but she had at least thought to grab one. That would appease him. She was trying, at least.

She went onto the patio, touching Vincent's back with her free hand.

"I didn't get to say goodbye," he whispered. "He's just gone."

"I know," she murmured, getting closer. In one second, it felt like an ocean was between them, and the next, they were crushed together, as close as two human beings could get. "I know, Vincent. It hurts. I'm so sorry."

"I can't...not say goodbye to Axel," he continued to say quietly. "I can't."

"I know."

"You shouldn't go-"

"I'm going. I'm not letting you go alone. Elijah is basically bedridden; Quinn is taking care of him. Zander needs to sleep and Jasper..."

"It's how he copes," Vincent said, sighing. "He's like me. Needs something to do."

"Yeah. Speaking of...things to do." She quickly explained what Naseem had said to her. What her suspicions were. How much she wanted to know who had secretly kicked this off.

"You and I both know the answer." He pulled away from her. "Sawyer...we both know the answer."

She was afraid he would say that.

"Tomorrow. Today...tonight...Thompson was right. We should...stay here and just...process it." He leaned on the rail, the sun hitting his face. She leaned to kiss his cheek softly.

"Get some sleep eventually," she whispered. "And eat this." She forced the sandwich in his hand. He had the stomach to take a bite, which meant he was doing a little better.

When she made it inside, she forced Zander to lie down and put a blanket over him. She didn't want him sleeping curled in an upright ball. It would only make him feel worse when he woke up.

They were all emotionally drained and physically exhausted. She ran her fingers through his wonderful red hair. She leaned down and kissed the freckled bridge of his nose. Her hands were shaking as she pulled away.

She found Jasper next, still in the kitchen, looking lost. "I'm going to try and lie down," she told him, kissing his cheek.

"Okay," he replied, not moving. "I'm going to try and keep everyone fed, and..."

"Come lie down," she ordered.

"I will in a bit," he promised.

She nodded. There was no forcing him to get any sleep and she knew better than to try. Eventually, exhaustion would claim him too.

Her hands were still shaking as she went into the guest bedroom. She stripped, just letting her things fall to the floor. The daggers, the kukri, and the throwing knives. Her clothing, messy. She stepped into the bathroom, wet a washcloth, and cleaned the slices Naseem had given her carefully. She should have seen a healer at the hospital, but she relished in the painful sting as she cared for them herself.

A physical reminder she was alive. They would scar, and then they would be a permanent reminder of the long night.

After that, she fell into the bed and didn't move.

The tears finally came as she curled into a ball, covering her head - the tears she'd held back, the tears she wished weren't so necessary. She didn't get under the blankets as the room got too cold and she fell into the quiet despair and hurt, her heart being ripped from her chest.

Sombra jumped on the bed with her, not pushing any of her own emotions into the bond. She just curled up with her Magi, a warm body in the cold room. A quiet love, an endless love, and a comfort that only the jaguar could offer her.

Eventually, she reached out and wrapped her arms around the big black cat, burying her face into the fur, and cried harder, gut-wrenching sobs taking over.

She stayed like that until the exhaustion took her.

"I'M DREAMING," Sawyer whispered, glaring at the body in front of her. "This isn't real."

She tried to look away to see another body.

And another.

And another.

All around her, she was surrounded by bodies. Nameless faces and those she knew. The ones she knew, she ignored, knowing they would just fuck with her. That those faces weren't the dead. They were alive, in the condo with her. They weren't dead, so she refused to look at them.

"This isn't real," she repeated. Sombra tugged on the bond, but she didn't leave the dream. She didn't wake up. She also wasn't sure she could. Her body was too tired and it needed the physical rest.

"Sawyer!" Jasper called, running for her, through the bodies around her. "You can't...you can't stay in this. Leave, like Sombra is asking you to."

"I can't," she said, nearly hysterical.

She laughed until tears fell from her eyes, then the sobs took over again.

Jasper grabbed her, clinging to her like she was going to collapse and become one of the bodies around them. "Let's change this," he whispered. She felt the magic sweep over the gruesome landscape and when she reopened her eyes, the field of bodies was gone.

Instead, they were in her room, back in Georgia. Back to normal and her life.

"Thank you," she whispered. She looked at the television and the couches. "Can we play video games?"

"Do you know any of them well enough to recall them perfectly?" he asked with a small smile.

"No."

"Then probably not. All of this is constructed from your memory. I can change it to other things but, really, this is your mind. If the information isn't there, I can't put it there." He pulled her to the bed. "Let's just lie down."

"You can leave...you don't have to stay."

"If I go, I'm worried it'll go back to what it was. I don't want you in that. Come on."

She nodded, nearly falling onto the bed next to him. His arms wrapped around her, holding her tight.

She needed this.

"Are you okay?" she asked softly.

"No," he admitted. "I'm very far from okay, but I don't know what else to do. I can do this. I can find...comfort in helping those still alive."

She pressed her face into his chest. "I just want to feel alive again," she murmured. "I just want this month to end. I want to go back to yesterday and tell him he was a good man. Tell him to take Dina to the hospital. Anything."

366

"Me too," he agreed. "I can only help with one of those things, and I need it too."

She would have asked what he meant, but when she looked up at him, confused, he just kissed her, desperate.

Tears welled up in her eyes.

Alive.

Yes, this was very alive.

She clung to his shirt, her tongue claiming his mouth. She pushed him back when she needed to catch her breath and swung her leg over his waist to straddle him. His hands massaged her ass and thighs as she leaned down to kiss him again.

Their clothing just disappeared.

She took the moment to appreciate that. Something light hit her heart and she began to laugh, turning her head so it wasn't in his face. When she looked back at him, he had such a wonderful smile.

For a moment, they could be home. They could be alive. They could be together. When they woke up, they would be confronted again by the grief, but for a moment, Jasper had given her a place to hide: her dreams. Something the real world couldn't touch, and as long as he was there, they would be wonderful dreams, not horrific nightmares.

"I love you so much," she murmured, kissing him again.

"I love you too," he said between her possessive kissing. God, she wanted to own him and keep him close. She wanted to keep them all right by her side, so that they never got hurt, so they never were lost to her.

Sawyer ran her hands over his chest, enjoying that he wasn't scarred. She had no problems with scars, on herself or anyone she loved, but she was glad he didn't have them. She looked back and grinned. He had both his legs here. Perfect. He deserved to be perfect.

"Sawyer," he moaned, wrapping a hand around the back of her head. She went back to kissing him as his other hand traveled down and he slid a finger into her, making her moan into his mouth.

They were suddenly in the middle of the bed and not on the edge. Dreams made this all so easy, she realized. As he fingered her, she nibbled and licked his neck, collarbone, and jaw, and every so often, she nipped his earlobe. Slowly, he built her up to a peak and she gasped at the soft finish she found, her muscles clenching on his fingers.

When it was over, he removed his fingers and grabbed her hips. She could feel him hard, ready to continue, ready to take it to the next step.

"Are you sure?" she asked softly, panting. She wanted it, but even in grief, she wasn't going to take it there without knowing he was okay with it.

"I want this," he whispered. "I wanted it the night this all started. And if people are going to be dying, I'm not waiting anymore."

She swallowed back tears at that. Death had a way of changing one's perspective.

She sank down on him slowly. "Let me," she murmured, riding him as he panted and groaned underneath her. Every sound was perfection. Everything about him was wonderful and golden.

She would try not to let this leave a dark stain on his soul.

She leaned over to kiss him as she continued. He held her close, the kiss becoming desperate between them.

Soft cries, soft words, soft sweet nothings. Everything about this moment was exactly what it needed to be. She didn't want rough or painful. Instead, she was glad that instead of the storm she knew was behind those eyes, she got calm waters.

Something peaceful and just for them, here in her dreams.

When her orgasm came like a wave, he followed her, groaning her name like a prayer.

She fell off of him and just curled tight into his side, feeling at peace for a moment.

"I love you," he whispered again.

"I love you too," she answered, feeling it to the very core of her being. "Thank you."

33

SAWYER

The next day, Sawyer was getting ready for a trip she was dreading. She didn't know why she agreed or wanted to do this. See Axel? She hadn't since that day in the hanger bay, the last time he tried to kill her and it got him arrested. Finally.

"Are you sure you two want to do this?" Zander asked, yawning. He looked worried and fearful for her. Not physically. Nothing was going to happen to her. There was more danger to her heart and her mental health now, when the entire team was already fragile.

"He was behind this somehow," she said, hoping that answered it. "I don't know how, but he's definitely had his hand in this. And because of that, James is dead - and I blame him. Do I want to go? No? Yes? But Vincent does, so I will."

"I understand," he said, wrapping a hand around her waist. "I've been in the room with an Axel and Vincent talk once. It's not pleasant."

"I didn't think it would be." She had a feeling it was

going to really fucking suck. "And it's not like we can arrest him again. I just want to look at him and...ask why."

"I know." He was so fucking understanding now. She wrapped her arms around him as well, and just held him for a moment. He rubbed her back. "If you need anything, though, call me. I'll raise some fucking hell for you. I promise."

"Oh, I know," she retorted, smiling a little. "Going to try and save the world?"

"Fuck the world. I'm just going to save you all. You're the only ones that fucking matter anymore."

She kissed his cheek and walked out of the bedroom, Sombra following her. The jaguar did pause to rub on his legs until he gave her a scratch behind her ears.

"Keep her safe," he whispered to the feline, who purred at the affection.

She walked out to find everyone, including Elijah in his wheelchair, eating breakfast. They were quiet, but she knew it was an improvement to the day before, where they would have all rather starved than anything else.

"Good morning." She bent over to kiss the cowboy's cheek. "How are you?"

"Been better," he said, pushing his spoon around the cereal he had. Probably something that was easier for him to eat? Or maybe it was something none of them needed to cook. That made more sense. "A little mad at Zander, but I was too drugged to handle it yesterday. They've worn off and I refuse to take any now. I need to be...here. Present." He tapped his temple.

"Okay. If you need anything-"

"Ask. I know, little lady. What I need right now is a kiss." He gave her a weak smile. He was trying so hard to be himself. It broke her heart.

She gave him what he asked for.

"I have some news for you, if you want to hear it right now or later." Vincent put down his newspaper. God, they were all trying so hard to be normal. She didn't have the heart to tell Vincent that the newspaper was upside down. He had probably just been staring at it, hoping he could pretend.

"Now." She sat down between Elijah and Jasper, who she sent a small smile to. He'd been in her bed when she woke up. Nothing happened physically, but it had been nice to find him there.

"Thompson called, with D'Angelo. The day...the day before James' funeral, they plan on pardoning you. For your efforts here to save the WMC."

She paused and she knew she should have felt happy. Some part of her did. Some part of her wanted to jump and cheer and cry.

It was a small, distant part.

"Why before his funeral?" she asked softly.

"Thompson thinks you should see him put to rest as the free woman he wanted you to be. I...agree with him. It'll be in a few days. Everything is hectic for all of them, so it'll take time for Thompson to nail the details of the funeral down. Dina is heading the issue of your pardon in the WMC." Vincent gave her a small smile. "It also saves them from the political drama of us."

"Congrats, love," Quinn said, smiling up at her.

"Thank you," she responded, swallowing on her emotion. It felt so anti-climactic and depressing. Oh, a friend of the team died. Pardon that one so they all stop being our problem.

What was she going to do? She grabbed a piece of toast,

buttered it, and took a bite. Bland - and perfect for the moment.

A pardon. The pardon. The thing that meant she could walk away and live whatever life she wanted to live.

She didn't know what she wanted after all of this. She looked up at Jasper. They had talked about the future before. Did he have any ideas?

"You don't need to make any decisions about the future right now," he said. "You don't. After this, we can all go home. You can keep working for the IMPO until you make a decision. You can...stay in New York and live with Charlie again. You don't need to have it all figured out right now, though."

"I'm...going to be free," she muttered to herself, a bubble of laughter hitting her chest after a moment. "Oh my god."

"Yes. And if you want to keep this good mood, you should stay here." Vincent was staring at her from across the table.

"Oh no," she retorted, grinning. "I'm rubbing his fucking face in this."

God, the idea felt so good. Even Vincent chuckled at her enthusiasm.

And damn, it was a good month for it.

THEY WENT ALONE, not even telling anyone except the team that they planned to. Vincent sent Thompson a text at the last moment before they got out of their car at the prison, letting him know.

"Do you think he'll be upset?" Sawyer asked, leaning back in her seat, staring at the foreboding building in front of her.

"No. They asked me if I wanted to see him. It was a request from him after being hurt and being a model prisoner. As long as we don't stir things up too much, no one will blink an eye." He sighed. "Time to say goodbye."

"For both of us," she agreed.

"The timing is pretty perfect," he said, getting out of the car. She followed and listened as he kept going. "You getting pardoned right after he had his hand in a scheme."

"What do you think he got out of this?"

"A good time. Proof that he could cause trouble. There's no evidence it was him, though. None at all. It's why I haven't taken it to Thompson. The only thing we can do is make sure to keep an eye on him to stop it from happening again." Vincent shrugged. "He's always liked testing his skills. He enjoys the mental work of playing people. He could have just been bored and wanted to see what would happen."

She agreed with all of that. Daring the Triad to take on such a big thing, to prove they were the best compared to his own assassin. Convincing a Councilman that he could take power if he followed a plan. It was an Axel sort of game.

They were admitted without question and led to a small meeting room, with a single table. They were held outside of it while someone retrieved Axel from protected custody.

Protected custody. She snorted.

"Do you think...James would have been proud of us for this?" Vincent asked softly.

She felt that question hit her like a bullet.

"Yes." She didn't see any reason why he wouldn't be.

"I just...he would have stood beside us here. It's moments like this where...he should be here."

"Maybe this is too soon after..."

"No. I need to do this now." Vincent swallowed. "I never want to come back after this."

They watched through a big window as he was led in and seated. He was handcuffed to the table. He had chains on his ankles. He had the inhibiting collar on his neck that stopped him from using his magic. He wore bright orange. Such a commercial prison color.

There had been a time when she thought she would be in that place. Chained and helpless, paying for her crimes.

She realized that she was paying for her crimes, but not in the ways she had always thought. She bled and fought for her crimes. She worked hard to put them behind her.

In the end, she and Axel were both prisoners in their own ways.

"Not for much longer," she whispered to herself, her eyes locked on his face, now scarred. Whoever had jumped him had fucked him up. A scar cut over an eye and cheek. Another down his neck. Another over the opposite cheek. They had been healed well, but someone had decided that Axel Castello wasn't allowed to be perfect anymore. "Did they catch who jumped him?"

"Yeah. They had stabbed him multiple times too." Vincent groaned. "I have...complicated feelings about it."

"He's still your brother." She couldn't blame him in any way for feeling somewhat bad for Axel being brutalized in prison. It was cruel. She didn't feel so bad, not really, but she wouldn't hold it against Vincent.

"No. He was once my brother."

She looked over his face. He said it with such confidence, such surety.

"And who are your brothers?"

"You should know. You love them." He smiled at her.

"Let's do this. Then we can leave this behind, once and for all, like James always wanted for us."

She liked that idea.

She followed him into the room and sat down next to him. Across from her, Axel's eyebrows went up at the sight of her. Oh, he hadn't been expecting her, not even a little.

"I'm glad to see you, brother," he said carefully, eyeing her like she was going to jump over the table and kill him at any moment.

"You wanted to see me. I came." Vincent raised his hands like it was obvious.

"Are you going to ask how I am? I was hurt."

"No. I can see how you are, and I've been kept updated on your recovery. I'm not here to play games."

"Than why did you come?" A tiny bit of rage in his voice. It wasn't normal for him, but she could assume that prison had changed him.

"To say goodbye, and that your fun little game with the WMC failed."

She grinned, and that caused her old master to glare at her.

"Failed?" he snapped. "Damn it. I wish anyone brought me any fucking news in this place."

Now she was uncomfortable. That wasn't a normal Axel. He was a model prisoner. He would have had people bringing him news every step of the way. And he didn't deny it was him. He failed and he had no idea.

"Well, there you have it." Vincent tilted his head, considering his brother through narrow eyes. She just watched the interaction, wondering what other out of character shit Axel was going to do. He was a different man than the one she used to know. "I won't be coming back. I'm here to say goodbye."

376

"Goodbye? I don't think they'll execute me for a long time. You'll be back." Axel grinned and it felt off-kilter to her.

"I'm getting pardoned in a few days. There's no reason for any of us to come back." It was the first and only thing she had planned to say here. "You failed because Vincent, the team, and I fucking stopped you. They think for the effort, I deserve to walk away. Thanks for the opportunity."

"You were supposed to DIE!" he roared, slamming his hands down on the metal table, breaking the chains that held him to it.

It bent. Not a dent. It *bent*.

She jumped up and pulled Vincent back with her, glaring at the table. Axel was never that strong. She wasn't that strong. No one she knew was that...

"Where is he?" she asked softly, looking back into the olive green eyes. They were wide, looking at his hands like he'd just made a terrible mistake.

"Sawyer..." Vincent sounded far away and stunned.

"We never found Missy's body," she snarled.

Axel gave them a twisted, angry sneer. "And you never will," he purred. "Not a body, anyway."

"WHERE IS HE?" she roared. "MISSY! WHERE IS HE?"

Missy just laughed, throwing 'Axel's' head back in the process. It was an insane laugh, a hysterical one. She shifted back into her normal form, still laughing as Vincent dragged Sawyer out of the room.

"WHERE IS HE?" she screamed, trying to keep diving for the doppelganger that haunted her.

"Oh my god," Vincent gasped, yanking her fully out of the room as guards ran in to grab the mad doppelganger, who just kept laughing. "How...That's why he didn't know...

Because no one is going to report those things to a minion. He's..."

"He's free," she snarled, glaring at the door to the room.

James was dead because Axel played a game with the WMC, behind the scenes, pulling the strings of people's emotions.

She knew what her future held. In every variation of it, it involved him.

34

VINCENT

Two days later, Vincent was numb. Not always. He had moments of anger and fear. He had moments of overwhelming sadness every time he thought about James.

But mostly, he was numb - because he shut it all down.

He had to drag Sawyer out of the prison that day. The next thing he knew, he was being interviewed and interviewing others, trying to figure out if it was true.

And it was. It was all true. Axel wasn't in the prison. He was free, somewhere out there, playing his games quietly.

It felt like everything he had ever worked for was slipping between his fingers. Vincent couldn't believe it, even with the whole story lined up in front of him on the table in James' condo.

He'd put it together easily enough. Axel had been in prison, until he was jumped and injured. From there, someone had helped get Missy in and Axel out.

Just a simple exchange.

Sawyer had helped him further. They had to give Axel a similar scar to Missy's, the one on the neck. Not hard to do, but it meant whoever was involved in the jump was a part of the conspiracy as well.

"It never ends," he mumbled. "It never fucking ends." This trip had been conspiracy after conspiracy. Starting from an angry IMPO agent who outed Sawyer, to assassins, the WMC, and finally to Axel, which had even more to it. Prison guards, Missy.

He was putting the pieces together already, little bits, but he knew he was behind. He was weeks behind. Axel had been injured a month before. Vincent closed his eyes. Was it a full month or three weeks? He didn't remember. He would need to make a better timeline, something on paper. Normally he could remember these sorts of things, but there was too much and he was too close to it.

"Vincent," Elijah called. "Are you ready to go?"

"I am," he answered. "Everyone else?"

"Yeah. They all headed down to our rides already. How are you?"

"I'm fine." He was lying. He was far from fine, but his emotional turmoil wasn't important. He needed to be focused. "How are you? You shouldn't be walking around."

"It hurts, but I'm not going to be wheeled into this. I'm going to stand on my own feet for this."

This. Sawyer's pardon. The WMC and Thompson had decided on no public ceremony, just the Council, Thompson, and the team, with her, watching her be granted her freedom from prosecution over her past crimes. Well, legally. The public saw her as a hero now, most of them, but there would always be some that only saw the killer.

"I understand." He grabbed his coat and threw it on as they walked out of the condo. After the funeral tomorrow, he had a meeting with Thompson over James' will.

When they got downstairs, he went to her side, but she

didn't acknowledge him. She barely acknowledged anyone. From James' death straight into Axel's freedom.

He was rocked by it too, but he had something to focus on. He needed to focus or he would *break*. He wondered what was going on in her head. Her freedom on the back of all of this. He desperately wanted to know.

They drove in silence to the WMC building and were escorted inside without any issue. Thompson waited for them outside the main chamber. He shook all their hands, congratulating them.

Pleasantries none of them cared about.

Once inside, Vincent and the team flanked her as she was directed to stand in the center of the chamber. There was no smile on her face. No inclination of how she felt in any way, just a blank, ready face.

He had a feeling he knew why. She was about to be free, certainly, but Axel was also free. She would be a part of the effort to catch him. It wasn't something to be excited about.

"Today, we've asked you all here to witness the pardon of Sawyer Cambrie Matthews from her past crimes as a criminal assassin under the moniker, Shadow." It was one of the Councilmen that Vincent had no experience with. "However, due to recent information, we cannot grant this at the current time."

Vincent let that hit him like a blow.

Everything that happened. All of them that had been hurt and bled. James had died. And they wouldn't give her the pardon?

"And why is that?" she asked softly, looking up. "Say it out loud for the class, please."

"We can't justify letting you walk free while Antonio 'Axel' Castello does." The Councilman shifted uncomfortably, looking away from them.

"You fucking promised!" Zander yelled. "Let go of me, Quinn! They fucking promised!"

"And what am I supposed to do about this?" she asked. He could hear the small quiver in her voice, but he figured only the team would. It was so small, so buried underneath her cold mask.

"He was sentenced to death."

"Say it," she demanded.

Vincent shook his head.

No. Not this. This couldn't be the thing standing between her and her future. She deserved so much better than this.

"Find him, catch him, and execute him, and you'll get your pardon...Shadow."

35

AXEL

Axel continued to shave in the mirror, staring at his scarred face. The things he had to do to get what he wanted. He would have been angry about it, but really, they were just the cost of his intelligence. He was smarter than all of them, and those were just a necessary evil to prove it.

"Sir," Felix called softly from the other side of the door. "Our source brought me news."

"Let me guess. They are sending her and Vincent, along with the rest of his little friends after me."

"Yes sir."

He figured. When the Triad failed to kill her and let the Councilman push them into mistakes, he knew it would come to this.

That was fine.

"I am almost amazed at her resilience," he murmured, then rinsed his face. He patted it down with a towel and smiled at himself. The scars almost looked good. They certainly didn't change how women treated him, and they made others fear him even more.

"Axel..." Felix hadn't left.

"Yes?" He was always kinder to Felix than the others. He liked the quiet young man. They were of similar age, but Felix seemed much younger. He was also loyal, and that was Axel's favorite quality in any person who had it.

"Missy has agreed to do as you asked since her reveal."

That was one problem taken care of.

"Does she know that I won't be visiting her?"

"Yes sir."

Good. He wasn't in the mood for it.

"Thank you for the foresight to bring her back, Felix. Have I said that to you recently?"

"Yes, Axel, you have, but thank you. Anything for our future."

"Yes, our future." He walked out of the bathroom and smiled patiently. "There's a couple things we need to get out of the way, but we have time."

"Sir, if I can be so bold..."

"Say what's on your mind." Nothing Felix ever said was offensive to him. If anything, the Magi with necromancy was too passive for him on occasion.

"I'm glad to see you back in your prime. You seem more focused than you were before...Before the incident in Atlanta. You seem more like you were when...she...worked for you."

Axel grinned. Yes. He felt focused. He felt like he could see his goals again and he knew how to play the slow game again.

Prison and his loss in Atlanta had reminded him of his best quality, one he'd thrown aside for his vendetta and anger at the bitch.

Patience.

DEAR READER,

Rest in peace, James.

Thank you for continuing this journey with me and Sawyer.

There's one more. Only one more. A Night of Redemption will be the last piece of Sawyer's journey.

I'm already beginning to miss her.

Whether you loved or hated the book, please consider leaving a review. Every review, even just a few words, is appreciated.

Continue on for a few more glossaries of information and my About the Author page, where you can find links to my social media.

ABILITIES

GLOSSARY

Note:

It's important to remember that every Magi is unique. Two Magi could have the same ability and use them in different ways due to their personal strength levels.

Legends are the exception. (ex. All Druids are exactly the same in power and abilities.)

Example: Sawyer can walk through a thick wall with Phasing but another Magi may only be able to pass through a thin door and push an arm through a window for a short time.

Ranking Code

Common- C, Uncommon-U, Rare-R, Mythic- M

- Air Manipulation-C- The ability to manipulate the element of air or wind.
- Animal bonds-C- The ability to bond with one to five animals. A person with this ability can feel emotional currents of the animal and use the

animal's senses by inserting themselves in the animal.

- Animation-C- The ability to make inanimate objects do tasks for time periods. I.e. Dancing brooms
- Astral Projection-R- The ability to use a non-corpeal form that can be seen by others. Renders physical body unconscious.
- Blinking-U- The ability to teleport short distances (10-20 feet) within eyesight.
- Cloaking-U- The ability to become invisible.
- Dream walking-U- The ability to walk through the dreams of others and go through the person's subconscious to reveal secrets and memories to the person.
- Earth Manipulation-C- The ability to manipulate the element of earth.
- Elemental Control-M- The ability to manipulate all elements and all combinations of them.
- Enchanting-C- The ability to enchant physical objects with specific properties, such as never losing a sharp edge for a blade.
- Fire Manipulation-C- The ability to manipulate the element of fire.
- Healing-C- The ability to heal physical wounds.
- Illusions-U- The ability to alter an individual's perception of reality.
- Magnetic Manipulation-U- The ability to control or generate magnetic fields, normally a very weak ability.
- Mind reading-M- The ability to read another's mind, normally requiring touch.

- Naturalism-C- The ability to control the growth of plant life and identify plants' properties.
- Petrification-R- The ability to freeze a person's movement without harming them by touching them. Can also be used to harm, by stopping basic life function for a short time.
- Phasing-C- The ability to walk through solid objects with concentration.
- Portals-U- Temporary holes through time and space to travel nearly instantly. (Not time travel)
- Reading-R- The ability to read the abilities of others, requires touching the individual.
- Shape-shifting-U- The ability to take the form of one animal, not chosen by the Magi.
- Shielding-C- The ability to create force fields that block physical interaction.
- Sound Manipulation-U- The ability to manipulate sound waves.
- Sublimation-R- The ability to transform into a gaseous form, normally looks like black smoke.
- Telekinesis-C- The ability to move objects physically with the mind.
- Telepathy-U- The ability to send thoughts to others for silent communication. Cannot invade the thoughts of others. This is a one-way ability, unless the other person also has telepathy.
- Tracking-R- The ability track a single individual by having a item that belongs to said individual.
- Water Manipulation-C- The ability to manipulate the element of water.

IMPO AND IMAS

Both organizations have a rank structure, but the IMPO is more relaxed than the IMAS.

International Magi Police Organization
Officer - Low level law enforcement officer

Detective - Case investigator isolated to the city they are assigned to.

Admin - Paper pushers, secretaries, assistants.

Lawyers - Self-explanatory. Magi lawyers who are experts in Magi law.

Special Agent - Case investigator that travels globally and carries out long-term investigations such as crime lords, internationally known criminals, and serial killers. Report to handlers and always work as a team.

Handlers- Normally retired Special Agents that act as liaisons between the Asst. Director/Director and Special Agents.

Assistant Director - Second in charge of the IMPO.

Director - The head of the IMPO. Reports directly to the WMC.

International Magi Armed Services
Chain of Command: 1 is the lowest rank,7 is the highest.
Generals report directly to the WMC.

Enlisted
E-1, Private (Pvt)
E-2, Private 1st Class (PFC)
E-3, Lance Corporal (LCpl)
E-4, Corporal (Cpl)
E-5, Sergeant (Sgt)
E-6, Gunnery Sergeant (GySgt)
E-7, Master Sergeant (MSgt)

Officer
O-1, Lieutenant (Lt)
O-2, Captain (Capt)
O-3, Major (Maj)
O-4, Lieutenant Colonel (LtCol)
O-5, Colonel (Col)
O-6, Lieutenant General (LtGen)
O-7, General (Gen)

IMAS Spec Ops
Special operations (or special forces). Teams are named for
gods and goddesses of war. (Ex. Team Ares or Team Mars)
Soldiers of all ranks may apply. Only the best succeed.

ABOUT THE AUTHOR

KristenBanetAuthor.com

Kristen Banet has a Diet Coke problem and smokes too much. She curses like a sailor (though, she used to be one, so she uses that as an excuse) and finds that many people don't know how to handle that. She loves to read, and before finally sitting to try her hand at writing, she had your normal kind of work history. From tattoo parlors, to the U.S. Navy, and freelance illustration, she's stumbled through her adult years and somehow, is still kicking.

She loves to read books that make people cry. She likes to write books that make people cry (and she wants to hear about it). She's a firm believer that nothing and no one in this world is perfect, and she enjoys exploring those imperfections—trying to make the characters seem real on the page and not just in her head.

She *might* be crazy, though. Her characters think so, but this can't be confirmed.

You can join her in being a little bit crazy in The Banet Pride, her facebook reader's group.

facebook.com/kristenbanetauthor

twitter.com/KristenBanet

instagram.com/Kbanetauthor

ALSO BY KRISTEN BANET

Made in the USA
Middletown, DE
09 February 2021

33429684R00225